ACCELERATION

L L
Larson

Cover Design

by Atrtink Covers

www.atrtinkcovers.com

<u>DEDICATION</u>

This book is dedicated to
my son, Timothy, and sister, Diane.

Thank you for your love, devotion, and kind hearts.
You are thelights of my life. I love you dearly.

LEGAL NOTES/ DISCLAIMER

Copyright © 2019 Linda Lou Larson as E- Book
Copyright © 2021 Linda Lou Larson as Paperback and Hardback Books Printed in the United States of America.
Paperback ISBN from Amazon #9798711660545
Published by- Amazon as E-Book and Paperback book with Sandy World LLC
Print Distribution by Ingram Sparks and Amazon

INTRODUCTION

ACCELERATION is an action/thriller story with a hero, Sam Stone, who is charming, brave, and dedicated to the right. He respects people and fights against those who crave power and superiority at the expense of others. He falls in love and experiences tragedy as he struggles to survive in the midst of violent and dangerous men.

Sam Stone battles a frightening and scientific and political conspiracy. It is one that can bring death to thousands and can destroy the United States of America. He must win.

Part 1:
CONFRONTATION

CHAPTER 1

"Hey, Sean, you are not home...Surprise! This message is from Sam. Remember me, the brother who writes books but is always too lazy to scribble letters? But then, you too, letters that is.... I miss ya. I'm still in Los Angeles. Same old condo. Call me, little brother. It's been too long."

"Sean, it's Sam again. Remember me? I really would like to hear from you, man. You still a big research honcho? Give me a call if they let you talk."

"Sean, you've got me worried now. You still well...and the family? It's Sam. I think I'm homesick for you. Call. Okay?"

Sam tossed his phone onto the bed-side table. He picked up his glass of Scotch, drained it, and smacked off the light.

As sleep enveloped him, dark memories reared up like angry monsters. "Remember your past. The Army, the Special Forces. Don't forget the death." The words echoed, snarled, and hissed. "You should have died too. That's what war is for."

"Buzz," Sam's phone erupted. He sat up suddenly and shouted, "NO!"

He gasped and struggled into reality as a huge, overly affectionate, Great Dane skittered into the room and plopped heavily onto his bed. It then lapped worriedly and profusely on Sam's face. Sam laughed between trying to breathe through the slobber and squirming up from his massive buddy. "Oh," he muttered, "I thought my nightmares had ended. Thanks, Pal, for the love, but you're not helping, and it's still night. Go back to sleep." Finally, he grabbed his phone with relief. "Hi, Sean. Just in time."

"You alone, Sammy?" whispered Sean.

"Yep. Just me and my big mutt, Caesar... You're hard to reach. Been on vacation?"

"No vacation… Come get me."

"Come get you?" Sam was stunned. "You...you never talked liked this before. What's wrong?"

ACCELERATION

"It's all turned. I'm losing. Come get me," Sean began to sob and then there was nothing. Silence hung in the air.

"Sean... Sean?" Sam listened intently, but there was no sound.

"You're gone. You hung up. Sean, I don't understand. What the hell is going on? You never cried before, even when Mom and Dad had died in the car crash." Sam felt like time stood still. He shook his head to clear his confusion.

Suddenly his phone rang again. Sam almost dropped it in his eagerness to answer.

It was Sean. He spoke almost mechanically. "I was rambling and being silly, Sam. I'm okay. You don't need to come. Don't come."

"What? Why?" Sam replied as the phone went dead again.

"What? The hell I don't, Sean. I'm coming. I'll leave in the morning... What's happened to you?"

Sam threw himself back onto the bed in frustration.

Caesar suddenly flopped upon him again, with his big lapping tongue.

"Oh, Caesar. I know you care. But slobbery affection is not needed. And move over, big ape. Susie, you are not." Sam heaved Caesar aside and fondly patted his shoulder. "Listen, we need to stop living alone. I think it's time for a change, for both of us. You like Susie. I like Susie." He chuckled as Caesar cocked his head. "I think I will ask her to move in, but it will have to wait to happen. In the morning, it looks like you're going to the dog sitter. I'll be back, but first, I have to help Sean. Something bad is happening. Something is terribly wrong."

CHAPTER 2

Sam stirred. His body ached. He felt he should open his eyes, but he really did not want to. He remembred taking Caesar to Cathy, the dog sitter. Caesar had jumped about her excitedly as she giggled with her big toothy grin. They both liked Cathy, a lot. He had told her hat she might be having him for awhile. She had said that she would keep him as long as needed. He had paid her for a month, although he hoped it would not be that long.

Sam kept trying to think. Why does his body hurt? And he felt cold." He jerked open his eyes and stared at the deluge of rain water that was smacking his windshield. "Interesting. I wonder why my car is not moving:" He turned his head, looked around slowly, and frowned.

"Oh no! I think I got into an accident. I just paid you off, car. You are a fantastic classic, beautiful, black jaguar, and I just wrapped your head in this cold-hearted gnarly tree. I apologize. Okay, now let me out."

Sam turned and pushed relentlessly until the door creaked heart-wrenching belches of sorrow and opened. He then untangled his long legs from the metal and yanked himself out.

The wind and rain immediately began to assault him. They ruthlessly hammered his face and drenched his body. The night chilled his bones. Sam shivered.

Sam slowly faced his car. He bent over and searched intently around the crushed front interior. "Where was help? Where was his phone?"

Ah, he found it, well, sort of. "My phone. Poor thing. You're smashed…Well, let's look at the bright side. It could be me."

Sam sighed. "I wonder how far help is."

He began to struggle over the trunk of his car, and pulled out his heavy jacket and flashlight.

His head still ached, but he felt stronger. "Now," he mused, "where was I going? Ah, I remembered it all now. I had intended to visit Sean. I had stopped at his office at Mekka Corporation. A man had said that Sean was on personal leave.

ACCELERATION

Sam had tried Sean's house. Sean's wife and kids were gone too, but the van and Toyota stood in the garage. I flashed on the thought of that old family cabin and had just headed out of town and towards it, when a massive truck had rammed me and shoved my car off the road. The drivegoing. I figure that I had passed out a few seconds later." His hand went to his head. "Yep, there's a knot on my forehead. It had been real. "

Sam thought in frustration. "Sean, this trip isn't going as planned, obviously."

He clawed his way up from the soggy ravine and stumbled out.

Sam now gazed ahead at the desolate pavement, as rain continued pelting him with gusto. "I wonder what's ahead," he thought. "It doesn't feel good. I'm just a writer, Sean, albeit a successful one, but I like knowing the endings upfront. My war is over. Danger is supposed to have ended also. Why are our lives suddenly getting so complicated and inexplicable? Why am I feeling that you are in big trouble? Little brother, I hope I can get you out, but I don't know... Where are you? Are you at the cabin? Maybe? Well, I'm coming. I'm going to get answers."

Sam yanked his jacket up, as the bitter wet wind reared up and angrily battered on his face. He began rapidly tramping down the gaping road. The flashlight beam slid hypnotically along the pavement.

The highway seemed endlessly in front of him, turn after turn. And no car appeared. On and on he walked, and then…he stopped short.

He had arrived, standing in exhaustion on the broken stone apron of the cabin's entrance. It was the childhood haven of Sam's memory. It was their special place. Sam was excited as he knocked and shouted.

"Sean, I've been through hell, open the door, Buddy... Sean, Kate, it's Sam. I'm wet and look disgusting at the moment, but I'm a relative." Sam laughed happily as he fumbled with the door. But his mood changed. Locked. He hit the door in frustration. "You have to be here. It's your favorite place."

Sam suddenly remember the hidden key and groped for it under the cobblestones. Feeling his prize and elated, he shouted.

ACCELERATION

"Hey, Buddy, I've got it. The key. I'm coming in. I hope you're dressed." He laughed, as he tore open the old creaky door.

A musty sad emptiness flooded and silently buried Sam's enthusiasm. No one and no sound pierced the reality. He stared into the darkness. He was alone.

In the room's core was a dusty old string attached to a naked light bulb. Sam reached into the gloom and pulled the cord. He released it and watched as it hypnotically swung back and forth and soft light gently bathed the interior.

Suddenly shivering, he gazed around and spotted the old wood, which was piled near the dirt covered fireplace. He brushed off the grate, heaped some of the fuel into the pit, and searched for a match. There at the back of the cupboard sat a half full box of matches and to Sam's delight- two old fashion cans of soup. Scrounging hungrily for a can opener, his stomach eagerly rumbled. "Aha! Gotcha," Sam gloated as his fingers closed on the metal of a rusty opener and eagerly sawed open one can. He wondered for a moment how old the soup was, since it didn't have a pop-open top. He brushed the thought away. Hell, he really didn't care, his stomach was churning with unfettered urgent expectation. Sam devoured the thick vegetable mix and sighed.

"Ah, delicious! Best soup I've ever had. Thanks, Sean. Now to light this fuel and I'll be warm and cozy. I appreciate the wood and the food. You know how to make a loving brother feel at home," He smiled as he lit the crumbling wood which sparkled and snapped into flames. Dragging his creaking chair over to the fire, Sam gulped down the second can of soup. Satiated, he leaned back in his chair and absorbed the enveloping warmth of the fire.

But his happy contentment suddenly dissolved into uneasiness. He loved mysteries, but this one bothered him terribly. This involved the only family he had left. He felt inadequate and helpless, and yet he knew that there was more to know, and he would find out. But for now, he had to make himself stop thinking. He was tired, really tired.

Sam dragged his body to the old cot at the side of the room and shook out the blanket at its foot. Dust flittered about in the air. He stared into the particles and tried to make sense of what he hoped would soon be explained. He wasn't sure if he'd like the true details, however. He brushed aside a foreboding, and sank onto the bed. He pulled up the old cover.

Sleep began to grab and wrap him into its protection, for this night anyway. He would rest, which was good. He needed the sleep, and yet he couldn't help but feel that the new day might bring great difficulties.

The night seemed to whisper into his dreams that he was probably right.

CHAPTER 3

Sam woke refreshed, physically, but his brother weighed heavily on his mind. Where was he?

He straightened the crumpled blanket and tucked it in with saddened carefulness. Suddenly his fingers touched an object under the mattress- a something that didn't belong. It felt like a small book. His heart raced as he tugged it out and opened it carefully. There was Sean's name in his familiar careful penmanship. Sam flipped to the first page. Sean's journal. His breath caught in his throat. Time seemed to stop, as he sank onto the bed. He read as he gently turned the pages.

Sam enters Sean's world. He beamed with brotherly joy as he read of Sean and Kate's love. But as the confessions continued, his exuberance dissolved. Sean's marriage turned rocky. They had worked together until he became ill. He had contracted an incurable cancerous growth.

"Whoa!" Sam jerked up, hitting his head on the slanted ceiling near the cot. "That can't be true!" he cried out. "Sean, you're a genetic engineer, you're brilliant. You're the picture of health, kindness, and domesticity. You can't be sick. You are also my brother and I love you." Sam's chest felt like it was viciously stomped upon.

He forced himself to continue reading- Sean was desperate for a cure, and then he began to have hope. He was running experiments on himself. The company had given him funding. He felt euphoria that his illness had been arrested and possibly cured. And then…he began gloating with superiority over the stupidity of his aides.

Cold cruel words now tumbled off the pages. Sean no longer had any use for Kate and the kids, but she refused to leave. She did, however, take the children to her mother's. She stayed for a time, and then returned. They fought, and she had cried. She finally left, and Sean was happy. He said that he no longer missed Kate and the children. He wanted to continue his work unhindered. He realized that he felt no love for them anymore, only indifference and pity. But his work- he needed and fed on his work.

"No, Sean, no!" Sam whispered in anguish as his hands trembled. He almost dropped the book. He forced himself to continue reading:

"July 5. I have made fantastic strides. Mekka has been supportive, but his intellect has not grown as fast as mine. He is not altering his serum at the stages that I apply. Foolish man. I have to take control. We are building a network beyond that which anyone has ever done before. And, people of power have become interested in my studies. I have selected further subjects also, so many that I am amused. They are all here…for my work and me! I am amazing myself.

July 10. I must make myself write every five days. However, I lose track of time. But then, maybe time is not important, certainly not compared with my experiments and observations… It's strange how I've changed. I notice that I am fascinated with colors in my environment. In fact, I've sensed auras in different colors and the bright colors are preferred. They excite and comfort me. The bland ones with black and tan shades create painful confusion in me and cannot be tolerated.

July 15. Time has begun to terrify me. I have covered all the clocks.

July 20. My subjects are so simple minded, compared to me. I am so far above them intellectually. I feel like a God. I'm special. I can't help but succeed.

July 25. I'm experiencing severe head pain. I am trying to control it. A genius should feel no pain, but I have faith that the pain is only temporary. I will overcome. I think that I must evolve and pass through barriers in order to be all powerful and superior."

Sam turned the page and gasped. The remaining pages were filled with chemical equations in a rainbow of colors, as if a child was playing with markers, but this child was one of genius capabilities. Sam closed the book sharply. These entries were those of a stranger. He felt sick.

Sean had been the nicest guy anyone could know. That talk with Sean so many years ago leaped into Sam's mind. He remembered.

Sean had grasped Sam's shoulders when he had started to shake violently. It was that night in the hospital. Sam had been badly injured during the Iraq War.

"I can't do it anymore, Sean, I …I…just can't…So much death. What could I have done better? I don't know. Tell me. Tell me."

Sean held him still, forcing Sam to look into his eyes. "You did everything right. You were a hero. Stop punishing yourself."

Sean's deep brown eyes, they were so kind and yet he fought them

"Look at me, Sam. You have a right to ask for a quiet assignment now. You've done enough for your country. The big shots will understand."

Sam pawed at his eyes with bandaged hands and struggled to sit up. "I couldn't save them. I was their leader. They trusted me. I keep seeing their faces. I wish I had died too."

"Stop it. You were all shot up." Sean snapped. "What do you expect of yourself? It was an ambush. The higher ups gave you bad intelligence. You're a Special Forces soldier who did his best. In fact, you did great. You're getting medals, and you deserve them." Sean wiped the sweat from Sam's face and eased him back on the bed.

Desperately Sam whispered back. "I don't want medals."

Sean poured some water into a cup at the bedside table. He held up Sam's head and brought the cup to his mouth. "Here drink this, relax, and then listen to me.'"

Sam still trembled as he tried to sip the drink, then lay back exhausted.

Sean continued. "It's not your fault. You made the right decision with the information you were given. The Big Brass agrees. You lost some men, but you saved so many more. You deserve the medals. You were a hero. You ran into the smoke and explosions, karate chopping and guns a blazing. You nut! And you took out a lot of bad guys. The ones that died would be proud of you and grateful for saving the rest. And remember, people die in war. You can't help them all. You can only try hard, and you did."

Sam had stared at the light above his head and then at his brother. He spoke softly. "I'm quitting the service. I want a quiet life now. I don't want to see people die anymore."

"I understand. But death, even during peace, isn't always pretty, serene, and free of pain. And we all just do our best to deal with it… Sam, you are not to blame. Remember that. You are one of the good guys, and you're my brother. Hey, I'm really proud of you. Now go to sleep. Dream of pretty girls and your new life. Then come visit me. I have a new job at a research hospital. And Kate and the kids will get to gush all over you too." Sean smiled.

Sam sighed heavily, but he understood. "Thanks, Sean. I'll try."

Sam remembered the long convalescence. Sean, Kate, and the kids had come often until Sean started working at his new job. Such a great family too. Sam felt a pang of envy, but he had enjoyed his new life, his quiet life, alone at first. He loved writing, but fame came quickly. He liked the money and freedom, no doubt about that. The attention, however, embarrassed him, but he was content. He married, but it didn't work out. He and his wife went their separate ways but stayed distant friends. Sam survived and basically recovered. He rebuilt his life. But now, Sean was in trouble. Sam may not be able to save his brother, but he would sure try.

Suddenly the sound of tires, on the gravel outside, cracked the air.

Sam shoved the journal back under the mattress. Who knew he was here? He rose and pulled open the old cabin door? A large van, with a huge Mekka Corporation Logo, seemed to glare hungrily back at him. His skin prickled? Sam blinked away his foreboding and walked firmly out of the cabin.

CHAPTER 4

"You Samuel Stone, the writer, Sean Stone's brother?"

"Yeah," Sam hedged.

"Get in," the driver grunted coldly.

"Why?" Sam stood his ground.

"I was just told to get you?

"Who are you? How did you know I was here?" Sam felt a gnawing sensation of increased wariness.

"You come now." The driver pointed close to Sean's face and evaded the question. He was a huge hefty brute. Sam had no wish to tangle with him.

"All right." No sooner had the words escaped him, but two men leaped from the van, shoved Sam onto a hard bench in the back and squeezed beside him. Sam felt his pulse racing.

"Are we going to see Sean?"

The men scowled and turned away.

Sam controlled his anger. "You're not answering me-means you are rude and uncooperative. I was treated politely when I inquired at the corporate building. Why so obnoxious now?"

"Just following orders. Now shut-up," the skinny one beside him said.

"I'll come, for the moment only." Sam wanted to punch them all in their swarthy faces and twist their tongues, but that wouldn't answer his questions. Not yet anyway. However, it sure would help him feel better. He fought the urge to strike back. He hadn't done physical self-defense since the war. He had wanted no part of physical violence ever again. He had been happy that his life had been peaceful, but now he was worried about the only family he had left, his brother. He couldn't turn away. Was his body ready and willing to fight back now? He thought so. To save Sean, yes; he had to do so. He could and would fight back. The skills would come back to him. He hoped so anyway.

It was a long two hours. Sam squirmed, but it only made the men crowd him tighter. He had about decided to elbow each hard, punch their ugly faces, and escape, but the van suddenly jerked in a turn and slowed to a stop. The men hurled him out the door and onto the ground. They smirked and roared with laughter.

Sam sat up. "Is this how you treat guests? Not funny. Is Sean your boss or this man, Mekka? They won't like you not being kind. Me neither." Sam staggered up and threw a steely punch. The bigger guy caught the hard impact directly on the center of his jaw. Unaffected, he turned, grinned at Sam, and hurled him against the van.

Stunned, Sam stood unsteadily. "So, creep, you're one of those freaks that don't feel pain. I'll have to change that." Sam threw his legs out to trip the thug and scrambled to hold the massive neck in a vice-like choke hold. I think I'll call you Loser, because you just lost."

Sam tightened his grip as the man gasped and sputtered. "Loser, don't treat guests like me with disrespect. You will promise to be sweet right?"

Sam suddenly felt a muzzle of a gun pressing hard on the side of his head. "Oh, protecting Loser, eh? Not good for me, is that what you're trying to say, in your own humble way?" Sam twisted and batted the gun down as it went off. Loser yelped and grasped his leg. Sam squirmed away. "Hey, Skinny, you hurt your Loser. Mekka won't like that. "

Sam stood up and glared at the men gasping on the ground. "It's been awhile since I've had so much exercise, fellas. My body's a bit achy, you too I imagine. Shall we quit and be civil now? …Take me to my brother and Mekka. Get up."

Sam immediately sensed a gun in his back. "Yes?" Sam said quietly. "I forgot about the driver. And you are?"

"Ratch," The swarthy driver grunted.

Sam nodded. "Well, Ratch, you may join us. Take me to your "Leader", you know, your little boss."

Ratch stared down at his men in scorn and lowered his gun. "Get up, men. Dr. Mekka won't like this."

Loser and Skinny struggled up and sputtered to the driver. "Give him to us."

"Later," Ratch spat out the words.

Sam stared up at this building in the rear. He had been to the small front one to inquire about Sean, but this one was huge and garish orange in color. This unusually colorful exterior puzzled him. "Your boss likes rather bright colors for his buildings!"

"Shut up. Move." Ratch gave him a shove.

Sam could feel Ratch's eyes bore into his back as he began to strut forward. "All right," he replied crisply. Reaching the door, he reached out to yank it open. "Oops, locked. I thought I was invited. I assume you charming fellows have a key?"

Ratch shoved him aside, inserted a key card, flung open the door, and snorted. "Yes, and I don't need your attempts at charm. Walk."

"Well, it would help," Sam muttered coldly, as he pushed down a heavy feeling. He wondered why he was facing such hostility. Something big was going on. It didn't look good, at least not for him. But why?

As the elevator climbed, Sam gazed at his brother's associates. He did not like them a bit.

The lift suddenly jerked to a stop. Sam emerged into sumptuous surroundings. It wasn't the expensive furnishings, however, that aroused his curiosity. He puzzled at the extent of the orange on the walls, that bright, brash, hard orange again! The walls were a bit of a travesty to the senses, he thought. Then it hit him with choking force- the serum, Sean's discovery! Either Mekka was possibly using it in here or Sean was or…both!

A small man, with a marmalade cane, interrupted Sam's thoughts. He peered at Sam with the curiosity of an evil mortician eying a dead human carcass. Sam felt a sudden nausea and the urge to run. He forced himself to not move and stared at icy blue eyes that never blinked. The man hoarsely whispered, "Sit."

Sam felt his breath catch and then rush back into his lungs. He cleared his throat. "I want to see my brother, Sean. He works for you, but you know that."

"He's busy and expresses his regrets. He wishes you to leave and not come back."

"I WILL SEE HIM NOW. THEN I WILL RETURN HOME." Sam had found his voice and strength.

"You will not see him. He's extremely busy. I don't repeat myself again. My daughter, Caroline, will see to your needs. You are excused. Caroline will join you in the lobby. Good day, Mr. Stone." Heavy doors opened as Mekka turned away.

Sam was amazed. "You are giving me your daughter. You under-estimate me."

Mekka turned. "You are an animal. She is an animal. You are worth nothing to me. She will be waiting and can make her own decisions. You are not wanted here. Go back to your own kind."

"My kind is here." Sam said curtly.

ACCELERATION

"No, you have made a big mistake, Stone. You don't belong. Your brother does not want you here. I do not want you here. Get out while you can." Mekka stared at him with distain, pivoted, and was gone.

Sam's thoughts scrambled as he struggled to control his anger.

Suddenly two men gripped hard on his arms and hustled him back to the elevator. Their vice-like grip held until they reached the parking lot. "Thanks guys for the tour, but next time, mind your manners. I hate to lose my sense of humor and break your ugly necks, but I could." Sam snapped as he jerked away.

"Mr. Stone?"

Sam turned to the voice and met the cool playful gaze of Miss Caroline Mekka.

"May I call you Sam?" she continued crisply, "You resemble your brother. I'm Caroline. My father says that Sean is well and regrets your wasted trip. Do return to your home. Your car is in the shop, but here is a new blue Jag loaner car. It should get you home. Yours was black but this one is terrific. You may use it or keep it, as you wish. However, we will let you know when your car is fully repaired and ready. In the meanwhile, we hope your journey home will be pleasant." She passed him the keys. "Good day, Sir."

Sam feared his mouth might be gaping. "I hate to be rude, but this won't work…Thank you for the car, but I need answers."

"Then let's go for a drive." Caroline flipped her long blonde hair and smiled charmingly. "I'll drive." She pointed to her white Jag. "We have similar tastes in cars, sort of. A good way to start our friendship. Get in."

"All right…Interesting," Sam was definitely fascinated. "Miss Caroline. I'm temporarily hooked. Don't betray me."

"Good, I'm harmless," Caroline laughed that lovely sound again. She gracefully entered the car and rolled down the windows. "I hope you don't mind if I open them; I enjoy the fresh air."

"I do also. Let's go," he replied as he joined her in the car.

Sam couldn't help but wonder if she was an unpredictable pawn or integral to the game she was playing. But he felt she had no cruelty and deception in her soul. He hoped he was correct.

"By the way, where are we going?"

ACCELERATION

Caroline turned to Sam and spoke softly, with a serious look on her face. "My place." She quickly threw the car into gear and sped away, as the wind tore at their clothes.

CHAPTER 5

The lady knew the hills. Sam wanted to shake her steely confidence; however, she was too damn sexy.

"You cold, Sam?" Caroline shouted in the wind.

"No, he returned.

She skidded onto a dirt road and began to traverse it with skill.

"Ever do any racing?" Sam yelled.

"No, you?" She grinned coyly.

"No… Is there a kind soul under that glaze, Miss?" Sam gazed at her seriously.

"Possibly," Caroline retorted and yanked the car into a turn. She then quickly pulled into the stone driveway of a small cottage. "My hideaway." She turned towards Sam with eyes flashing. "Don't get me wrong, Stone. I don't bring all my father's friends here, just the ones I'm attracted to."

He had to admit, he was aroused.

Caroline ran up the steps and cocked her head in his direction. "Come, we need to go inside."

ACCELERATION

Sam felt drawn to follow and did. Once inside, Sam closed the door firmly and looked at her gravely.

"You are confused, angry, or delighted?" She replied softly.

"Delighted, of course, but why am I really here?" Sam definitely needed more honesty than he was getting.

"I need you to help my father," Caroline said quietly.

"Your father seems very much in control. He doesn't need my help," Sam said flatly.

"He's wrong. You'll see." She whispered as she moved close to Sam and touched his mouth with her fingertips.

Sam kissed them gently and smoothed her silky hair. "You are beautiful," he breathed softly, as he looked deeply into her eyes. She was one of the good guys, he was fairly sure of that now. Sean could wait until morning.

Sam woke and gazed into the darkness. He had forgotten where he was. He stared with slow comprehension at the shadowy figure framed in the moonlight by the window. "Caroline?" he whispered.

Caroline turned. "I didn't mean to wake you. I couldn't sleep. I'm sorry, Sam. I'm using you. I'm not being fair."

"Using me, I'm also using you, but enjoying every minute."

Caroline stared back.

Sam could feel the tremendous sadness, even at the distance. "What's wrong? There's more?"

She slowly walked to him, lowered herself on the bed, and curled up in Sam's arms. As she lay beside him, tears filled her eyes. "I can't, Sam. I can't handle…" Her slim shoulders began to shake with overwhelmed emotion, and she began to sob.

"Easy, honey. Take your time." He felt suddenly very close to this lady, closer than he had felt towards anyone in a long time, even with Susie. It wasn't just physical attraction, although she was lovely as hell, but there was something else. He wanted to stay with her and never leave.

Caroline began to calm and grow quiet. She swallowed and smoothed out her emotional chaos. "Sam, my father is dying."

"I would not have guessed that." Sam was genuinely shocked. "He seemed so…"

"Sure and hard," she said.

"Well, yes, and very self-centered. How can you care about him?"

"Because… I just do." She turned her face away.

Sam sensed that he had gone too far. "I'm sorry. I was blunt and uncaring."

ACCELERATION

"No, you're right." She rose quickly and began to dress. "Time for you to go," she said coldly.

"Whoa, come back. Where are you, Caroline?" He sat up on the edge of the bed. "I'm listening. Talk to me."

She stopped and turned away. "It's difficult... Sean was supposed to help my father, but something went wrong. Dad is worried, and it's changed him. He won't tell me anything. I don't know how to help...Maybe you can go back tomorrow and try to talk to him again."

"You really think he'd tell me, Caroline?"

"Maybe not, but if you want to find, Sean, we could team up and there might be a chance." Caroline turned back and said softly, "I don't know what else to do."

Sam took her hand gently. "I would love to help but please consider -we may lose and it may be dangerous." He felt a heavy silence as he looked at Caroline's grave face. "Oh, Caroline...All right. You love your father and I love my brother. Maybe, just maybe, we can win. We'll find Sean and get some answers. Maybe we can help them both."

Caroline sat beside Sam and sighed in relief. "We'll succeed or die trying. Thank you."

Sam kissed her gently and smoothed her silky hair. "I don't want you to die… You are very beautiful and loving," he whispered softly. She was one of the innocent, he was sure of that…Sean and Mekka would have to wait until morning.

Caroline grinned mischievously as she began slowly removing Sam's blanket.

He chuckled as he pulled her gently down onto the bed.

She crawled on top of him and ran her hands across his chest and down his sides. She felt the rippling of his hard muscles. She also felt his scars. "What are these from?" she said softly and then kissed them gently.

"War memories from another time. But you are now." He was very attracted to this lady, very, and aroused. He didn't expect more sleep, but she was definitely special and worth it. He felt like Sean would joyfully approve, wherever he was.

Sam gathered Caroline into his arms, and both felt the tremendous sexual electricity between them. He pulled away briefly as he tore off her clothes. They then joyfully caught fire.

They would remember this night.

CHAPTER 6

Sam and Caroline rose in the morning light and dressed in silence.

Suddenly Sam felt something unspoken. "There's more, isn't there?"

Caroline sat and breathed deeply. "My father isn't usually cold and cruel to people. I don't know why he's acting this way now. He's always been a kind man. Maybe the pressure is getting to him. But I realize that may be a flimsy excuse to you." She shook her head, rose, and slipped into her clothes. She hurriedly tucked in her blouse.

Even in a simple outfit, she looked breath-taking, he mused.

"I'm awfully worried, Sam."

"I know. I'm sorry, honey…Let's go, back to the company and the labs. We'll find Sean. Then maybe we can help your father, if they'll let us. After all, we're smart." Sam's eyes twinkled.

Caroline couldn't help but laugh.

"Ready?" Sam asked. "Sean will have answers or leave us with more questions, hopefully the former."

Caroline leaned over and kissed him gently. "I really like you, Sam, as if you didn't notice from last night. And thank you."

"You like me, eh?... And I noticed," Sam teased."

Caroline laughed. "Now Sean has two floors, a lab and temporary apartment in the east wing, below my father's floor," Caroline gathered up her small purse. "Lately my father has refused to let me see Sean and won't explain why."

"We'll figure it out. Ready, partner?" His eyes twinkled.

"Charmed, and yes," Caroline laughed and kissed him on the cheek.

"Oh, only a cheek kiss?" Sam teased.

"The best comes later." Caroline flounced out the door.

Sam laughed and followed. But suddenly he stopped and felt an uneasiness descend. His joy at being with Caroline was smacked by a bad feeling. There was real danger ahead. But, he could face whatever was to come. He knew that he had healed from his brokenness after being so badly hurt during the war. He was strong now mentally and physically. But he couldn't help feeling a nagging worry about Caroline. He prayed she wouldn't get hurt.

Sam and Caroline arrived at the Mekka complex and decided to plow ahead confidently and without secrecy, for now anyway. It was Saturday, and they met only one guard at the main door.

Caroline waved at the man, "Hi, George, my new boyfriend here."

The guard grunted, "Ok, Miss Caroline."

They breezed through.

Sam looked around. "Now where?"

"Sean's probably in his lab or apartment on the fourteenth floor. He uses the whole floor. Follow me."

Sam strutted beside Caroline as they traveled the maze and nodded to an occasional worker. "Piece of cake so far, beautiful. Oops, spoke too soon." They pulled up a short distance from the guard at the elevator. "Do you have a pass note or key- card?" He looked at Caroline expectantly.

"My father took it away. I think he knew I was getting curious that something was wrong. He knows how headstrong I am. And, I don't know this guard."

"Okay. Let's see." Sam thought of his novels. He usually cured this hitch with a gun or stolen pass key. But he actually now preferred not to use a gun, unless necessary. But then, he had no gun anyway. "We'll get the keycard non-violently, maybe, and sort of. Is there a coffee machine near here?"

"Coffee? You want to take a break now?" Caroline said with surprise.

"Nope," Sam explained. "You do. You need coffee. It's morning. We all need coffee, and you want it so as to tease the guard and accidently toss it onto him." Sam explained. "I saw it in the movies, well, in lots of movies." He grinned. "But it can be effective."

"But it will be hot." Caroline said earnestly.

"All right, I'll handle the coffee. Be sure to flirt, and I'll play the jealous lover. I'll throw the coffee on the guard, and you can mop him off with a little napkin. Then I'll pilfer the key, or you will, if you can do it."

"I can do it. I feel a bit badly about the poor guy though, but I'll do it. Actually, it might, sort of, be fun. Let's go. This way to coffee!" Caroline led Sam through the halls, and they grabbed their hot cups of coffee.

ACCELERATION

Sam thought aloud. "We'll start out arguing about something…ah, our last date, how about… like… you flirted with the bartender and I was perturbed."

Caroline laughed. "Perturbed? You perturbed? All right. It's not exactly a high espionage approach, is it? But I can do this. I once wanted to be an actress, although I doubt I will be doing great acting now, but yes, I can do this." She planted a quick playful kiss on his lips. "I'm ready, I think." She picked up the hot coffee and took a deep breath.

"You'll do fine, and maybe I'll get a longer kiss afterwards," Sam teased.

"You will, I promise." Caroline took a deep breath again.

"Ah, I accept. Let's go," said Sam. "We are a real team now… like Bonnie and Clyde," Sam grabbed her other hand as they wound through the corridors and back to the guard.

They stopped behind a corner near the guard.

"Who are Bonnie and Clyde?" Caroline whispered, as she tried to steady her cup from splashing. "Oh, I know, they were gangsters. But we're fighting for the right," Caroline replied, as she giggled.

"Yep, but they were smart and crazy about each other," said Sam while cradling his own coffee carefully also.

"But they were killed in a rain of bullets," said Caroline.

"Oh, yeah," said Sam. "Well, maybe they weren't that smart. But, we'll be fine, I think." He gave her a quick kiss. "Now, I'm ready. You ready? It will be enjoyable for us, although maybe not for him. But again, it's for a good cause."

"Yes." Caroline said softly, nodded, and then staggered forward, as she changed into character and swaggered with drunken charm. "Hi, you good looking sexy guy. I want you, instead of this creep. You are so cuddly. I like chubby men. Kiss me, handsome," she teased.

Sam played the jealous and also inebriated lover with gusto. "Lay off my girl," he threw his coffee at the startled guard. "Leave my baby alone."

"Hey man, that's hot! You burned me!" The guard cried out. "OW. Hey, you bitch! I know you. Aren't you Dr. Mekka's daughter?"

Caroline cooed and pulled the guard to her as she swabbed him with her little napkin and sat seductively on his lap. Sloshing her words, she fawned over him, caressing his face and kissing him all over. "Me, hell no. I wish I had her money. You poor thing, sorry Mister, but you are very sexy." Caroline hugged him and coyly swiped the key card from his pocket.

ACCELERATION

"Get off of me, you dumb broad. Now I gotta call for help and change clothes, and you hurt me with that coffee. You stupid drunks. I'm calling Dr. Mekka and get you arrested."

Sam grabbed Caroline's hand as she dropped her coffee on the guard also.

The guard howled.

Words slurring, Sam pretended fierce regret. "Buddy, I'm sorry. I just thought you was messing with my lady. She belongs to me. We're leaving. We don't want no trouble."

"Ow, I'm still hurting," the guard moaned.

"I'm really sorry, you cute thing. We're leaving now, right now." Caroline also pretended repentance. "Let's go, Clyde."

"Right, Bonnie." Sam turned and winked at Caroline. "We're going…Mister. Don't tell the big boss that we made you messy, ok?… Girl, tuck in your blouse, you whore. The boss won't like it."

Sam grabbed Caroline's hand. They spurted forward, rounded a corner and hid, falling against the wall. Looking fondly at Caroline, Sam whispered, "You were a terrific bad girl."

Caroline felt great. "And you were a terribly ornery jealous lover."

He laughed. "Elevator, over there. Let's go."

They ran.

CHAPTER 7

The elevator door opened. Sam and Caroline moved a few steps forward into the huge dark laboratory.

"This is it. I haven't been here in a long time." Caroline squeezed Sam's hand. "You lead, please."

"I suppose we should knock," Sam said. "Good idea, yeah?"

"Brilliant," Caroline smiled.

"Here we go." Sam knocked on the wall. No answer. He knocked again. Silence. Feeling for a switch, they walked forward, hand in hand into the semi-darkness. "Where's the light switch?'"

"I don't know. The lights were always on when I was here."

"Humm." Sam sighed. "I think the windows must be covered or there aren't any."

"There aren't any," said Caroline. "I think I'm nervous."

"Klunk!"

Sam turned. "I think the second elevator came up. Only the lights were off on it." He suddenly turned to Caroline and squeezed her hand.

"What's wrong?" She whispered nervously.

"Um," said Sam as his body stiffened and he dropped her hand. "I think there's a gun in my back."

A crisp callous voice seemed to echo in the darkness, "Mr. Stone, where is your brother?"

Sam spoke much more calmly than he felt, "I was hoping you could tell me that,"

"Don't get smart!" The man hissed as light suddenly flooded the room.

Sam was then smashed into a chair, and four men piled upon him, holding his arms and legs fast. Caroline started to protest, when suddenly she was shoved into a second chair, as another man gripped her hard.

A buff woman walked up, and punched Sam in the gut, and quickly tied them down.

"Ah, a lady, or maybe not. What was that for?" asked Sam with disgust.

"I hate men. Don't come back," She grunted.

"Perhaps you haven't met the right man. But then you're not my type either. I'm here to find out where my brother is," said Sam firmly.

"You're a spy."

ACCELERATION

"Why would I do that? Nah, no spy, I'm a nice…" Sam never got the rest out. A chunky first rammed into his face again.

"What are you protecting here?"

Sam's felt himself fading and lost consciousness.

"Sam, Sam wake up? It's Caroline. They're gone."

Sam gasped. He licked his dry lips. "My face hurts, but I'm sort of back. Those women were very hostile. Do you know what they are protecting?"

"I don't," said Caroline. "You were out a long time. I was so frightened when you didn't answer. I'm so glad you're alive and back."

"Well, honestly speaking, me too. But I'm not feeling too well. Give me a minute, I guess my fighting skills have slipped a bit." He inhaled deeply a couple of times. "Okay, Caroline," Sam said softly, "why don't you scoot your chair over to me. Push with your feet, but don't tip over. When you get to me, I'll try and untie you. Or you can wait until I feel better and go to you, or we can compromise," Sam chuckles. "Ow, it hurts to smile."

"I'll try," Caroline whispers. "I hope I can do it."

Caroline begin to move her chair slowly, and they met. They struggled to untie each other, and finally, they were free. They stood and held each other tightly.

"Ok." Sam released Caroline and looked around. "We need light. They never did turn them on. Maybe they didn't know where the lights were either. I'm going to open the elevator door again," Sam walked to the door unsteadily and propped it open. "I don't think they'll be back, at least not just yet. Did they hurt you?"

"No, just you. I'm sorry," Caroline said sadly.

"I'll be fine. It's just a nasty hiccup on our way to answers…Let me hold you." Sam reached over and pulled her gently to him. He hugged her and smiled. "You okay?"

"Yes, I'll be fine. I'm just not used to violence," she said softly.

"No one is, well, most people, or some people. We just must try to forget and go on." Sam kissed her hand, and gazed around. "There must be a light switch somewhere."

Caroline turned around. "I think I remember now, where it is." She found the switch, "Here." The lights flooded the room. "Now I feel better."

ACCELERATION

Sam looked at her warmly, "Me too…And in the darkness and amidst my pain and suffering, I forgot how beautiful you are."

"Thank you, I must look pretty messed up though."

"You will always be lovely," said Sam with a bruised grin. "Now to business. Sean must have left some clue or notes, unless he didn't want anyone to find them. Let's take the former idea and look around."

Caroline picked up Sam's hand and drew him to her. She closed her eyes and hugged him, then pulled away and smiled. "I'll check his apartment behind this lab."

"Good," said Sam, "And thanks for the embrace, but what was that for?"

"For not dying on me while they beat you. I don't want to be alone, and I kind of like you," Caroline said solemnly.

"Kind of, good, I like that. Then last night was worth it…and don't worry."

"Thank you, Sam." Caroline felt tears filling her eyes. "I'd better go check that lab, handsome."

"Handsome, eh. You like me."

Caroline laughed, "A little bit and sometimes more, lots more." Caroline trotted off to the open apartment door and scooted in.

"There are no notes," Sam joined Caroline in the apartment. "I sure hope you found something."

"Not yet, but I'm not giving up. Help me pull the bed apart." Caroline brushed her hair back from her face. "I'm getting tired, but we can't quit." She picked up the pillow and took off the case. "Nothing here."

"We are not giving up yet. Under the mattress. There might be a journal." Sam grabbed the covers and yanked them off. He shook them, and pulled off the mattress. An orange journal seemed to stare teasingly back at them.

Caroline gasped, "How did you know?"

"Sean is a man of habits," Sam replied with relief as he picked up the journal, flopped the mattress back onto the bed, and sat down. "Sit. We need to read this now, before someone takes it from us."

Caroline sat and clasped his hand as they read:

"Oct.1. The headaches are stronger. I fear the injections cause them, but the results are too tremendous to warrant their discontinuance. The cancer is gone. I'm cured. I rejoice. I have also made fantastic jumps in my mathematical abilities. I am sure that Dr. Mekka must be envious. I've tried to explain the new results, but he doesn't understand. I have progressed much further in my intellect than he has. I feel some pity. Such a foolish man. He stopped his injections. He should have continued. Work progresses somewhat with the other subjects, but I'm getting superior results with me. I am better than them anyway, and more important.

Oct. 3. I scream in pain. The headaches are hourly today, but my mental test results continue to soar beyond ordinary human belief. My brain scan shows increased size; however, my bones have not grown. The pressure in my skull is great, but I can't stop experimenting. Soon I'll be the smartest human in the world.

Oct. 4. My head hurts terribly. I'm hoping the bones will grow soon.

Oct. 5. I see through walls and hear voices. Mekka is jealous. He doesn't hear them. They praise me but are also often evil and insult me. I must constantly fight them. I've considered how to kill them, but they may take me in the end.

Oct. 10. I felt suddenly smothered today, so I slipped out and drove to a town. The light burned my eyes terribly, and there were shadows of monsters everywhere. They stared at me in the streets and wherever I turned. I yelled at them to get out of my way. Then I decided that they were not worth my wrath. I'm the superior one, not them. I then drove back to my office. I like it better here.

Oct. 11. Mekka has stolen my formulas. He uses it on his other subjects. It's not fair. It should be only mine now. I don't want to share. But I can't think right today. I hurt badly. I pleaded with Mekka to let me have the next stage. I want it. I need it. But, I don't have to listen to him anymore. I'm smarter than he is. So I've taken the new improved medicine. I am in the new stage now. I'm thrilled.

Oct. 15. I have been receiving phone calls from my brother. I'm amused. I called him when I was in pain and depression, so I worried him. But now I don't want him here. He will try to stop me. But I decide. I choose. No one tells me what to do anymore. I do wonder, however, if Sam is coming. He will be frightened. Should I give him the drug so he won't be afraid? Then he'll see how wonderful it is to be the smartest person in the world."

The journal ended. Sam and Caroline sat very still.

ACCELERATION

Slowly Sam began to pace. I think I need to go back to Sam's house. I'd love to have you come, but I don't think you'll be safe with me. I don't want you hurt. Go back to your place and stay there. I don't think your father and his men will hurt you. I'm not giving up, and I'm not deserting you. Wait there for me. You are very important to me."

"All right, Sam. I'll go home now. Someone here will take me. Be careful. I think I'm falling in love with you, and I don't want to lose you."

"And I you," Sam said quietly. He gently reached over and pulled Caroline into his arms and softly kissed her. "Will you be all right?"

"Yes, Sam. I'll be fine. You're right. Neither my father or Sean will hurt me. I'll be waiting and hoping that you'll find a way to end this nightmare."

"Me too. If I can't do it, we'll leave together and for good. I promise. Goodbye for now, darling." Sam kissed her, turned, and walked down the hall. He didn't dare look back or he would change his mind.

Caroline stepped back into the lab and sat down. Suddenly she stood. She bounded out the door and down the hallway calling, "Sam, wait! I've changed my mind. Take me with you." Abruptly she stopped. He was gone. It was too late. "But," she whispered to herself, "Sam, I know you'll come back at the end. You promised."

CHAPTER 8

It felt good to be in the familiarity of his black Jag. It was parked outside the Mekka Corporation building. Sam sighed with relief. They had performed a Band-Aid repair job on it, but it functioned well. The car had always seemed a superficial part of him, but now it felt like family, old and safe. He suddenly realized that he was driving fast, he slowed down. His old family home, that's where he planned on going.

There was a Chinese restaurant near the old house. He always liked Asian food and his rumbling stomach reminded him that he was very hungry. There it was, the restaurant. He pulled over and went in.

The food helped. Sam felt hopeful. He was looking forward to visiting that old homestead. They never sold it. Sam had stayed there when he visited. Sometimes it was rented out. He hoped that it might be empty.

Now it was flooding back. On that fishing trip, when they were kids, the brothers had caught a myriad of very tiny fish. Their father had thrown them all back. Sean had cried, and Sam had put his arms around him and said that it wouldn't be fair to eat the kids. Sean had sniffled and looked up at him with adoration, but the feeling was mutual. Sean was a great little brother. Sam had said, at the time, that he would help his brother aim for the big ones the next day. But- they never did catch any.

Sam remembered so clearly. Sean had sighed and said he didn't care anymore, and that he was just happy that his big brother was fishing with him. Sam had laughed and said, "All you need to do is ask." But Sean never did ask again, and Sam, being older, didn't really play with him a lot. There was, however, an unspoken agreement that Sam would be there if Sean ever needed him.

Sam never felt that close to his brother again, until the hospital ordeal, and that was years later. And then it was Sam needing Sean. "I owe him big time," Sam spoke aloud to himself.

Sam rubbed his eyes, he was very tired.

All of a sudden, there was the house. He'd arrived. The family house, now Sean's, was dark. A huge maple tree secluded the old colonial homestead from the eyes of strangers. The home was occasionally Sean's refuge from the material world. Of course, he also had his home from his marriage, and guests usually visited his apartment at the lab.

Sam started to unlock the door, but it wasn't necessary. It swung open easily on its hinges and rocked in the late November breeze. A figure hovered in the shadows. Sam tensed as he squinted to make out the shape. He seemed to be resting in a chair in the corner.

"Sean, that you?" Sam started for the lights.

"No, no light," a voice softly said. It was Sean.

"Okay, Sean." Sam pulled a chair up to face him. "I'm here. Can I help?"

There was silence.

"Tell me what to do, Sean? I want to help." Sam listened, but the only answer was the sound of the door flopping on its hinges in the wind. Sam reached over and put his hand on Sean's shoulder. "Sean? Let me help."

Sean began to whimper. "I'm sick...very sick."

"I know. I'm here. I don't know what I can do, but I'm here," said Sam softly.

Sean started crying softly. "I gotta take my medicine." Hands trembled as he pulled out a syringe and a vile from his pocket.

Sam put his hand gently upon the hand of his brother. "Please don't take it. That's what is making you sick. Let me keep it for you. It will be safe."

"NO!" Sean screamed out and pushed Sam's hand away. "It's mine not yours!" Suddenly, he shoved Sam and his chair backwards.

"What the hell!" Sam stammered as he climbed off the floor. "Sean, give it to me. I'm here to help. I care about you."

"You can't have it. It's mine. YOU GET YOUR OWN!" Sean screamed out as he injected himself.

Sam was stunned and just stood still staring. His brother was definitely the man in the journal. He shook away the image. Sam reached out and grabbed the needle protruding from Sean's arm. Sean looked at it and began to whimper.

"Sean," Sam said softly. "Please stop taking your injections. Your medicine is killing you. Listen to me. I would never lie to you. I want you to stay alive. The medicine won't do it. Trust me. You helped me at the military hospital. You helped me to live again. Now I want to help you. We're brothers, I care about you. Trust me. Stop taking your medicine. You are poisoning yourself."

ACCELERATION

Sean rubbed his arm and stood trembling. "You hurt me. Nobody is supposed to hurt me. I'm special. I'm a genius."

Suddenly Sam found himself hurling towards the wall and smashing into it. Sam wasn't prepared for Sean's surge of strength. They hadn't fought physically in years, not since they had discovered that they could truly hurt each other. He remembered seeing Sean with a bloody nose that he had given him when they were wrestling. He was shocked and vowed never to fight him again. Now Sam was the victim of brotherly aggression. He didn't like it but knew it wasn't the real Sean.

"Who are you?" Sean yelled and lunged.

Sam was taller and more physically fit than his brother, but the look on Sean's face was dangerous. "I'm your brother, the one who went fishing with you, the one you held in the hospital. You saved me from severe depression. Because of you, I have a life again. I owe you a lot. Let me help."

Sean paused and a confused expression raced across his face. "I remember him, not you." He cried out and clutched his head.

"Sean, please let me help you." Sam reached out.

"Don't touch me! They told me not to talk to anyone. My work is mine. My medicine is mine!"

"Yes, it is yours. Sit down here, Sean, and tell me about them. Who are they?" Sam implored.

"Perhaps he means us," a voice spoke coldly from the doorway. Sam turned and watched as three men in suits walked into the room. "We were correct. We figured that he'd be here," the tall one continued. He lit a cigarette and threw the match on the floor. "Nice house kids."

"Kids? How flattering. Now, get out of our nice house… gentlemen." Despite his bravado, Sam was feeling uneasy.

"This really won't do," the small man spoke in a shrill voice as he chewed on a tooth pick.

"Do, for what? Get out," Sam was angry now. They had invaded his privacy, his family home. "Tall man, Shrill, and you, Tatoo, get out.

"We just need your crazy brilliant brother, and then we leave." The third man with tattoos all over his face spoke. "And don't call me Tatoo."

"Sean's staying here. He's ill," Sam replied as he tried to pull back his temper.

"We own your brother. We're here to collect," Tall Man spoke carefully.

ACCELERATION

"I thought Dr. Mekka owned him, if anyone could own a person." Sam was confused.

"Mekka is a desperate puppet." There was that third man, Shrill, again.

"We've said enough," Tattooed boomed. "Face the wall."

Sam stared at them uneasily and rocked forward, ready to spring into action. "Why?", he said cautiously.

"Acceleration says why," Shrill hissed.

"Acceleration?" Sam retorted quickly. "What is that?"

"Shut up," Tattooed was enjoying his position of boss. "Face the wall."

"I don't think so," Sam started to speak, when suddenly a chair was hurled into their midst. "What the…"

"RUN WITH ME, BROTHER!" Sean shouted as he rushed out the door.

The thugs were a short breath behind Sean, who paused and kicked Tall Man in the knees and pitched Tattoo over his shoulder. Shrill held a gun, but Sean was wildly possessed as he ran towards it. Shrill was too stunned to fire or perhaps he knew that he shouldn't. Sean hurled Shrill into a maple tree and then screamed madly at Tall Man, as he picked him up effortlessly and tossed him into a second tree. Then all of a sudden, Sean stopped his rampage. He stood dazed and still.

Sam caught up and punched the rising Tattoo out cold and breathlessly looked at Sean. "Wow, you were amazing!"

"Amazing, yes," Sean said woodenly. The fire had gone out.

"You hurt?" Sam gasped.

"You hurt?" Sean repeated.

"No," Sam turned and glanced at Sean's now still body, standing beside him.

"No," Sean mimicked.

Sam felt an overwhelming sorrow, as if a fist had smashed into his soul. His brown eyes glistened. "Sean, get in the car. I'll drive."

Sean woodenly walked to the car, got in, and stared ahead. They drove, neither speaking. Much later Sam noted that Sean had curled himself into a ball on the seat and had slipped mercifully into sleep.

"Oh, Sean, why did you do this to yourself?" Sam whispered painfully. "I wonder, what this Acceleration is. Is it just a bad drug or is there more? And where the hell are we going?" Sam shook his head and started laughing. "How did our world get so complicated and crazy?"

CHAPTER 9

"Sean," Sam stopped the car and turned towards his brother. "We're going to Caroline's house. It's the only place left to turn. They won't think we'd go back there. We can hide you there and get you off the drugs you're taking."

Sean was staring straight ahead and not moving.

"Do you hear me and understand?" Sam continued. "There are other things I need to know. You have to help me out. What is Acceleration?"

Sean began examining his hands and mumbling.

Sam spoke again. "What is Acceleration? I need to know that. Also who were those men and what do they plan to do with you." Sam got out of his car and crossed to Sean's side. He opened the door and knelt beside him as he clasped Sean's shaking hands. "Sean, I need to know the answers. Clear your head."

Sean raised his head and seemed to focus. "It's what I am," he said.

"What you are? Is this your experiment? Who are those people that want you?" Sam said.

"They want what I know. I'm very smart, you see. I am smarter than you and everybody. They try to make it work with others, but I am smarter, you see." Sam clutched his head and whimpered. "You see you see you see."

"Don't cry, please. You are smart," Sam was baffled, but he'd play along.

"Are you my brother, Sammy? Do you want to see my pictures?" Sean was getting more childish by the minute.

"Yes, sure," Sam was feeling frustrated. This was leading nowhere.

"Lost. Want. Me. Give me?" Sean seems to be at toddler stage, Sam thought sadly.

"Where did you leave them last, Sean?"

Sean grinned. "Book. Mine. Pretty. Me write. Num-ber-s."

Sam was thinking hard. The pictures, maybe they were of his scientific discoveries. "Sean, can you make those numbers and pictures again?"

"Num..ber..s." Sean's face lit up with another bright smile, as he nodded his head.

ACCELERATION

"That's wonderful, Sean." Sam excitedly searched for a pen in his glove compartment and handed it to Sean. "This will draw. You can make the numbers on the back of this envelope. There are more paper envelopes in this box, that I had placed in the glove compartment. I forgot that I bought them and had left them in the car. I'll find even more paper, if you need it. I like that you can do this."

"Okay," said Sean.

But the numbers that grew on the page were childish scratches. They seemed like nothing to Sam.

He stepped back in discouragement and walked over to a nearby tree. He leaned against it and exhaled sadly. He then sat down in the grass as he stared at the car, watching quietly, as his brother giggled and continued to draw his pre-school pictures on envelopes.

What should he do? Should he retrieve the journals with the notes and take Sean out of the state? He'd then have other scientists who could try reversing the drug process, or was that impossible? Should he destroy the notes? Will Sean survive this experimental poison and come back or was it too late?

Sam lay back. If he could just close his eyes for a minute, maybe he could make a decision." That thought had barely formed, when Sam fell asleep.

Sam woke suddenly. Sean was standing over him. He was angry. He had also aged mentally, but his skin was sallow. Even in the moonlight, Sean looked unfriendly and sick.

"Where is my medicine?" Sean demanded with eyes flashing in anger.

"I don't have any, but you don't need it anymore. It makes you sick. You are better already and without it," Sam said as he stood up.

"I need it now." Sean stomped his foot.

"All right, Sean. Get in the car. We'll drive to our old family's house instead and look for it. It's not rented right now, I think, and it's still furnished. Maybe you left some there, and hopefully, we'll be safe there, for a brief time anyway." Sam quickly walked to the other side of the car.

Sean slowly climbed onto the car seat and sat stiffly, anger seething.

After some time, they reached their destination. Sean rose, no longer upset, just sleepy. He was behaving somewhat older, but also seemed to be pouting. The house was locked. They found an unlocked window and crawled through.

Once inside, Sean hurried to a table and planted himself and his pen and envelopes before him. He began to write and draw furiously. Suddenly he spoke softly, "Need more paper, sir."

"Right," Sam answered. Bewildered but excited, Sam grabbed a stack of paper from a desk and handed it to Sean's eager hands. Sam sat back and watched. This was his brother who now felt like a stranger. But he would always be his brother. Maybe the writing would bring him back along with answers. Sam hoped beyond hope that he was right.

Suddenly Sam thought of Caroline and sat straight up. Where was she? Oh God, I hope she's all right. I left her on her own. Doctor Mekka wouldn't hurt his own daughter, would he? He sat back. No, she had to be fine. Stop worrying.

Sam was dreaming nightmares of a screaming Sean. He sat up suddenly, feeling cold and disoriented. Then he saw Sean, still writing. Relieved, Sam looked at his watch. "Had it really been two hours?" He gazed back at Sean who was sweating profusely.

"Are you tired, Sean?" Sam got up and walked quietly over to Sean.

Sean stopped writing and looked intently at his papers. "Yes. I am very tired." He walked to the couch and closed his eyes. "Sammy?"

Was that really Sean calling him by name? Was he returning to normal? Sam walked over to him eagerly and sat at the foot of the couch. "Yes, oh Sean, it's good to have you back."

Through closed eyes, Sean spoke softly. "You've been a good brother to me. I'm sorry I got you into this. It wasn't supposed to be so difficult and horrible."

"I understand. It wasn't all your fault. Just rest."

"I'm fine now," Sean whispered as he closed his eyes. He looked so young now, lying there. The lines that had deepened in his face over the last few days seemed to have vanished. He's my dear brother again. Sam found an afghan blanket and covered him. He started to cross to a chair. Suddenly he was stopped by a terrible feeling. He stared at Sean as he felt his forehead. It was cool, no fever. That's good. Then his fingers slid to his pulse. "No, oh no!" There was no pulse. Sam pulled back stunned and fell against the table.

ACCELERATION

Sam starred at his brother in anguish. "Oh, no. You can't die. You're getting better. You're going to be just fine. I need you. We just connected with each other again, after all these years." Sam rushed over and shook his brother furiously. "Stop it. Look at me. What the hell are you doing, trying to scare me like this? Stop!"

Sam sank to the floor beside his quiet brother's still form. "Sean, oh Sean. I didn't get here in time. I'm sorry." He gently took Sean's hand and looked at it through dazed eyes. "I never paid any attention to you over the years, since we grew up. But I'm looking at you now." Tears rolled down Sam's cheeks. "You can forgive me and talk to me now. You helped me. Let me help you. Please come back."

Sam looked at his dead brother face and realization came. There was no more to be done. It was over. "Why didn't I call you sooner, Sean? Why didn't I keep in touch, all these years? I could have been there for you."

Sam began to hyperventilate. He rose unsteadily and crossed to the door. He threw it opened. A soft breeze flooded the room and quieted him. Sam turned back to look at Sean, one last time. "At least the pain is over now. Nobody will hurt you again."

Sam crossed to the table and gathered up the notes. He would have to hide them for now. He wanted to destroy them, but then again, perhaps some good could come from these last experiments, although he doubted it. Sometimes people aren't meant to know everything. But he was going to find out what Acceleration had become. Was there more to it than just Sean's abilities? Were there others that will die like Sean? He felt there was more to know. And if it needed to be stopped, he was going to do it.

Sam's mouth set tightly now, and his eyes started burning with his anger. He had to do something. He wasn't about to just take Sean's death lightly. His mind leaped to the pictures of the destruction from the war that had created such a monstrous fear of death in him. It had lasted years. He thought death was only after him, but he was wrong. It was also pursuing the innocent which is awfully sad. But – Death, you don't scare anymore! Death will be a happy place for my brother. He won, not you.

Sam steamed out the door and slammed it shut. He walked in angry determination to the back yard. He quickly spread apart the weeds around a large rock by a fat tree. He pulled up the rock and crammed Sean's papers under it. This was what

ACCELERATION

Sam had done as a child. Sam had buried his secret stash of writings under a rock by this old tree. He had created stories but never showed them to anyone. Sean had wanted to see them, but he resisted. He was afraid that Sean would think they were silly stories. Years later Sam had checked for them, but they had disintegrated into mere scraps in the earth. Maybe it was for the best. And if he never returned this time, these notes would also turn to dust. Perhaps they should stay in the past with his treasured childish stories.

Sam then walked to the car. He could not go back into the house and look at his dead brother again. His sorrow and anger over Sean's death was exploding in his mind again.

He skidded his tires as he turned onto the road, going faster and faster. Suddenly headlights beamed in the distance. They seemed to be coming straight for him. "Is this chicken you wish to play. Fine. Have we begun?"

Sam floored the gas pedal and shot forward, straight for the approaching cars in the distance. The two in the lead spun sidewise and stopped, blocking the path.

Sam shook away his tears that blinded him. "Yep, I knew you were the bad guys. Damn you!" he cried out, as he jammed on his brakes. "I want to live after all!"

Suddenly his head cracked against the steering column. His car soon became silent and still. Sam stared out and tried to raise his head, but he could not. Blood streamed down from his nose and a gaping cut on his forehead.

Three passengers burst from the front car and raised rifles and a handgun.

"Why?" Sam could barely speak out the word.

The men didn't answer as they yanked him from his car and jammed a steel gun muzzle into his mouth.

Sam gagged. He was stunned by their brutality.

"Where is Sean Stone? You will answer me now," Thin Man growled.

The gun had a numbing effect on Sam's mouth. He felt like he would throw up in their faces. He was hoping anyway.

Suddenly, the gun was removed. Tattoo snorted. "You like the feel of this power of death, eh, Stone? Would you like to feel your guts splattered all over your fancy car? No, I think you don't; so where is your brother now?"

Thin Man jerked his gun back up to Sam's head and waited.

Sam let out the breath he had been holding. "He's dead. Isn't that what you wanted?" he replied fiercely. "You and your fellow criminals killed him, you and Acceleration." Sam immediately kicked out the man's legs and lunged away, but the others were too close and alert. And Sam felt weak and dizzy. They grabbed him again and began pulling off his jacket. "What are you doing?" Sam gasped as they pulled up his sleeve.

Tattoo gave a sadistic half smile, reached into his pocket, and pulled out a syringe. He shot a bubble from it up into the air and growled. "So, you know about Acceleration. That is too bad. He jammed the needle into Sam's arm.

Sam grimaced and began to feel disoriented. "You creep, take your hands off…" but his lips felt like they weren't there, and further words wouldn't come out. His mind was present, but he couldn't seem to understand.

The men were laughing at him. Why? What had he done? What was he doing now? Why were they talking so slowly? He was confused and tired. He couldn't even remember who he was.

Where was he now? Seeing shadows… carry…what? Sam tried to understand. Who? Tired. Eyes heavy. In back seat. Mind dark. "Am I dead?"

<u>CHAPTER 10</u>

Sam, looked around. He felt lost, confused, and afraid. He was very cold and everywhere he turned were the faces of dying screaming men. His eyes began to focus. Those are his old buddies- Carl and big Emmanuel. They are here too, or is he in a nightmare with them. "And Sean, you're here too. I'm so happy to see you, but I thought… you were dead. You're alive? Am I alive? Or... are we all dead?"

"Get out, Sam! Get out! Don't stay here. Run."

"I hear you, Sean, but I can't run. I can't move. I want to stay with you? I'm going to stay." Sam felt himself suddenly flaying his ms and legs about uncontrollably. "I'm convulsing. Oh! Make it stop…" And then, the shaking was over. He stared out, unable to move.

Suddenly, he was seeing… something happening. Sam watched in confusion. Was it real? It couldn't be. Sean was clinging to a rope, suspended from a helicopter. Sam looked around. He could move again, and he was operating the copter and desperately trying to hold the rope. "Sean, hold on. Don't let go!" But Sean was losing his grip.

ACCELERATION

"Sam!" he was shouting into the wind. "I can't hold on. I'm not strong enough. Let me die." His voice seemed to echo and whirl as Sean began falling into the thick blackness below. "NO!" Sam shouted but he couldn't hear his voice or stop the pictures that he was seeing.

Suddenly darkness was rolling over him. He was floating in that blackness. There was no longer a helicopter. All had disappeared. Sam couldn't seem to see anything. Before him was inky nothingness. He kept jerking to find an anchor of some sort, but there was none. Then the faces shot forward, alternating rapidly.

"I know you all," Sam cried out. "Mom! Dad! My army buddies. You can't all be here. Are you, are you all here?" You're talking to me, but I don't hear you. What are you saying? "Speak louder. TELL ME!" I know I was shouting, but I can't hear me either. And I'm trying to move, but I can't. You need to know that I'm here. I don't know what to do. Tell me… Your faces are zooming at me, forward and backward quickly, and they are blending into each other. Why don't you hear or see me? You're getting smaller. "Don't" go! Don't leave me here alone"… What are you saying? I can't move. I want to follow you. But you can't hear me. I'm fighting hard. But…I'm getting hot… too hot. Should I be afraid again? No, I won't be afraid. I think, I think I'm better now. The room is getting brighter and brighter. My friends and Sean are disappearing into a tiny speck. My eyes are burning, but they are staying open. They hurt.

Am I getting real again or am I still lost in madness? That must be what it is. I'm having delusions or nightmares? There are white shadows swimming in front of me. I can't touch them, but oh now- they're beginning to hold still. I can almost see what they are. Almost. Oh, almost is over. I see. I know what they are. But, it's funny. The white are not people. They are walls and floor. I am on the floor and all's now staying still. I'm in a white padded room, and the crazy visions are gone. I'm alone, and all is real again.

I must remember now. Someone had injected me with something. I've been hallucinating, but it's over. I feel exhaustion…and relief. But I'm still trapped. Sam sighed and closed his eyes. I'll just rest briefly. I feel alone, very alone."

Hours passed, no one has come. Have they forgotten me? Am I worth so little? No, they are saving me. Why? What for?

Questions keep exploding in my consciousness. I want answers."

Suddenly, one huge wall slid back. Sam struggled up and stood weakly.

A chubby elfin little man walked up and pointed a huge gun at Sam. He muttered sourly, "Come, Stone. I'm small, but I have a big gun. I shoot quickly. Obey me." Elf shot at the floor and a giant hole appeared in it. "That could be you."

Sam gaped at the hole's size. "I guess I get the message. Big hole. Where are we going? Is there anything good that I can look forward to?"

"No," the little man replied.

"Well, anything is better than this room, I think," said Sam as he balanced unsteadily on his feet. Sam began to lunge at the gun, but Elf was fast. He fired at Sam. Sam jumped and hurled himself to the side, just in time. He stared at Elf and then at another huge hole, inches from his body. He slowly got up and moved to the side of the hole.

"I think I got your message a little better this time. I'll come," Sam muttered flatly.

"Good choice, Stone. I enjoy killing. I forgot to tell you that," said Elf with a sadistic smile.

"I believe you," Sam grunted. He straightened. Elf circled Sam and then jammed the gun into his back.

"Walk," Elf screeched.

"Calm down, and yes, I'll do that," Sam muttered.

They walked down multiple empty hallways. Sam tried to remember the route. Why, he wasn't sure, but he felt it might be important later. They finally emerged from the maze of corridors and into a large room, bursting with very old people of various nationalities.

The huge crowd turned when he entered and rushed over, pawing and fawning over him. "Help me," each implored. Their pleas tumbled over and over as they kept turning Sam around. He yanked away in his confusion. "Why, what's going to happen to you?"

Elf suddenly barked and waved his gun, "Back up, ladies and gentlemen."

The mob stepped back against the walls. Their eyes bored into Sam. They stood, as if programmed by a mysterious force.

"Why are they just standing there, looking at us?" Sam asked in awe.

"They await orders," Elf said curtly.

"What kind of orders?" Sam replied hesitantly.

ACCELERATION

"You are only passing through. Walk," Elf continued.

Sam walked. He had a bad feeling though. They entered another large room, all white, with a desk and chair rising from the middle. Windows set high in the ceiling seemed to stare down at him. Nothing else lined the room.

Sam felt like he was in some kind of hospital, but there were no beds. Nothing fit the stereotype. Of course, the last few days didn't fit the stereotype of his world either. He felt on the edge now. He feared that he wouldn't be able to return to his old life and self, even if he ever wanted to.

Elf gestured to a solitary chair. Sam sat feigning calmness. Elf grunted, "Good Day," and then was gone.

"Hmm," Sam called, "You're leaving me alone. Was it something I said?" Sam stood up, paced, and then sat tentatively in the chair again.

Suddenly the walls changed color. They were now lavender. Sam's mouth fell open in surprise. He quickly shook off his shock. Feeling stronger, He began to pace the room, over and over again in frustration.

Then, he stopped. A man had entered, this time a very tall massive one. Elf and his gun followed him and, to Sam's surprise, Mekka trailed behind. But Sam could quickly see that this Mekka was not the self-possessed and domineering man that he remembered. Mekka's eyes were now staring within a withered body. A large cataract-like film covered one eye, and his back had hunched over.

Elf followed with his gun and spoke, "Sit on the floor, Stone. That is now the boss's chair. Get out of the chair!"

"And if I say no?" Sam queried in his sweetest voice.

"Max will throw you against the wall." Elf pointed to the massive hulk who stood glaring beside him. "Then I'll destroy your head with my big gun. Now sit, there," Elf waved his gun to a spot on the floor.

"Max is big. All right. I'll give up my chair to Dr. Mekka," Sam said pleasantly. He felt trepidation, but he wasn't about to show it.

Sam got up and stood aside. Dr. Mekka did not move.

Elf grunted. It is not for Dr. Mekka.

They all waited silently. Suddenly, a door opened, and a man, puffing on a stinky cigar, lumbered over to the chair and sat. He stared at Sam. No one moved.

Then Cigar Man spoke in a low voice. "Mr. Stone, I am the Executioner. We have a problem. You... Your brother was an asset, you are not. Prove me wrong. What do you know about

ACCELERATION

Acceleration? You did not respond well to drugs, this time, perhaps because of your former military training. We would prefer to not experiment on you further, unless necessary. So, perhaps you could be a gentleman and tell us. You have the floor, Mr. Stone."

Sam chose his words carefully. "You killed my brother."

Cigar Man grinned malevolently. "Your brother was brilliant. Did he give you his notes?"

Sam glared back. He hated evil men on power trips. "I repeat," Sam replied crisply. "You killed my brother. And, do you really think that Sean would show or give me his notes? I guess that you aren't as smart as you think you are. You're a fool."

Cigar Man's face seemed to freeze the room. He nodded at Elf.

Sam backed up as Elf crossed with his large gun and then started to slam it across Sam's head. Sam caught it in the air, but Elf was strong and they stood facing each other with equal strength.

"Met your match, eh Elf. Surprised?" Sam taunted.

Elf nodded and four huge men entered the room. Despite Sam's usual good blocking skills, he knew that he'd probably lose this one. The strong burly foes shoved Sam back and pinned him against the wall. Elf sat his gun on the floor, smiled with repulsion and crashed his iron fist into Sam's face.

Sam coughed and tried hard to see and recover. He felt blood gushing from his nose and mouth and swiped his face with his hand.

Cigar Man looked at Sam with contempt. "Do you think I need the gun? I have steel in my hands, but I like to preserve them normally. Where are the notes?"

"Temper temper, big guy. I'll show you my secrets if you show me yours!" Sam felt
total revulsion for this man.

Suddenly Cigar Man simpered. "I doubt that your evasions will help you. Sometimes I enjoy eliminating people in other ways."

As if on an unseen cue, Elf led Mekka slowly out the door.

Cigar Man started to walk out also. Suddenly he turned and grunted, "Stone, you will soon be going to a terribly painful death. A small pity. Very small. We will enjoy watching."

Elf and his four nasty assistants turned to Stone, gave obscene grins, and followed their boss out of the room. The door noisily locked behind him.

ACCELERATION

Sam listened warily to the silence. Then he suddenly turned and whirled about the room. Something was happening. Were the lights growing dim? A moment later Sam was enveloped in blackness, except for the slight shadowing from the high windows. He let out a breath and stumbled for the exit. He grasped the cool metal of the door knob. It turned too easy now, he thought. But he continued to inch along the outside corridor. The walls seemed to be getting closer, or was his imagination working overtime? No, he thought, it was definite! They were moving and faster now. He would soon be crushed. Now would be a good time for prayer and a miracle.

Cigar Man's low harsh voice boomed from all sides. "Stone Stone Stone…." The voice repeated over and over again. Suddenly the walls and Cigar Man's voice stopped. "Stone, here is your only stop on your tour to freedom or oblivion. I suppose you choose death. Your loss. This is where you and others are released from your life's burdens. You have outlived your usefulness." His obscene laugh shook the walls.

Sam saw the flames leaping out at the end of the hallway tunnel. They seemed to get closer every second. Sam jerked away from the walls as his arm sizzled at the touch of the heat.

"My God!" Sam choked and tried to hold down the surging panic. "All right. Stop. I have Sean's notes!" Sam yelled out. "You want them. You need to keep me alive for that!" Sam desperately hoped he was heard over the roaring flames. He feared his adversary had left him, the prey, to die painfully and alone, but then… No. Someone that sadistic would want to watch or at least listen to the death screams of his victims.

"You can hear me, I know you're watching, you bastard," Sam yelled. "You kill me and the notes are lost forever, or someone more evil and smarter than you will find them!" Sam's voice felt raw, and it was hard to breathe now.

Cigar Man's voice boomed back. "We'll find them without your help."

"But what if you don't. Can you take that chance, can you?" Sam tried to sound confident, but his stomach was knotting up and he was feeling a crushing weakness as well as unbearable heat.

Suddenly…it was like being slapped awake from a nightmare. Sam blinked and coughed as the noise and flames stopped their hungry assault. An arm reached out and grabbed him out of the hell on Earth that was to be his tomb. He was tossed into the now blinding lavender meeting room of his previous encounter.

Sam coughed and gasped for air as he struggled to stand on the floor. He sensed Cigar Man perched triumphantly in the doorway. "Are you always this unpleasant with guests?" Sam shouted painfully and then coughed again.

"Only with people I don't like," Cigar Man leered back.

"Oh my," Sam said sarcastically. He definitely hated this guy. He had a feeling, however, that despite his nastiness, the guy was not the brains of this insane outfit.

Suddenly the walls and floor fell away, and Cigar Man was gone. In fact, Sam's gravity was also gone. He felt disoriented, like he was floating chaotically over an abyss. He shouted as he struggled to stay upright. "No floor, no walls. Clever design but unusable, not very creative. I expected more from an ugly man who smokes stinky cigars."

Cigar Man boomed over a speaker again, "Shut up, Stone."

"I may do that. It is hard to hold an intelligent conversation with a pawn instead of the big shot." Sam was enjoying taunting him now.

"You are mistaken." Cigar Man replied with venom. "You, Stone, are the pawn."

Suddenly the walls reformed in a bright orange color. Sam swallowed hard.

"Thanks for the walls," he shouted, "but I hate orange. It's getting boring."

No one responded. Sam felt movement, however, and turned to see a figure at the end of the room. A cot and desk sparkled with a garish orange florescence in this crazy orange Oz-land. An orange computer sat on the desk with a matching whining printer. As Sam moved slowly across the room, the form reclined on the cot. He solidified slowly in Sam's vision.

Sam wiped his eyes and starred. "Dr. Mekka!" he said in surprise and then rushed to the cot.

Dr. Mekka did not respond. He seemed unconscious or asleep. Sam peered over at the printout. It seemed to be mathematical gibberish. Sam sat on the edge of Mekka's bed. He shook him, but Mekka did not awaken. The minutes passed.

"I'm alive but confused". Sam thought out loud. He looked around with worry about what had happened to Caroline, hoping she was at home. He was glad she's wasn't with him now in this pseudo-Frankenstein den.

ACCELERATION

Mekka's computer suddenly stopped its cryptic paper printing blitz. Sam picked up the mass of pages and sat down. He began to read and got lost in their complexity.

CHAPTER 11

Two hours of studying the notes and still Sam didn't have the foggiest idea of what they meant. He knew that he was being watched. The watchers were probably disappointed and bored to death. That's justice. Sam laughed to himself.

Mekka began to stir.

"Dr. Mekka, are you well?" Sam sat at the side of the bed and quietly asked.

"I'm functioning. Mr. Stone, why are you here? Is Sean with you?" Mekka looked across the room. "I see not. Too bad," Mekka's voice trembled as he tried to sit up on the edge of the cot. "I could use his assistance in my work." Sam reached out his hand to help.

"Thank you, young man. I'm sorry for my abrupt behavior when we first met, but secrecy was necessary." He frowned and looked around. "You shouldn't be here. Where's Sean?" His voice suddenly lost its warmth, as he noticed the papers in Sam's hands, "Give me those papers. They're mine and not yours." He jerked them away as Sam relented. "Get out, Mr. Stone, now."

ACCELERATION

Sam wasn't afraid or angry. He just felt pity at the tragedy of the doctor's dedication to his dangerous experiments. "I'd love to leave, but I'm a prisoner now, possibly just like you, and Sean is dead. Explain why and what's going on here."

"Dead, no!" Mekka was stunned. "He's a fine young man. He's like a son. What...what happened?"

"First I must tell you that we are being watched by your men and a big obnoxious lug with a cigar," said Sam quietly.

"Understood. Why is Sean dead?" Mekka replied dryly.

"It was from your damned experimental medicine." Sam said icily. "You and your nasty friends were slowly killing him."

Mekka stood up uneasily and moved to a chair. "No, it was Sean's design. It should have worked. Where had he erred? Did he tell you, did he leave anything for me?" Mekka was clearly agitated and not nearly as formidable. He now looked only like a sick and lost old man.

"He left his last notes?" Sam was not about to say more or where.

"You have them with you?" Mekka asked eagerly.

"No," Sam said quietly. "And I don't plan to bring them unless you tell me what is going on and why your awful drugs should ever see the light again. Also, the notes are my insurance from not being murdered by your organization."

"Murder you, oh no. They only want your help."

"No. Not true. I thought that they had arrested you." Sam said.

"On, no. They merely brought me here to work." Mekka replied. "OOOW!". He suddenly grabbed his head. "Headache, bad one. I need my medicine. Excuse me, please." Mekka struggled to get up from the chair, but Sam grabbed his arm. "Don't you see. It's happening to you too, just like with Sean. The headaches will get worse, then you'll die, Dr. Mekka. You must stop the experiments."

"Then I will surely die. The experimental medicine is my cure." Mekka said tiredly, as the headache subsided.

"The side effects will kill you, Sir. Something is wrong," Sam said firmly.

Suddenly a door sprang open and two men in white coats walked quietly into the room. They carried a needle and a syringe. Sam backed up and watched as they injected the doctor. Mekka closed his eyes and smiled as the medicine began to lessen his pain.

"Thank you, gentlemen," Mekka replied.

ACCELERATION

"Yes, Doctor," they answered without emotion and strutted out.

Sam watched their exit with sadness. "Doctor, don't you realize that they're watching your every move. Why?"

"They want to help me." Mekka said simply. "They also want some of the side effects. You see, Mr. Stone, these notes, could you decipher them?"

"No," Sam replied curiously.

"Well, I couldn't write them or understand them either before the drugs, but now I can. This is what they and I both want. We are improving intelligence. The headaches are a small price to pay for brilliance and a cure. A potent combination, wouldn't you say? Think how we can help and change the world." He crinkled his grey skin into a smile.

"Sir, it's potent but lethal," Sam said simply. "You'll die, along with the others here. Your hopes are admirable, but speeding up evolution is deadly."

"It's my choice to try and there are no other people taking the medicine here," Mekka said in confusion. "Why should you say that?"

"Because I feel it, Doctor. There are too many nasty guys here. It has a giant crematorium. The walls move and fire can flood a hallway. When they have learned all they can from you, they will eliminate you and I think others. It is set up for many. I suspect that if you examine the whole facility, you'll see what I think is going on. Do your total research. Learn more. These are not good people here. You have to stop your experiments and get out."

Sam knew he had said too much. The guards would be here soon, but then doing nothing yields nothing, better to get this ball rolling. He only regretted what would happen to Mekka. Sam was beginning to feel pity for the old man. He, like Sean, had missed the whole deadly impact of their vision. He also hated to think of anyone going through Sean's anguish and pain at his death.

"Come with me, please sir. We can try and escape." Sam implored.

"No," Mekka said firmly. "I still have hope and am here for the duration. They won't let me die. And they won't hurt others. I trust them."

"They will. You are foolish to believe otherwise, Sir. I'm sorry." At that, Sam whirled around to see guards closing in from all directions. Three doors, Sam noticed. He had not realized there were so many doors. He shoved Mekka into two

ACCELERATION

of the white coats and skidded around the bed, pushing it towards them. Dodging to the computer, he hurled it at the other guard, who grabbed it fearfully from the air.

"No, don't hurt my computer!" Mekka shrieked.

Sam didn't in the least care. He only wanted to leave this mausoleum. He bolted for a door and slid into the next room. He yanked the door shut, crept into the darkness and found another door. This place is a maze of doors, he thought as he darted from room to room, each as barren as the last.

The rooms felt like cells in the catacombs, Sam thought as he ran. Like cells for victims before being thrown to the lions, and he was the runner.

In the last cell, he found a corridor and stumbled through the blackness, falling onto a wall with a selection of buttons. He gingerly felt the outline of an elevator and pushed a button. The elevator's light burst upon the corridor as Sam plunged into the refuge. He slammed the bottom floor indicator. He wanted to leave but also learn more. Sam scanned the trap door in the ceiling. He leaped up and shoved it open. He boosted himself up into the overhead tunnel of the elevator shaft and shoved down the cover. Now to think and be safe. He steadied his breathing. He would wait, give it some time for the static of his absence to pass. Hopefully they'll think he got out and look outside and elsewhere for him.

At times men would come into the elevator and talk of the search. They seemed to think he had escaped. "Good," he thought, "so perhaps I'm safe, for now."

Suddenly a red light and a beeping sound came on in the elevator. He hoped it indicated that the facility was shutting down for the night but not the elevator. He wanted time to explore the floors. Sam figured that he needed to wait just a bit longer before he moved.

"Orders are to terminate them at 3 A.M. You need to bring your men and meet me in Area C- Room 3," a man spoke gruffly as he strutted from the elevator.

"Yes, sir. Area C- Room 3." The second man trotted after him and out into the hallway.

The voices woke Sam. He must have dozed off. It had been so long since he last slept safely. He remembered now, it was at the cabin and earlier with Caroline, he smiled. He hoped she was at her home. Dear Caroline. He promised to come back to her. He hoped he'd be able to do it. What did he get himself into? Well, he knew that he had to see this horrible situation to the end, hopefully a good ending, but he was worried.

More voices interrupted his thoughts.

Two other males continued in conversation. "Have they found the brother?"

"No, he may have escaped. The search has been extended to the entire building."

"What do we do if we find him? Interrogate?"

"No," he's to be taken straight to Area C- Room 3 with the others, Orders from the big guy." The elevator door closed as the men left.

"Others!" Sam repeated in his mind as his mouth fell open. He was right, but he had hoped not. There were other victims of experimentation. That must be what the guards meant. And he wondered who the big guy was. Was he the big boss and not Cigar Man?

Sam wanted to stop thinking and sleep again, but he knew it would be fatal. He had fallen asleep for a moment, but he would not do it again. He stretched and managed to stand up in the shaft. Suddenly he heard a voice and froze.

"And then. Don't sleep again. Termination. Is that correct?"

Other men were in the elevator! There weren't two before, there were perhaps four instead, or did the elevator stop and others get in while he slept? Sam berated himself silently. He hoped he hadn't been heard while standing. He listened. No, he didn't think so. Well, regardless, termination was meant for him, and probably others. In this day and age, how could this happen? Were they all drugged? Sam shook his head in shock and listened. The elevator was opening. The men's footsteps seemed to indicate that they were leaving. The elevator must now be empty. And he was tired of cowering here. Time to move.

Sam jumped down through the roof and back into the elevator. He pressed basement. Area C- Room 3 had to be there, near the crematorium, maybe. A place that burns bodies had to be hidden in the basement. The whole thing made him feel sick, but he had to know. Could he perhaps help to rescue them? That was a big perhaps, he realized that. After all, he was being pursued and had been **sentenced to the same** fate, probably. He had to find out who were the next victims, besides himself. He shuddered...The elevator came to a stop. Time to find out.

ACCELERATION

The doors opened to a dimly lit hallway. He peeked into the first room. There were tables set up. It was a large long room with about a hundred people playing bridge. Were they crazy? Who plays bridge at this hour. He drew closer and stared at them. They were all so old, so very old.

"A new player. How nice. Join us, won't you, sir," a sweet old lady sat in her nightgown and piped up.

"I'd like to, but who are you? And where did you come from?" Sam smiled.

"We live here. We are valuable clients of the big guy. I haven't met him but I'm sure he's very handsome, like you," she giggled. "Tonight we're having a pajama bridge party. Isn't that a fun idea?"

"Yes, that sounds delightful, Miss. Is the big guy the leader of Acceleration?" Sam said expectantly.

"Shh! Sir," she whispered fearfully. "That is a forbidden word,"

An old bearded man, with a walker beside him, spoke up. "Mary, does he have a pass to our party? He should be with the younger ones."

"Yes, I think so," Sam lied. "Which pass?"

"The one for our party, of course," Mary felt joyful again and laughed. "We don't care, George. He's a nice man."

"You don't care because he's young and good looking. You can wait. Tomorrow we'll be young like him. Then you'll want me," George whispered and chuckled through his scruffy beard.

"I like you too, Georgie," Mary said happily. She looked at Sam. "Do you want to play, Sir?"

Sam was enjoying talking with them but feared their future. "No, I'm sorry. I don't know the game. But you shouldn't be here. You need to dress and leave. Bad things will happen to you in this facility, to you Mary, George, and all of your friends here."

Mary frowned. "No, young man. You need to trust. I heard that the leader, the big guy, is going to make us young, intelligent and beautiful. And then, I'll flirt with you again." She winked.

"Hey! Mary and George, you are holding up the game. Sit down. Leave that man alone. We're waiting. Hurry up or I win," a frail old Asian woman howled with glee as she playfully punched the withered man next to her.

ACCELERATION

"No, I win," said Mary, as she blinked rapidly and sat down suddenly as if programmed.

"No no, I win," said George, as he too blinked rapidly and plopped down into his seat and stared out.

Suddenly all the old people in the room put down their cards, blinked, and stayed still. As if hearing a terrible sound, they all grabbed their heads and began to wail.

"What's wrong?" Sam shouted over the roar.

"It's the knowledge!' George shouted. "We write now."

"I don't understand," Sam yelled to George over the noise, but George turned his head away as if in a trance and grasped his pencil and a tablet.

Sam looked around. All stopped crying out and were holding their heads and then also picking up their writing materials. He was stunned as he listened to the pencils scratching on the pads and no other sounds in the room. He moved to the side of the room and waited. The writing continued for forty-five minutes exactly. Then all pencils went down. The entranced old people simultaneously moved and picked up their tablets and pencils again. They rose as one and walked to the doors, and placed their writing. materials within metal boxes on the front tables.

"Why are you doing this?" Sam asked a group, but no one answered. No one even

acknowledged that he stood there. They were robotic victims who would die in minutes; Sam was sure of this.

"Come with me, all of you. You're all going to die!" Sam shouted urgently.

"They all just turned as one and sat back at their tables. They looked up and waited.

Sam noticed that the overhead lights were changing to red. "Could there be a key word, He thought." "Wake," he shouted. Nothing happened. "Play". Nothing. "Run." Nothing. "Acceleration." "Mr. Big needs you to wake up." Nothing. "Children." That was it! They turned.

Sam gasped with relief. "Children, follow me." They all got up, turned to face him, and followed. Sam led them to the elevators, where they suddenly relaxed and crowded together shyly.

A spindly old man tugged at Sam's sleeve. "It's my birthday today."

Sam curiously asked. "How old are you, sir?"

The old man whooped, "I'm eight years old. I'm Herman. I like games."

ACCELERATION

Shocked, Sam stared for a second and then forced a smile. "Me too."

Sam looked at the huge group in amazement and then cleared his throat. "Okay, everyone. Now, Sam said, we'll ride in groups. When your group comes up and the elevator opens, get win. I'll point to the button for you, and you'll push the first floor button. You'll ride up quietly. When the doors open, I want you to run out as fast as you can to the front doors and through them to the outside. Don't stop. Go through the door and outside. It's a game. Run as far as you can. Run to your homes. I will try to catch you. You must keep running. Don't let me or anyone else tag or catch you. If they do, just laugh and keep running. I am your teacher and leader. It will be fun. Promise to follow my instructions." The old people all nodded. "Now, let's begin our game. Walk to the elevators."

"Yes." They smiled and replied in unison. The first group quietly entered the elevator. Sam pointed to the button as a lady reached for the button and the doors closed. Sam watched as the lift rose.

He repeated and grouped others for the elevators. The old people quietly and obediently did as Sam had told them. Sam joined the last group, encouraged them on, and watched. The doors opened, and Sam watched the old ones for a moment. The crowds were exploding chaotically about the hospital entrance, through the doors, and onto the grounds. The feeble men and women were laughing and weakly trotting as best they could. Most didn't make it past the hospital perimeter, but they enjoyed being caught.

Mary was scooped up. Old George with his walker made it to the second step by the doorway where he froze and kept blinking his eyes. Herman and three others reached the street. There they stopped, managed to sit down, and waited, blinking soundlessly. Sam ran and tried frantically to get them to rise. A guard that was holding a frail, blue haired lady saw Sam and started laughing.

"They're finished, man. Can't you see that? Stupid old people!" the guard shouted.

"They're not old or stupid," Sam retorted angrily. Oops. Sam regretted saying that immediately.

"Who are you?" The guard narrowed his eyes in the sunlight. "Hold it! You're Stone, that brother."

Sam started to run. A gunshot roared and nicked his shoulder. He paused for a fatal second, turned, and stumbled into an old man. He set the old guy quickly onto his feet and

ACCELERATION

suddenly gasped, as three men quickly surrounded him. They stood for a moment, and then Sam kicked into his famous Bruce Lee moves. He almost succeeded as well as Bruce. He was able to down the trio rapidly and started to run again. Suddenly a fourth shot stung his leg and another propelled Sam's head back. He sensed that none of the wounds were life threatening, but they were enough to stop him for a moment. Quickly a fifth man jammed a gun at his temple.

"Stop," the owner of the last gun yelled out. "Or we'll kill you now."

Sam gasped for breath. "Well, if you put it like that, nah. I'll stop. I can sometimes take directions," Sam felt his head. Blood coated his hand, but he figured he'd live, although he now had a terrific headache, and his shoulder and leg were achy and dripping blood. Most of all, he felt like a fool for getting caught. The gunmen were fairly fast though. They must have had orders to wound and not kill. Maybe he'd try one more time with his Bruce Lee, he started to make his move, but stopped abruptly. Three more guns were pointed closely at various parts of his anatomy. These guys were good. They must have been warned. They were ready for him and his style. Lousy for him.

Sam walked with the six guards, who still pointed their guns at him. Thoughts were whirling in his head. "Why did I stay? Stupid of me... How can people be so evil? I thought I could save these people. Don't be so egotistical and confident next time, if there is a next time. And who in the hell is Mr. Big?"

CHAPTER 12

Sam was beginning to feel awful physically, however. He was hurting, exhausted and hungry, as he stumbled along. Maybe he'd get a last meal anyway. He hated to lose and felt badly for the old people, but he was unsure of any next move. He had no idea what to do as an encore. Plus, the gunmen traveling closely around him were good convincer of his perhaps fatal options. He hated guns, especially when turned on him. They usually have no heart and style. Now Bruce was cool. Oh, well, the guns won this time. I'll probably die by one. That was justice for me. He felt resignation. Of course, he did sort of leap into all this trouble or was somewhat dragged into it by Sean. Soon time will show me what the next surprise will be. Death or Death. Lousy options. I can do better, I hope.

Sam was now ushered into a small red room. These guys sure have a thing for colors, he thought. But then, it did match his blood dripping on the floor from his wounds. They probably like that. Suddenly he was tied to a chair, and the lights dimmed. He felt like a pig waiting to be cooked or eaten.

"Mr. Stone, welcome back to us." A voice boomed over a speaker.

"You missed me, how nice." Sam simpered.

"You assume too much. Now. Where are your brother's notes?" The speaker spewed out angrily.

"Where you'll never find them. You have to be kinder than this." Sam yanked at his ropes. "And by the way, what is your problem with colors? I really prefer blue or heroic white in room décor."

"This ruby red is my favorite color," the voice said with an ugly glee. "Does it remind you of your fear of death, Samuel."

"Just get out of here and leave me alone. You've got a lot of guts. You can't even face me, so go away." Sam said vehemently and meant it.

"Oh my, the rat protests. You do have a point, however. We'll leave you alone shortly. Perhaps we should meet." The voice laughed. It was an icy laugh, yet familiar. A shadow walked towards him, and the lights got brighter. Sam blinked as his eyes watered.

"Sean, you're here. It's you? But you died. Are you real?" Sam sputtered and sank back. "I saw you die. How could you

ACCELERATION

be here?" Sam stared at him, and recognition of this person as his brother suddenly frightened him. This wasn't the brother he loved. This man seemed soulless. Sam groped for another more terrifying word. Evil, that's the aura he gave off. But this was also his brother. He couldn't change like that. He couldn't become a totally opposite person, could he?

"Sean, what happened to you? Sam leaned back in his chair and felt sick.

"Sean half formed a smile with his lips but there was no warmth for Sam. "It's exciting, isn't it? I've changed. I am a new me, and none of my weaknesses remain. I have only strength and intellect. I stumbled on a fragmented organization, when I was trying to cure my illness. Together I, and my associates, have built a spider web that can lead the world. I understand my amazing changes now. You saw me last in my cocoon level. I can't help but laugh at your reaction to our wonderful colorful environment. You see colors signify and encourage our level of development. They spark a chemical reaction in our brains. We work better under our lovely colors. Orange is our best, then violet, and red. Each color assists us in aspects of our brain development."

"Mekka is not going to fully cross over and neither are the wrinkled old subjects you
encountered on Level C. We experimented many times with them. They have become the failures- waste material and a nuisance. They will soon be exterminated. But we think we now know how to balance dosages correctly, and the new subjects will soon never experience old age, and will have eternally brilliant minds. The danger, right now, is that the serum mutates. I'll fix that. I'm very smart, perhaps the smartest person in the world."

"Sean, these are human beings you are treating like insects. They don't understand fully. They have their own lives, hopes, and dreams. You've become an obscene killer," Sam said softly. "They don't truly understand. Stop what you're doing."

"No," Sean snapped. "They like being a part of my great adventure to the unknown. My subjects have flashes of brilliance, during which we allow them to record their knowledge before they experience their periodic regression. Their dedication will help me and my people to lead mankind into a new future. Our intelligence will rule the world, and they will like it. It's too bad that Hitler never lived to see my success. He'd be proud of me.

"Hitler, Sean, you can't be serious. He went down in history as a mass murderer. Is that what you want?"

"People sometimes must die for good causes. Mine is a great cause. I find my success to be extraordinary and fascinating, don't you?... My Samuel, I think you are finally without a wise-crack or sentiment!... And I'm afraid that I don't really need you now. The past is gone. My notes were an important key, but I am managing exceedingly well without them now. However, you amuse me, so I'll keep you around for a while. Store you, so to speak."

Sean turned his back and began to stroll away.

Sam shouted. "I don't understand. Keep me around? Store me?"

Sean turned and spread his hands palms up. "No, I don't expect you do. You are eons behind me in intellect, big brother. You are nothing but amusement now."

Sam was speechless. "My God. How can you like what you've become? "

Sean turned. "I love me." He laughed with obscene joy as he walked away.

Two guards came slowly to Sam. Sam felt he wasn't going to like what came next and he didn't. One man poured a liquid from a bottle onto a cloth, the other grabbed Sam's head and held it back in a vise-like grip.

"Come on, guys," Sam choked out. "I believe you, you're strong. Don't do this." And then it came; the wet cloth and its solution covered his nose and mouth. Sam fought, but he had to breathe, and he had to inhale the fumes. But he also knew that he wasn't going to die, not yet.

CHAPTER 13

Sam's pilot landed his copter in the clearing beside the village. They waited for the patrol. Suddenly the sunlight seemed to explode. He squinted across the seat into the blinding light. He needed to check his pilot. He was dead. Sam saw shapes of color swirling in the distance. Screams filled the stillness. Sam fought to change positions with the dead pilot. He gasped as rotting carcasses seemed to crash through the ceiling and fell upon him. They extending their mutilated arms and hands and clawed at his face and legs. He fought for balance and tried to start his copter. He gasped in terror as the bodies dragged him from his seat, tugged him out of the plane, and covered him....

"NO!" Sam jerked desperately in the bed. The vision in his dreams were choking him and he fought for air. Suddenly he gasped and was awake. He could breathe again. He shivered and tried to pull up the blanket, but restraints tugged at his wrists. He turned and realized where he was. No copter, no battlefield, no bodies. He was in a hospital? There was an intravenous solution hanging at the side of his bed. But fear gripped him.

"What are you giving me?" he whispered. "I gave you no permission for this." He cleared his throat, tried to shout in protest, and jerked at his bindings. But no one answered. No one was there. The room was empty.

Sam quieted and felt his world swirling around him. He tried closing his eyes to keep down his whirling vision but it didn't help. Another nightmare took over.

Caroline was standing on a windy desert battlefield a few feet away. She held a stack of his books. Looking at him, she was desperately trying to say something, but there were no sounds. Sam didn't understand. Suddenly a faceless body rose up from the sand and grabbed onto Caroline's feet. She dropped the books and struggled in terror. Sam heard the cries of soldiers on a nearby hill as they motioned frantically for him to come to them. The faceless form in the sand extended one of his hands to Sam's foot and began yanking him under. Sam looked at the men on the hill and back at Caroline. He felt paralyzed and couldn't move. Was he dying? The now violent wind seemed to call out affirmation. Sam whispered into the wind, "I can't die, not yet. They mustn't win." The words repeated louder and louder in his mind. "I can fight and win. I can save them. I have to. I have to."

Sam tossed violently, and felt men holding him down. He jerked awake, but felt an oxygen mask covering his face. He reached up to pull it off.

"Not yet," Sam heard the words and felt for the hand, following it slowly up to a face.

"Sean?" Sam inhaled repeatedly and calmed.

Suddenly the mask was removed, and Sam opened his eyes.

"Sam," Sean stared without warmth. "You are having a tough time. Too bad. We just have a few more data tests to do on you. I hope you can handle it, big brother," he laughed psychotically. "You don't want to stand in the way of our research."

Sam felt resignation and exhaustion as the drugs dragged him back into sleep.

Sam's eyes slowly opened again. How long had it been? He had no idea. He blinked repeatedly and tried to clear his mind. He remembered everything. He did not tell them where Sean's notes were. He was sure of that. A new plan, he needed a good one. Got it. Get out, get back to the car, retrieve the notes, and hightail it to a government security agency. He smiled. He wasn't sure how good this plan really was, but it could work if he could achieve it. And if the government believed him. And he was all on his own. No one else will get hurt anyway. Does anyone here care? Probably not. First, how to get out of his bed and off the I.V. If he could just stay awake until someone checks on him...

It was a short wait. A large shadow entered the room. Sam squinted up at a huge scarred face. Poor guy. I wonder how he got so scarred. I better not think about it. He probably beat someone in a fight but got cut up in the process, and scarred, or then maybe he lost and got cut up as punishment. Ouch! Either way, he is big. He mused. But I'm tough. Yeah right, not so much now, but I have to be. The bigger they come, the harder they fall. I like that old motto. Cliché but might be appropriate, and I'm not feeling very creative right now. Simple and to the point, he couldn't help laughing out loud.

"What's so funny?" Scar Man snorted.

ACCELERATION

Sam's mind whirled fast, "Um, oh...I just need to use the John. I feel silly asking... But, I don't think you really want to clean up after me."

"Who said I was going to clean up." Scar Man grunted and then looked around. "All right, but don't try anything sneaky."

"Who me, I can barely stand up," Sam said feigning weakness, which he kind of felt.

Scar Man unfastened Sam's wrists and helped him up. Sam felt a little dizzy and used it. Bending over, he grabbed a heavy basin and crowned his aide.

"Sorry, man, but we're talking survival here."

Disoriented, Scar Man struggled to get up.

"Stay down." His adversary tried to rise again. "Oh fellow, this is gonna hurt, again."

Sam brought down the basin one more time, but harder. Scar man slipped to the floor. Sam felt his pulse. "You'll live, fella. And thanks for helping me up."

Sam eased the needle out of his arm and threw it on the floor. He looked at his unconscious guard, "This all is too easy now. I might start feeling lucky. Thanks."

Sam then knelt. Ah, oh! His bullet wounds still hurt, but he was alive and that was good. He pulled Scar Man's keys from his belt. He got up too fast, however. Suddenly dizzy, he sat down on the bed. He groaned as he shook his head to clear it. He then got up slowly and peeked through the door.

Only one guard at the end, and he looked asleep. Sam padded softly down the hall towards the guard. He grinned at the empty beer bottle in the man's hand and quietly eased the bottle down to the floor, slipped off the drinking man's white coat, and hauled him onto the bed.

"Night night. Sleep tight, Bad Guy," he said as he tucked him in tightly."

Sam turned and was suddenly assaulted by dizziness again. He forced himself to see and stand straight.

Again, he peeked out the door. Sam then staggered into an adjacent room. It was empty, no window or door outlet. He tried again and plunged into the next one. This one held a patient. He gazed at the bed quickly and started to creep out the door. Suddenly he was drawn to look back and was shocked. This wasn't what he expected at all.

"Caroline! Oh no…" He was speechless. Sam moved closer and sat on the edge of the bed. He stared at her quietly and his heart ached. Her long blond hair was damp and lay limply on her pillow. Her face no longer was radiant with life. She looked pale and gaunt.

"Oh, honey," he said, as tears welled up in his eyes. He moved and sat and cradled her head.

"Caroline suddenly inhaled deeply and opened her blue eyes. Sam eased her back onto the pillow and kissed her softly. She stared in awe at him and tried to speak.

"You don't have to talk. I'm here," he said softly. "I'll get you out. I had no idea that they had you too. Don't try to talk."

Caroline smiled and whispered, "Sam." She brought her hand up and touched his cheek.

Sam kissed her fingers tenderly. "Dear Caroline. Let me help you up." He started to assist her, but she leaned on him completely.

"I can't," she stammered as tears glistened in her eyes.

Sam gently helped her to sit back upon the bed. He rested her head on his shoulder. "Never mind," he said. "We have lots of time. Just rest. Let me help you to lie back down." He was overwhelmed by her frailty as he gently lowered her down.

"It's all my fault," she said softly.

"Shh, it's their fault," He said furiously. "They've moved on from the willing to the innocent."

I found out that my father is here, but he's changed." Her eyes opened wide. "Oh, Sean's not dead. He's here."

"I know. I saw him."

"He's the boss now, Sam, but he's crazy." Caroline looked deeply into his eyes. "I'm sorry."

"Me too. Why don't these people fight him?" He said angrily. He calmed down. "How
do you feel, any better?"

"I'm only in the beginning stage. I feel weak and nauseous, but my father is euphoric. He thinks that I'll be fine. I'm not so sure. He also believes that he can cure the world. I think we all are fighting bad odds. I don't think any of us will live."

"If they weren't so sadistic and ruthless, maybe it could have led to some kind of success," said Sam. But the side effects…They are too dangerous. We've sure got another super-race ideal here. One that might kill a lot of people." Sam stood up. "Caroline, can you walk with my help?"

"No, I'm sorry," she said regretfully.

"Then I'll carry you," Sam said.

Caroline studied his face, so handsome but carved now with worry. She reached up and took his strong hands. "No, you won't. You'll come back for me though, before Dr. Frankenstein has too much fun."

Sam kissed her gently. "Are you sure?"

Caroline said softly, "Yes, you'll never make it with me. Maybe I'll be stronger when you come back. But, I want you to live and destroy this place and this cult. If our loved ones die in the process, so be it. It's necessary. You can do it, Sam. I'm too weak now. I may be better later, when you come back for me. I'll be fine here. I'll just sleep."

"I will come back. I promise. We'll either meet here or in the hereafter. Now rest," he tried to look positive but felt horrible despair at the thought of leaving her. He knew she was right, however. Sam tucked the covers around Caroline's slim body and held her hand. "Bye, darling. I'll be back with the cavalry. I love you." Suddenly the tears burst forth, and he began cry. "I shouldn't have left you. I'm sorry."

"It was my idea too. You thought I'd be safe," she said as she reached for his hand. "Don't cry for me. We'll make it, and I have found the love of my life in you. I could have lived forever and never found such happiness as you bring me… Am I getting too sloppy with my sentiment? We've only known each other a few days."

Sam bent over and kissed her softly. "I like it. Thank you."

"I can't stay awake. I'm sorry, I want to. Be careful, Sam." She closed her eyes and slipped into sleep." Sam kissed her again gently, and quietly crossed to the door.

He turned back for a moment, closed his eyes and fought back his emotions. He then turned and forced himself to walk out the door.

CHAPTER 14

Sam knew that leaving Caroline behind meant that he would return. He hoped they would let her just rest for now. Maybe after all this is over, there will be something other doctors could do. He would not let her die here. But he had to explore and find their way out. Then he could carry her without their being captured or maybe she'll be up to walking when he returns. He prayed he was doing the right thing by leaving her in that bed.

He raced down the dark halls, ducking into closets filled with medical supplies, but nothing he could use. Sam was consumed now with the need to escape, for both of them. He made his way easily until he heard voices and slipped into a utility closet stuffed with boxes of bindings for violent patients. If he could just connect the bindings together, he'd have a way to lower them to the ground floor. He found an unlocked window but it faced the front of the building. He would need to find another. He grabbed what he needed.

After traveling endless mazes of hallways, he found the best window. It was in the rear of the building and perfect except for the activity in the next room and posted guards. He could lower himself quietly though and be out. But with Caroline being so sleepy, she might fall. And could she run, no. Not yet. She needs to sleep first. She's safe here for a brief time. But he would have to return soon. He hoped to bring help, a whole army, if possible. And Jensen was coming.

Suddenly Sam heard shouting in the next room and crying. He crouched behind a bed in an empty room. What was happening? Could he turn his back on suffering? But he had to hurry for Caroline's sake. He was torn. Leaning close to the wall, he strained to hear more clearly. There was now silence. He waited. A commotion erupted in the hallway and it sounded like a gurney was swishing by. Sam pulled the door slightly ajar and peered through. A sheet covered a silent heap on the table. Was it the source of the cries? Had they just killed a subject? Were these people murdering in this area also? Were they so obsessed and heartless that…Oh, he had to stop thinking and just get out.

Sam climbed into his binding ropes, turned, and mounted the window sill nearby. "No," he thought. "This would be too hard for Caroline. She's too weak." He had to go it alone for now. With barely perceptible rustling, he lowered himself slowly down. He almost fell a couple of times, as the rope bit into his hands and he started to lose his grip. His hands burned. He hadn't climbed down a rope since his army days, but he remembered the technique. Once down, he darted into a side shed. Footsteps crunched on the gravel and passed by.

This place is an armed camp," he muttered. He started to fall upon a large bag. Sam felt about quietly in the darkness. There were many such bundles. He was hesitant to look inside, but he couldn't leave without knowing their contents.

The men outside had passed now. He had no excuse but to look. He wandered his hand over the end of the bag until he found the opening and slowly yanked it wider. He couldn't see well in the shed, but he could feel the contents. His hands touched something clammy and realization caused him to frantically yank his hands back.

Bodies. Sam shuttered. But who were these people? The old ones? He opened the door slightly and let the moonlight filter in. Sam swallowed hard to calm himself and turned to the bags again, bracing himself for what he would find.

The first bag held the body of an old man. Others bore ashes. He sat back and for the moment was overcome by the tragic coldness and indifference of such human acts. Their bodies were now mutilated or burned, and all were now disposable trash. Sam had seen death in war but this was different. It was supposed to be a peaceful era.

Sam suddenly felt like he was going to be sick, and then he was. When he was finished, he stood slowly and walked silently out the door and into the surrounding trees. He threw up again and began to sob. He cried for Caroline, For Sean, for Mekka, for those poor people, and lastly that he had come too late.

Sam finally pulled himself up and out of the shelter of the cool vegetation and began walking. He wasn't even sure of his destination. He couldn't free Caroline and destroy this place by himself. He needed help.

Hours passed. Sam had distanced himself from the hospital. He had not been pursued, he wasn't sure why? Surely they must know that he had escaped. Then he felt a sudden weakness and fell to the ground. His head felt like it would explode. He clutched it desperately.

Sam reached out to grab an outstretched tree, but his hand seemed to pass through it. He tried to touch the ground and sit but there seemed to be nothing beneath him. He waved his arms about and suddenly he felt better. He laughed hysterically. He felt much better. In fact, he felt overcome by intense power and

ACCELERATION

alone in his existence. He was surprised that he was unafraid. In fact, it was a glorious feeling. Who would want to give this up? It was like a oneness with the universe? No, it was more, it was power over the universe. He stood up and felt the breeze. He reached up to the sky and seemed to tower above his corporal world. Sam suddenly began to pace and talk rapidly to himself. He lectured himself with delight on the meaning of the universe. Moving closer to the tall hills and rock formations, he felt that he could climb them. He had supreme powers now. It was exhilarating.

Sam began to run, passing trees and clearings. He mounted a steep hill and whooped with joy. He began climbing, further and further, higher and higher, up boulders perched upon boulders. His hands became scrapped raw, but he never wanted to stop until he could greet the sun and be as one in its power. It was an amazing feeling to be so possessed. He sensed in the back of his mind that something was wrong with him, but he didn't care. He wanted to feel this way forever.

And in the back of his mind, he wondered if this was how Sean and Mekka felt, at the beginning.

Sam woke up. He felt fiercely cold and it was dark except for a half moon peering down upon him. It did make him feel less alone. He had lost his shirt somewhere, and the winds easily whipped through his light hospital trousers. But it wasn't only the clothes that made him feel so unbearably isolated, it was the absence of that essence that had briefly empowered him. It was gone now, the drugs seemed to have left his system, and he was plunging into a hellish depth both physically and mentally. He shivered and hugged his body. He was physically fit, but still he trembled in the rugged wilderness of October.

He looked around, sighed, and shook off the depression that hovered and tried to reign. He needed to go forward physical and mentally. The one should help the latter. This place was great for macho rock climbing but not so hot for being ill dressed for the elements and unsupplied for rescuing the fair damsel, as well as himself. He was relieved now that he hadn't brought Caroline. She might have died.

Well, time to try to get up, somehow. Oh! He had stood too fast, he realized, as his head felt dizzy and his legs wobbled. He rubbed his forehead and absently looked at his hands. They were a bit grimy. He was obviously no longer the God-like being of his drug induced euphoria. The sense of power was gone. He accomplished nothing so far.

He regretted, even with the bad odds, that he had left Caroline. He kept thinking about it. He had to stop, stop damning himself for his decision. He knew it was hers also. But he ached inside from the choice. Oh Caroline, I hope I can still save you. No that's wrong. I will be back.

He frowned as he started down the tall cliffs. He was surprised he was even up that high. I must have been a basket case to be so stupid and reckless," he muttered to himself. Inching his way down, he forced himself to not move too fast. He brushed away the flashing image of his body hurling down the cliff. "Nope, rather not see that," he thought. He slipped suddenly, but caught himself on a jutting root, pulled himself up, and continued on. After what seemed like too long, he took a deep breath and jumped down to the floor of the cliffs.

Sam slumped, as he looked out at the rapidly spreading darkness. Gathering up his energy, he rose, walked, and planned. His strides grew bigger, and his eyes blazed their intent. He was thinking more clearly now; should he call the FBI, CIA or who? "Somebody must be aware of this group and be investigating them. If he could get more help, he could rescue Caroline safely. He was well aware now that he might not be able to do it alone. The authorities had to come and crush this group.

Then he saw it, the small gas station light. It seemed to welcome him. "Good, a telephone. Now we are getting somewhere," he nodded in relief, as a scruffy old man stumbled out to great him.

"Where did you come from, Mister? You sure ain't dressed for our mountains and hills. No, Sir. Come on in."

"Long story. I'm Sam." Sam shook his hand and followed the kind man inside. "I got into a situation and then an accident. I'm very relieved to stumble onto you and your place, May I use your phone?" Sam said wearily."

"I'm Jessup, Yep, you can use my phone. You don't look like you got any money, though," he said. "You better pay me back."

"I promise, Jessup. I really need your help here and appreciate it," Sam said warmly.

Jessup's eyes twinkled through his beard. "It's over here. You can sit down while you talk, if you want. You look bushed. Hey, you calling your girlfriend or wife to pick you up? I ain't seen a pretty girl here for a long time. That would be nice."

Sam picked up the phone and paused. "No, somebody else, sorry. I need more than a ride."

He thought, "Who would he call?" The he remembered an old fraternity guy in college. He'd read that he was now a big shot in Washington and working for the FBI. Would he remember me and trust my information, and would he help? It can't hurt to try. Maybe he'll believe me. I've got to try."

Sam picked up the phone. "It's to Washington D.C. Okay? Jessup? I will pay you back, Please, trust me. I won't forget."

"Wow. Oh, all right. Sounds important," Jessup nodded and handed him the phone.

"It is." He picked up the phone. "Operator, I'm unable to make a call, would you find it and connect me, please. It's to Washington D.C., the FBI, Mr. Silas Jensen. Say it's from Sam Stone, from college."

"No problem, Sir," the operator answered.

Sam waited nervously. He hoped that Jensen would remember him. They had been in the same frat house, but not good buds, and it was a long time ago. He looked outside the window. Dawn seemed so beautiful. He wished for a minute that he was still that young innocent fraternity kid again.

"Sir, your Mr. Jenson is on the line. You may go ahead."

"Thank you, Miss."

"You're welcome, Sir," The operator said happily. It made Sam feel good just to hear her calm friendly voice. Sometimes he missed old phones and connecting with human operators instead of automated computers, especially now.

"Agent Silas Jensen here''

"I'm Sam Stone. Do you remember me from college, Sir?"

"You are kidding, of course," Jensen replied. "You were my idol. I studied your every move with the ladies. When you spoke to me, I was the star of our class."

Sam laughed. "Thanks, Sir. I don't know about the star. I was young and having too much fun, I guess."

"I hear you're a famous writer now. Congratulations… So now, what can the FBI do for you? I have to admit that I'm surprised by your call." Jensen continued.

"Agent Jensen," Sam spoke gravely, choosing his words carefully. "My life has turned upside down in the last few days. I've fallen into the middle of a dangerous situation for our country, which top echelons may or may not be aware of. Either way, could we meet right away?"

"Sam, where are you? I'll do what I can."

"I'm on the other side of the country. I'm in a small grocery store and gas station in Utah. It's owned by a guy named Jessup."

"Hold on, please, Sir." Sam turned to Jessup, "What's the name of your town and store?"

Jessup proudly shouted. "Barkley Flats and this is Jessup's Store near Old Creek Road. I like to use my own name in the title. It makes me feel important," Jessup proudly answered.

Sam smiled. "Did you get that Agent Jensen?"

"I did." Jensen laughed. "Barkley Flats, Jessup's Store in Utah, on Old Creek Road."

"Good," said Sam. "I know it's a long way from D.C., but you and a lot of your men need to come. It's a life and death mess of illegal activity, and innocent people are dying here."

"All right. I'll trust you on this. It better be worth the trip. Now, I can't get there faster than ten or twelve hours, but maybe less. Regardless, I'll be there." Jensen paused. "Be careful, Sam."

"Right. Thanks, Sir. I'm going to explore the town while I wait for you. If I don't return, look for me at the town or the hospital. But both may be dangerous places."

"I'll do that, Sam. But why don't you wait where you are until I get there?" Jensen said.

"No, Sir, I'll explain my reasons when you get here. So, see you then." Sam replied.

"All right. I'm on my way." Jensen disconnected.

Sam nodded to Jessup. "Thank you. I don't feel so alone now."

"It's sounds kind of scary. You better hide if a car comes. I won't tell anyone you're here." Jessup grabbed a bottle of whiskey and two glasses from the shelf. "Want a drink?" He poured two drinks and gulped one down. "My quiet life just got kind of exciting."

"I hope you'll stay out of it, Jessup. Be careful." Sam downed the other drink. "Thanks, I needed that." Sam said seriously.

Jessup grabbed a cigar from his shelf and started thinking. "Now you go pick out a shirt and jacket, clean britches, and maybe a hat from what I got in the store. You look cold. And you can have a cigar too, if you want one. Then wash up and go sleep in the back. You look like you might need it. I'll leave a sandwich and glass by the bedside. Help yourself to milk from my refrigerator here, if you want some. And I'll keep watch. Oh, and you can pay me later, But, don't forget, I ain't rich."

"Thank you, Jessup," Sam replied.

Sam was exhausted. He quickly selected clothes and crossed into the back room. He showered and devoured the sandwich and glass of milk. He realized how long it had been since he'd eaten. Then Sam fell upon the bed. He was relieved that he was getting help. Now maybe with Jensen, they could help Caroline and the experimental subjects. He hoped so. He knew he'd fall asleep fast. He was pretty sure Jessup would keep good watch though, and he did.

The hours ticked by.

Sam jerked awake and sat up. Where was he? He looked around but suddenly felt relief. Ah, Jessup's back room. Good. But time to move. The shower felt great, and he was refreshed as he tossed on his new clothes. He walked into the store area and saw Jessup sleeping on a stool with his head resting on the counter. Sam glanced at a wall clock. Good, he still had time to explore the town before Jensen got here.

"Jessup," Sam taped him gently. "You can have your bed now. I'm sorry you had to sleep here."

Jessup jerked up. "I'm just nappin'." Jessup grabbed his drink glass and poured in some more whiskey. "I guess I should wake up. I'm not a very good lookout. This will get me tingling and alert, or it will make me sleep more," he chuckled. "You better now, Mister Sam?"

"Lots better. I was wondering, how big is Barkley Flats?"

"Actually just me and that hospital. I lived here a long time as kind of a hermit on my Social Security pension. There were people here when the hospital opened, so I opened the gas station and store. The people all moved away though. I don't know why. I don't get many visitor, but I keep the store and station open just in case. I figure they'll get tired of city living and come back. Them hospital people come here sometimes for supplies and gas, but they are kind of a crabby group. They customers, though."

"Interesting. I'm going to explore a bit. Tell Jensen that I'll be back, although I should return before he gets here. Maybe he and his men will buy some things from you, and you'll make some money," Sam said.

"Sounds good. But you be careful. That hospital is kinda... a secretive place now. It don't sound too safe for you, if you have to call in the FBI." Jessup took another drink.

Sam smiled and then frowned. "Listen, it may not be safe here either after Jensen and I are gone. Take a vacation, if you can. Return in a few weeks or a month. All should be righted then, hopefully. I'll come back also, as soon as I can, and share that whiskey with you, and pay you." Sam said warmly.

"Ah, Jessup, I was sort of in a battered state when I came. I've forgotten- Do I turn left or right to get to the town and the hospital?"

Jessup was thinking. "I could go visit my daughter and her family Salt Lake. They ain't seen me in a long time...Oh, you turn right, then make another right at the first road you meet. The town is first. ...You'd like my kid. I'll introduce you when we both return."

"I bet I'll like her and her family. I'd love to meet them. Thanks for the clothes, food, definitely the shower, and all your help, Jessup, I have to say, that you are someone special. I'm glad we met, although I wish it were under happier circumstances."

"I kinda of think I'm pretty fine and special too." Jessup grinned broadly through his whiskers. Thank ya. Sam…" He extended his hand.

"Yep," Sam said, as he shook his hand hardily. "Really special, and fine." Sam turned, and confidently walked out the door.

Immediately, memories flooded him as he walked, however, and the tension and worry returned.

Sam arrived at the edge of the town. Walking quickly, he kept to the shadows of the
buildings. Peeking into the window of the first house, he saw pink curtains, but it was empty of furniture.

"You didn't like being near this hospital, eh, Miss Pink? Pretty curtains though," Sam thought as he moved on and crept down below the window of a second larger frame house with blue striped curtains. Again, he saw nothing inside. He checked out the whole block of houses, and then the next. All were empty of people and possessions.

ACCELERATION

Who were the people and what happened to them? Were they the horrid people he met or were they once ordinary hospital workers? Were they the old people who were victims? Or maybe there were never any people here. He had an upset feeling in his gut. He looked up at the sun to figure out the time. No, probably there's not enough time to go to the hospital.

Then he saw it, a large warehouse behind the town. He had to see what was there. Jessup would understand, but worry. Jensen would have to wait or maybe he'd come looking for him. Regardless, he couldn't skip this building. He had a queer feeling that it was important.

CHAPTER 16

Entering the structure quietly, Sam listened intently. Nothing, so far, no one was there, good.

His eyes immediately fell upon an array of brightly colored cartons. They had to be associated with the hospital. Their colors were too obviously a clue. He slit open the side of a red box and felt amongst the paper filling. He felt an object and pulled it out. A vile. Sam read the complex chemical formula on the label. It meant nothing to him, but then his college chem course was not enough preparation for what he suspected the serum was for. He tore off the label and carefully secured it in his pocket. Suddenly Sam turned at the sound of scraping. He crouched behind a tower of cardboard, as two men rose up from the floor.

"We've got a lot to bring down before the truck comes," a gravelly voice groused.

"Hey, how come it's just you and me doing this?" a squeaky fellow replied.

ACCELERATION

"Because the rest of the team are at the hospital," Gravel grunted with irritation. "Some guy has been infiltrating, so they're moving this new batch of meds immediately to the hospital and burning the carcasses in the pit this afternoon. They want us to pile the black cartons outside in the pit.

"They got bodies in them?" Squeaky asked with horror. "I don't want to touch them."

"You want to get paid? You touch them but only the boxes, understand? That ain't so hard. Now get movin', Stupid."

"Hey, don't get mean. I'm young and new."

"Well, you'll be old fast, once you see all that's goin' on here. Now move it." Gravel boomed as he popped some tobacco chew into his mouth, then chewed loudly and spit.

"Got it, Boss. I's sorry." Squeaky lowered his head ashamed. "Hey, Sir, can I have some of that chew? I got to quit cigarettes."

"Sure," said Gravel, "My girl hates it. But, who listens to her? I don't." He boomed with laughter and then started to choke. "Oh, Shit, I almost inhaled my chew." He coughed, cleared his throat noisily, and continued to chomp between his next words. "Now, you hand up the black boxes first from down there, and I'll stack them up here. Then I'll pass down the orange ones and you pile them beside you. Then we haul the orange ones to the lab. Now move it. I ain't got any more patience."

Sam settled back behind the orange boxes and watched. He then shifted to behind the huge black pile, before he was noticed.

The men moved quickly, despite the spitting and coughing. Sam had to stifle a laugh at the absurdity of these villains and their stinky chew tobacco.

When they had finished, the orange cartons were gone and mountains of black boxes stood in their places. The "mole" men then returned to their holes in the ground and slammed down the trap door.

A dense quiet wrapped up the room. Sam broke the trance that held him, and stood. He hadn't realized how cramped he'd been 'til he stretched.

He paced. I should follow them, he thought. I also should wait for Jensen. Maybe I can snoop around for just a short while though; I think I have time. After that, Jensen can take over. If they capture me and I disappear, I'll know that Jensen will still investigate and look for me. I've got to learn more now. Sam paused for only a second, then opened the trap door into the floor. He quickly climbed into the hole and disappeared.

Silence again permeated the building like nothing had occurred. Only those black boxes seemed to ominously stare back.

Sam climbed quietly down the ladder and emerged near the piles of oranges boxes and a maze of vats and tubes. Bright colors blazed on the walls. A motor hummed amidst the voices of Gravel and Squeaky in the distance. They seemed to be back to chattering about the brands of chew. Then their voices faded.

Sam crouched in the gaudy room. His foot brushed a dirty book of matches. He gasped. Well, thank you, person who dropped it, he thought. Could it work? he wondered. His eyes drifted up to the fire alarm switch above his head. Destroying acceleration could start here. He didn't need to wait for Jensen. But he couldn't kill everyone outright; maybe some haven't realized the monstrous group they were part of. He'd warn them. His eyes burned with intensity as he yanked down the alarm switch.

The room filled with voices and screams of terror. People erupted from the corridors as if their puppet strings had been

ACCELERATION

violently pulled. Lights changed quickly to emergency red. Workers swarmed and smashed into each other.

Finally, it eerily grew still, except for the incessant whining of the siren. The people had disappeared into various exits. He didn't know where they were. He only knew his exit, back where he had come from.

Now the climax, Sam was determined. Time for fire, fury, and destruction; His adrenalin rose as he pulled out the laces from his shoes and tied them together. He draped one end over the edge of a vat. He lit his little fuse and ran. He doubted the results would be simple, however.

The explosion wrecked its havoc; it's force hurled Sam against a hot vat. He could feel his skin burn. The fire was raging now. Sam stumbled painfully towards the exit ladder. He cringed as his hands touched the heat of the ladder. He tore off his shredded shirt and wrapped it across his hands furiously. He'd make it if he could just hold on to the ladder's bars.

Sam propelled himself up painfully, rung by rung. His hands stung unbearably through the cloth, and he smelled the scorching rubber of his shoes. But he managed to continue his climb. Suddenly a hand reached out and grabbed onto his as he mounted the last rung. It vaulted him over and into the room. It dragged him away through the choking smoke.

Sam had no idea if his benefactor was friend or foe. He only knew that the pain in his hands was awful, and that he could breathe again and wasn't dead. Suddenly a final explosion hit, blew out the trap door in the floor and tossed his rescuer and Sam into the air. They slammed down onto the concrete floor with violent force. Sam felt nothing more. He was out.

\#

Sam groaned as light blinded him. He squinted up into the face of Squeaky chomping his chew. He wanted to laugh at the craziness of seeing him, but his face hurt and a solitary gasp escaped in its place.   "Hey, man, you just made it. They never told us this stuff could explode. We are lucky sons of bitches. "We sure are. You saved my life, Mister. That was some explosion." Sam pushed the flashlight from his face and sat up painfully. "I thank ya."

"Shucks, it weren't nothin'."

"It were a big somethin'." Sam really was grateful. "You're my hero."

"Aw, wow. That's cool. I ain't never been a hero before. I gotta tell my lady. Maybe I'll get me a little more somethin' in bed tonight, you think so?" Squeaky said as he stood up.

"Yep. I think so," Sam smiled weakly through his soot and stood up slowly beside him.

"Thank ya again, friend," I thought I was gonna die." Sam said as they sat on the step outside the fire room.

Squeaky was breathing hard. "Which section were you in? Didn't you hear the alarm? I ain't workin' here no more. That was scary. I'm quitten" I don't care how much they pay us. I ain't eatin' that stinkin chew anymore either." He spit out the chew and pulled out a cigarette. He started to light it, but his hands shook and he couldn't find a match. "You got a light for your rescuer, buddy?"

"Yeh, but maybe just one. I been tryin' to quit." Sam pulled out one of his left over matches from which he had lit the inferno. He started to stand up, but he swayed with dizziness.

"Mister, you don't look good."

"I be fine, but I think I'm gonna leave this place too. It's hard on the health," Sam said as he coughed and cleared the smoke residue from his lungs and throat.

ACCELERATION

"You sure ain't kiddin'." Squeaky continued. "Hey, I haven't seen you around. You from the hospital?"

"Yep, I just started today. I was at the hospital for too long. But this place might kill us," Sam continued.

"Hey, I heard stories about Mekka. He's crazy now and ready for the ovens, I bet. It sure must be exciting over there. We get bodies, but you got to see them all baby-like."

Now Sam was feeling sick again. He no longer liked this guy. He was a sadist, but Sam knew he had to play along. "Yep, babies, and then they burn. It's fun to see them all babble and then cook." Sam was making himself sick. He felt like vomiting. "Friend, I'm sick. I gotta get out and away from here. Thanks for saving me." Sam bolted for the trees and leaned against them. He was then very sick.

After it was over, Sam lay on the ground and stared at the sky. He could still hear the fire crackling and exploding. He felt himself smile though. He had done the place major damage.

People were huddled in groups about the lawn, but Sam just lay with exhausted relief by the trees. He felt better getting away from them. He still needed to return to Caroline, but he had to disappear here in the trees for a while and regain his strength. And where was Jensen?

Sam dozed off but was awaken by the rumble of a steady stream of Army vehicles. Good, very good, he thought. Quite a show of power. They'll really investigate. I hope Jensen understands my being late to talk with him. Sam got up and started walking towards the vehicles, but stopped suddenly and stepped back. Jensen was holding a cloth to the side of his face and shaking hands with Dr. Mekka. He was patting him on the back. Why isn't he arresting him? Is he taken in by lies here? No. He couldn't be. He's a government official. He's fighting for the people, isn't he?

Sam noted Jensen now had prematurely grey hair flowing down his back and a slight middle-aged spread. He didn't look like a government agent, but it was the handshake that puzzled him. Maybe he was just trying to trick them for information before arresting them? Or maybe I have him all wrong. Sam frowned. And is that cloth to keep away the stench of death or is he burned. Was he there before his men?

Sam's mind raced. He moved in closer and grabbed a blanket from a pile in the medical trucks parked nearby.

ACCELERATION

Jensen must have brought these trucks. He dropped the covering over his head and shoulders and blended in with the other casualties. The fire had left him pretty beaten up and singed anyway.

Suddenly Sam saw Sean and his insides turned over. His brother that he loved was causing all this horror. He sauntered near Sean and bent to adjust his shoes, which moved clumsily without laces. The voices were barely audible, but he understood the words.

"Sean, where is that brother of yours? It will take us months to get on our feet again. You've got a big loose end. Fix it," Jensen rasped.

"Agent Jensen, your people have failed to adequately secure my project. I do not need to listen to your pouting and orders. You find my brother and execute him. My project must continue. I'll need full security at the hospital now and new quarters. Arrange them immediately. Do it now!" Sean shouted and entered a vehicle.

Jensen glowered with eyes blazing. "Damn scientists!" he hurls out the words. Then he snapped at his men. "Gordon, clean up this mess. I also want a detail sent over to the hospital. You need to watch for this man, Sam Stone, the brother." He grabbed a picture from his aide's hand. "Make copies and pass it out at the hospital. Then set up a command post over there." Silas Jensen turned and steamed off to his limo.

Oh my, a limo, Jensen. You're getting rich off this. I wonder, how and who pays you? Sam mused. His thoughts then began tumbling, as he clutched his blanket more closely and made his way to an empty van. He suddenly forced himself to calm the pounding of anger in his head. Okay, think. Car keys. He looked under the mat. None. He felt under the dash for the ignition wires and hot-wired the car. He chuckled sarcastically to himself. His old teen years, spent working part-time in an auto shop, weren't a waste. Slowly he started the motor, just as Squeaky lumbered up to the window.

"Hey, you got room for me? I'm supposed to go on duty at the hospital now. I didn't quit. You too?"

"Nah, I'm still here too, but I got orders to hurry back to pick up more supplies, like fast…Sorry, pal. I can't take you with me." Sam didn't dare tempt fate any further and drive near the hospital. He still might get caught.

ACCELERATION

Squeaky's ruddy face dissolved into anger. "Sure, right, you say so. You ain't my friend no more." He slammed his fist on the car.

"Friend, it's just my job, I'm sorry. The boss said he'd dock me if I don't hurry," Sam said in his most regretful manner, then pulled away.

Well, what's another enemy? He thought. At this rate he won't have any friends left at all. His face became glum but determined as he drove quickly away.

Sam was going to finish this mess and bring Caroline out somehow, even if it meant by himself. He was overwhelmed, however, at how big this conspiracy was. How many important Washington people are involved in this mad plot? What do they want to accomplish? And who's paying all the bills for this? Someone always pays. Is it the FBI? Or has Jensen gone rogue? And how is Caroline doing? I have to stop getting side-tracked and go for her now. Is she still alive? I've taken so long. I can't depend on Jensen now to help in her rescue. It's all up to me.

CHAPTER 17

Sam wasn't sure how to find the hospital entrance by the road, but if it led to it, no problem. If there was a turn off, he'd have to go blind and trust his hunches. But the road led only to one place. Sam slowed as he saw the lights of the hospital. He pulled off and into the brush. He quickly doused his car lights.

This was going to be a seat of the pants mission. He hoped to get Caroline out and back to the car, but he wasn't sure they'd survive. Oh Caroline, he missed her. Was she changed now and would she come? He wished that he had just tried to carry her out from the beginning, but he felt deeply that they wouldn't have made it. He had to stop doubting himself. He just hoped that if they got out, that she would be able to get good medical treatment and get well. As for Sean, Sam doubted he'd ever have his brother back, and he didn't want what Sean had become. Was his brother still buried inside the egomaniac or was he lost forever? Sam ached at the thought. He suddenly looked down at his raw hands. They had been gripping the wheel so tightly that he felt pain at removing them. "Move it, soldier. Get Caroline out now." he said grimly as he got out of the car and tore off pieces of his shirt. He used the pieces to bind his shoes so he could run. He really missed those laces.

He headed for the lights. First, he'd get Caroline out, and then destroy everything, including Sean and Jensen, if possible. He doubted the fire alarm bit would work again. He'd have to play a different card this time, and he'd show no mercy. It was too late for that.

Sean saw a sentry guard and came up behind him. His adrenalin was pumping now. He grabbed the guard from behind. He squeezed his neck but hoped he hadn't actually broken it. He may be just an innocent guard, but he couldn't take a chance now of the guy alerting someone. Sam pulled the man behind a bush and stripped him of his uniform and shoes. The pants and shirt fit satisfactorily, but the shoes were another matter. They were painfully too small but would have to do. He was happy to donate his own torn, raggedy pants and floppy shoes to the man on the ground. He dropped them onto the man's chest. Well, at least the poor guy will have something to wear when and, regretfully, if he awakens.

He stayed at the fellow's post for a few minutes and then strolled purposefully towards the entrance. He'd walk right in. Why not? Hell, who'd expect Sam to come from the front?

It all seemed to be working. He mingled with the crowd of guards in the front and then passed through. Next Sam found the stairs and made his way to the sixth floor. He remembered that Caroline was there. He nervously watched as the floors passed by. Then six. Slowly the door opened into a crowded corridor. Patients were being led down the hall to another elevator, and then he gasped in shock. There was Caroline! She was smiling as she took the arm of her young guard. Her face shown with immense energy and gayety.

"Thank you, kind Sir," she laughed as she flirted with the young recruit.

Sam joined the march and swaggered up beside the guard. "That's a pretty lady you got there, young man," Sam winked.

The lad nodded with delight. "We're going to meet the leader. I've been doing a good job. He's proud of me and the other guards here. I think he's going to praise and reward us. You too, I'm sure he wants to see this lady also."

Caroline stared with confused at Sam, as she walked.

"You go ahead. I'm assigned to bring Miss Caroline."

"Are you sure. I actually like bringing her. She's so nice and beautiful," the youth stammered.

ACCELERATION

"You'll see lots of pretty girls up there and you are getting rewarded, just remember that kid. You'll probably see her later. Now hurry and catch up to the others. You're falling behind," Sam said curtly.

"Yes, I suppose you're right," the youth spurted forward and caught the elevator.

Caroline stopped walking as the boy left. "Do I know you? Are you, Sam?"

"Yes, honey. I am." Sam looked around. "Duck in here." Sam guided her into a small closet.

Caroline smiled, "I'm on medication, but I know you now. Sam, you came back for me. I'm so happy to see you.," Suddenly she closed her eyes and went limp.

"Oh, no, Caroline, this is all we need!" Sam pulled over a pail and turned it upside down. He sat and cradled her in his lap. "Baby, wake up, you gotta walk with me."

She looked so frail now. Her long blond hair caressed her pale cheeks. She was so lovely and helpless. He kissed her once gently. He shouldn't have left her. Now they were back where they started. "Okay, honey, now wake up," Sam shook her gently.

Caroline opened her eyes slowly and blinked repeatedly. "Sam, I don't think I feel well."

"I know, baby, I know. Come on, we have to get out of here before they realize you're gone." He took her arms and helped her up.

Caroline leaned on him precariously for a minute and then stood firmly. "Let's go, before I slip back…Oh, Sam, I love you, you know." She beamed and quickly kissed him.

"Wait a minute, we've got time for one more. And it may be our last." Sam caught her up into his arms and kissed her passionately. Suddenly he broke away, "Wow. I love you too."

Caroline started to laugh but then covered her mouth. "I guess I should be quiet. I'm so happy with you. All right. I'm ready to move. Where? Down the elevator?"

"Sounds good." Sam grinned and kissed her tenderly again. "Now we can travel." And they did.

It was all too simple. He was afraid of that. Why? They had gone down two floors on a stairway, when they heard voices above on the steps.

"Oh, no!"

"What?" whispered Caroline.

ACCELERATION

"Trouble. Out of the stairway, fast!" Sam grabbed her arm and pulled her through the

doorway.

"Fourth floor. Quick, in here," Sam said anxiously. They ducked into a room.

Caroline and Sam relaxed.

But suddenly, they felt it. There was something in this room. And Caroline was trembling beside him.

"I'll get the lights," said Sam.

Sam reached out and flicked on the light. Caroline froze. Sam gasped at what he saw.

There sat Sean. But he had changed. This man had a brain that had grown and broken through the bones of his skull. Attached to his head were wires that stretched across the room to a wall of computers which hummed ominously.

"Let's get out of here, Caroline," Sam reached out for the door handle, but Sean's computer voice stopped him.

"Sam, you don't want to leave." Sean boomed out. "I'm glad you came to see me. "I'm powerful." Sean waved his arms, "I'll never die and I'm brilliant." His eyes glistened. "I keep evolving further and further. It's incredible. Surely you must see the benefits."

"No," Sam replied nervously, "I see danger. Sean, you've become selfish and cruel. You've lost your humanity."

"NO!" Sean's voice boomed. "You're jealous. I am a genius. It's what all people want to be."

Sam felt suddenly calm. "Not me. I don't want to be you. I was afraid of you, for a while, but not anymore. Now I'm afraid for you. This place you've made and you are terrifying. You can't see what you've become. We're leaving."

"Stay with me. I'm lonely." Sean implored, suddenly quiet.

"No. We're leaving. We're going to live our normal lives."

CLICK. "You locked the door. Unlock it Sean. Let us go."

"No!" Sean's voice boomed. "I can destroy you if I want to."

"Yes," Sam replied quietly. "But you won't. Unlock the door."

"I don't want to be alone anymore. No No NO NO!" Sean's voice seemed to speed and go into a high register. He kept turning his head back and forth, back and forth, pulling on the wires which suddenly burst into flames. The fire traveled in a split second to the computer. Suddenly the fire sizzled and exploded into a massively flaming computer wall. It began to crawl, snapping and sizzling to the other walls.

ACCELERATION

Sam stared. "Pull out the wires, Sean. Get out, please Sean. Get out before you catch fire too."

Caroline grabbed Sam hand and cried out. "Run." She pulled him to the door. "It's still locked!"

Sam turned to Sean and the now three burning walls. "Open the door, Sean. You can still hear us. Don't take us with you. I'm Sammy, your brother. You remember me."

Suddenly the door unlocked. Caroline took Sam's hand and pulled him through the door and into the hallway.

"To the elevator," Caroline yelled as she yanked the stunned Sam along.

They reached the lift and ran in. Caroline slammed the button to close the doors and the other button for the first floor. The lift began to move.

"I should have saved him," Sam stared and mumbled.

"You couldn't. He killed himself." Caroline said as she panted and tried to catch her breath.

Sam stared at the doors. His brother was now truly dead.

They faced the front of the elevator and waited nervously for first floor.

Sam said absently. "Lately I have this thing for fires."

Caroline didn't understand. Was he in shock?

Sam shook himself. "Sorry. I'm okay."

The lift doors opened onto the third floor. The backs of two men with ugly automatic weapons hung from their sides. They were turned slightly away from the lift doors.

"Oops, wrong floor." Sam said as he pounded the close and the elevator suddenly descended. "I think we're going to the basement. Someone else pushed it first."

The elevator doors suddenly opened upon the basement floor and madness. People of all sizes, with withered-aging bodies, stormed into the elevator and threatened to crush Sam and Caroline against the walls. Sam held tight to Caroline's hand and pushed forward. They reached the button, but the doors would not close. More people shoved to get in.

"We have to get out, Caroline!" Sam shouted. "Hang onto me!" He felt like he was being smothered as they squeezed through the crushing mob. It seemed that they would never get clear without falling, but he finally felt space and yanked Caroline after him. Gasping with relief, they turned and scanned the crowd. The multitude seemed to be crazy with fear as they wailed and pushed madly.

"Calm down!" Sam shouted. "You'll be all right. You're too many for the elevator. Some of you pull back towards me. We need to let one load go and then the rest of us will follow! Some of you come out." But Sam's words were lost in their plaintiff wailings for life. He couldn't blame them. The sirens were blaring. He wasn't sure exactly how all would escape.

"Stairs! Over there. It's on a different side from Sean." They ran, but the crowd was one step behind them, pushing them aside, and pounding on the stairway door.

"Locked, they can't get through!" Caroline's voice was beginning to show fear.

"There's got to be a way out. Let's try the ventilation system and see if there's a way through. I hope it's big enough. If it is, you game?"

"Well, I'm not terribly athletic and healthy right now, but…" Caroline winced. "Are you sure we'll find a way out that way?"

"No," Sam shrugged, "but, otherwise, we're trapped." He looked back at the mob, now attacking and fighting the people still in the elevator.

Caroline followed his look and heard the screams. "You're right. Lead on Tarzan. We need to climb up, I'll try." She looked up worriedly.

"Right, Jane. We can do this, honey." He tried to smile with reassurance.

The crowd was so bewildered and frantic that it paid no attention to a couple climbing a chair from a side room and Sam held Caroline up to the ceiling vent.

"Can you get the panel off?"

"I can't reach it," Caroline stammered.

"Hold on. I'm going to try and balance you up on my shoulders." Sam tensed as he held Caroline up, and she mounted his shoulders.

"I think I've got it. Ouch!"

"What happened?" Sam braced for her fall.

"I broke my nail. It's okay, I've got it," and the panel fell open onto Caroline's head as she lost her balance and fell.

Sam managed to break most of her fall. He held her closely as they sat on the chair. "We may be clumsy but we try," he laughed. "You okay?"

"Yep." Caroline grinned. "Now you get to climb up and pull me up. Ready, Clyde?"

Sam chuckled. "Yes, dear Bonnie. We are a good team. However, you said Bonnie and Clyde died in a hail of bullets.

Let's hope we are luckier." He sat her on her feet. "Hold the chair tightly. I may knock it over when I reach up."

"I'll hold it, I think," Caroline said nervously.

"Wait. He grabbed a sheet from a nearby laundry basket and twisted it as best he could and tied it around his waist. "A rope would be better but we are resourceful. Now I'm going to climb up and extend our sheet rope. Grab on and I'll pull you up. Don't let go. Do you think you can hold on?"

"I have to," said Caroline.

"Yes, we have to," said Sam as he hugged her. "Let's go."

Sam made it up. Caroline climbed quickly onto the chair and grabbed the sheet rope.

He hauled her up and pulled her over the top and into the shaft. They looked down. The mob was attacking and killing each other. He left the ceiling grate open just in case they wanted to try and escape their way, but he didn't have time to help them. And they were so frail and so many. Also, Sam could feel heat building in the vent. They might not make it themselves.

"Sam, it's getting warm on the floor," Caroline said nervously.

"I noticed. Let's go." Sam looked. "Wait." He scooted up to Caroline and gave her a long lingering kiss. "If we're going to die, we need a last moment of joy first. Thanks, my love."

"My love. That's sweet. You're welcome. Now we crawl. You're bribing me with affection first." she laughed.

He nodded his head with a laugh, and they began to crawl quickly. Their hands and knees stung as the heat intensified. There were wrong turns and backtracking. They finally opened a ceiling door which led to the first floor of the building. Boosting each other up, they made it. Pausing for a minute, they then stood up, and yanked open the last door. They sprang out into dense smoke. It also was very dark.

"Where now? Right or left or straight?" Caroline coughed as she muttered the words.

"Mind if I cough with you?" Sam followed with his own coughing burst. "Okay, how about forward." He coughed again and grabbed her hand. Sam saw a faint light in the distance. He hoped it was an exit sign and not a stairwell. They inched along in the darkness. They felt a glass doorway and a handle. It opened and they rammed into a crowd of moving bodies. The people carried them along as they fought to keep hold of their hands. Finally, they plunged out a door into the cold air and darkness of night. The people began to scatter and then fall in relief upon the ground. Sam and Caroline felt the same way and found a secluded spot further away from the masses.

For the first time in days Sam felt no fear and dread as he collapsed onto the grass. He happily pulled Caroline down next to him. She then turned away and curled into a ball.

Catching his breath, he laughed. "You look cute. Do you realize that we actually made it, honey?"

Caroline didn't answer. Sam looked at her tenderly as she lay on the ground. "Darling?" There was no answer.

Sam nudged her playfully. "Caroline, we made it." He turned her gently towards him. "Are you asleep already?" he said teasingly. Then his gasped and stared. She wasn't seeing him. Her eyes had veiled themselves in an opaque shield. Her skin was turning in upon itself and drying up. Even in the moonlight he could see in horror as she aged at grotesque speed.

"Oh, no. Baby, no. Stop, not now…" He held her close as if his will could stop the terrible process. "I love you." He rocked her gently as tears glistened in his eyes and flowed down his face. He sobbed as he held her tightly.

"Tell me what to do, darling. I don't know what to do," Sam whispered over and over until his voice was lost to the wind. He finally eased his body beside her and grasped his hand on hers. Exhausted, he closed his eyes. There was nothing more that he could do, just lie beside her. He'd hold her hand though and not let go.

Caroline died. Perhaps she wasn't as strong as Sean and the others or did she not want to live like she was at the end? She had awakened once, looked at her hand, felt her face, and then put her hand back in his.

He had felt it and opened his eyes. He brought their hands up, kissed hers, and then he noticed. He looked from their hands to her face. She knew and tried not to cry.

"Darling, you are still very beautiful inside and out… Caroline, don't leave me."

"I'm in love with you, Sam, but I guess I'm too old for you now," she whispered.

"Never too old for me. I love you too. Don't leave me." He blurted out the words.

Her fingers went to his lips. "Shh, it's okay. I got myself into this mess. It's not your fault. Plus, it led me to you."

ACCELERATION

"I should have taken you with me the first time. It's my fault that you got worse." His voice shook with emotion.

"It was my choice to stay. And I couldn't have left that first time." She smiled. "Sam, we stopped them, didn't we?"

"We sure did." Sam kissed her cheek;

She smiled faintly and died.

Sam sat up. "Oh no, don't go." He took her body in his arms, as if he could transfer his life into hers. "Take me with you if you have to leave," he said softly. "Please." But there was no answer. Sam held her, and the stars watched.

When morning came, Sam stood and blinked in surprise at the bright sunlight. Why was he still alive? He felt ravaged and empty. He looked at Caroline, but he had to look away. It hurt too much. He turned back to stare at the hospital site. The rubble seemed to glare back at him. He felt satisfaction at its destruction, but heavy regret at the cost. Sean's work had caused the fire and brought it all down. It caused many deaths, but it was over. The madness was gone or was it? There was still Silas Jenson. A shiver flooded his body. Jensen. He needs to be stopped and prosecuted. Can it be done? Yes, and he would make sure of it. But how?

Silas Jensen was still alive. Could his network be rebuilt? Was he the top gun or another? Sam was going to find out, but he wasn't the same person who called Jensen those hours before. Something had died inside Sam, at least for now. He felt cold. He was that soldier from years before, but one filled with a hatred he had never known.

Sam noticed that the local authorities were on the scene now also. He walked up to a young police officer as the man covered a body. Sam was sure that he must look a mess. His shirt and pants were torn and filthy, and he needed a shave. He'd last cleaned himself up while at Jessup's. It seemed so long ago now. He'd have to just approach the cop like he was an important person. He kind of was. He had added to the destruction.

"Mister, there's a body of a young girl, a Caroline Mekka, on the ridge in the trees over there." He pointed. "Can you see that she's taken care of, please? She was an innocent victim."

"Sure. Yes, of course. Sir, do you know what happened here? No one tells us beat cops anything," he asked.

He's so young, Sam thought.

ACCELERATION

"I don't know, sorry. I just stumbled on her body and recognized her. I need to see a guy named Silas Jensen from the FBI. Have you seen him?" Sam asked authoritatively.

The cop looked at Sam strangely. "How'd you get so messed up, Mister?"

"I was sent to help organize transfer of the people last night. We didn't expect the explosion." Sam's eyes took on a faraway look.

"Must have been awful, Sir. Sorry I asked." The young cop looked sincerely concerned.

"It's fine, but it was hell," he said grimly.

"Yeah," the cop replied as he shifted his feet uncomfortably.

"You were saying where Mr. Jensen is?" Sam said sternly.

"The guys were talking about him. I think he's gone to meet some other big shots."

Sam snapped. "You still haven't answered my question, Mister. Where?"

"Sorry, Sir. I think he said in Washington. Yeah. I'm sure of it. He said he had to catch a plane and that his bosses are going to be very unhappy."

"I'm sure they will be. You have a vehicle?" Sam asked.

"Yes, Sir."

"The keys? I'll inform your superiors that I have it," said Sam. The cop hesitated. "Now, young man," Sam continued, "Unless you want heavy trouble on yourself, I'd give me the keys, now." Sam's face was like iron.

The young cop blanched. "Sorry, Sir, yes Sir. Here, I'm parked over there." He pointed a short distance.

"Thank you. I will remember to commend you to your superiors. Your name is?"

"Kellogg, Sir. Officer Andrew Kellogg," he replied.

"Thank you, Officer Kellogg. Now take care of the girl's body." Sam quickly turned on his heels, walked to the appointed car, and drove away.

Kellogg, standing in the ruins, swallowed hard and grabbed a blanket. He walked towards the ridge and approached the trees. Looking down at the body, he stared as thoughts meandered through his head. That guy's playing some sort of joke on me. This isn't a young girl. It's an old dame. He snorted and covered the body. He carried it carefully towards the others, near a truck. What did he say her name was, oh yes, Caroline Mekka. I wonder if she was related to this Mekka Corporation. Maybe she was the Grandmother of the founder.

ACCELERATION

Oh, well, she's dead now. He wrote out a tag and   pinned it to her clothes.

How did he ever get placed on this job? He sure wished that he were home with his wife. Right now he wanted to touch a loving hand. He yearned to be away from this carnage. He had a half hour left on this shift. He wondered briefly about the strange man he'd met. He sure hoped his boss didn't get upset about his losing his vehicle to the guy. He didn't even get his name."

He looked at the old woman's body again and gently pulled the blanket over her face. He wondered briefly what happened to her. He pushed it out of his mind, as he wrapped the blanket around her more securely. "Rest in peace lady," he whispered, as he picked her up and carried her to a truck, where she would join the rest of the dead.

Sam had been just driving forward. He needed a plan. This was crazy to just drive. All right, he'd drive north and then cross over into California and aim for San Francisco, where he'd call his friend and agent, Ben. He looked at the gas gauge. "Umm, a pretty full tank. Good. He might just make it. He muttered emotionally. "Thank you."

He suddenly thought about Jessup. He hoped he was okay. When this was over, he needed to go back and tell him he survived and thank him properly. He couldn't go back now. Jensen's men may be watching for him. Returning would have to be in the future, whenever that might be. But for now, he would keep going.

He did. Sam drove on and on.

CHAPTER 18

"Ben?"

"Yes."

"It's Sam."

"Sam, where are you?" Ben implored. "What happened? You've been all over the news. The police and FBI are all chattering and demanding your surrender. What the blazes did you do?"

"It's complicated. I'm on my way to San Francisco. I stumbled on horrible activities created by the government and involving my brother. I'm trying to figure out what to do now. There are a lot of bad guys involved. You know me, Ben, I'm not one of them." Sam sighed. He felt awfully tired.

"I'm sorry, Sam. I didn't mean to accuse you. I am on your side. What's important is that you're not hurt. I've been very worried about you. How can I help?"

Sam was relieved. "Thanks, Ben. Your help and belief in me means a lot." He still had one friend. Ben had been his agent from the beginning, and they also had become long-time friends. He had taken Sam under his wing and stood by him through his adjustment after the Army, family amused at Sam's reluctance to speak with people who recognized him, but Sam was always respectful to his fans. He just treasured his privacy. Ben, however, loved the parties, and he definitely liked the money. But then, Sam had to admit that he wasn't tragedy, and his discomfort with being a now famous writer. He had always been opposed to the money either.

"Sam, where are you?" Ben interrupted his thoughts. "What can I do?"

"I hate to ask, but can you lend me an advance on my sales, say two thousand for now?" Sam said. "I've lost my wallet and might get arrested, if they find out that I'm still alive, and if it's true that I'm a wanted man now. I might get caught. if I try to access my bank account. Eventually I hope to clear myself. You know I'm good for the money. I'll come to you to get it. I hate to ask when you just paid me with a big royalty check, however."

"Sure. No problem. I like your big royalties and my cut also, I also know that the checks will keep coming," Ben said. "But why would they arrest you. I hoped that they just want to talk to you."

ACCELERATION

"You'd better not know the details just yet, my friend. Are you home for a while?" Sam said.

"Yes, but I'll have to get cash at the bank since you probably don't want a check, right?"

"Yes. Thanks," Sam said. "I'm coming then. I can be there in about two hours. I'm not very close. I'm on a bus. Is anyone watching your house?" Sam said anxiously.

"Oh my goodness, I don't think so. If it is that dangerous, be careful, Sam. I don't want to lose my wonderful old friend and best client." Now Ben sounded worried.

"I'll be careful. Thanks, Ben, for your friendship. I'll pay it back."

"I know you will. See you soon." Ben hung up.

Sam felt a little less anxious.

"Sam, I was very worried," Benjamin Gallagher opened the door eagerly. "Rumor has it that you're now dead."

"Really?" Sam said tiredly. "Nope, I'm indestructible, so far anyway and hopefully in the future. Missed you, my good friend."

"You look awful, and I missed you too. When did you decide to go the derelict route? The whiskers are a bit scruffy."

Ben's face crinkled into a grin. He sincerely liked Sam. They had maintained a long friendship, aside from the business. He knew that he was Sam's dearest friend, except for his kid brother and Susie. They didn't always associate with the same crowd, but there was honest affection, respect, and loyalty, which was bread over the years.

"Razor, clothes, and a bath await you. Fast man, before the neighbors begin to talk," Ben teased.

Sam smiled. "I owe you," and he clasped Ben's hand.

"You owe me nothing. Your friendship and talent have been a gift to me, plus we crusaders need to stick together." Ben spoke warmly with that old twinkle in his eye.

"Crusaders? For what?" replied Sam curiously.

"Justice, money and women." Benjamin joked. He enjoyed surrounding himself in life's finery, but he retained memories of his poor upbringing and class struggle. Despite his jovial front, he was about as down to earth and humble as a man could be. Sam had deep respect for his friend.

"Hey, speak for yourself, chauvinist!" Sam countered. He needed to laugh and was enjoying the banter. Ben must have known that. He pushed all the right buttons. Sam's broad shoulders relaxed. He suddenly felt very tired. He turned back to Ben, who was just fixing a drink. "I've got to sleep for an hour. May I use your couch or bedroom. Throw a drink on me if I go longer, will you?" he said.

"Right, use any bedroom. There's an alarm clock in each. But throwing the drink would be fun." Ben's smile faded as he suddenly turned serious. "Then, when you wake, we'll talk, young man."

"Yes, then we'll talk." Sam said sadly. He never quite made it to a shower first. He mounted the stairs, lay across the bed, and was out. Sleep was just what he needed.

Sam's eyes sprang open. He stared at a disembodied head with a gaping mouth. His body tensed but couldn't move. A bloody grey mass oozed from the head and spilled over his body. It was seeping into his orifices. He wanted to scream, but it was in his mouth and now choking the life from his body. Sam was flinging his arms about, but they were caught in its tendrils. Hideous gurgling sounds were coming from its mouth. Suddenly he was free, but something was shaking him. He would kill it, if he could see it. He squeezed his eyes shut and open them again. If he could just clear his vision, and then suddenly he could.

Ben was holding his arms or rather trying to. "My God, Sam. It's just a dream. I'm here."

"Here?" Sam tried to sit up but fell back. "Where?" He couldn't quite understand. Why was Ben looking at him with such pity? "Hey, I'm fine now. I just had a nightmare. I'm bloody happy that it was a dream and not happening here and now though." He smiled tightly. A lock of dark hair had fallen over his forehead. Despite his rugged strength, Sam looked like a young boy in that moment.

Ben swallowed hard. "You need a drink. If what you've been through caused that nightmare, I'm very sorry, Sam. Can I help with more than money and a drink?"

"You are helping by just believing in me, and with the money. Thanks. The memories of the past week and the mess is getting to me. And I need a shower." Sam was feeling better as he managed to stand. He took a towel and wiped the sweat from his face. Out now, while I clean up. Okay?"

"I'm going. I just feel like a worried father." I'll meet you downstairs." Ben moved out and closed the door.

Sam stepped into the shower. He shook his head to rid himself of his horrible memories. The water soothed his cuts and bruises. He wondered about Jensen. What was he doing now? Is more happening with his experiments or is it all over? Why were they after me? I can't write about the hospital and the horror. No one would believe me. He wasn't going to let it all blow over though. Maybe Jensen realized that. Sam just didn't know what to do. How was he going to end this Jensen madness? He feared there was more to follow on Acceleration and that it wasn't over. He always finished what he started. But it wasn't over as long as Jensen lived, and he wasn't about to stop finding out more information on Jensen and the drugs. He turned off the shower. He felt better.

When Sam joined Ben he was no longer the terrified little boy with the bad dream. He took the offered scotch and eased his lanky body into an old leather chair. He downed the drink with gusto.

"You're a good bartender, my friend," Sam said quietly.

Ben nodded his head proudly. "Thank you, and by the way, here's some coffee also and a sandwich. And you probably won't have to pay me back for the loan because your books just shot up on the bestseller list. The publicity has made lots of people want your books and that means, I'll get lots of royalties also. I brought you $5000. Being poor is never fun." Ben's eyes twinkled and then he sobered. "Now give. I just listened to the news. One minute you are public enemy number one, and the next, you are declared dead. You are now dead? Why? Can you tell me? I won't judge you, Sam."

"All right." Sam began at the beginning. After he'd finished, neither said a word, but rather they stared into their drinks, as the fire in the fireplace sparked and shadowed the room with the demons of Sam's tale.

Finally, Ben cleared his throat and spoke. "Why did it kill Caroline and not you?"

"Maybe because I wasn't on it very long. Perhaps you need it after a while in order to survive. I didn't need it after my hallucinations and craziness in the wilderness area. I don't know all the answers. I hope it doesn't affect me later. I don't think it will. It hasn't so far."

Sam buried his face in his hands. "Ben, I should have gone back sooner, I killed as sure as they did. I shouldn't have left her."

"You said she was too weak, and it was her choice too." Ben rested his broad hand on Sam's arm. You didn't kill her."

"I should have carried her the first time." Sam's eyes burned with the pain of the memory and choice.

ACCELERATION

"Then you'd probably both be dead or brains preserved in their anatomy boxes or jars. You did what was right at the time. Also, you caused a lot of destruction to their chemicals and hospital. In a way, you were a hero. Maybe you stopped the experiments." Ben said.

"I wish I could feel that inside." Sam stood and shook his head. "Look at me, I'm a bundle of self-pity. So what now? I think I have to investigate further. Knowledge isn't worth destroying human lives in such a cruel way." He sighed sadly. "Why did those subjects volunteer?"

Ben thought for a moment and then said, "Maybe they were too excited and greedy. Science can bring wonderful results, but not all experiments end well. The effects seemed worth it to them. They just didn't expect death or Sean's results which changed his personality. He was obsessed. You couldn't have saved him or them. They all made their choices."

Sam passed his fingers through his hair and thought. "Do you think it's over? I have a feeling that it's not. And do you think it just involves Silas Jensen now or the whole FBI?"

"Damned if I know. Even speculating is frightening. All right. Enough knowledge here for my poor old brain. Do you think this is enough money?" Ben dug the money out of his wallet on the table and handed it to Sam. "What else can I do?'

"You did a lot. I owe you big time. You also made me feel sane again." Sam stood up. "I guess I have to go and rejoin the world once more, sort of. I'll have to see if I'm still wanted as a criminal or dead."

"Oh, here." Ben said as he handed Sam the morning paper. "You might want to read the fiction that Jensen created and is putting out. It's fascinating but not as interesting as the bloody truth."

Sam reached out for it just as Ben enveloped him in a bear hug. "Be careful, kid."

"Kid," Sam laughed. "You'll be calling me that when I'm eighty."

"Yep," Ben said playfully and then froze. He turned to being serious. "I hope so. Now go before I get emotional. By the way, where are you headed?"

Sam smiled. "Washington, D.C." He turned and walked out the door.

CHAPTER 19

"**Ladies and Gentlemen, please remain in your** seats until we have come to a full stop. Enjoy your stay in our nation's capital, Washington D.C. Sam woke with a start at the giggle of his five-year-old seatmate.

"Wake up, Mister. My name is Sarah. I'm going to see my daddy. I was visiting my grandma." She certainly was a cute little urchin, but too cheerful. She did let him sleep, however, which was wonderful. He needed the rest.

Sam stifled a yawn. "Are you? That's nice, Sarah." She hadn't made a sound all through the trip. He usually hated sitting next to kids, but he was amazed at how good she was. It sent a pang through Sam. He and his ex-wife, Mandy, had lost their little girl, Annie, years ago. On reflecting, he knew that the loss caused their break-up. It was when he sold his first book. They lost their baby through meningitis. Mandy had gone into heavy depression for months afterwards. She just couldn't look at Sam after that. Their happiness together was over. It couldn't survive losing Annie. Mandy never remarried, at least so far, he thought. Sam secretly hoped someday they could go back to what they were, but that was a long time ago. He hadn't seen her since the

divorce, though they wrote ever Christmas. Annie died at the age of one. He missed her.

He closed his eyes for a minute. He could still see her in his mind and remember her giggle. He smiled and opened his eyes again.

Sam looked around. The plane had stopped. Little Sarah was gone. He was alone except for the two tired stewardesses that were staring at him. He apologized and shrugged. He cheerfully walked off the plane and through the airport crowds. He felt renewed energy. Suddenly he froze.

Next to the street exit stood little Sarah with Silas Jensen. She was hugging him and calling him "Daddy." Sam felt shocked, as he quickly turned away. He was shaking inside. He hated Jensen, but seeing the child changed the whole scenario. Jensen suddenly had become a human being. But no, a human couldn't be so twisted and still have this innocent kid. But then Hitler was gentle with kids too, as long as they weren't Jewish and other minority groups. No, this wasn't going to make him quit investigating the man. He was hiding the evil inside him.

ACCELERATION

Jensen didn't notice Sam as he walked out of the terminal with his child and boarded a taxi.

Sam quickly grabbed the next taxi in the line and delighted the driver with the famous words, "Follow that car." Sam then turned on his charm as he spoke to the driver. "It's just a game," he said, "a game with a dear friend. Try not to let them see us, however."

"Sure, if you say so," the guy grinned, as his metallic front tooth glinted in the headlights of the oncoming cars.

For twenty minutes they wove through the traffic. They suddenly came to a colonial estate where Jensen stopped in his taxi. Jensen pulled through the front gate. Sam's driver pulled over on the next block.

"You want me to turn around and park in front," he said.

"No, this is fine. Thanks. I can't wait to surprise him." Sam winked and handed the driver the fare and a big tip. "Is that enough?"

"Sure is. Have fun, Mister." The driver winked back and dissolved into guffaws. "I wish I could see the guy's face. Thanks, Mister." Sam laughed too and got out, as his still grinning driver drove off.

He had made Sam felt good. The driver was so genuine and one of many colorful and happy people that delight our world but do not change the grand scheme of history. Was Sam one of those people or part of the Sean and Jensen master plan? He wished he could just be one of the ordinary ones living their lives, but he felt like he was obligated to affect the present and stop what he feared might be a threat to people. Feeling this way, he couldn't just crawl back and be a little satellite of his own. He didn't need power or immortality, but he felt he had to do something. He was part of the hurricane that was coming whether he liked it or not.

The people Jensen hurt didn't even realize the cruelty of their fates. They were being lied to, used, murdered, and then thrown into the trash. They were walking to their deaths and possibly wouldn't comprehend it until it was too late. Sam had to do something but what?

He stood alone on the dark street as the cold winds stung his face.

Sam finally began to move. He crept through the dark grounds at Jensen's home. He touched the study window and crouched in the shadows as he listened.

ACCELERATION

Kaupman pursed his lips in distain. "Hell, it's only spit. So, how do we start over? It's all destroyed." He bent down with a crumpled tissue from his pocket; wiped the spit; and dropped the tissue on the antique table.

"No, it isn't. We still have Grandpa and Sean Stone's notes. We'll begin again."

"We don't have Stone's notes yet."

"We'll find them, but then again, we may not need them." Jensen said curtly.

"And what about money? We've lost millions." Krieder added, as he coughed noisily and inserted his cigar back into his mouth.

"The organization will be reinstated. The President is still our ace in the hole. He will do anything I ask. He wants the power, and I can give it to him. He knows this. He's just waiting for the media dust to settle. You see- he's tired of being told that he got the presidency based on his looks and charisma. He wants the intellect, so he can gain power and adoration, and then he can hold onto his job. He also wants all the problems worked out with the serum." Jensen preened as he sat, enjoying his kingpin status. We have many people waiting on our serum."

"But Mekka's kid and Sean Stone are dead. What was the kid's name? Was it Caroline? She was a fox. They found her body outside the hospital. Doesn't that mean that the serum's not ready yet?" Krieder was sharp despite his smelly cigars. "Anyway, we need more research. Does the President know that? Some people come out of the hibernation, some don't. What if we give it to the President and he dies?"

Jensen walked to his bar and fixed himself a shot of whiskey. "That's his choice," Jensen said smoothly. Don't worry, Mr. Krieder. Mekka will fix it."

"Mekka? We're going to rely on him? Frankly he scares me, Mr. Jensen."

"It's under control. I have a bigger vision, and we have all the time we need."'

"No, you don't," Sam thought. "I'll see to that. He crept around the outside of the house. He had to find Mekka. He must still be alive, one of those who came out of hibernation. With Sean gone, they needed Mekka, and Sam needed to convince him of the right thing to do. He might be able to handle Mekka if he could only just talk to him again.

Sam heard a car pull up and burrowed further into the bushes near the house. Suddenly shocked, he saw the face of the man exiting the limo, despite the shielding of the multiple muscular bodies. It was the President. "Shit! It's the President of the United States! He's involved. He just lost my vote," thought Sam. "Here he's so pretty and friendly too."

"I guess if they're going to be busy, I'll find Mekka," Sam murmured to himself. He gazed up at the second floor window and measured the distance to the nearby tree. He rustled the trees as he boosted himself up. He froze for a few moments as he waited to see if the house and men would notice the noise he was making. When sure that he was still alone, Sam climbed and swung over to the second story ledge and slid open the window.

Well, it's being unlocked seemed a good omen. However, he climbed through fairly quietly, or at least he hoped so. He had to admit he'd been creeping around an awful lot lately. He would love to be welcomed again and come through a doorway, but then, maybe not to this house.

Sam lowered himself carefully into a bright orange colored bedroom. It was the little "Shirley Temple's" room, Sarah's room. He looked down at the sleeping child and smiled. The kid was going to be a knock-out someday, he was sure of it.

She also had the sweet heart to go with it. "How could such twisted scum as Jensen have such a wonderful child?"

Sam softly passed the bed. He hesitated only to gently pull Sarah's blanket up under her chin. "Really cute," he thought. "You yearn for a child again when you see them like this." Sam then continued his silent prowl.

Thoughts tumbled through his head. Where was Grandpa housed? Where was Mekka? How could Mekka be related to Silas Jensen? Mekka had such a fine daughter, Caroline.

He had just entered a darkened room when the lights suddenly played brightly over his eyes. Sam jerked around, stared, and gasped. "Caroline?" he whispered.

CHAPTER 20

"No, but I might ask who you are?" The beautiful lady said.

"You first," Sam countered.

"But I live here."

"Oh... Sam Stone." Sam extended his hand. "I'm here to find Dr. Mekka. Less than

two days ago, a terrific young lady named Caroline Mekka died in my arms. You sure as hell look like her." Sam's eyes held a pain that was not lost on the young lady.

"Caroline's dead? She was my twin sister. I'm Alex." She leaned weakly against the wall as tears glistened in her blue eyes. "What happened?"

"I'm sorry... Alex, are you sure you can handle the details? She had a rough time. Silas Jensen didn't help. Who is he to you?" Sam said quietly.

"He's my husband." Alex found a chair and sat. I loved him once. But he's changed. He wasn't always cruel like he is now. But, how could he hurt Caroline?" The tears began to roll down.

Sam knelt down beside her and held her hand. "Alex, I loved her too." Sam turned from Alex, the resemblance shook him. He cleared his throat. "Who is the little girl? I met her on the plane here."

"My daughter, Sarah."

"She's beautiful. Where's Dr. Mekka?" He replied.

"He's upstairs on the third floor. They converted the top floor for him, but I'm not allowed to see him. They brought Dad in two days ago." Her voice broke. "I didn't mean to cry."

"Maybe we should both cry. Alex, something is very wrong. Let's go talk to your Dad." Sam stood and gestured towards the upper floor.

"Good idea." Alex swept her wet cheeks with her hand. "I could use a Dad right now."

Sam walked quietly down the hall with Alex. He kept seeing Caroline with her hair hanging softly about her face and the confident swing to her body as she moved. He thought of the way she tipped her head when she smiled. He missed her.

"You were going to tell me about Caroline's death," Alex said quietly.

"Later, please Alex." Sam said as he stopped at the attic steps. "You put his bed in an attic?" Sam was puzzled.

"It's not that bad. It's all fixed up and very private. I do love my Dad. Silas doesn't, but I do."

ACCELERATION

Alex was angry now. She had tried so hard to get them to like each other, Dad and Silas, but Dad refused. Why he was finally convinced to give up his independence and move here, Alex was mystified. She was happy about it though, so why couldn't she see him?

They arrived up the stairs. "Dad. Dad. It's Alex. May I come up? Dad, are you busy?" There was no answer.

Alex turned to Sam. "Maybe he's asleep."

They entered the room as Alex spoke quietly. "Dad, I'm bringing up a friend of Caroline's." She turned towards the bed and suddenly stared at her father. Horror flooded her face. "What!" Alex stepped back, ready to faint.

Sam grabbed Alex's arm as she crumbled and began to fall. He slid her into a chair at the side of the room and away from the bed. "Easy, Alex. Don't cry out. I'm afraid I've seen this before. I was hoping I was wrong and that he was doing well. I'm sorry."

"Oh, no," he thought. "It's not over." Sam had definitely seen this before, but this time it was different. This time a brain was suspended in a huge chamber on a bed, with a maze of tubing leading to a computer in a small orange colored bedroom.

"What is this?" Alex sobbed. "Where is my father? That's not him." She jumped up.

"Shh, Alex. Quiet." Sam reached out for her. He held her mouth as she began to sob uncontrollably. "Hush," he whispered. "Please don't make noise, they can't find me here."

Alex quieted. He removed his hand from her mouth. He eased her back into the chair and pulled up another for himself.

He spoke quietly. "Mr. Jensen and others are trying to preserve his thought processes, his genius, but what he discovered killed what he was and took my brother and Caroline's lives. Do you want your father to continue like this?"

Alex shook her head as the tears continued to roll down on her pale cheeks.

"Help me to disconnect the machines and give him peace, Alex." Sam said softly.

"No," Alex tried to stand. "I don't want him to die. Maybe he still feels and understands," she whimpered.

"If he does, it will not be rational. He became as crazy as my brother did. The drugs advance brain intelligence, but in a twisted way, and kills the body. They also killed a lot of people in their quest." Sam talked firmly and clearly, and Alex seemed to be listening.

"Alex, I'm curious. Who painted your daughter's bedroom?" Sam hated to hurt her more, but he had to know.

Alex was stunned. "Silas, why?"

"Has he been giving her any medication?" Sam said softly.

"Yes, special vitamins. Why? Sam, you've got to tell me. Is he hurting my daughter?" The fear in her eyes was tortuous for Sam to see.

"I can't be sure, but if he's been giving her his serum as vitamins, she builds up a preference to specific bright colors in her surroundings."

"What happens if she doesn't have the colors around her?" Alex said.

"I don't know." Sam replied.

"Well, Mr. Stone, you are still alive and interfering."

Sam and Alex whirled around.

"Silas, what are you doing to our daughter and my father?" Alex cried out.

"Alex, my dear, your father is continuing his work, and Sarah is my first truly young subject. She will be very grateful when she is older."

"Silas, if she gets older! What if you kill our child? You're crazy." Alex said with despair.

"I am not crazy, just brilliant. I'm doing something great, and we will become rich beyond our dreams, darling. And Sarah will be super intelligent."

"Why didn't YOU take the medicine, Silas? You aren't taking it, are you?" She said with total distain.

Silas stared at Alex. "I ah, I …"

"Because you're afraid," Alex snapped. "You would give it to your daughter instead. I hate you, Silas… I'm taking Sarah and hope that God is merciful and she lives. This monstrous research with my father ends now." Alex picked up a chair and hurled it at the container holding the last remains of Dr. Mekka. "Father, I love you!" She cried out. The container shattered. Alex wildly slammed the chair again on the brain as it oozed in the glass shards on the floor and ceased throbbing.

Silas started to grab her, but Sam intercepted him and delivered his infamous right cross punch. "This is from Sean also."

Silas fell into Mekka's remains, and lay inert on the floor. Sam then walked over to the computer. He stared at it and began to removed discs and flash drives. He then stomped upon them and kicked apart the computer. "We need to destroy everything here. Perhaps we can then bury it all somewhere."

Alex knelt down and yanked out the heinous tubbing from her father's now deceased brain. She then took off her sweater and wrapped up the remains.

"What are you doing, Alex?" Sam said gently.

"I'm going to give him a proper burial."

"Okay. Then let me take an extra minute with your soon to be ex-husband here," Sam replied, as he rescued the discarded tubing and wound it tightly around Silas Jensen. "That should hold him. By the way, Alex, what happened to his face? I guess I only saw his good side when I was at the hospital site."

"Silas was burned in the fire. He deserved it," Alex replied bitterly.

The task of burying Mekka's remains and the computer parts was completed in the shadow of the massive tree that Sam had climbed. Afterwards, Sam stared at the tree. "It seems to be watching us sadly."

"Dad planted that tree when I was born," Alex said. "He loved it. Thank you for burying him there for me and for Sarah."

Alex knelt down and patted the soil. Tears rolled down her pale cheeks. "He'd like it here. I'll miss you, Daddy. I love you."

Alex took a moment and then turned to Sam. "Let's go. Let's get Sarah and get out of here. Either we go now or you'll be watching me kill my husband. We can take my car," she said.

"Good, because I came in a taxi," Sam grinned and then grew serious. "Alex, your husband is a powerful and dangerous man. He may try to take revenge. Are you sure you want to leave and with me? I'm a wanted man. And your husband hates me."

"I want and have to go," said Alex.

"He may try to have us all killed," Sam continued quietly.

"I know. He knows that I know how guilty he is. I have no choice. Also, I respect you, Sam. In the short time you've been here, I can see why Caroline fell in love with you. I trust you. If you'll have us, we'll go with you. I know we'll be a burden though. I'm sorry."

"I think you'll be more of a gift than a burden…All right, get ready fast. I'll check out your car."

ACCELERATION

"I'll get the keys. Then, will you carry Sarah to the car, and I'll throw some things together quickly…Thank you, Sam"

"And you," Sam said. "I'll enjoy the company. Let's go. By the way, would you like to travel to Utah first. I need to get my brother's notes and computer. We must destroy them all.

"Whatever you decide is fine with me," said Alex. "I've never been to Utah. It will be an adventure."

"Good." Sam said as he took Alex's hand, and they walked quietly back into the house.

Sam, Alex, and little Sarah had traveled to Utah for a number of days and nights. They had traded the Cadillac on the way for a used car. It was a bit of a shady car dealer, who loved the Cadillac so much that he didn't care if he got the papers for it. They picked out an old Buick, and Sam and Alex were happy to no longer have a car that Jensen could trace.

He parked a quarter of a mile away from the old family cabin. Sam left the sleeping Alex and Sarah in the Buick and walked alone over the last distance in the darkness. He hoped Sean's journal was still here. Sam found the hidden key and entered the cabin. He turned on the light switch. The lighting played harshly on the rustic furniture. He walked over to the old bed and extended his hand to feel under the mattress. Fumbling for only a moment, he stopped. He had found it. It was still there. He pulled out the book of notes from its cache and ran his hands over it gently. He opened to the first page and then closed the book quickly.

It was better to not dwell on the past heartaches. Better to dispose of them now. He crossed to the fireplace. Sam began to rip out the pages furiously until the tears began to well up in his deep set eyes. He shook away the grief and set his mouth in a thin line. He piled the pages together and lit them with a match. "For you, Sean. Rest now."

The flames rose up into images in his mind that couldn't be forgotten. He stared at the ghost of Sean as a little boy, sharing the tree house with his older brother. He remembered the shock and loneliness they'd shared after their parents' death. He smiled at Sean's excitement over receiving his Phi Beta Kappa award and later his research grant. He remembered Sean's reassuring hand that reached out for Sam when his child died and when he had been broken by his war experiences and lost all hope.

Sam felt the pain in Sean when he thought he was dying. He saw Sean's tortured eyes as he flayed with feeble arms and caught fire. Sam closed his eyes to this last image, then blinked in relief to see the fire lick up the last remnants of Sean's notes. "Die Acceleration."

Sam sat back. "Little brother. It was not all your fault. You just got lost. Now your soul is healing."

Sam wiped his tears on his jacket. It was done The ghosts were disappearing. He woke Alex in the car and gently carried Sarah into the cabin and placed her on the bed. He rested his hand on her small soft forehead. She was cool and her breathing was regular. She slept with the innocent. She was young, she would be fine. He hoped that he had made it in time to help her.

Sam lay across the small bed next to Alex, who cuddled her sleeping child. He was near the warmth of humanity as it was intended. He was sick of death and nightmares. He wanted a normal life again. Perhaps he could still have it. Alex squeezed his hand. Time would still the terror and ache of the last few days, and he hoped he could continue just living. He'd stay with Alex, for now. Early tomorrow they would depart for a place and new lives.

He felt the breathing beside him of two sweet souls. Sam smiled, closed his eyes, and slept until the next day, a new day. That was his new plan.

ACCELERATION

"Sarah, go to bed now. I need to talk to these gentlemen." Silas Jensen bent down and patted her head.

"Daddy, I drew you a picture."

"Yes, it's very pretty, now go to bed." He spoke without looking closely. Suddenly he turned back, stared at the picture and drew back. "Sarah, what is this?"

"It's Grandpa in his room." Her clear blue eyes noted her Daddy's frown. "Daddy, don't get mad at me." Her lips began to quiver.

"I'm not mad. Your picture is well done, but don't draw him next time."

"Okay. I like orange. Or..an..ge." She played with the word.

"I like orange too. Now go to bed." Silas said sharply.

"Yes, Daddy." Sarah said, as she sadly walked out.

Sam's face was motionless. He didn't care if Jensen had twenty Shirley Temples. This was the same man from Mekka's conspiracy.

A tall man with a sandwich rose from a nearby chair. "Jensen, what's in the kid's picture?" He said, as he chewed his bite of the food and threw the remains of his sandwich on the table. "Kaupman, watch the table. It's eighteenth century French."

"Who cares? It's just a stinkin' table." He slid the sandwich along the table and licked his sticky fingers.

"Kaupman," Sam's mouth fell open. He was also "tall man."

"Kaupman, you're disgusting," Jensen sneered. "You can be replaced."

"Ignore him, Jensen," a second man said in a deep voice as he stood up and chewed a fat cigar. Sam froze. "Here was cruel Cigar Man, from the hospital. Cigar Man started talking again. "So, what's in your kid's picture? You even got me curious."

"It's her grandpa's room, Mr. Krieder," Jensen spoke angrily.

Cigar Man was Krieder. So Jensen's hanging out with the hospital's executioner now. Not very classy.

Sam listened again.

"What was she doing in his room?" Keep your damn kid out of there?" Kaupman said as he spit, aiming for the basket but landed it on the floor.

"Watch your mouth and don't spit on my floor, you pig. She won't be doing it again. Now forget about my kid. Understand? And Mister Kaupman, clean up your disgusting saliva." Jensen snapped.

PART 2:

SANCTUARY

CHAPTER 21

Sam froze. He could almost see the eyes, but they were veiled in the semi-light. He knew the outline of the face, however. It had at one time been very dear to him. Now he cringed. "Sean, it's you, what's wrong?" Sam reached out and brushed the space. He touched a warmth. "You can't be real, can you be, Sean? Why have you come? What do you want from me now" Tell me!" His voice had risen to a shout, and he was shaking.

"Sam, stop it, you're hurting me. Sam! Wake up."

Sam stopped. The shadows of morning now bathed Sean's face and remolded it into a different shape. "Alex? What the…? Where's Sean? He was here." The sweat had beaded on his forehead and crept around his beard.

Alex was gathering her composure now. "Hey," she brushed his beard playfully, "scruffy old man of the mid-west." Sean's gone. He's not coming back He wouldn't recognize you if he did. By the way, you're going to be late for your 8 o'clock class, Professor Sinclair."

"Sinclair, hum," Sam's confusion was clearing. He felt relieved. "I guess I'll resume this scruffy old geezer's happy mundane life. He started pulling himself up and out of the twisted mass of bedding.

"Scruffy old geezer, my eye. You are feisty for your age," said Alex. She twinkled with giddiness, as she wrapped her arms around his neck and perched on top of him. "I could devour you here and now, but your students would complain. Their mysterious hunky heartthrob would be gone."

"Let's not project too much. Deep down they probably detest me. I crucified some of their essays." Sam grinned."

"No! Really? Even sexy Heather's heartfelt exploration on passion in pornographic literature?" cooed Alex teasingly.

Sam laughed. "Even nubile Heather's."

Alex started kissing his chest. Sam flipped her over and pinned her down. "Listen lady, you'll make me late." He kissed her quickly, then bent again to really enjoy her. He came up, finally, and took a deep breath. "Your sweet little youngster just might walk in."

"My darling child is already at school slaving over her desk, but I understand. All right, get off of me, you big brut, or you may attack, but make up your mind. But remember, I can arouse you to passions that Heather has never read about or lived through." She smiled wickedly.

"Oh, really, let's find out." Sam leaned forward. "On second thought, give me a rain check. I am really late." He heaved himself off of her slight frame."

Alex was beautiful, he thought. She was so like Caroline, but also different. He was beginning to enjoy those differences. Caroline was straight-forward, Alex – more playful, but both were and are terribly sexy. He regretfully headed for his shower as he talked. "Thanks for waking me, my lady. I never did trust alarm clocks. This fresh country air and stillness makes me want to sleep forever." The last lines were muffled by the roar of the water.

Alex sat on the edge of the bed. She felt warm and safe. It was all too perfect. She tried to hide from that twinge of guilt. Was she enjoying their seclusion too much? Should they have shouted to the world about their past? No, it was too dangerous. They were wanted by the people in power. They knew too much.

Thank God for Ben, Sam's publisher. They'd have been caught, if it hadn't been for him. When they'd descended on Ben that following night like battered humanity, he had welcomed them, wanted to help, and patched their wounds. He had also refurbished their wrecked lives with new identities and looks.

Alex now had her short brown, bobbed hair. She liked it now. It had taken some getting used to at first. She'd had always been fiercely independent, despite being a twin. She had enjoyed attracting men with her blonde mane. Now she was someone else, who enjoyed blending in. Occasionally her old style had slipped through though, like with Sam on the bed. But now it was back to being sedate Jill, wife to Professor Sinclair and mother to daughter Lizzie? Sam wondered. Was he a coward to hide in this little university town that was hidden so beautifully in the middle of Midwestern cornfields. Why did he leave Jensen alive? Was it a mistake? Jensen was crazy and ruthless. Would he let them continue to be loose ends? Would he decide that Sam and Alex would be too dangerous to his plan? And what would be the plan now? Could Mekka and Jenkin's scheme rise from the ashes? Sam's head was spinning. He turned the water to cool.

"Turn on the news, Alex," he shouted as he shivered and turned off the water.

"News again," said Alex. "Face it, honey, we are no longer famous. We've been replaced by our playboy President."

Alex flicked on the television, however, and played with the remote. "No news," she
muttered. "I'm really getting sick of it." Suddenly she straightened. "Wait, Sam, come here. Listen."

Sam entered the room while wrapped in his towel. He too had been brought up short by the words echoing across the room from the set.

"President William Quint, on vacation from his ranch, has hosted a luncheon for FBI
personnel to show his appreciation for their diligence and patriotism over the years. A celebrity from the latest hospital bombing is attending. He is FBI director Silas Jensen."

"Director Jensen, is there any progress on the search for perpetrator, Samuel Stone, the famous writer? Do they know yet why he and his brother, a scientist, would cause such destruction and death?"

Alex felt sick as the face shifted to that of Silas Jensen. He looks so cool and confident, she thought, as she nervously ran her fingers along her silently parted lips.

"We'll find him," Jensen said with no warmth. "In time. He can't hide forever."

ACCELERATION

"Could you still answer my why question?" The female reporter was tenacious, Sam had to credit her with spunk.

"We don't know why. We think that he was having Iraq War flashbacks and just went off the deep end, taking his brother with him," said Jensen.

"What a crock!" Sam's old anger was seething. Alex slipped her hand in his.

Jensen continued. "Sam Stone is a dangerous man, to others and himself."

Sam's picture was flashed on the screen. "Come on," Sam said in frustration. "America knows me by now, how many times do you have to show my picture, Jensen?"

A hot line number crept across the bottom of the screen. Sam sat dejectedly on the edge of the couch. "They never give up."

"Thank you, Director Jensen," said the reporter. "Oh, Sir, we hear the hospital will be rebuilt."

Sam's mouth fell open and a chill fell over him.

"Yes, it just got a huge grant for its philanthropic research. We lost some good men in the explosion, however. So it will take time to get it back to its former success in research and care." It was then that Jensen turned full view to the audience of millions.

Jensen's face was still scared horribly on one side.

"Did Stone hurt your face, Sir?" the interviewer's lovely eyes could not mask her repulsion too successfully.

"Yes, when he killed my wife and daughter."

Killed! Sam hadn't heard that accusation before. Alex exchanged a silent look of sympathetic understanding with him.

Alex said softly, "I'm sorry, Sam."

Sam held her hand and whispered, "I know."

The show continued

The reporter pursued coyly. She could be sweet when she wanted something and she wanted fame. "How, Sir? You've never told the media exactly what happened."

"It's classified information for now, honey," Jensen replied.

"Honey," bad choice of words, he thought. Too patronizing.

Alex turned towards Sam. There was a different look on his face. "What are you thinking, Sam," she asked.

"Nothing."

"Ah, no. You're germinating with ideas," Alex countered.

"Let's use her." He said calmly.

ACCELERATION

"Who? That lady?"

"Yep. Why not? She's smart and independent, and she doesn't trust Jensen," said Sam.

Alex's mouth fell open. "She could turn us in for the scoop of the century."

"Or not, for the scoop of the century. Maybe she'll want the truth." Sam was thinking fast now.

"You think that you can trust her from just that telecast?" said Alex.

"Yeah, but let's put out a feeler first."

"I hope you're right." She shrugged. "Are you going to class first?"

"I thought I might." Sam got up. "I'd better throw on clothes though. Heather may not be able to handle my macho beauty." He grinned triumphantly. "Silas Jensen, you made your first mistake. You acted like an ass. It's going to come back and bite you. I'm going to see to that."

Alex laughed. It was good to see him gaining his old strength.

Sam gave her a quick kiss and turned to finish dressing hurriedly. "I'm late. I'm late. For a very important date, with…Heather."

Alex threw a pillow at him.

"Oh, patience, pretty lady. I'm just enjoying my cover." He picked up the pillow and threw it back. "Eh, I'm too old for Heather. Guess it will just be you and me, and Lizzy."

"I rather like that, that's better. Now out into the cold."

"Yes, Ma'am, I'm going." He grabbed his sweater and was gone.

"Sam, take your jacket!" Alex ran to the door, but he was gone. She muttered to herself. "Samuel, you forgot you were no longer in California." Her eyes grew sad. "Be careful, Sam."

CHAPTER 22

"Professor Sinclair, do you think an author must only write about what he knows? What if he is fascinated with another field? Can he become affective writing about it?"

"Mis-ter?" Sam squinted across the stage lights. "What is your name, young man? I like to know who I'm addressing, and I consider your question important."

"Edward Allen, Sir." The young man's voice responded eagerly.

"Mr. Allen, absolutely he may write about other fields, given the prerequisites of research and interest in it. Both are usually recommended. You must care deeply about your subject." What a hypocrite I am, thought Sam. I stopped caring. However, I do write about characters I like or ideas or issues. I guess, I do care.

"Gentlemen and Ladies," Sam said. "Our time is up and enough on my opinions. Tomorrow we'll consider in depth a true giant in the field, Mr. John Steinbeck. Please consult your syllabus for reading background and be prepared."

Sam tried to exit the stage quickly, but his students bound up and detoured him from getting near the door with their human barricade. It wasn't that he didn't enjoy talking to them, but he was suddenly tired. Maybe it was watching the news. He shouldn't do that before class.

"Professor Sinclair…Professor, do you expect…Sir…"

Sam held up his hand. He felt exhausted. "We'll talk more Tuesday. I'll answer all your questions then. Make a note of them. Thank you."

Sam pulled his grey sweater across his broad chest and crashed through the assemblage that swarmed excitedly in his path. He managed to get to the door and exited quickly into a swirling snow storm. "Just what I need to get out of my mood, a blizzard," he laughed at the irony. It might clear his mind, however. He felt refreshed at the thought of walking in the beautiful falling snow.

Sam sprinted towards the student union. Coffee, hot brew, and a sandwich. That's what he wanted. And perhaps he'd get a daily paper. That should cheer him up, he mused sarcastically. He actually wanted to be alone. Feeling the bitter cold outside, Sam buttoned his sweater tighter. I wonder if I stand out like a trans-planted Californian?

ACCELERATION

By the time he had eaten his quick lunch, the winter had gathered even more force. Sam started out the door, but a student stopped him.

"Professor!"

Sam turned.

"Sir, may I stop you for a minute. It's me again, Edward Allen, from class. I usually go just by Eddie though."

Sam groaned inside. "Eddie, I'm rather tired today. Would you mind if we talked before or after the next session?"

"It's just that…" Eddie began hesitantly. "I just want to read your books." He gained confidence. "Could you give me a list of them?"

Sam suddenly felt the danger of his cover falling off. "Eddie, I don't mean to be rude, but my books are not what you should be reading."

"Sir, let me be the judge of that. I've read the authors for your class, now I wish to read your works, assuming you have any." Eddie lowered his head. "I'm sorry, Sir. I was being rude."

Sam couldn't help but let a smile escape. "Whoa, you are gutsy and honest. Let's start over. Maybe I'll get my energy back. Join me for coffee, Mr. Eddie Allen?"

"Yes, Sir, I'd like that very much." Eddie took a deep breath and followed Sam back into the cafeteria area and its line.

Neither said a word for a few minutes. Sam finally cleared his throat. "Eddie, tell me, are you writing now and/or planning to do so?"

"I'm writing now but haven't published."

"Do you want to get rich at it?"

"Yes, Sir." The boy looked so happy. Sam felt old.

"Don't write. Very few get rich from writing."

"I know there are no guarantees," said Edward. "I also like writing, a lot."

"Good. It can be satisfying." Sam stirred his coffee absently. He rather wished the kid would find another idol. His writing career was a thing of the past. He was another person then. Now he was like a colt in a stable that didn't know where or how to run. He didn't want to talk and maybe he shouldn't. He couldn't let anyone get to know him, not yet, and certainly not this innocent kid. Sam started to get up. I need to take off. We can talk more next week. Don't worry. Just enjoy writing."

"Sir, wait, you remind me of someone." The boy looked honestly puzzled.

"Sure, Hemingway. It's the beard." Sam rubbed his beard and chuckled playfully.

"No." Eddie shifted in his seat. "Did you ever write mysteries?"

Sam felt that he'd forgotten how to breathe. "No. Not my field of interest. Well, Mr. Allen, it's been pleasant meeting you. I don't mean to be mysterious or rude. I just don't like to talk about my work."

"But…" said Eddie.

"Keep writing. You're a fine young man." Sam said. "We'll talk next week, I promise." Sam rose and hurried out the door.

Eddie stared after him in confusion. What had he said wrong? Was he too much of a pest? He figured he'd just slammed his grade deep into the pits. On top of that, the man he'd grown to idolize over the months probably now figured that he was an irritating little jerk. Eddie sank his elbows on the table and groaned.

A voice piped up. "You didn't do any better than I did."

Eddie looked up into the gorgeous eyes of the school's most famous female, Heather St. James. "Yeah?" He looked back down at his now cold coffee. "I struck out pretty badly."

"Hey, don't feel that way. I don't. He's special. Let's compare notes," said Heather.

"What notes," Eddie said dejectedly. "I didn't even get to first base."

"Neither did I. Now the why is intriguing. Come on, let's go to my place. There's something I want to show you."

Eddie looked up warily.

"No no, it's not what you think. I just want to talk. I'm really very serious," Heather said quietly.

"Me too. "Eddie scrambled up and stood beside her. He figured he was a good head shorter. "Let's go," he said.

"Let's do it," Heather needed a partner in her quest for answers.

"It's him, I know it is." Heather held out the book jacket to Edward. "Do you really go by Edward? It's a bit stuffy." Heather gathered her long legs under her body as she sat and leaned against the wall by her small bed. "He might be very handsome under that beard, and what a terrific disguise. If it's true, we've got one hell of a story." She threw up her arms in excitement.

ACCELERATION

"Eddie," Eddie said softly. "I sometimes go by Eddie. Now, I think you're nuts here. I know he looks familiar, but Sam Stone, the writer and now murderer, here in Middletown U.S.A. Sure!... I said that sarcastically, sorry." Eddie stood up and tossed the book back on the shelf. "Anyway, how could he get a job here as a professor so fast and without a background check."

"The man had money. And probably he has friends in high places." Heather returned.

"If he has such friends, how did he get into such a mess?"

"Yeah. Hey, did you ever see him on a talk show? I have. His voice is just like the Professor's. I'm very good with voices, among other things." She laughed and flipped her long red hair. "Just kidding about the other things, Eddie. But really, the voice is the same. Look I made a disc of his interview last year. He's talking about writing. I wanted to save it so I did. Listen and think about the lecture today. I taped that on my phone. I'll play both." She crawled off the bed and plopped in the disc.

They listened intently as Heather repeatedly punched between the disc recording and her phone recording. Sam's voice played:

"You must care deeply about your subjects, but probably every writer does." Sam Stone laughed with his host.

"He's right," Eddie quipped. "Every writer does. It sounds like him."

"Now listen to his voice and look at his eyes and the book jacket picture. It's him, I know it." She paused the picture. "I've wanted to do this. Heather pulled out assorted colored pencils and began sketching over Stone's face. "See grey hair and a beard."

"Hemingway," said Eddie.

"Yeah," She laughed, but Eddie wasn't smiling.

Eddie looked at her "I think you've got something, but why would a famous writer do the terrible things that guy did?"

"Let's ask him." Heather's eyes were deadly serious.

"When?"

"Now." She jumped off the couch. "I know where he lives."

"Are you crazy? He'll either kill us or laugh in our faces." Eddie shook his head.

"I have protection." She proudly pulled a gun from her drawer by the bed.

"Whoa! Where did you get that? Do you know how to use it? Anyway, I think he's innocent," said Eddie.

"So do I. I just have a feeling though, that it's him. Plus, my mom works for the news network. She'd die for this story. We could become famous or get rich. Either way- are you with me?"

Eddie nodded his head, as he put on his jacket.

Heather jammed the gun into her coat pocket and grabbed her hat and gloves. "I wish it were a little warmer out. I hate confronting a terrorist when I'm freezing my body?"

"Yep," Eddie was amazed. Heather was not the sex-crazed airhead of her reputation.

CHAPTER 23

Sam's face was burning from the cold. Rather stupid of him to not wear a jacket. He spied the lights from the town businesses ahead. They seemed to glow invitingly. His feet padded quietly on the soft blanket of snow beneath him. He held out his arms and stretched. Hey, cold is a state of mind and body; then he shivered. More like the body. The temperature must have plunged.

His first mid-western winter. New York snowfalls were exciting, but this is gorgeous. He might grow to like it, if he had a jacket, he thought. He felt like he was back in time, when life was simple, all black and white, no greys. There were bad guys that were caught, at least in the movies. Even death was dignified. There was no fuss, no mess. True, there were tears, but that went with living. Physical pain, he could understand, but not madness, idyllically speaking that is. At least that's the way I like to remember it.

Oh, Caroline, I miss you. And dear Alex, are you home safe and warm. I'm cold. I'll get warm for a few minutes in this shop.

ACCELERATION

Sam swept into the small store and stomped the snow from his feet in the doorway. Rows of books met his sweeping gaze. A bookstore, delightful!

"You still open?" He felt a need to respond to the quiet look of the clerk. "Pretty snowfall, isn't it?" Sam felt relaxed here and rather jovial. He loved being around books, just holding them made him tingle inside. There was so much to learn. He wished he could read them all. Funny, he felt that way when he was a kid. It never seemed to go away- that crazy curiosity.

He stopped abruptly and stared. In front of him stood a six-foot tall poster of himself. "Sam Stone Mysteries," the sign said beside it. I'm famous, he almost blurted out the words. He felt like laughing insanely. He couldn't take his eyes off the poster. The eyes seemed to follow and return to him.

He casually picked up one of the books, his books, and read a jacket title- "Mystery Writer's Last Novel Before Insanity," Sam quietly lowered the book down onto the pile. He didn't authorize that book jacket, did Ben Gallagher, or the publisher? Well, at least we're both getting rich, sort of. He shrugged. He needed to stop taking everything so seriously. He was stuck over a thousand miles from his life, a life he had thought he didn't want. Now he wasn't so sure.

He wondered what Susie was thinking about all this. Had she found someone else? Why not, she deserved better than he could give right now. Anyway, he was nuts about Alex. He'd been very lucky to have met such fascinating ladies. No need to complain, except for the horror at the hospital. Sam suddenly felt eyes on him. He turned around and met the eyes of the shopkeeper.

Sam thought fast. "Ma'am, you wouldn't like to sell me a cup of that magnificent smelling coffee, would you?" he said. It sure felt like a good idea. He offered his most charming smile. Actually, he really would like some hot coffee. And it worked.

"All right, Mister. I guess I can spare a bit. I really want to hear the news though. You want to sit and listen too?" The lady was old but sharp. "Be nice though. I won't put up with anything but good manners... I'm Agnes." She extended her hand. He clasped it firmly.

"I promise," Sam chuckled. He liked her. "I'll be very nice." He turned toward the television and settled on a vacant stool.

Agnes poured him a cup of coffee and handed it to him carefully. She continued, "This is that reporter Elizabeth Martin. She's looking into the disappearance of that novelist,

ACCELERATION

Sam Stone. You were looking at his book over there. He's a smart fellow, handsome man too. I can't believe he could do all those terrible things that they say. I saw him once on a talk show. He was real nice, charming too. Oh, here she comes on again, quiet now." She waved her slim arthritic-marred hands to hush him.

"Yes ma'am." Sam found her enchanting.

She turned to the television, however, and his delight quickly vanished.

"Who is Samuel Stone? People have been asking this for months, ever since his strange disappearance. Could a person in the public eye seem to be so sane and do such tragic and horrific acts?"

We are standing here next to his girlfriend. Miss Suzanne Colton, can you tell us about this man, Mr. Stone? Why would he bomb a hospital and kill innocent people?"

Sam's Susie looked frightened and confused. "No comment. I don't know anything. I just think that he would not do those things. He wouldn't hurt anyone. Excuse me, please." She tried to pull away from the microphone.

"Wait. Did he tell you why he left town, Miss Colton?" Elizabeth Martin was not about to let Susie get away.

"He said that his brother was in trouble and he needed to see him," Susie said quickly.

"Did he seem sane?" Martin jumped in again.

"Yes, of course, very."

"Did he ever have war flashbacks?" Martin pushed further.

"No comment." Susie said as she tried to move away. Poor Susie, Sam thought. I'm so sorry they're doing this to you.

Martin followed her. "Do you still love him? Would you take him back?"

"None of your business, Miss Martin." Susie fired back. She'd had it. "This interview is over." Susie pushed the microphone aside and turned her back to the cameras.

That a girl! Sam felt better. Don't let anyone push you around, Susie. Sam felt sad though. He wondered if he'd ever see her again.

"Thank you," Miss Colton. We did learn something. Tomorrow we shall interview Silas Jensen of the FBI. Will he fill in the missing pieces? Tune in for my special report on- "The Disappearance of Writer Sam Stone."

"That's one pushy dame. I like her." Agnes grunted.

"You know, I do too." Sam stood and stretched his legs. "I've got to brave the Arctic blizzard again."

ACCELERATION

"You are not going out in only that sweater, young man. Here, this old coat belonged to my husband. Borrow it and bring it back tomorrow, you hear. I trust ya." She rose and draped a long topcoat over his shoulders. Sam could just imagine the old lady trudging through the snow drifts to give it to her husband."

"Young man, eh?" He smiled with amusement as he rubbed his grey beard. He imagined by morning that his beard would be dark brown again. The snow would probably sop his dye job. Then Sam got serious "But what will you wear? I don't see another coat hanging there."

She waved him off. "I'll just stay here for the night. It's too cold outside for my old bones and arthritis anyway." Her face wrinkled into an affectionate look. "I like you, Mister. Come back tomorrow, and we'll watch the rest of that lady reporter's interviews."

"I just might do that. But I will definitely return the coat. Thank you." He bent and lifted up her small frail hand and kissed it lightly. "Thank you, Ma'am."

She giggled like a school girl. "Get on now. You men. You sure know how to flirt with an old crone."

Sam felt such admiration for this woman. "Never a crone. You are a lovely and very kind lady. I'm so happy that I met you. You cheered me up. Thank you again.".

Sam heaved the door open, looked at the roaring blizzard and stepped out. He shut the door firmly behind him. The wind was fighting his every step now, but he rather enjoyed it. He pulled himself along and cleared his mind of only one thing. He would write to Elizabeth Martin upon reaching home. She just might believe him. He'd have to mail the envelope from somewhere else though. Yes, he'd take the train to Chicago and send it from there. He wondered though- Do they have trains to Chicago from this small a town? Or an airport? He could maybe fly to Chicago in the morning and hope he wasn't recognized.

Over and over he formed the words to his letter in his mind, as he walked. He feared that Elizabeth Martin might not believe all he had to say. It would sound absurd. But she'd have to believe it. He would see to it. If he had to meet her in some dark alley, he'd do so. He was sick of hiding. He clutched the coat tighter around him. It must be getting colder, he speculated. Nice weather for a walk in the outdoors. Sam laughed to himself. He thought of Agnes. I am so grateful for

ACCELERATION

her coat. Good people turn up in the most unexpected places, like when you need them.

The snow was piling up now into massive drifts. Sam's feet were beginning to feel numb. California's warmth seemed far away. He wanted to look at the magical wonderland being created about him, but he felt forced by the pounding wind to lower his head. It seemed to say that he didn't belong so don't bother to enjoy it. He was going to take it all in, however, because he felt he might never return and certainly not to this moment, when no matter how much you fight to assert your power, nature always wins. It deserved to conquer; nature brought order, even in death. Man brought chaos. He could stop here near this old maple tree and just disappear into the whiteness which rose up beside it. But maybe the snow wasn't meant to bury the ugliness and hide it forever, perhaps it cleaned it away and left everything in life new and fresh.

Sam inhaled the crisp moist air. He felt good. He'd been walking around like a wounded animal, but no more. The dizziness he felt at the lecture was probably caused by his feeling of guilt. But what had he to feel guilty for? Let's leave that to Jensen. Of course, Jensen was too insane to feel remorse.

He couldn't wait now to get home to Alex. He turned the corner of his last block and increased his pace. The little faculty cottage nestled in the drifts like a toy house in a bowl of marshmallows. It seemed so unreal compared to his apartment in L.A. with all its adobe stylings and Spanish décor. He turned the cold doorknob with his numb fingers. It's great not having to lock the doors here; it's the way people should always live, free from fear. Sam stomped his snow-caked feet on the mat and looked up, just as Sarah leaped into his arms.

CHAPTER 24

"Daddy Matt do you see the snow? Will you play with me in it? Mommy says you'll help me make a snowman, please please." Sarah's clear blue eyes pleaded. "I did all my work today in school. Please?"

Sam gave her a squeeze and quick kiss and then sat his squirming little girl on her feet. "It's dark and cold outside, wouldn't you rather go out in the morning. We might build our Frosty cockeyed."

"What's cockeyed?" She liked the word and giggled as she jumped up and down.

"Well," Sam's eyes twinkled, "Frosty's carrot nose might be where his ears are, and his eyes might look out the back of his head. He would look very funny. We would laugh at him, and he would cry big icicle tears."

"I wouldn't laugh at Frosty," Sarah's little face became serious.

"I would, I would go- ho, ho, ho!"

"No, you wouldn't Daddy," she laughed brightly.

Sam liked when she omitted the Matt on Daddy. He adored this little girl, but who wouldn't? Jensen must miss her terribly, if he still has a heart.

Sam scooped up Sarah again. She planted a sweet kiss on his face. "I love you, Daddy. Can I see how dark it is outside?"

"Sure, let's open this door slowly though, so we don't wake it up. The darkness wants to sleep like little girls." Sam opened the door, and they peered out at the lovely snow-covered bushes, trees, and street, lying cuddled in their veil of darkness. "It's so pretty, like you."

"Shh, Daddy, we don't want to wake it up," Sarah whispered.

"Okay" Sam spoke softly and heaved Sarah up to his shoulders, just as Alex poked her head in the doorway.

"You two sure are quiet. Weren't you supposed to be in bed, Angel?" Alex teased.

"I was waiting for Daddy Matt, so we could make a snowman," Sarah said sweetly.

"Daddy Matt can help you make one in the morning," she said.

"Daddy said the dark is sleeping," whispered Sarah, as she brought her finger up to her mouth like a hush sound.

ACCELERATION

"Oh, he did, did he? He's clever, and he must be right," Alex chuckled, as she took Sarah into her arms. "Say Night Night to Daddy Matt now."

"I want Daddy to take me to bed too, please Mommy," Sarah coaxed as she held onto Sam's neck.

"Daddy's got company, he'll say good-night now, and he'll carry you up tomorrow night." Alex looked at Sam and nodded to the living room behind the partition.

"Who is it?" Sam curiously mouthed the words.

"Heather and Company," Alex whispered back and batted her eyelashes coyly.

"Not now," he grimaced and whispered. "It's late."

"I agree, good luck, sexy," she said softly. Alex pulled Sarah's little hands from around Sam's neck. "Say night, Daddy," said Alex, as she bounced Sarah in her arms as they mounted the stairs.

"Night, Daddy," Sarah called back.

"Night, Sarah," Sam called back. He loved this child. He didn't want to ever lose her.

Sam strolled into his small comfortable living room and sank into the old leather chair. "Okay, kids, what's so important that you have to interrupt my privacy on a gorgeous night like this?" Sam spoke as a friend, but he was annoyed. He lit a cigarette from the small box by the lamp. He usually didn't smoke, the cigarettes were mainly for Alex, but tonight, facing these eager youngsters, he felt like bracing himself with a cancer stick. He didn't ask if they minded. He almost hoped that they did, so they'd leave and he could enjoy being with Alex.

He flashed on the idea that he had never made love in a snowstorm, not since his marriage to Mandy, in New York. That was a lifetime ago. Sex with someone you're crazy about, as the wind bellow and rattles the walls, now that sounds better than chatting with these kids. Plus, he was suddenly exhausted.

Sam exhaled slowly from the cigarette. "Okay now, we shouldn't sit in silence. What's up? What's the problem, kids?"

"Sir, our problem may just be yours." Heather fingered the cold muzzle of the gun in her skirt pocket. She hoped the bulge didn't show. She felt a little ridiculous but also scared. What if her teacher is a cold-blooded killer? She glanced over at Eddie. His upper lip glistened with sweat on this cold night.

Sam sat forward. "You've captured my interest, young lady. Go for it." Sam figured it was about teaching, his teaching, but a strange sensation of uneasiness tickled his neck. He rubbed it involuntarily.

"Professor, I'll be blunt." Despite Heather's bravado, she swallowed hard and took a deep breath.

"Please do, Miss St. John." Sam smiled through his beard. He rather enjoyed her uneasiness.

Heather pulled a strand of her long red hair behind her ear and paused.

Eddie watched in fascination.

Then she dropped her bombshell. "Are you Sam Stone, the writer?"

Sam didn't say a word. The air seemed so heavy that no one in the room could breathe. Finally, he spoke. He could have like lied, but he didn't want to, not anymore. "Yes."

Heather and Eddie almost fell out of their chairs. They scrambled in unison to their feet.

"Oh, now, you don't want to leave so soon after opening Pandora's box?" Sam did not rise, but his voice stopped Heather and Edward.

Heather was trembling. Eddie grabbed her hand, and together they fumbled for the gun.

"Don't move, sir!" Eddie held the handle tightly. "Heather, call somebody, the cops." He felt like he was in a movie. Eddie held the gun and pointed it straight at the tall bearded man in the chair.

Sam's deep brown eyes looked steadily through the billowing smoke from his cigarette. He took a last drag and then smashed the stem in the ashtray. "No, don't do that. Don't call anyone. I'm simply a writer who stumbled on a national threat and tried to destroy it. I failed to eliminate the big guy. That was my mistake and why I'm here. I'm not the perpetrator. I am a victim." Sam rubbed is beard slowly. "How did you recognize me?"

"You're famous," Eddie murmured while still holding tightly to the gun. "Doesn't eliminate sound rather nasty?"

Sam chuckled at the absurdity of his situation. Here he was caught, not by Jensen but by his students. "Yes, it does, and it is."

Heather slowly took the gun from Eddie. She cleared her throat and enunciated with determination. "We need to know more before we help you."

"Oh, you're going to help me." Sam's amusement turned introspective. "No, you might get hurt. Where did you get the gun?"

"It's my mom's," she said simply.

"Put it away, I'm not going to hurt you." Heather nervously put the gun in her pocket.

Suddenly there was nothing to say except pour out his story, and so Sam did.

Eddie was the first to respond "Wow! That would make a great book."

Heather nudged him. "I'm sorry about your girlfriend and brother," she said.

Sam, finally stood. He walked aimlessly toward the window and viewed the snow outside. His life no longer appeared simple and inviting.

"Me too. I'm sorry too." He spoke almost to the window, and not so much to his students. "Have you heard that reporter, Elizabeth Martin, on television? She might see our side, if I can get it out. Can you try and get to her in the morning if I write it all down?"

Heather spoke too quickly. "No problem."

Sam turned back. "It might not be that easy, getting to her."

"Sure it will. She, she's my mother." Heather said merrily.

Even Eddie turned in awe. "She's your mother?" Eddie gulped. "She's a super reporter."

My mom thinks so too." Heather retorted. "That's our problem. I have to measure up."

"You will," Sam said. He was beginning to like Heather. There was more to her than just great looks and a silly surface personality. "Heather, you can prove yourself without getting mixed up in this. Maybe you shouldn't; I have no right to ask."

"Ah, but I'll get a great story from it, as Eddie says, or my mother will or you. Either way, I'll be respected."

"Yes, you will be," Sam smiled warmly. "Thanks, but we are up against a tyrannosaurus rex of a nasty guy."

"Nothing's too big, with friends helping you." Heather proclaimed.

"Heather you have a wonderful heart," Sam felt moved.

"You bet I do, Sir." She leaned over and shook his hand. "Mr. Stone, I've always wanted to meet you."

He bowed his head. "And I you, Heather," Sam said honestly. "There might be danger here though."

"I'll be fine," Heather said quietly.

ACCELERATION

"Okay," Sam tucked in his emotions. "Let's get some sleep. Can you navigate through the snow? We'll meet in the morning at say 8 A.M." unless you call me. Sam wrote the number down on a pad of paper and ripped off the number. He handed it to Heather. Heather handed it to Eddie, "Eddie will hold it. Right, Eddie." A smile filled Eddie's face. "Yes, I'll hold it, Heather."

"Professor? Um, Mr. Stone?" Heather dug in her pocket.

"Yes?" said Sam.

"You take this. You may need it more than I do." She handed Sam her gun. "My mom probably forgot she had it anyway."

"Thank you, Heather." He emptied the barrel of bullets. "You trust me."

"Yes, I do. I am never wrong."

"You have courage, Heather. You too, Eddie."

Heather bit her lip with embarrassment and then walked to the door, opened it, and skipped down the snow-covered steps. She looked back at Eddie. "Come on, Eddie. The snow's not yet slippery. It's beautiful."

Eddie beamed and followed her.

"Be careful, kids."

"We will. We were born here," They said in unison and laughed. They were children again, relieved of the sometimes terrible burden of adulthood, for a time.

Heather leaned over and molded a snowball. "Good packing, but light." She looked at Sam and then mischievously aimed one at Eddie. "He's cute, isn't he?"

"Yep" Sam roared with laughter. "Go get him, kid, and she did."

Sam closed the door and smiled at the thought of their horseplay. He leaned against the door and relaxed.

He ran his hand through his shaggy grey haircut. This annoying disguise isn't very effective with kids, he thought.

"Sam," Alex stifled a yawn, as she sat on the old stair step. "Did you enjoy lovely Heather."

"Yes, I ripped off her clothes and quoted Carl Sandberg." Sam said wickedly. 'Maybe that was my mistake. She seems to have thrown me over for her young fellow, Eddie."

"She's young." Alex continued the tease.

"Yes, but oh, Heather has that glorious red hair."

Alex flipped her short curls. "But, you love brunettes."

"Yes, that's true. I think I do," Sam scooped her up. "Now, how will I get the lights?" He looked around.

ACCELERATION

"Do we have to?"

"Yeah, I'm shy." He chuckled and carried her and twisted and turned precariously at each light switch. Finally, they teetered up the stairs, and he threw her on the bed. "Do you feel like a jolly newlywed?"

"As a matter of fact, yes. But, I'm not too innocent." Alex said as she pulled Sam down beside her.

"Neither am I," Sam returned, as he smiled and then frowned.

Alex could feel a sudden distance between them. "What's wrong?"

"The kids. They know who I am."

"What!" Alex bolted up.

"Easy." He pulled her down. "They're on our side, I think."

Alex responded slowly. "Sam, is it going to come down again? Are we in danger?"

"Not yet. Did you know that Heather's mom is Elizabeth Martin, the newswoman?"

Alex jumped up again. "What? This is crazy. They'll find us!"

"No, no. I have a feeling about the mother." He slowly pulled her back down, this time onto of him. Sam kissed her gently at first. "I've been looking forward to you all day."

Alex came up for air. "You asked for it." She sat up and pulled her sweater off over her soft curls, and she came back to him.

"Is this all I get?" Sam said teasingly.

"Patience, more is coming." She slid down and took off Sam's shoes. "Now it's your turn. You give a piece. I give one in return. All's fair. It's an old game, but sometimes old games are the best." She continued her game.

Sam stopped. "I'd like to give more than one necessity at a time."

"Oh, you would, would you, Mr. Stone. But, you don't' have much left, do you?" Alex grinned.

Suddenly they were no longer polite. They boldly enjoyed each other.

Afterwards, Sam lay listening to the walls creaking in the storm. It must be a blizzard now. He never thought he'd like being snowbound. He felt Alex's light body curled against his.

ACCELERATION

He was wrong. He'd have to put this into his next book, if he lived to write one.

CHAPTER 25

The room was heavy in darkness, but he couldn't sleep. Sam kept tossing in his bed. He was afraid he'd wake Alex. He rose and threw on his robe. The old wooden floor was cold now. Better turn up the heat. He moved quietly down the steps and adjusted the thermostat. He entered the study and sat in the darkness. How would he begin? Would Martin believe him? He switched on the old lamp. Ben had said that Sam would like the old study lamp. He did. He swiveled thoughtfully in his chair. Ben used to live here in his teaching days. Maybe that's why Sam fit in so well. He tried to imagine burly Ben in his youth, sitting in this simple chair and planning his lectures. His students probably adored him. Ben was an honest and caring man. Sam missed hm.

Sam pulled out a pad of paper and wrote out his story in longhand. When he was finished, he folded the pages into an envelope and addressed it. He couldn't read it over. He hoped he'd watched his p's and q's, but he felt emotionally beaten. The old pain had returned.

It came, despair flooded over him. He turned in his chair and cried. He hadn't cried since Caroline died. He had to get hold of himself. He had more to do. He grabbed the envelope and placed it in the old overcoat hanging by the door. He'd have to return the coat in the morning.

Suddenly he flashed on a moment in the past. The formula! He had left the drug label in his pocket. He wondered if Jessup had found it in Sam's old clothes. Maybe Jessup just trashed them. He hoped he was doing well and not hurt. He still had to thank and pay him. Oh, stop thinking. It's in the future, when and if this all ends well. I'll ask him then about the label. I'm going to stop worrying and go back to bed.

Sam turned out the lights and padded softly up the stairs. He stole a look at Sarah on the way. She looked so sweet. Her pert nose barely reached above the soft quilt. He brushed aside the copper ringlet that had fallen across her forehead. He kissed her lightly. He couldn't resist, he felt like her father. He stopped short and placed his hand on her head. Was she unusually warm? He was beginning to feel his role and his obligations as a guardian. Sam went back and woke Alex.

"What's the matter?" Alex said sleepily.

"Sarah feels warm."

"Is she crying?" Alex stumbled quickly into her robe.

"No," said Sam.

"New Poppa, she's probably fine." Alex punched him playfully on the arm.

She checked anyway. Sam was right, he wished he wasn't.

Alex worked all night on Sarah's fever. She tried Tylenol and then changed to aspirin. She used cold towels, nothing worked. Sarah became lethargic and tolerated her mother's frantic efforts. Finally, they bundled her up for the hospital. Sam scribbled a note on the door for Heather and Eddie, and they left.

"Did you poison your daughter?" The doctor said angrily.

"Of course not." Alex was terrified. "What's wrong with her?"

"We don't' know, but whatever it is, her illness is not naturally caused."

"Oh God, no. I love her so much." Alex began to cry hysterically.

Sam put his arm around her.

"Who are you, sir?" The doctor snapped.

"I'm a professor at the University, and Sarah's stepfather." Sam didn't blink with his lie. Her natural father had given her special vitamins, but that was months ago. Could it still be in her system and cause a reaction?"

"I don't know. Can you bring the vitamins for testing?" the doctor said.

"I don't know. Alex, calm down, honey. Think. Do you still have some of Silas' vitamins, the ones he gave Sarah?"

Alex stopped crying and looked up in shock. "You think it's the vitamins. I stopped giving them to her. Are you sure it's not the flu or an ear ache?"

"No. Your daughter is in a coma."

"What, oh, no!" Alex screamed. "No, no, oh, Sam…Do something, please!"

Sam sat her down. "Did you save any of the vitamins? Could Sarah have found them?"

Alex looked up stunned. "Do you think she did? No, not my baby! Why would Silas give her dangerous medicine and hurt our baby?"

Sam took her hand firmly. "Alex, he was crazy. Doctor, I'll go home and look for the pills. Alex, where do you remember last seeing them?"

"In my letter box. I don't know why I save them. I don't know why, oh, no!" Alex was inconsolable now.

"Doctor, can you give her something 'til I get back?
"Yes, sit down, Mrs. Sinclair. Nurse…."

"Oh, Alex, why did you save them?" Sam muttered as he hurled himself up the icy steps. He fumbled with the door in the semi-light of dawn and then tore it open. He took the old steps to the second floor in leaps. Grabbing the antique box on the dresser, he dumped it violently on the bed. No pills! He felt desperate. Alex, where did you put them? You didn't take them, did you? Tears formed in his eyes, he shook them away and launched himself at their little girl's room. Sam started with the bed, then the closet and dresser. He was throwing possessions like a madman. He saw it suddenly, the bottle, on the floor under the side of the blanket. He pulled it towards himself and shook the container. Empty! Sam extended his arm wildly under the small bed. His fingers touched a scatter of objects. The pills. He pulled them in. Thank God, he had them. He sat his large frame on the edge of the little bed and exhaled deeply. He loved Alex's little girl. Jensen, what did you do to your own child? What kind of stinking monster are you?

He reflected only for a moment and then rushed to the door. He grabbed the overcoat as an afterthought and threw it in the backseat of the old black Chevy of Ben's. He crunched down the driveway and hurried off. Sam's mind was only on a small girl with bright copper curls.

Sam had delivered the pills to the doctor and then quietly opened the door of Sarah's hospital room. Alex slept with exhaustion on the side chair. Her head rested on the bed and her hand clutched the small hand of her only child. An I.V. tube penetrated Sarah's other helpless limb.

Sarah was so young. She had a whole life ahead of her. How could Silas have poisoned his own child with his horrible obsession? What kind of man does that?

Sam pulled up another chair and sat softly beside Sarah and Alex.

The young doctor suddenly taped him on the shoulder.

Mr. Sinclair, Professor, may we talk?"

Sam nodded. "Outside."

They stood facing each other. Doctor Hernandez was no longer angry but instead, very sad.

Sam sensed the change. "Will she live?" Sam feared the answer.

"I don't think so. I'm so very sorry." He paused and lowered his eyes. "I had the pills analyzed, as thoroughly as we could with the time necessity. I've never seen that combination of chemicals before. We don't quite know how to treat the child. We are not giving up, but, well, I have a specialist on poisons coming from Chicago. The pills worked awfully fast, however. Do you know the manufacturer? There was no brand stamped on them and no label on the bottle."

Sam frowned. "I think it was experimental. His father is a powerful man. He did this to her, and we can't touch him. Not yet anyway."

"I don't understand," The doctor said.

Sam changed the subject. "Have you told her mother?

"Not yet. Do you want me to wake her and explain the situation?"

"No, thanks, I will, but not yet. Let her sleep, if time makes no difference."

Sam braced himself and crept back into the child's room. He pulled the chair back up next to Alex. He stared at their unconscious child. At least there seemed to be no pain, he thought.

Sam rubbed his eyes. He must be tired. His hand suddenly went to his mouth. Sarah was changing just as Caroline had. Her beautiful sweet face was aging at incredible speed, as if

ACCELERATION

years took seconds. Sam burst into tears. "Oh, sweetie!" He stumbled from the room and leaned against the wall.

"An outstretched arm kept him from falling. "Professor, let me help you sit down."

Sam turned his tortured eyes towards the doctor. "It's Sarah!" His voice broke.

Dr. Hernandez dropped Sam's arm and sprang into the room. Sam slipped slowly to the floor and sat there stunned with his head against the wall.

A few minutes later the doctor joined Sam and helped him up. "She's still alive. I've never seen anything like it. Can you help your wife? She's just staring at her daughter."

I will try." Sam said emotionally and turned back to the room. He then looked back
to the doctor. "If she'll leave the bedside, do you have a spare room that my wife can rest in?"

"Yes, two doors down in room 609."

"Thank you." Sam quietly brought Alex out. Neither said a word. They just walked down the hall. Sam stopped at the door and took a deep breath. It all seemed like a horrible dream and so final. He slowly pushed open the door, and they entered.

Hernandez understood. He felt useless, however. He did not want to return to the unconscious child's room, but he did.

Sam helped Alex to lie down in the spare hospital room. She stared out for some time and then finally closed her eyes. He had to pry her fingers from his arm in order to leave her side. He left a note by her tear-streaked pillow. She looked so broken. Sam was sick of the people he loved being hurt.

Sam slowly walked into the restroom and splashed his face with cold water. He looked at himself warily in the mirror. He was different. He recognized immediately the change. He was filled with hate. All the politeness of his planned offensive using Elizabeth Martin had disappeared with the youth of his child. No one should hurt a child. Jensen was going to die, the sooner, the better. Sam went into the hall to seek out the doctor. He had to see Hernandez before he left.

He found the doctor in the lab looking over the chemical reports. Sam sensed the young man's bewilderment and frustration. "I know how you feel. Doctor, I've been dealing with it for months, but for the first time with a child. Let me explain." He did.

"Mr. Stone, what do you plan to do now?"

ACCELERATION

"You're with me then?" said Sam.

"If I hadn't seen that little girl, I would have called the authorities at the mention of your name. I believe you, crazy as it all sounds." Hernandez extended his hand.

Sam shook it quietly, and they walked down the hall.

Sam stopped and leveled with the doctor. "Is there any hope of finding an antidote or cure, or is it a foolish question?"

"In time?" The doctor sighed. "I doubt it, but I'm going to try. I promise you that. What are you going to do? You are in one hell of a mess."

"Yep." Sam started walking again. "I'll go for the media, then Jensen. Maybe if the head honcho falls, the dominoes will follow and the money vultures will scatter. It's the President's involvement that might be dangerously sticky."

"Yeah, sort of. I can't believe he's involved. He's slick but not very bright. Why would he join in?"

"That's just it," Sam countered. "He wants to be smarter, he's power hungry and a follower. He's probably more dangerous than Jensen, and I'm sure he's taking the drugs. A drug controlled man who has the power to push the annihilation button is scary."

"You are pulling the rug out from under me. Good luck, sir."

"Thanks. Take care of Alex and my little girl for me. I love them both, very much." Sam said as his eyes teared up. He quickly brushed them away. "Sorry."

"Don't apologize for having feelings. I'll do my best, Mr. Stone. By the way, I am a big fan of your books.

Sam smiled. "Thanks. You just reminded me that I'm not a total nut." Sam clasped his hand for the last time and covered the hall in big strides. He disappeared shortly into the snow covered streets. Day had come and Sam had things to do, and it was almost 8 A.M.

CHAPTER 26

Sam pulled up to the empty house just minutes before the kids. He threw belongings into his suitcase and headed back to the door as the sound of a car signaled its arrival. He paused as he heard Heather and Eddie talking, settling on the icy step, and reading Sam's note aloud. He yanked open the heavy storm door and looked into their concerned faces. "I'm glad you're here," said Sam quietly.

"Is Sarah all right, sir?" Heather piped up.

"Nope." Sam tried not to show his pain as he explained, but it was all over his face. "She was given dangerous experimental vitamins by her real father in the past. We didn't realize that last night she found an old bottle of them in her toys and then ate almost all of the pills. Now her body is reacting to the poison. The effect is causing the aging process to move with tremendous speed. She was unconscious all night and then- an hour ago her face and body rapidly aged. My sweet little six-year-old girl now looks like a very old woman. She is dying fast. It's so awful." Sam gasped and fought back tears. "Let's go. We have to tell people what is really going on in our country. We have to warn them. Ready?"

"Yes," said Eddie softly. Heather nodded.

"Good, thank you." Sam turned, grabbed his suitcase, and burst down the steps and across the walk. "We'll take my car."

Then suddenly he stopped and turned to the kids. "Do you both have money to get home if I have to leave you in Chicago? Should our plan fall apart, I don't want you hurt. I want you to go home. I don't want you in danger. Understood?"

"Yes," answered Heather softly.

"I agree, sir," said Eddie.

Heather then leaped into the front seat, Eddie in the back.

"Thank you," said Sam, as he handed Heather the letter from his overcoat pocket. "This is for your mother. You both should read it, and I have to make a short stop on the way."

"Okay." Heather nervously nodded her head and began reading.

Sam soon stopped, dropped off the coat, and began to drive again.

Heather looked back at Eddie and handed him the letter. He read it as she turned to Sam and proudly said, "I called my mother. She has a restaurant near the lake front and is meeting me there. Here's the address." She handed the paper to Sam.

"Good, thanks Heather." He then returned to his silence and drove on.

Heather and Eddie leaned back and slept.

For five hours not another word was spoken.

Heather thought she was dreaming when Sam finally said, "Heather. Eddie. We are about an hour away now."

They arrived at the restaurant as planned.

Eddie and Sam settled in a booth with their backs to Heather. All three were beginning to feel the excitement of the confrontation. Would it end positively or all turn afoul? So much hung on Heather, her hands shook. Sam leaned around and hugged her briefly. "You'll be fine, honey. If I forgot to tell you, you're terrific, and thank you."

Heather relaxed momentarily, then she saw her mom. Heather froze for a few seconds and then, feigned relaxation again. She pasted a blazing smile on her face and stood up.

"Mom, thanks for coming."

"I love seeing you, sweetie, but I'm running ragged with this Stone story. I can't stay long." Elizabeth Martin pulled an expensive silk scarf from her long dark hair and shook her head. "The winds are really tossing me around today, but it feels good. Did you order? I've got to eat fast. There have been rumors that Stone has been sighted in Florida." Martin summoned the waiter and ordered for the two of them.

"Mother, I have something that you should read."

"What is it, your term paper? Dear, I know you're smart. I really don't have time." She smiled her perfect smile.

"No, it's not a term paper, and you do have time. Please." Heather fished the envelope from her pocket and handed it over with trembling hands. She hoped that her mother would believe and side with Sam, but she wasn't sure of her mom's reporting ethics. She got her stories but maybe at the expense of others and possibly the truth. Hopefully, Sam wouldn't end up her victim.

"Who is this from?" Martin was puzzled.

"Sam Stone," Heather said calmly, she was starting to gain control.

"What? You've seen him? Is he here?" Martin jerked out of her seat.

"Mom, relax. Just read the letter and believe it. Let's eat too, I'm starved." The waiter had brought the food, and Heather dug into her pastrami sandwich. She was enjoying seeing her mom squirm in shock.

Finally, Martin relaxed and settled back to read the letter.

Heather took a bite of her food and then lost her appetite. She watched her mother's face carefully as the pages were slowly turned. The ending finally came. Heather and her mother sat back almost simultaneously.

"Well?"

"It's terrific fiction. I always did think Stone was a good writer." Martin stuffed the pages back into the envelope. "Do you really expect me to believe this and print it? I thought you were smarter than that."

"Mom, he's not a fool, he's a famous man. Why would he make it all up?"

"To cover his tail. He committed murder. Why, no one knows. He killed his brother and a hospital full of patients."

"Mom, who's the fool now? Did you ever ask why? And what kind of patients?"

"It's hard when the records were destroyed?"

"Were they? The key is Jensen. Do you trust him?" Heather asked.

"No, but that's beside the point. I don't have to like a man to believe him?" said Martin.

"Heather was adamant. "I didn't say like him, I said trust him?"

Martin leaned back in sudden awe of her forceful daughter. "You really believe Stone, don't you?"

"Yes, I do. Mom. His stepdaughter, Sarah, has been given the drug. Jensen fed it to her. She is six-years-old and dying from old age now."

"You saw her? What hospital?"

"Mom, if I tell you, you can't let him be caught." Heather put her hand over her mother's hand as she pulled out her notepad and pen.

"I won't, if he's innocent."

"But you think he's guilty." Heather said, as she shifted her position in discouragement and put down the pen.

"I'm a reporter, Heather. I regret to say that we always go for the guilty verdict until proven innocent. It's a fatal flaw, probably in this case. Okay, for the sake of argument, suppose this fantastic tale is true. What do you want me to do?"

"Just print his side for now. It should stir up the soup. It might prove exciting, Mother. You also might just have the story of a lifetime."

ACCELERATION

"Where did you learn to be so convincing?" Martin smiled genuinely.

"I watched you carefully because," Heather paused, "because I always wanted to impress you." Heather bit her lip. "I didn't mean to sound so maudlin."

"I rather like it, Heather. By the way, I always was impressed with you." Martin did love her daughter. "I guess I tried too hard to compete in my job. I forgot sometimes that I have this wonderful kid. How about a hug. I'm sorry."

"Sure." Heather stood. "In front of everyone."

"Why not?" Martin stood, embraced her daughter, and gave her a quick kiss on the cheek. "But perhaps we shouldn't overdo it, or people will talk." She laughed.

"I'm glad I had this excuse to see you, Mother."

"Me too. So now, introduce me to the elusive Mr. Samuel Stone. Is he here? Why didn't you bring him?"

Sam rose and stood before her. He extended his hand. "She did. A pleasure to meet you, Ms. Martin."

Martin was truly stunned. "And I you," She stumbled to her feet. "Please, sit down. I hate looking up to a wanted killer."

Sam frowned and still stood.

"You are too old for my daughter, you know. I do see her fascination, however. It must be the disguise. She always did like a good mystery, but I hope she didn't overbite here." Martin scanned Sam thoughtfully. "I need to call my editor and tell him that I will be late. You may take longer than this pastrami, Mister." Martin adjusted her elegantly tailored suit. "Excuse me."

When her mother was out of site, Heather cleared her throat. "What do you think of old mom?"

Sam picked up the checks from both tables and aimlessly laid down bills. "She's a strong lady, Heather." He couldn't seem to put down a foreboding, however. The minutes ticked by, Sam got more restless. Then all hell broke loose.

Sam saw the cop car and bolted for the back door. He wasn't sure which way to go, but it was definitely not to the front. He crashed into a waiter and sent the plates upside down on a group of businessmen. He plowed through a service door and slid on the kitchen floor. He'd never had people terrified of him before. He hated the sensation. Sam burst into the alley but ducked down at the scream to "freeze." He pushed over a barrel of trash and seized a fire escape. The bar chilled his fingers, and he knew he was being followed. This can't be happening.

ACCELERATION

Thoughts raced through his head. This was real. He'd been betrayed. He had trusted foolishly. Keep running.

Sam tore up the ladder and across the roof to the edge. The distance to the adjacent roof was a good four feet. He doubted he'd make it, but what was the alternative? He took a running start and hurled his body across the yawning cavity. He landed near the edge and lost his footing. Sam grabbed with his fingers and clawed his way back onto the flat cold haven's surface.

He gasped and clung only a second, then sprang to his feet. A gun cracked in the wind, and Sam felt an intense burning in his arm. He was hit, but he'd been through worse. Then he felt himself thrown forward as a second shot skimmed his skull. He didn't have time to feel his head, only to get up and leap for the second roof. He would make it; he just knew it. He wasn't finished.

Life was hard sometimes, and it just seemed to get harder. He sprinted the third roof. That's it. He wouldn't tempt fate on a fourth. He yanked on the roof door. It wouldn't budge. He took out Heather's gun, which had rested so long in his pocket and thankfully not fallen out. He blew out the lock, and it moved easily. He was vaguely aware of a throbbing and dizziness rising and falling in his consciousness, but he hadn't the time to dwell on it. He buried the gun again in his pocket and leaped down the stairs.

Sam reached the street and mingled in the crowds. No one saw the tall lean man, with blood on his face, pulling up his jacket collar and heading into the wind. No one really cared. The few people who stopped the flow of their lives were interested in the mass of police that had surrounded a restaurant. The glitzy lake front establishments did not recognize figures that weren't their own. Certainly criminal elements would be caught and sent to the other side of the city. That did not concern them. Sam kept walking and walking.

The distance from the restaurant widened. Sam slumped on a park bench. He needed to think and gather his strength. He didn't know where he was going, and he needed to rest. His hand went to the side of his head. He felt a crusting of blood, not too serious, but it sure carried a headache. He eased his aching arm from the sleeve of his jacket. He jerked off his tie and bound the bleeding extremity. He knew the tie was good for something; it sure didn't impress Elizabeth Martin.

Poor Heather, he thought. She's probably mad as hell. He was too tired to be angry at her mother.

ACCELERATION

He would have to lose himself in the city. He hoped it was possible. He would go for his car later. Now to find a place to crash. He headed away from the posh and towards the real people of the city. He could belong, if he could just think clearly for a little longer.

CHAPTER 27

Sam paid the chubby ruddy-faced man for two days. He had stumbled on the steps of the sleazy hotel. He hoped that the desk clerk would think him drunk. The man had grunted an obscene order about not throwing up on his carpet. Sam figured the place had been through too many sick men and women. Who would search for him here? No one, and that was good, sort of.

Sam climbed the steps to the room. He didn't care what it looked like. He would take a hole in the ground as long as it had a bed and was warm. The room almost fit the technical requirements. Sam banged on the heater which managed only a faint glow. He flicked on the light, and roaches scampered to their respective walls.

"Sorry fellows," Sam tiredly stared at the insects. "You gotta share this place. I paid, you are freeloaders." Sam fell across the worn sheets of the murphy bed. "Stay down bed." He muttered. "I really don't want to bounce up and join the insects in that wall." He couldn't stay awake for any more casual conversation with the pesky inhabitants. His arm had stopped bleeding, although it still held its deadly bullet. He would attend to it later. If he could just sleep first…Sam passed out.

"Mother, I trusted you!" Heather sputtered with anger.

"Quiet, dear; it's time for my broadcast." Martin turned to the camera and gave her hair one last pat. Snow had begun to shower her with white flakes. She did not belong in this wonderland, and she obviously wasn't enjoying it.

Neither was her daughter. "Mother, don't call me dear, not after what you did!" Heather tossed the paper cup with its brown liquid at her mother's rich grey suit. "My coffee's cold." She started to flounce away but stopped. "Mother, when did you get to be such a bitch? And, when did a story become more important than the truth?" Heather grabbed Eddie's arm furiously. "Eddie, I have to get away from here." Heather couldn't see now; tears were flooding her vision. She swiped at them and pulled Eddie away from the film crew and leaned against the building. She could hear her mother's voice proudly snapping out her story.

"Sam Stone, the writer and fugitive has been sighted here in Chicago. He has given me a fantastic story of government cover up. Is it fact or some of Mr. Stone's exciting fiction? We have not verified his claims so you, the listener, must consider that. He is also a wanted criminal, perhaps wounded and hiding in the streets of this city. A heavy storm has begun to pound on this windy city. Will he survive it? This reporter will bring you reports, as they come in. We do know that a beard covers his features; here is our artist's conception. Any information on his whereabouts will be rewarded by this reporter and the network. We are committed to learning the truth, be it fact or fiction. Here is Mr. Stone's story, as he revealed it to me not two hours ago." The polished Ms. Martin read the contents of Sam's letter.

Heather listened intently from the distance. She could remember his voice and the words. Sam's story was being told, at least her mother hadn't discarded it. Soon the real news vultures will cut loose. They will devour and dissect the story. Truth will come out, somehow. Heather had to cling to this hope.

ACCELERATION

Heather thought of Sam, she huddled deeper within her fancy fur parka. He was hurt, and they had his picture. "Eddie, what do we do now?"

Eddie must be thinking her same thoughts. "The car."

"The car." Heather chimed in, simultaneously. "The police may not know about it. Do you think Sam can get back to it?"

"Yeah, eventually." Eddie said. His eyes peeked through his wire rimmed glasses. Snowflakes melted on the glass, and he smeared them with his coat sleeve. "It's the eventually that worries me. We may have quite a wait. We could take shifts."

"It's going to be cold in that car." Her eyes suddenly got wide. "Eddie, do you think it's locked?"

Eddie was having trouble seeing now. He took off his glasses, buried them in his pocket, and squinted at Heather. "I have an extra key. He gave me one just in case there was trouble. He told me to take you home."

"No way, we are sticking together. This is too exciting. I'm not a helpless female," she said proudly, "in case you didn't notice."

"I noticed."

"Eddie, can you see without your glasses?"

"Not really." He shrugged and put them back on.

"Here," Heather reached out and eased them from his hands. She pulled out an exquisitely painted scarf and wiped his glasses. "I bought this for my mom, but she doesn't really need another scarf. She doesn't need anything, and she sure doesn't want me. Let's go friend." She handed Eddie back his eyewear.

Eddie fumbled with the glasses. Heather took them back and perched them on his nose, for him. She gazed fondly at the gawky youth. Snow had plastered his hair and he looked bedraggled, but he would someday be a fine looking guy. He just needed a little more time to find himself, Heather thought. She kind of liked him this way anyway.

"Come on, where's that car? All the streets look alike, they're all white," Heather said.

"Snow does that." Eddie said seriously.

"Hey, don't look so glum, we've got a plan."

"We do?" Eddie said in confusion.

"Yep. The car is a good start. We'll figure out the rest as we go along." Heather grabbed off Eddie's knit cap and raced ahead playfully, as the huge fluffy wads of snow continued to blind and conceal the dirty streets.

CHAPTER 28

Sam's delirium struggled to rip down the heavy dark curtain that seemed to be smothering his life and his memories? Why couldn't he see faces? Were they to forever be forgotten? Was he dead? Had he slipped into a void? No, he lived, he suddenly felt pain. He was relieved. He could see now. He could watch the small little forms scooting around and exploring the floor near his bedtable. He was lying on his stomach with his clothes still soiled in his blood. The heater must have come on in the night because at least he and his crawly friends were warm and toasty. He boosted himself into a sitting position. His body ached, but it would pass. His arm was a problem, however. He examined it closely and grimaced. He knew he would have to dig out the bullet himself. The thought didn't exactly elevate his situation. He would need more than was in this stark room to even inadequately complete the butchery. Sam grabbed his key and struggled into his coat.

He felt the eyes of the desk clerk on his back and turned. I really don't feel like dealing with the storm. Could I buy a bottle of booze and a knife from you, mister? Sam said in his best drunk imitation.

"You going to carve up a body and eat it with your booze, wino?" The skinny clerk simpered. "How much you pay?"

"Twenty bucks is all I got? I ain't going to cut anybody. I got me a little bread, and I want to be dainty when I eat it." Sam was enjoying his acting part. "I'll give back the knife afterwards, you'll see. I ain't no liar." Oops, he thought. A double negative in grammar. This would be more fun though if his arm weren't throbbing so badly. Sam lowered his head subserviently. "Please, mister?"

"Okay. But you give the knife back." He took a swig from the bottle of cheap whiskey that he pulled from under the counter. "You can keep the bottle," the man said as he leaned into Sam's face and exhaled a foul odor.

"Thanks," Sam choked and grabbed the half empty bottle. It would do. "The knife?" he added.

"Sure?" The weasel waved the point toward Sam. "Don't cut your ugly self."

Sam carefully unwrapped it from the clerk's fingers and stuck it in his pocket. "I'll be careful," he replied innocently. Sam returned to his room.

He poured the whiskey over the knife and unwrapped his arm. He gulped twice on his drink, then soaked his tie and dabbed at his wound. It definitely burned. He gathered his courage and grasped the knife.

"Oh boy, I know I'm going to hate this." He gritted his teeth and dug into his injured arm. Red blood flowed freely onto the faded sheet. He paused.

"At least I still have lots of red blood left. One more time, you masochistic bastard!" He jammed the knife into the throbbing arm again and pulled out the offensive bullet. He poured the remainder of the bottle into the wound and cried out. Sam hurled the knife against the wall.

"Go to hell, Jensen! It's your fault, all of this."

Sam collapsed on the bed and squeezed his eyes shut for a moment. The pain eased slightly. He rose and removed a sleeve from his shirt, then the other one. He shredded them into strips and packing and bound his arm. Now if it doesn't get infected, he'd be fine. That is if he lived that long to find out. He didn't plan to stay here forever. He would kill Jensen and his buddies, all by himself. He laughed at the absurdity of his vow. Maybe I'm getting to be as crazy as he is, Sam thought.

He leaned back. He would wait out the storm for one night. Then tomorrow he would seek his car, if they hadn't impounded it. There were a mighty lot of ifs. But Sam slept.

Heather had just approached the old Chevy with her bags of donuts and coffee. They were deep in conversation over their salivary preferences, when Heather felt a hand on her shoulder. She spun around to give a tongue lashing to the annoying bystander. She gasped, and suddenly her face beamed at the sight of Sam.

"You're alive!"

"In the flesh," Sam said. He reached out and drew her towards him for a hug. "I missed my partners."

"Mr. Stone, we worried a lot." Eddie bounced in excitement.

"Let's get into the car and get out of here before anyone important, like cops, see us."

"A good idea, sir."

Sam slid behind the wheel. It felt very good to his touch. Heather and Eddie scrambled to their respective places. No one breathed easily until they were on the interstate headed east.

"Mr. Stone, where are we going?" Eddie piped up.

"I think it's time you called me Sam."

Eddie bounced his head in agreement.

"Sam, sir, are you going to tell us?"

ACCELERATION

"Young man, no one will ever accuse you of being impolite. Yes, I am driving to Washington. Do you want to come too?"

"Yes," Eddie nodded at Heather, "but why?"

"To see the President," Sam smiled broadly.

"To see the President!" Eddie nearly spilled his coffee. "You mean of the United States?"

"That's right, kid. Let's go straight to the top."

"Wow, yeh, why not? Eddie settled back in his seat. Heather smiled and nestled her head on his shoulder. They rode on and on.

Sam watched row after row of ice-covered trees spin by. Hours whirled into days. They stopped only for gas, food, and to switch drivers. He ignored the pain that occasionally shot through his arm. He refused to acknowledge the building fever it caused. Heather argued once for proper disinfectant. So they stopped. He bought disinfectant and a newspaper. Sam's face jumped from its pages. He quietly entered the washroom and disposed of the beard. He kept the moustache. He hoped he would soon have no need for it as well.

Heather was still in the car sleeping. She tossed fitfully in the car's seat. She saw her face crumbling into dust. Suddenly she awoke to Sam's shaking her shoulders. He was still standing outside the car and beside her. The door was open. He was kneeling down. His eyes held such sadness.

"You okay, Heather. I'm sorry. I added nightmares to your peaceful youth."

Heather clutched his hand tightly, then relaxed. "I'm fine now." She sat up straight and looked around. She blinked at the bright lights. "Where are we?"

"Washington," Sam said soberly.

"Wow," said Heather. "I've never been here."

"It's quite a city. Now we find a motel. We all need rest." Sam nodded at the sleeping Eddie in the back seat. "Do you want to get out and stretch before we leave here?" said Sam.

"Yep." She stood and did three jumping jacks and plopped back into the car. "I'm ready," Heather said eagerly.

"I wish I felt like that, jumping around that is. All right. We go." Sam walked to the car. He wiped his face with his sleeve. He was sweating! It was freezing outside, and he was hot. Oh, not a good sign. Perhaps his fever would go away on its own. Maybe?

ACCELERATION

The weary travelers skidded the vehicle next to the pale green door of their small motel room and deposited themselves haphazardly about the basic, cheap, cream-colored room. The two simple double beds were most inviting. Even a refreshing shower couldn't tempt them from the soft refuge.

"I promise I'll hit the bath later," Heather puffed her pillow and yawned.

"Me too, whatever you said," Eddie mumbled back through closed eyes. I'll sleep on top of the bedspread tonight, if you want. You did it last time, Heather. Our parents may be pleased. Like we are never awake enough to even stare at each other. I'm asleep. Night." Eddie closed his eyes and was out.

Sam shook his thoughts to clear them and stumbled to turn on the television. He turned it on softly. "Sorry kids. I have to listen here." He lay back down with the remote control. The lights from the television broadcast flashed hypnotically before him. He swallowed and closed his eyes. His throat felt raw and his body felt hot. He was sick, and the timing was lousy. He shivered and yanked the blanket to his chin, as the commentator babbled.

"So, Ellie, I think the President has given some snappy answers. What do you think? Isn't this atypical? Has he been hitting the books or have his advisors finally been briefing him properly? This is not the man of four years ago."

"No, Tom, I agree. The President has been trying very hard, especially since the election is coming. He has taken seriously the comments that he is charming but absent-minded and that his wife runs the country. He has been on a self-improvement crusade. We are seeing the difference."

"What is this regime?" Ellie pursued. "We all should follow it."

"Maybe he just eats right and reads a lot," Tom replied. "He also believes ritualistically in special vitamins."

"Special vitamins. Oh, no." Sam quickly sat up on the bed. His head started swimming, and he abruptly slipped back to his position. Heather noticed.

Ellie was again talking. "Most Presidents age terribly. He almost looks younger than when he was a congressman. His office must be treating him well."

She and her partner, Tom, laughed.

ACCELERATION

Sam pressed the remote and changed the channel.

An announcer was speaking. "President Wilson Quint will attend a funeral for his dog, Peaches, tomorrow at an undisclosed cemetery location. He does so to promote animal kindness and respect. He will miss the funeral of Congressman Reynolds, however. He expresses his condolences to the family of Mr. Reynolds."

Sam flipped the channel again.

"Mr. President," the lady of the television press asked, "what are your budget plans?"

The President answered hotly. "And what are yours? Are you cutting spending? Do you expect your country to take care of everyone's needs? We have far too many examples of human trash feeding on our goodwill."

The President's aide tried to usher off the President. "President Quint will be available for questioning again next week."

Quint cut in. "Mister, I'm not finished!"

The aide interrupted again. "Sir, we are out of time."

Quint furiously responded. "Make time."

"No, Sir," the aide continued. "I can't."

The camera caught a glimpse of the anger seething from the leader of the land.

Sam changed the picture again. Cartoons, sitcoms, crime and mysteries shows, violent live action, more news. Then he stopped. It was Elizabeth Martin concluding her report with the question that had not been answered. "When will I meet you, Mr. Jensen Are you afraid of me?" Her dark eyes flashed suggestively.

Sam sighed. Perhaps it's been worth it. Martin was carrying the ball pretty well without him. He shut down the chatter of the television and slept.

Heather contemplated the darkness for a short time and then she too drifted into sleep. She suddenly awoke to Sam and Eddie's voices.

Sam was shouting, and Eddie was frantically trying to quiet him.

ACCELERATION

Heather smoothed Sam's tousled dark hair and pulled back her hand, as if stung. "Eddie, he's on fire with fever. Wet the towels I'll call for an ambulance.

The manager of the tiny motel now pounded on the door for quiet, as if intensifying the noise would help.

'Sir," Heather cracked open the door ever so slightly. It's my friend. He's delirious with fever. We're calling an ambulance now. It will be quiet soon."

The little man's anger evaporated, and he shifted his demeanor to a jittery twitch. "He better not die here. It's bad for my business. Be out by morning."

Heather pursed her lips. "Of course, we will." She almost shut the door in his face. She wished she had.

CHAPTER 29

Strong arms lifted Sam onto a table. Sam pulled the hazy face of the medic to him. "Corporal, it's my crew. We went down near the canyon. You have to get them out." He pushed the body back. "Who are you? What is this place? Corporal, I want out?" He jerked, but the strong arms were back, holding him in place.

"Hold him while I look at his arm. See the striations. Here's the source of the mass infection."

"Infection!" Sam's voice boomed in his ears. "I've been shot, but I took care of it."

"You sure did, Mister Sinclair. Nurse, hand me that syringe."

Sam felt the sting, but he was confused. Sinclair? Then he remembered the kids must have entered him under his cover.

"The police want to know what happened?" The doctor had heavy bushy eyebrows. Sam stared at them. His head was still groggy.

"I had a hunting accident a few days ago. My son tripped and shot me. It was nothing, so I didn't report it." Voices raged behind the partition. Sam doubted that Doctor Eyebrows even heard his answer.

The doctor shouted to his nurse. "Keep Mr. Sinclair strapped down for now. I need to stop that noise on the other side of this room. It's a crazy night."

The doctor yanked the partition open and then back as he made his exit to the other side and switched patients. His presence was certainly still heard, however.

Sam drifted in and out of sleep, as he tried to make sense of the clamor.

"What's going on?" Sam mumbled as he felt the nurse giving him a shot and covering him with a blanket.

"You are next door to the President of the United States. They just brought him in. He had a seizure at a funeral. I think he's going to be okay though. Exciting, isn't it?" The stocky little nurse pulled her hair behind her ears and patted it down. "I better see if they need my help. I'll be back. You just rest now. I gave you a shot for the infection. Now, you need rest." She dimmed the exam light and tilted it from his face. She quickly disappeared behind the partition and joined the voices.

Sam's mind caught fire in the darkness. He couldn't have planned this better. He wanted to laugh insanely, but instead he would simply listen and definitely enjoy it.

"Gentlemen, we do not need everyone in here. Please, this is a hospital." The doctor's deep voice split the air. "Now get out while I examine the President."

"We can't do that, Doctor?" A man's voice returned.

"Then stay, but please, shut up."

"Excuse me. Nurse, you may leave. My people will assist the doctor. Remove yourself now."

"Doctor Kelly, do you want me to leave?" the nurse said to the doctor.

"No," he replied.

"Nurse, leave, or I'll have you arrested. I am Mr. Kreider, I will take responsibility ."

"What? You will not," Dr. Kelly interrupted.

"Nurse, go."

"Doctor… Mr. Jensen will be here momentarily with the medicine he needs. I was informed that Mr. President only wishes to rest here until the serum comes."

ACCELERATION

"I see. Well, let me look at him anyway. This is our job, you know."

"Doctor, I can't allow that. His doctor is on the way."

"Then why did you bring him here if you don't want us to treat him? He is a patient. It is my job to examine him. Look at how pale he is. He is barely breathing."

"Doctor, I am saying again. Don't touch him!"

"Then take this man from my hospital. I won't have him die here, when I am forbidden to help. Take your grey suited mob with you also." The doctor groused vehemently.

Suddenly a different voice sweetly interrupted. "Please, Doctor, we don't mean to usurp your authority. We merely are more familiar with our leader's medical condition. I have his insulin here."

"He is diabetic then," The doctor said. "That makes for an even stronger argument for me to attend to this patient."

"Sir, it is not exactly insulin. I use that term only to simulate the importance to this patient. It is experimental."

"You are using experimental drugs on the President of the United States! That is a terribly dangerous action."

"We know, Doctor. Sir, I am losing my patience. Gentlemen, remove the kind Doctor."

"What are you talking about?" The doctor was angry now. "Remove me from my own hospital? Get your hands off of me!" The doctor's voice was suddenly muffled. Sam heard a brief struggle, then a sound of someone being dragged. The doctor?" Sam yanked at his bindings. He hoped that Kreider and his men didn't realize there was a roommate behind the partition.

"Where's that ugly nurse?" A scratchy voice piped up

"Mr. President, I told her to leave and to hold the press. She was very flustered," the man laughed boisterously. "Oh, sorry, Sir. I should be more quiet."

Sam heard a door open and then Jensen's voice. "Roll up the President's sleeve or we may be too late. This is serious, men."

"Yes, sir," Kreider, in his low voice, seemed to be the one answering.

Sam heard a rustling and a groaning. Sam felt like he was holding his breath. He let it out slowly.

"He's coming out of it, Mr. Jensen, sir. His color is coming back."

ACCELERATION

"Good. Mr. President? Wilson? Do you hear me? It's Silas. We've just given you your medicine. You forgot to take it this morning."

"I'm better."

Sam recognized the President's smooth simpering voice. "Thank you, Silas. I knew you would fix me up." Suddenly his personality changed and he fired out his words at machine-gun speed. "What does the media say? Are they talking sympathy? Am I up in the polls?"

"Mr. President," Silas returned coldly. "You may let go of my tie, so that I can answer your questions. Thank you. Yes, everyone is worried and your polls are up. They love you, Mr. President."

"Good, Men, I'm ready to leave. Call my security council. We need to plan the attack. Silas, where are my pills? I need my pills!" He screamed out.

Sam could hear the bed being torn apart. A pillow fell against the partition. Sam prayed that it would continue standing. It did.

"Your men stole them from me, Jensen. Give them back or I'll have you killed." The President's voice had become shrill with panic.

"Relax, Mr. President, you're upset for no reason. Your pills are now in your pocket. See, I am putting them in, right now. Remember to take them. Now sit here and relax while we prepare for your departure."

"Jensen, you are my friend, aren't you?"

"Of course. In fact, I think we should move up our plans for the military. I think we should meet with our faithful congressmen and generals and discuss the infiltrations and the coup. Can you clear your schedule for next Monday, Mr. President? I don't think we should fool with the elections at all. You are too good for the American people. You don't need to subject yourself to their whims."

The President simpered proudly. "I believe you are correct. I'll show them to not belittle and laugh at me. Move up our plans. I'll arrange for the holiday, on your splendid yacht. Yes, I like that, I do."

A door opened. A different voice spoke. "Mr. Jensen, the halls are cleared of reporters. We can exit smoothly to the front lobby. Do you wish to talk with them there? And perhaps you would like to reassure them of your good health, Mr. President?"

"I would like that," said the President.

A gaggle of footsteps then plodded out of the room.

Sam felt the perspiration beads roll down the sides of his face. That was too close, he thought, as he stretched his aching muscles as best he could. He hoped the nurse hadn't totally forgotten him. He wondered nervously on how they had disposed of the doctor. The man meant well, he was only doing his job.

One thing was sure. President Quint was psychotic from the drugs. What did the rest mean? Infiltrate who or what? Who else was involved? He didn't like the sound of what he heard. The hornet's nest was growing.

It seemed like hours, but he knew it had only been minutes. The little jittery nurse returned and popped her head from behind the screen. "That was frustrating but exciting. They're gone. Did you hear anything juicy?"

"No, just the usual pleasantries. Can you undo these straps now? I feel much better?" Sam smiled charmingly.

"I don't know. I should ask the doctor first, but I can't find him."

"Please. I need to use the john, and I'm embarrassed." Sam said sweetly. This ploy worked before, maybe it will work again, he thought.

"Oh, I understand. Well, I guess it will be all right. If I help you down, do you need more help in the john? I need to also check the other patients. I'm the only one here right now. I hope the doctor comes back. I can't take care of this place alone." She ran out flustered, then darted back

"Oh, your straps, yes. She unfastened them and helped him to his feet. "Can you walk?" She squinted at him with her eyes and her plump face crinkled in concern.

Sam leaned on her briefly and slipped the keys from her pocket. He straightened and grinned. Thanks, Miss. I'll be fine. You're a wonderful nurse."

"Oh, thank you. I try hard. I'll come back and check on you," She smiled broadly and scurried out of the room.

Sam waited only a second, then examined the waste container where the doctor had tossed the empty ampule he had used for Sam's injection. Sam hoped he had found the right one. It looked correct. He peeked out the door and then slowly walked down the hall, eying each door's name until he got to the pharmacy area. No one was there. He slipped among the shelves and found the correct ampule, then grabbed a couple of extras and some syringes. He hoped that they were the correct ones. He had the directions and info pamphlets also. They would have to do. He grabbed some pills that seemed to have the same name, just in case.

Sam was about to walk out when he thought of the poor nurse without her keys. He slipped back into his room and dropped the keys on the floor by the bed.

Done. It sure was quiet here now.

He made his way to the lobby and found Heather and Eddie curled up in the chairs facing each other. He knelt and tapped them quietly. Heather opened her lovely eyes, and then jumped up with a start.

"Sam," she yelped, "you're here. Are you okay now?"

"Sort of." He nudged Eddie. "Eddie and Heather, let's go. Don't talk."

Eddie yawned and then scrambled up. Bewildered but obedient, he followed.

They silently passed through the empty lobby, which had only a short time ago been a bubbling mass of reporters and presidential aides.

The sun was now up. It looked like it would be a clear day, a good day for a new plan. Sam definitely needed a new plan.

CHAPTER 30

As Sam drove the endless roads back to the University, he realized nothing had really changed. He knew, however, that he wanted to drag no one else into it. He was taking the kids home. He then would find Jensen and destroy him and his plans. He had to learn the location of Jensen's yacht first. Perhaps Elizabeth Martin could help him out there. Surely she had an investigative team behind her. Also, she might have changed her feelings about Sam's story after encountering all the wrenches to her inquiries. And he desperately wanted to see Alex and Sarah one more time. He hoped Doctor Hernandez had found an antidote or cure for Sarah. He grew frightened at the thought that she might have died while he was gone. NO, he would have felt it, she was still alive. Could he even hope that a cure would be found for the President? That was probably too much positive thinking.

He sipped from a paper coffee cup as the icy hills rolled by. What had the President meant by meeting with the congressmen and power magnets? Were there more people involved? Infiltrations were meant for who? Innocent people again, he cringed at the thought. Was the attack just the ravings of drug-induced insanity? Sam felt his head was spinning. When would it end? When would the questions all be answered in neat packages?

Sam popped a couple of antibiotic pills into his mouth and gulped down the last of his caffeine.

"Heather, we'll be at the house in a few minutes. I need you to call your Mom. Do you want to do that?"

"Won't she just make trouble?" She said bitterly. "My mother in not ethical."

"But she craves a good story. She has no fear about where to tread. That is obvious from her reports. I think she is on our side without admitting it."

"You've forgiven her, haven't you? Sam, she almost had you killed. I can't talk to her again. I hate her."

"Honey…" Sam pulled the car into the drive and turned. "We need her. It will work out for the best, at least I hope." His eyes seemed to smile. "You two are very much alike, both independent, stubborn, and extremely attractive."

Heather gave a half smile in return. "You think so. I always did like older men."

ACCELERATION

"I'm flattered." His light mood vanished suddenly as he gazed at the darkened Victorian house that had been his home over the bitter winter months. It's heavy cream shutters glared back, as if he were an intruder from the future.

Sam inserted his key and entered the old home with foreboding. Heather and Eddie followed.

Something was wrong. He felt it. It was as if no one had lived there in weeks, dust now covered the tables and sills. He bounded the stairs to the bedrooms. They had been stripped clean; only the barren furniture remained downstairs. Closets were empty. Beds were perfectly neat and unrumpled. He felt like he was in an early American museum. Here lived the Sinclairs from two hundred years ago, he thought. They disappeared and were never heard from again. His mind kept rambling the nonsense. He went back down the stairs, with the kids faithfully following. He searched for the hospital number. He had lost his cell phone so used his home's land line. Alex always like this old phone. Now he was happy they kept it. Sam put in the hospital number and asked to speak to the mother of the young girl in room 607. The mother is Alex Sinclair. The child's name is Sarah. Her doctor was Hernandez." He paced, then sat down, waited, and tapped his foot involuntarily.

He froze. What if she died? She was admitted two weeks ago. He knew he shouldn't have left. They were all alone, and he had deserted them for his stupid quest to establish his innocence and gain revenge. He stood up and paced a small path in the living room.

Suddenly the operator came back on. "I'm sorry. Dr. Hernandez has left the staff. We also have or had no patient by that name."

Sam felt stunned and panicky. "Lady, I saw them, and the little girl was dying."

"You must have the wrong hospital. Try another town," the operator continued.

"You are the one who is wrong, ma'am. Where is the doctor working now?" said Sam.

"I believe he left no information on that," the operator said and hung up.

Sam slammed down the phone. "There's no further information on the doctor." Sam said as he stared out, dazed. "The lady said that Sarah never was there."

Heather spoke in a small voice. "I'm sorry, Sam. What do we do now?"

ACCELERATION

"I don't know. Go home." He leaned his large frame against the dusty window with the pink flowered drapes. "Alex loved these silly curtains," he said. "She said that they made her feel like picnics and cotton candy." He remembered that she had followed those words with virginal, and winked. Sam squeezed his eyes shut. "Heather, I'm sorry. I can't do any more. Please go home. Thank you, for all you and Eddie have done for me."

Heather rested her small hand on Sam's arm. "I'll call my mom and make her listen. We'll be back. Right, Eddie?"

"Yes," Eddie said quietly and trotted after Heather.

Sam listened to their retreating footsteps and the creaking of their closing the heavy front door. Where were Alex and Sarah? The house had brought the three of them together as a family. He looked around at its century old interior. Now it meant only painful memories.

Pacing the empty hallway and longing for the past staggered Sam. He had to get out. He ran out the door and down the stoop. He circled the two story structure. It's very presence haunted him. He pulled away and staggered to the ancient apple tree, now naked in the freezing snow. He knew how it felt, exposed to forces it couldn't control. Sarah had tried to climb this mother of trees. He ran his hand along the tough bark. It was only three months ago. Sam looked up and memory pictures and sounds assailed him.

"Daddy Matt," Sarah had giggled, "push me up!" Her little arms had tried to reach the thick branch, but each time she jumped up, it was a near miss.

"Sarah, you're too little," your mother has said.

"No, I'm not. Daddy Matt will you help me." She had stretched out her arms expectantly.

Sam had boosted her up and turned to Alex. He had only taken his eyes off the bubbling child for a minute, when she fell. There were no broken bones, but the tears were very real. It tore him up to see her sob in her mommy's arms. Alex had kissed and bandaged the bumped and cut arm, and Sarah was off, ready to challenge the monster tree again. She was fearless, and he was in awe of her childish courage, but he was shaken by the accident. Sarah had seemed so fragile to him. Could he protect her from evil? Alex had teased that he was just like a new father. Sarah was a strong cookie, she had bantered.

Alex and Sam had flopped on the frozen ground near the evergreens that speckled the yard. The late November wind had swirled about their light jackets and tossed their hair.

ACCELERATION

Sarah had found a stray orange striped Tom cat and pursued his every turn. The Tom had patiently settled under a spindly bush. Then Sarah had curled beside it and talked blissfully to the cat's marble eyes. The Tom cat gazed clearly back, as if he understood her giddy chatter.

Alex had cuddled under Sam's husky arm and rested her head on his broad chest. "It's electric and rather sexy, isn't it? And cold."

"What?" Sam mumbled comfortably.

"Winters in the Midwest." Alex said, as she glanced over to see Sarah, who continued her cat communion. Alex put her hand under Sam's shirt, pulled it up, and kissed him hungrily. She paused after a moment, leaned back and propped herself on her arm. She ran her fingers over Sam's mouth. "I am very attracted to you, Mr. Stone. It's pure animal attraction with an awful lot of love thrown in. Am I being deceitful to Caroline's memory. You can tell me to leave this platonic if you like, but it will be hard on me, Sam."

Sam sat up. "Stone is another person. His life is over for now, along with Caroline's. We are different people here." Sam turned, braced himself, and held his weight above her. "I like you a lot, Alex." He lowered himself and kissed her tenderly.

"Momma, the big kitty likes me," Sarah knelt down beside them.

"Oops," Sam said as he rolled off Alex.

"Sarah, that's nice." Alex was flustered also. "Come on, Daddy Matt, let's see the big kitty." She scrambled up and took Sam's hand, as she pulled him up. "Later for us," she whispered in his ear. She noted Sarah scampering ahead. Alex roamed her hand flirtatiously over Sam's body and played with the snap on his jeans. "Tonight at 10 P.M., my place, the only adult bed." She popped open the snap.

Sam smiled. "It's a date." He pulled up her slim hand and clasped it firmly. With his free hand, he closed the fastening. They then joined their excited child.

Sam shook away his memories and turned away from the trees. It was a sad-looking house now, and he was discouraged.

Sam settled back on the old oak bed. It creaked noisily, as he pulled his arms under his head and interlocked his fingers. He thought for a moment, then stretched out his arms and smiled. Alex and he had tried to stifle the creaks but seldom succeeded. Once they had held their laughter 'til they were ready to explode.

Sarah had awakened and jumped between them. She wanted to be told the joke. They then told her every children's riddle and gag that they could think of.

He inhaled deeply of the memory. They had giggled, and Sarah had bounced up and down with glee. Finally, she had kissed her mommy and Daddy Matt on the cheeks and he carried this lovely child to her little bed. They had all been happy then, except for the nightmares.

Sam remembered. They had had no problem at the beginning, but Alex was tortured nightly by the vision of her father's brain floating about the room. She described huge eyes bulging and erupting from the throbbing mass. She thought that it watched her during sleep and times awake. She felt like it followed her everywhere. She would often cry herself to sleep hysterically. She couldn't keep it from Sarah.

"Momma's seeing the monster again, Daddy Matt!" Sarah would rush to the den as Sam was reading late, and she would bury herself in his lap. Sam would comfort her and carry her up to Alex. Alex would see Sarah's tears and stop her own. She would reach out. Sam would crawl into bed also and together they cuddled Sarah between them.

At other times, Sam would hear Alex crying and mount the stairs in seconds. He would often find her in a corner, covering her head with her arms. "He's here," Alex would sob. "Father is mad at me for not letting him live. I killed him!"

Sam had caressed her soft brown hair and eased her bangs away from her delicate pale features, now damp with tears. "Honey, you did nothing wrong. He killed himself way before you found him that night. Please, you have to stop blaming yourself. Blame me instead, or better yet, Silas. Silas encouraged the experiments and helped make your dad into this horrible remembrance. It was also your dad's fault. He didn't realize how bad things would become for him and how wrong it was to go further. Alex, think of him instead as he was before, he would want that. He loved you, he wouldn't want to leave you like this. And he's very happy buried under that tree that he had planted. You did good."

Alex would grow quiet. He would then scoop her up and carry her to the bed to rest. Sam would say, "Sarah, go play in your room while I take care of Mommy."

ACCELERATION

Sarah would plant a sweet kiss on her mother's anguished face and then very seriously enter and close the door to her room. She was a good little girl.

Alex experienced the ritual repeatedly. It had begun occasionally in the night and then occurred daily, and finally it would happen a couple of times each day. But when the news started splashing the reports on Sam Stone by Elizabeth Martin, the visions began to cease. It was as if she was brought back to reality. Alex got better and became carefree and truly happy in the big old house.

It was strange that as Alex improved, Sam began to get worse. The past began to relive itself in the nightly broadcasts. To him, he was living a lie. To Alex, her life with him became a lovely dream come true.

Alex blossomed when she helped him plan his lectures and grade his mountains of paperwork. She was a true Professor's wife now, a storybook life. They would conscientiously fulfill their roles.

Sam even began writing again. He wondered about the manuscript for his new novel. Was it still hidden in the den? He thought of Alex and how she had perched herself at the table and eagerly awaited each new handwritten page. She identified with the young lovers in the story. The character of Alice was her. Alex said that through Alice, she realized that a person is never too old to forget or identify with young love. She cried and then smiled mysteriously when Alice and lover Ethan had grown old in the story. She thought it was an exquisite ending for all love. She said once that she would never grow old with anyone, however. She just felt it. She had walked over to him at that time and embraced him sadly. He had seen a faraway look in her eyes when she broke away. She had laughed and said that she had to have everything in life now, and she couldn't wait.

Sam rubbed his face and gasped for air. He felt that he was smothering, and that the walls were swallowing him. He yanked himself from the bed and suddenly hesitated. Could that story, that Alex liked so much, could it still be in their secret place? He walked through the empty house which seemed to reverberate with memories with each lonely step. Sam didn't want to wake those memories, but he felt driven to see if the story was still there, or if it was all a dream.

Was it in its special place? He pulled up the edge of the faded carpet under the roll-top desk. Alex had called it their magic carpet, which would hide all their secrets. The manuscript had been nearly completed. He slid it out and settled in the old chair. He reread it, page after page until there was no more.

Sam then moved over to the huge black manual typewriter. He inserted a sheet of paper. He stared at the white page. He had handwritten the manuscript, and now he wanted to type the ending. But was it too late now? He didn't know how to end his story. It needed an epilogue or ending. His eyes fixed upon the large glowing moon, suspended over his little kingdom. He brushed his hair away from his eyes. It had grown long, he felt he would get it cut soon. Most of the grey dye had washed out, now to get rid of the moustache and he could stop hiding. He reached into a bottom drawer of the desk and pulled out an electric razor. Alex had put it there, saying that she wanted to shave away the disguise when they were free of the past. No point in waiting now, she was gone. He ran the razor over his face and brushed the remains into the waiting trash container. He slid his hand along the face of the old Sam Stone. Welcome back, he thought. I missed you fellow.

He lay his fingers on the keys of the typewriter. He grinned as he remembered Alex again.

"Oh, more, give me more," she had demanded at the typewriter with her arms extended. "I'll give you a plenty good time if you do, handsome." She had batted her eyelashes and shaken her short curls. "You can't resist me, I hope."

"No, Beautiful, I can't," he quipped, as he threw her the newly scribbled pages." She would scramble for them and eagerly read them with delight.

Once she had crawled onto his lap, as he sat watching an old sad western on the television. She kept scanning his face and wiping the tears that were forming in his eyes until he had thrown her over onto the floor in embarrassment. She had stayed there spread-eagle and very serious. She said that it was good to see a grown man mist over when he watches death, even if it was only on television. It showed he had heart. She said she liked that and had yanked him down to join her on the floor. They had consummated their love many times over, but that night was special. He had let his guard down and showed his feelings, and she had welcomed them.

When they were both exhausted, Alex had asked Sam to write her a poem. He had said he was lousy at poetry. Together they had created a silly verse, indulgent with verbs. He'd forgotten it now, he wished he had written it down.

ACCELERATION

Sam rose and lit a fire in the cold damp den. He watched the flames snap hungrily at the wood and then seemed to be dying out. He had set the logs in place weeks ago. It was the night when Sarah had gotten sick. He had intended to help her build her snowman the following day. Now that will never happen. He poked angrily at the dying embers. A flame ignited briefly with life.

Sarah loved having a fire in the fireplace. She kept saying how much she loved her mommy and Daddy Matt. She saw Silas once on the television and said that daddy was dead and in heaven with Grandpa. Alex had never really told her that Grandpa had died or Silas. She had just said the Grandpa was not coming back. Sarah had created her own happy explanation that Jesus had come, and he had walked happily away with him. Alex was relieved. It was for the best. She never corrected her daughter's illusion. And who knows, perhaps after he was buried, she was right.

Sam was getting sleepy. He stared at the flames in the fireplace. Sarah's form seemed to coalesce and lay down on the floor beside Sam. She seemed to be coloring in her booklet intently. Alex sat across from her in a chair, trying to figure out how to knit. Alex finally grabbed a marshmallow from a bag that she had been eating from, and plopped on the floor. She carefully stuck the ball of marshmallow fluff onto one of her knitting needles and said cooking was more to her liking. She had then held the marshmallow over the fireplace flames and set it ablaze atop the needle. Sam had slid down on the floor and joined them. They had blown out the flame excitedly on the marshmallow and stuck their fingers in the sticky warm goo. They roasted more of the gooey balls and devoured them in delight. Sarah then had jumped up, said she was a big girl now, kissed them both, and walked sleepily up the stairs to bed. Alex and Sam had continued their picnic. They ate from each other's fingers. It had become another moment of intimacy.

Sam stared as the flames shrank and disappeared. He felt melancholy wrap it's heavy quilt around his senses now. He didn't want reality or sleep. He wanted to wake the happy remembrances and live again those cherished moments. The ugliness of reality would raise its deformed head and shake his stability and happiness soon enough. But sleep came, and he was right. He would wake to his sad reality. But he knew that Alex, Caroline, and Sarah would not want him to give up. Neither would Ben, Heather, and Eddie. He wasn't totally alone. He wouldn't give up. But, Alex and Sarah, where are you?

Sarah's sweet face dissolved into dust. "Daddy Matt!" she screamed. The voice change to that of Alex, and then of Silas Jensen as he sarcastically mimicked the words, "Daddy Matt!" Sam clutched at his face and searched the darkness. Something woke him. There it was again. It was a telephone and very real. Sam almost knocked the old telephone over as he grabbed the receiver. Relief chased away the cloud of ugly blackness and confusion as he recognized the voice.

"Sam, are you awake? It's me, Heather."

"Sam cleared his sleep away, "Hi. Yes, Heather?"

"I talked to my mom," she gushed excitedly. "She says that Jensen's yacht is in Los Angeles at the Marina...ah...?

"Del Rey?" Sam filled in.

"Yeah, that's the one. She hadn't heard about a big meeting there. She wants to meet you again."

"Oh sure. No! I don't think I'd like to do that. Tell her to interview some other fool, try Jensen."

"Funny? I said just that, Sam. She said she tried to see Jensen. She also said that President Quint has been behaving strangely and that all the news people have been talking about him. She thinks your theory might now be correct. She wants to apologize to you in person." Heather trailed off.

"No," Sam said quietly.

"Okay. Can I come over?"

"No." Sam wanted to see no one. Anyway, he'd be leaving in the morning.

"Sam?" Heather gathered back her confidence. "The news people and the cops think you're dead. They found a body washed up on the lake front in Chicago. It had two police bullets in it. Jensen identified the body as yours."

"Man, he is crazy and maybe desperate." Sam was sincerely shocked. This was a direction he hadn't expected from Jensen, but then Jensen was full of surprises. "He possibly wants to dissipate the media attention. Thanks for the information. I plan to be gone in the morning. Heather, I'll never forget all you've done for me."

"I hope you never forget me. I like you a lot, Sam." Her voice sounded so vulnerable.

"I know, honey. Thanks. I care about you too, but as a very special friend. Stick with Eddie, he's got guts and a lot of promise. I hope to read your prize winning books someday."

ACCELERATION

"When this is over," Heather continued softly, "and if I finish my great American novel, will you read it?"

"You bet, Miss St. John. By the way, how come you don't go by Martin?"

"St. John is my writing pseudonym. It has mystery, don't you think?" Heather giggled.

"Ah, yes, it does. I like it. I have to go now. I'll talk to you again when it's all over. By Miss Heather St. John." Sam hung up the phone.

"I bet you will write a famous novel, Heather," Sam thought, "but it will probably be a pot-boiler of intrigue." It was hard not to like Heather. He stretched in his chair. But he felt every bit of his years.

Then all hell shattered his sanctuary.

CHAPTER 31

Actually, it was worse than hell. It was real.

Gunfire began exploding through the windows of the house. Splinters coated Sam's hair and back, as he hurled himself to the floor. He crawled through the glass fragments

in the hallway. He bit back the pain as glass sliced into his extremities. He had almost made it to the doorway, when suddenly armed men hauled him to his feet and threw him up against the wall. Fists slammed into his face and chest. Over and over they repeated the blows. Sam choked with spasms. They tossed his blood spattered body to the glass encrusted floor. A shoe stepped on Sam's head as he lay coughing and retching.

"Hey, friend," the voice of the shoe rasped out vehemently. "You need help? Too bad." The shoe then kicked, as Sam wrenched his face from its path."

"You are dead, you know," the voice simpered, "so I can do what I want with you, hot shot. This is for stealing my wife." He kicked Sam in the back. "This is for my kid." He aimed his foot again. "And this is for me!"

ACCELERATION

This time Sam grabbed his foot and tipped his tormentor, yes Jensen, backwards. He spilled him noisily onto the treacherous carpet of glass shreds and smashed his face into it. His hate raged but was short lived. Jensen's men reacted and cracked their weapons twice on Sam's skull. He remembered the first shock of pain, but the second exploded his brain into immediate unconsciousness. He hoped the battle would end but not this way.

Sam awoke to the surprise that he still lived. He was again in his den, and he remembered it was no dream. Sam's face and body were swimming in pain and he was bound to his chair by leather straps.

He forced his head up and words through his swollen lips. He stared at the face of Jensen. "Hum, thoughtful of you, to bring your own fashionable leather straps."

Jensen leered at him. The lights were suddenly bright in the room. Sam squinted through his cut flesh and lowered his head.

"Lights hurt your eyes, Bastard? Good. Let me watch." Jensen roared. "Who do you think you are that you can try to beat me? You think you can walk in and destroy all I've worked for. You think you can then disappear. To hell with you!"

Sam felt his head being jerked up by his hair. He sputtered. "Don't you think your jealousy is pretentious. And that entrance not classy."

Jensen answered by twisting his hands in Sam's hair.

Sam breathed deeply. "If you hate me so much, just kill me now and have it done with. If you don't, I'll have to eliminate you. I promise you that, old buddy."

"You do?" Jensen hissed. "I was never your buddy. I hated you back in college. You with your women and your success. You never had to work, it was handed to you."

"Wrong," Sam said. "I worked hard. You were just too green with envy to see it. You were a loser and still are." Sam clenched his teeth with hatred. "You can't just plot and experiment against the laws of God and nature, then murder the innocent, and go free. You'll die just like Hitler. If I don't get you, someone else will."

"There is no one else." Jensen's eyes glinted in the bright lights. "Stone, I think I'll keep you alive. I want to observe you squirm and die inside a bit each day. I have a network and power that you could never imagine. It will defeat you to watch."

ACCELERATION

Sam leveled his gaze into Hensen's dark hungry eyes. "What are you trying to prove in the end? Is it all for power?"

"Oh, I already have that." Jensen preened.

"The authorities will get you." Sam countered.

"I own the authorities, as you say." Jensen roared with crazed laughter.

"All right. Where are Alex and Sarah? Did you hurt Alex? I know you hurt Sarah, you bastard."

"Shut up…Later. I may tell you later. Maybe." Jensen cooed. "Let's watch your little

television." He fondled the control switch. "I'm missing my favorite programs."

"What are they?"

"Shut up, I say. I watch the news." He smirked and leaned forward.

Sam saw something he hadn't noticed before. Jensen had covered it beautifully to the casual observer, but here in the confines of a normal living environment, it raged. The guy was insane with obsession. He wanted power to own people. He wanted control like a pimp, but his junkies were world leaders. He lied, he didn't just want limited power. He wanted it all.

"Jensen," Sam said with exhaustion, "How many more people are addicted to your drugs?"

"My little vitamins?" Jensen laughed obscenely. "Thousands."

"The drug is unstable; you'll never hold what you want," said Sam calmly.

"I was doing fine until you came along. I will continue until we've secured our position."

"What position, and how will you do that?" Sam said.

"You'll see. Shut up." Jensen turned towards the broadcast and pumped up the volume until it blasted in Sam's ears.

"This is Elizabeth Martin in Chicago. The body of Sam Stone has been definitely identified by his closest friend, Silas Jensen of the FBI. The writer was experiencing severe emotional problems, which led to his killing his brother and Jensen's wife and daughter. The hospital tragedy was the insane man's rampage.

The case is officially closed. We now turn to exciting news from our Congress and President Quint. A gala dinner is planned off the California coast to reward the leaders for a job well done in balancing the budget. Also, military expenditures have been increased so as to defend our great nation against foreign terrorists from the world's hot spots. I hope to bring in our cameras and film the gala celebration for you. This is Elizabeth Martin from Washington."

"I like her, don't you? Silas Jensen looked far too happy.

"Then there must be something wrong with her." Sam snipped.

"Elizabeth and I have known each other for a long time. She's only beginning to benefit from my hard work. In fact, Stone, you brought us together."

"Me? Oh, I see, when I asked to see her. So she's your girlfriend. When did you get her hooked on your poisoned vitamins?"

"They are miracle pills. Why do you say my girlfriend? Jensen was actually puzzled.

"On the news. I gave her more credit than she deserved. You called her honey on the air. She became irritated. I figured she didn't like the condescension. I didn't realize it was because she was your whore."

Jensen's face clouded. "Shut up, Stone." He stood up and took his red handkerchief from a once dapper suitcoat which was now streaked with blood. He wadded the cloth and jammed it into Sam's mouth.

Sam gaged and choked for a time. Then he breathed easier and watched Jensen.

Jensen tore out the telephone cord and wrapped it around Sam's head and over the cloth.

Sam's eyes filled with hate.

"You don't like not talking, do you? Do you, Stone? Get comfortable; you probably have charmed your last woman and certainly written your final book. You look funny. The great Sam Stone, is all trussed up like a piece of garbage." He snorted and turned to a new station.

"Cartoons! You wouldn't think that I would enjoy them, but I do. You learn a lot about
winning. I never lose." Jensen became transfixed with a Road Runner cartoon and roared with glee.

Sam started testing his bindings. Jensen noticed.

"Oh, you won't get free." Jensen said gleefully. "By the way, no one will come to this house. The whole neighborhood has been lured away on a hoax. They got the word that a truck with poisonous gas had tipped over a short distance away. See all the work I went to, Stone. I know you don't deserve it." He laughed too loudly again and returned to his program.

Sam waited and wondered what the men in the next room must be doing. And he worried about what this mad man's next big move would be?

"I like how they put my shows on so late at night. Cartoons aren't just for kids, you know. Actually, I pulled some strings to get this program. Many people would thank me, if they knew. They will eventually, but not yet. It was nice of you to wait so patiently on my whims. My show is over now," Jensen said smoothly. Then his face turned ugly. "Let's go." He called his men.

"No drugs this time. I want you to feel every painful moment, Stone." Sam was dragged outside and thrown down into the snow. The coldness numbed his swollen bruised face. He almost wished they'd leave him there, but he doubted he would be so lucky. Hell, he sure must have been in worst messes, well maybe."

Sam heard Jensen talking on a phone. Then the noise of two helicopters drowned his senses. The blades whipped the wind into a blinding frenzy as it landed. Sam tried to see through the shower of snow. It was some kind of hi-tech military copter.

He would travel in style, he hoped. That feeling was quickly negated as he was pitched to the floor in the first copter. Jensen took the second one. Huge army boots held him down in the small enclosure. It was going to be a hell of a ride somewhere. He wondered if Jensen was toying with him. Was he really keeping him alive or would he just drop him off in midair? He probably would have obliged if it had been Jensen on the floor instead. But then, Jensen wanted him around. Sam felt better, that was a stupid move on Jensen's part- the wanting him around. Jensen had made other mistakes. He'd kill Jensen and his terrible plans, but first he had to find Alex and Sarah.

Sam's head ached. Better to sleep while he could, if it was possible that is- with the huge foot in his face. He would sure like to amputate that guy from "his" face.

CHAPTER 32

Heather and Eddie had come too late. Looking around, they doubted Sam had survived.

The door had been open and swinging in the night wind when they arrived. They had evaded the mass evacuation and had hidden in the shadows of the homes they knew well. They doubted the general populace had heard the gunfire; the townspeople were too far away. Heather had cried as the guns shattered the house.

"Oh, God, Eddie, they're killing him." She had buried her head in Eddie's arms and sobbed in silence.

They didn't dare be caught; it would do Sam no good. They had crouched long after the helicopters had gone and the cars departed. They had seen a bound and gagged body dragged and dumped onto the floor of the copter. They hoped that Sam had lived and that they would not see him dumped from the sky. The young people were too far away to be sure.

Crunching their feet along the glass, they gingerly entered each room. Heather never let go of Eddie's hand. She feared that if she let go, the spell would be broken and they would find Sam's bullet riddled body or those of his wife and child. They saw the marks of struggle in the hallway and the blood. Heather let go of her lifeline, Eddie, and sprang to the bathroom. She leaned over the sink and waited for her body's revulsion to subside.

"Heather," Eddie said simply, "do you want me to look around and you wait outside?"

"Heather looked out with grief-stricken eyes and pale face. "Yes, please."

Eddie guided her to the back door. She collapsed her body on the small step. She couldn't quite believe that the night could now be so quiet. The air should be vibrating from shock, but instead it was as if nothing had happened. It seemed to say that the old house had always been shattered to its core by violence. The wreckage would be brushed aside by the cruel elements, as if it never existed. It did, however, exist for now. How can the government cover up this brutal intrusion and destruction? She sighed in despair and wandered aimlessly among the trees. That's when she saw it. Heather screamed, and she couldn't seem to stop.

Eddie exploded from the house and grabbed her shoulders. "What is it? Stop it!" Then he too saw it, his mouth fell open. He wanted to yell also, but he couldn't seem to move.

ACCELERATION

Hanging from a tree was the body of a young lovely woman with soft brown curls.

"Please, don't tell me that it's Mrs. Sinclair, Alex." Heather gasped out the words.

"Heather, I think it is. There's a sign on her. Oh, shit."

"What does it say?" Heather couldn't look at those eyes or Alex. They were frozen open.

"It-ah- says- bitch."

Eddie turned and grabbed Heather. "Let's go back to the house."

"Eddie, we can't just leave her there." Heather couldn't seem to stop crying.

"We better leave her for the authorities," said Eddie quietly.

"The authorities! They probably did this!" Heather shrieked.

"Heather, stop it!" Eddie shook her violently. "You are losing control. You can't do that, not now."

"Oh, Eddie. Do you think Sam knew she was here?"

"No, I don't think so, but I could be wrong."

"What do we do now?" She looked helplessly up at Eddie, whose glasses sparkled in the moonlight. "Should we call my mom?"

"No. Heather, I have a bad feeling about your mom and this thing."

"You think she caused this? You're crazy. My mom may be sly, but she wouldn't intentionally hurt someone." Heather felt helpless. She hated that feeling. "Eddie, you've got to be wrong."

"She almost got Sam killed before."

"I know but she…she apologized."

"Oh, yeah, that really helps if you're dead. Just say, "Hey man, I'm really sorry," Eddie said sarcastically.

"You're making fun of me." Heather sat right where she had stood, there in the middle of the alabaster snow-covered yard.

Eddie knelt beside her. "I'm acting like a jerk. I apologize."

She absently scooped up a handful of flakes of snow and tossed them up into the shadowy night. "There's a dead lady over there, and I'm feeling sorry for myself. I'm sorry. Poor Sam."

"Yeah. Come on. Let's get out of here." Eddie said sadly.

"Where to?" said Heather plaintively.

"Away from here. Sam said you might get hurt if you tried to help. I think he was right. You stay here. I'm going to California."

ACCELERATION

"Without me, no you're not." Heather jumped up.

"Heather," he turned her to him. "What if your mother is a big part of the wrong side? Could you turn her in?"

"I …I don't know."

"You'll have to decide first." He waited. "I know it's a pretty lousy decision to make."

"Yes, it is." Heather felt awful. "But if it's true, she needs help and I want to be there for her."

"She may be too far along for you to help."

"Darn it! Okay, I'd turn her in. Is that what you want to hear?" She pulled away.

"Not really. I want to hear that you'll stay out of it."

"Eddie," Heather turned and stood still. "I am in it. Let's stop being hypothetical and get some facts. Don't worry about me, I won't cave in on you again. And…I won't cop out. I'm in. I'm also freezing, let's head for the car."

"Heather!" Eddie stopped her. "I'm crazy about you."

"Isn't everyone?" Heather smiled. "Did I really say that?" She planted a quick kiss on his lips and stomped her way through the snow.

Eddie pushed his glasses further up on his nose and followed her in a gallop. He felt like a very unlikely hero at the moment. He hoped that the strangling in his chest would go away. He doubted it. It probably would be there for some time.

"Heather, wait up!" His voice bounced off of the deserted house and was absorbed by the indifferent night.

CHAPTER 33

Sam was beginning to feel a huge cramp in his leg. But, his stretching seemed to activate his captor's foot. It began kicking his head.

Suddenly, in a flurry of movement, Sam heard the side door being dragged open. The wind roared in response and tore through the plane. Sam was suddenly jerked up and over to the gapping opening.

"Stone, we want you to remember your flight," Kreider shouted. "You will fly now without using your arms, legs, or even a plane." Kreider roared with laughter.

"Hey, Buddy." Sam desperately yelled back as the raging wind slapped and stung his face. "You don't want to kill me." Sam's mind was whirling. Why? Why? There had to be a good reason, ah… "Tell Jensen I'll give him the diaries, and that I've changed my mind. Tell him that I'm scared and I don't want to die! Kreider, he'll lose everything and he doesn't like losing. Then you'll pay. He'll kill you. You need to at least tell him my offer."

"You're making this up!" Kreider shouted. "You don't want to die. I don't blame you. Terrible way to go, your brain and body all eaten by fish."

"Funny." Sam desperately threw his next words back. "Tell Jensen. Tell him now. He'll be very angry with you if you hold back this information. He may even splatter your stinking body to the fish instead. You won't like it either," Sam taunted. He hated this creep.

Kreider took his good old time making a decision.

Sam shivered in the freezing wind. Oh, man! Well, at least he wasn't still squashed on the floor! He wanted to laugh insanely. Instead he squirmed and fought his bindings... But he also saw Kreider talk to the pilot.

"Hold still!" A voice whined. "Your squirming ploy might be for nothing. I'm very clumsy. I may just drop you," Sam could see this guy's profile. It was a kid dressed to the teeth in military hardware.

"Thanks. Aren't you a bit young for a terrible life like this?"

"Ha! Nah. It will be a kick, dropping you from a plane," he said sarcastically.

ACCELERATION

"Oh, okay. It's nice to learn that it's not personal, I think." Sam was amazed that he was feeling so clever, while dangling on the edge of the clouds.

"I kinda like you, man. But, a job is a job. And I like it," the lanky kid gloated.

"There must be better kinds of employment," said Sam. "What does your mother say? Probably, my handsome son drops nice guys from helicopters."

"Leave my mom outa this… You think I'm handsome? Thanks, creep."

"Name's Stone. I like to be remembered as more than just a streak of blood in the water."

The kid cocked his head but said nothing.

"What'd you say your name was?" Sam said sweetly.

"Hell, I didn't and I ain't!" the kid shouted gleefully.

Sam turned his head as far as he could. "This is a dirty job. You should quit."

"Shut up," the kid's stocky partner grunted.

The pilot turned. "You can pull him back in. The guy's got a reprieve."

"Cap him up," Kreider snorted.

Sam was roughly yanked back and the familiar gag reinserted. This time he was
allowed a portion of the seat. The leather straps were tightened. But he figured it would be a short trip. Helicopters weren't made for long cross-country flights. However, he mused, some of the high tech ones go pretty far. Well, at least he's not hurling into into the mouths of hungry sharks, the fish kind that is.

Sam had nothing to do but think now. Questions with no answers tumbled fast. He guessed that his life as Sinclair was definitely over. So what of Alex and Sarah? It hurt too much to think of them. We're they dead or alive? Could he hope to see them ever again? He suddenly shivered uncontrollably. He should have brought a coat. Like he had time to get a coat. Maybe remembering Alex will make him forget his physical misery. He could almost smell her sweetness, lying beside him. He could feel her touch on his body. Damn, Jensen, why couldn't you just leave us alone? You couldn't let us go. …No. Stop it, Sam. These thoughts won't help you escape. Forget the past for the moment. Think ahead. You may need to move fast soon.

ACCELERATION

Suddenly the copter began descending. He could see an airstrip with a solitary building below. Time to change planes. Suddenly Sam felt intensely sad again. He was leaving the memory of serene farm country, the university, his Victorian house, the school kids, and his beloved wonderful family. They were now in his past. He was Sam Stone, trying to change the future of his country and save people. He must be as crazy as the bad guys are. He braced himself for what lay ahead. Somehow he'd handle it. He had to.

PART III:

<u>COMBUSTION</u>

CHAPTER 34

The landing was uneventful. His guards untied Sam's ankles and pushed him onto the frozen dirt. He would have pried more info from the kid, but they neglected to take out his mouth stuffing. Sam tried sputtering for attention, but the guardians merely grunted their amusement and made no effort to ease or extract the irritating material in his mouth. Sam was then dumped into a large crate for safe keeping.

Time crawled. Hours passed. He decided that he must be feeling better because his stomach rumblings reminded Sam that he was damn hungry. How long had it been since he'd eaten? It was just before he'd entered town with the kids. It seemed so long ago. Sam started kicking the sides of the box. Hell, why not? Starvation was no way to treat the holder of Sean's precious diaries. Sam stretched as best he could. All he gained was a terrific headache and sore legs, like they weren't hurting already. Either the men had deserted him or they were ignoring his pesky ruckus. He wanted to know what was going on. He was beginning to hate mysteries, he mused sarcastically.

He thought about laughing insanely, but he still had his disgusting gag in his mouth. Jensen was definitely letting Sam squirm.

Sam dozed. Suddenly the crate was ripped open. He tried to focus, but a light blinded him. He grunted his protest and was greeted by the "joyous" removal of the hated rag in his mouth. He felt like vomiting immediately afterwards, however. His dry mouth took a moment to adjust. The gagging stopped, and he managed to whisper.

"Thanks, guys. I knew you cared."

Hands reached out and yanked Sam from his horrid box. A cup of water was held to his lips. He drank greedily.

"More, please," Sam voice croaked.

"You are polite. No more."

Sam was hauled to his feet and cut loose except for his hands. Arms from the darkness pushed him forward and into the inky depths of the outdoors.

Night, it was dark again. He had to have been in that crate for twenty-some hours. No wonder his body felt mistreated. He didn't feel like talking anymore, at least not without helpful responses.

ACCELERATION

Sam followed in silence, as he was led to a military aircraft that seemed to suddenly appear in the darkness. Bright ground lights quickly turned on and focused on the plane. It's wings and body were like gleaming black marble. He was prodded up the stairs and cuffed into a seat in the rear of the plane. Voices rattled from the front, but he could not understand the words. His stomach rumbled and reminded him that he could be human again. He was amused and wondered if they served meals on the flight. Sam's wish came true as a tray was set in front of him and his one hand released. The other was still cuffed to the chair, however. It was the usual airline prepackaged fare, but Sam downed it greedily. He even wished that he had a few more platefuls. It was definitely a good idea to feed the condemned man a last meal. He's less likely to make a fuss, Sam rationalized. The plane was now airborne, and no one deigned to chat. So he settled back. California might be its destination if they want the diaries. If so, it would take a while, so he might as well relax. Things will pick up later, he was sure of that.

His mind drifted aimlessly. I wonder if Ben still wants his house back. He should have paid him a huge cleaning fee. Or, is Alex stuck with the mess? Alex, they wouldn't hurt her. She must have been visiting friends. She's fine or is she? He had a sick feeling in his chest. He hadn't prayed in years, maybe he'd give it a try.

A voice interrupted. "I see that you're still alive. Why?"'

Sam opened his eyes, as Elizabeth Martin slid into a seat next to Sam.

"What a surprise," Sam said with shock. "You do get around, sweetheart." She was the last person he expected to run into on this flight.

"Don't call me that!" she snapped.

"You mean "sweetheart." Oh, macho revulsion. I should have guessed. So why glue yourself to a stinker like Jensen? Oh, I know, he pays well with his little pills."

"I used to think that way," said Martin. "But I've changed, and I like it. You'll see. Maybe you won't though. I don't really care." She took down her hair and flipped it about her face. "You men have begun to bore me."

"Give me a chance to change that. If you'll just unlock these pretty bracelets?" Sam said as he held up his handcuffs and taunted. He had definitely lost respect for this lady.

"I bet you are a male chauvinist," she eyed him haughtily.

"Try me." He smiled, but inside he felt revulsion.

"Maybe later." She uncrossed her legs seductively. "I'm not exactly unattractive or

inexperienced myself."

"No. I can see that." Sam placated with as much charm as he could muster, considering his battered body and the fact that he didn't trust her. She obviously was with Jensen and was part of his gang now.

"Did you sleep with my daughter?" she said quietly.

Sam was stunned by that question, but he recovered quickly. "No. She's a kid. Would that bother you as a mother or as a jealous female?"

"Both," she said as she leaned over and kissed him. She then crawled on top of him and began to pull open his clothes.

"Is this some kinky game you play?" Sam drank in the air.

"Suddenly Martin was pulled roughly from Sam. A hand impacted on her flesh with a sound that reverberated in the air. Martin gasped and shrank back into the seat across the aisle. Her eyes peeked through her tumbled hair like a wounded animal.

"Jensen, wouldn't like you messing with Stone. He's being saved," Kaupman sneered.

"Jensen doesn't tell me what to do. Don't you touch me again." Martin's voice trembled as she straightened her red silk dress.

"Ah. Excuse me. Would you mind terribly, if Ms. Martin put me back together," piped up Sam.

"Embarrassed, Mr. Stone? Allow me." Kaupman leered.

"I prefer her." Sam said with a wink.

"Yes, I'm sure you do. Go right ahead, lady." He laughed lewdly.

Martin slid seductively from her chair and slowly put Sam together, piece by piece. He had to admit to himself that he rather enjoyed it. His body felt like it would incinerate, if she touched him any longer.

"I'm finished," she whispered in his ear.

"Thank you." Sam mouthed the words.

"Anytime." She crawled out of the seat and stood in front of Kaupman.

"Enjoy the show? Too bad all you can do is watch." She reached out and grabbed a cup of coffee from an ogling guard's hand. Smiling shyly, she quickly dumped the steaming liquid into Kaupman's lap.

ACCELERATION

Kaupman howled and sputtered incoherently, as he sprang from his seat. He raised his fist at the willful woman who dared to humiliate him, but she had run down the aisle laughing maniacally.

"The bitch is crazy. I used to think she was one smart dame," Kaupman grunted as he brushed frantically at the hot coffee running down his trousers.

"Yeah. Well, I had a good time. Too bad she blistered your manhood." Sam couldn't help but reply.

It was a mistake. Sam knew it but he loved saying it. He did have a physical regret, however. Large hands pulled him up and nearly broke his neck with the whiplash from the blow. Not his face again, he gasped in his mind. It already hurt like hell. He then felt his arm being twisted and tried to see the syringe needle which was jammed into his vein.

"Jensen said I could start you on this, when I was sick of your face." Kaupman said.

"My face, yeah, me too, you." Sam's tongue felt thick. "What are you giving me?" he slurred.

"What you've always wanted to try. The stuff, Mr. Stone, the stuff."

Sam wanted to fire back that he'd already had the brief pleasure of the hellish drug, but his mouth wouldn't articulate. He suddenly was out.

Sam awoke feeling very seasick. Was it his head that was churning or the floor? "I'm sick!" He muttered through numb lips. He was surprised when a voice answered.

Yes, you are and you're going to feel much worse if you don't let me help you. Tell me. Where are the diaries?"

"Where am I?" Sam twisted in his chair and noticed that he had been divested of his clothes, and an intravenous solution was dripping into his arm. He stared at the wooden floor; it seemed to rise up and meet him.

"You are on a ship. You will go swimming soon; we didn't want your clothes to get wet."

Sam heard a chuckle and swallowed. "I'm cold. A blanket would be nice," he said.

"Your evasions won't work here. Where are the diaries?" The heavy man's sunburned face swam into Sam's view. "There aren't any, are there?"

"There are diaries," another voice said.

ACCELERATION

Sam knew what he was up against now. He remembered his military training and fought the drugs. He gritted his teeth and pulled back his head.

"Stone's resisting. This won't work. Just kill him." A thin anemic face came forward. "Jensen said to give you a few minutes only. Hurry up, fellow. We plan to drag you for the fish after we shoot you. You won't like it."

"No, I don't expect so. I'm sick, I'm going to throw up. I'm going to mess up your little boat. Oh, here it comes...." Sam screwed up his face.

Sunburn man sprang into action. "He's right. Un-cuff him. I don't want to scrub this boat or smell his mess. Let's get him up on top, come-on.

They dragged Sam's limp body to the top. Sam moaned and leaned into the scrawny anemic one and tripped him. Sunburn man reacted too late. Sam chopped his neck and then finished off Scrawny. Sam collapsed on the rail and breathed deeply. "You guys don't know how close you came to me barfing in your faces." He stayed on top for a while, despite the cold spray chilling his body. He needed to get the drugs out of his system and think. He looked at the empty horizon. "Where the hell am I? I'll figure it out." He turned and gazed at the small boat crew.

Skinny and Sunburn were still out. "Silas, you should have sent more men," muttered Sam, "Don't you know me yet? Well, actually that's good." Sam sighed and proceeded to strip the ship's unconscious men, tied them up, and put them in the ship's dingy. He felt it only right to reciprocate as he was treated, by the removing of their clothes. He lowered the raft and tied the tow rope to the ship's stern.

Sam turned back to the cabin. He was alone and the ship was anchored. He needed to study the maps and compass before he set off.

It was a clear night so the constellations should help his sense of direction. Sam played with the ship's radio and got mainly static.

He decided that now would be a good time to find his clothes, before he froze or he began to relish the nudist mentality. His jeans were in a heap with his blood stained shirt. Sam threw them back in the corner. He tried on the clothes removed from his guards. Sunburn's simple shirt and slacks weren't a bad fit. He tucked in the shirt and tried the shoes. The feet must have been tiny. He'd use Skinny's "gunboat" shoes instead. Thanks, fellows. At least you stayed rather clean.

ACCELERATION

Sam could hear the distraught bellowing from the crew in the dingy. He decided to ignore them. He figured his coordinates, plotted his course, and pulled up the anchor. They were off.

Sam steered all night. By dawn he was in sight of the harbor. He unwrapped the tow rope and set the raft adrift.

"I hope the sun doesn't burn your pretty skin, men. Have a good trip." Sam yelled and gave his best Navy salute.

Sam turned back to the map. There was a spot circled near Santa Barbara. Could the LA Marina have been a ruse or earlier decision which was changed? Sam corrected his course for Santa Barbara. The breezes were building up. A storm was coming. It would be nice, if it veered towards the south. On second thought, keep coming. The storm could mask Sam's investigations. He'd love to learn what the big pow wow was about on Jensen's yacht.

Now which yacht? Sam tried the radio again. He was close to the coast. It worked.

'Harbor Master, this is Kentucky Rose. I'm meeting a Silas Jensen on his yacht near Santa Barbara. I've forgotten the name of the boat, and I'm bringing the wine. Could you do a lonely sailor a favor and check your registry for Mr. Jensen?"

"Kentucky Rose. This is the Harbor Patrol. Only do it if you save us some refreshments or send a card of appreciation."

"The card is in the mail. Refreshments may follow," Sam replied. This was too easy.

"Mr. Jensen has docked a big one. It's the Excelsior Star. You need to be government cleared to board. Are you Big Time?"

"You bet. Thanks Harbor Patrol. I'll put in for more government funding."

Sam chuckled. He wished he could really help out those guys and gals.

"Kentucky Rose out." Sam disconnected. Eh, little Rose, let's go get 'em.

Sam had no idea who really owned the Excelsior Star. He'd seen the boat in Santa Barbara. He had been there with Susie at the time, and they had rented a small sail- boat for the day. It had been the first time that both of them had tried a sailboat. He chuckled and remembered.

Sam had studied the book as prep for their small water adventure, but nothing was like the real thing. It was a very windy day. He was doing well driving their little sailboat, or so he thought, when suddenly he veered right too sharply and quickly, the boat lost its balance, and capsized. They had finally managed to right the craft with advice from laughing experienced sailors on a nearby boat. Susie had maintained her sense of humor throughout it all. They had returned the boat and vowed to maybe check out a speed boat next time…Well, actually, they did later try a sailboat again and did well, but he would never forget that first time. Sam chuckled and it felt good. He'd forgotten the good times he had shared with Suzanne, his Susie.

Kentucky Rose, he was pretty sure he had read the side of his boat correctly. He wondered who really owned her and what she had to offer him besides a ride. Sam scanned the compartments. The only papers were his captors' wallets, but they might come in handy. He found snorkel gear under the seats. Scuba tanks would have been better, but the fins would help. Sam fished out a wet suit. Maybe it would all come together. He'd wait until dark and hopefully the end of the storm.

Sam was nearing Santa Barbara. He scanned the boats carefully with the cabin's binoculars. He found it easily. The Excelsior Star was a monster of a ship and very well lit. It was also surrounded by dozens of military crafts. It was going to be tricky. Sam sat back and rolled with the waves. Night was a good two hours away, but the storm was already blackening the sky. It was definitely the beginning of the storm and not the end as he had hoped for. The small boat was beginning to pitch. He was no longer seasick, however. He was in control.

CHAPTER 35

The sky was unleashing all of its impatience and revenge. Rain shelled the small craft and threatened to submerge it from existence. Sam stripped off his borrowed clothes and pulled on the rubber suit and gear. He sealed his clothes and Sunburn's gun in a waterproof bag and jammed the bulk into the wetsuit. It was a grotesquely uncomfortable fit, but he needed his hands free. Sam had barely slipped into the freezing blackness of the water, when it yanked him into its hellish depths.

Sam sputtered and nearly panicked. He finally found the surface and gasped insanely for air. The deadly ritual of drowning the human intruder, Sam, and throwing him back to the surface continued unabated. Sam's extremities screamed with exhaustion. It would have been so easy to just let the devil win. He need merely to give up and not fight, but he couldn't.

He banged into the Excelsior Star with shattering force. He clawed madly for a ladder or rope as he inched along the side. Each second brought fresh beatings. Then he found it. He clung to the lifeline. He felt as close to death's jaws as he had ever been. This death was not the loving climbing of the stairwell to heaven that he dreamed of in his childhood fantasies, but instead it was an insatiable hunger to devour and extinguish the living spirit. Sam found the strength to rebel and slowly pulled himself up the ladder.

Finally reaching the top, Sam rolled onto the deck. He needed time to regain his strength. He frantically searched for a refuge and found it amongst the lifeboats and riggings. He trembled severely from the shock of his undertaking. His heart was pounding madly. Then his body found its pace and he was back in control. Sam struggled out of the clinging rubber and into the warmth of Sunburn's cotton clothes. He felt part of humanity again, no longer a prisoner of angry waters. He rammed the gun into the waist of his trousers and emerged from his cocoon transformed into a hunter.

Sam prowled the empty deck until he found the door he wanted. This one led to passenger cabins. Sam darted along from door to door, each with locked secrets. A steward asked if he could be of service. Sam bumped him drunkenly and thanked the man profusely. Sam slipped the passkey from the innocent soul's pocket and was on his way.

ACCELERATION

Sam began his meticulous search. Each room was carefully examined. He found out more than he wanted to know. The ship held artifacts and drugs belonging to a broad spectrum of the rich and powerful. Sam had never been a part of this population. These people had a reason for being here. It was greed. The drugs and riches were abundant. However, he saw no clues as to where it was all going.

He had to mingle and learn more. Sam found an expensive suit of an approximate fit. He climbed into the rich material and repaired his hair and face as best he could. He caught a look at himself in the mirror and examine himself in disbelief. His face and figure were gaunt and bruised. His eyes had a hollow cold look. It fit his insides. He dabbed from the make-up jar and concealed the savages of the past. A new man emerged into the hallway of the elite ship.

The maze of corridors challenged his patience. Where was the party or board room? Voices rose in the distance. He forged a maze of hallway and finally threw open carved wooden doors to the main event. A huge gaggle of people swarmed around him, as he aimed for the center of the room. He felt it held importance, for the throngs were deeper at the core of the huge richly draped room. Expensive decorative pieces provided further resplendency for the crowd. Finally, he reached the destination and blinked in amazement.

The apex of the banquet room held the master plan of the noxious group. A large table, holding a large, glass-enclosed, relief map, sat in its midst. Sam studied the table. Burning flags marked military hot spots throughout the world. Each also bore a number. Signatures of the rich and famous bordered the map. Sam read with awe the names- congressmen, politicians, ex-presidents, corporate heads, military generals, actors, writers, rich corporate heads, and the list went on. Sam rocked back on his heels and studied the names closely. What did it mean? What were they all doing? What were they celebrating or planning?

Suddenly Sam was struck by the décor of the room. He whirled around and drank it all in. Orange colored drapes, orange table cloths, orange shades on the light fixtures- were they all coincidences? Sam remembered his first meeting with Dr. Mekka and his orange cane. Were these people addicted to the medication? Were they all now obsessed with power? His insides felt queasy. The drugs were unstable just as they would be. All of these important people, did they really know what they were taking? Was it too late to tell them?

ACCELERATION

The image of the map dragged Sam back. What did it all mean? He felt a bumping of his shoulder. Sam's eyes traveled up to meet those of an enormously gigantic man. The guy's frame was also heavily padded with muscle. He was a formidable sight with his long blonde hair, Adonis-like physique, and penetrating blue eyes. The presence of the huge young fellow would have made some people nervous and evasive, if it wasn't for something he sensed. Was it sensitivity and caring? He wasn't sure, but he liked the guy immediately.

"Hey!" Adonis poked Sam again. "You understand all this?"

"Nope." Sam said, "But I was afraid to show my stupidity."

"Name's Eon Gustafson." The man extended his huge hand. "I'm a physicist, and you?"

Sam scrambled about in his head for a name. "Adolf," he pulled out the name too fast. He berated himself for his hokey choice, but figured he'd better stick with it now. A last name? His favorite old country singer/actor popped into his mind- "Kristofferson's the last. I'm a corporate executive of a global company. I'm Adolf Kristofferson."

"I never heard of you, but then I'm usually stuck in my lab. I feel out of place here. Actually, my boss doesn't even know. A friend had a ticket and asked me to take his place."

He continued on. "I know I look like a weight lifter. Actually I do like the sport, but
science is my vocation. You don't look like an executive, if I may reciprocate? What happened to your face, sir?"

"Oh, you noticed. I was in a slight accident. Want a drink?" Sam reached for an orange liquid on a waiter's tray.

"Are you kidding? That stuff has a strange aftertaste. I'd love to put it through a chemical analysis."

Sam put down the glass and thanked the waiter. "You convinced me. So what's on the night's agenda?"

"The President makes his speech soon. I always liked the guy. It's going to be a big kick seeing him in person."

"Oh, yeah, me too." Sam said thoughtfully. "It should be interesting; I hear he's changed a lot."

"There sure are rumors, and they've stopped interviewing him on live coverage. All we get are newspaper statements. I'd like to see the real guy." Eon said cheerfully.

"Yes." Sam said. "What's your friend like- the one whose pass you borrowed?"

ACCELERATION

"He's a good buddy. We've been friends since college. He's gotten a bit eccentric lately though, which is why I got to go to this. He stays in his lab like it's his life. I usually have to resort to bribery to get him to leave. He claims his studies will save mankind. He's a little naïve. Most scientist go through the savior cycle in their youth, but Hector must be a late bloomer." Eon laughed heartily and then ran his fingers around his constricting collar. "I hate wearing a tux. Men were not meant for this punishment. Let us be free to wear grubbies, right?"

"I couldn't agree more," Sam replied. He liked this guy, but he wasn't yet sure if he could trust him. He was looking forward to Eon's reaction to the President's speech. He imagined that the guy was in for a huge jolt. Quint was bound to be crazier than ever, and where was Jensen? Sam had better be careful in this room.

He looked around and noticed the uniformed armed guards for the first time. They were stationed by the podium and by the exterior doors. Sam had entered through a cabin hallway, so he had missed the pleasure of their scrutiny. The guys looked polished and well-dressed, but their intent was obviously threatening. Sam hoped he could stay anonymous; he really didn't want to mess with the muscle guards here.

Lights began to flicker in the huge room.

"It must be speech time." Eon beamed excitedly.

The men watched as an Honor Guard presented the American flag, and the familiar strains of the national anthem echoed through the room. A solo spotlight held the flag in its grasp, and a crash of symbols signaled suspense and a blackening of the room. A spotlight then suddenly came up upon President Quint, who smiled and waved to the cheering crowd. The light then widened to introduce Sam's old adversary, Mr. Silas Jensen. The masses quieted as Jensen spoke. His words became almost hypnotic. Jenson's changed, Sam thought ruefully. The man had clearly learned the game well; he was a controller now and a rather enigmatic one. He was now all the more dangerous. Jensen spoke in a low smooth voice.

"You have been chosen. You are privileged to be given the new medicines that will enhance your innate abilities beyond your wildest dreams. With your new skills and leadership, we will guide the world to new levels. Your President and I salute YOU!" President Quint and Jensen raised their arms in Nazi salutes.

ACCELERATION

They lowered their arms as Jensen continued. "The torches we planted on the map will blaze and destroy the world's Sodom and Gomorrahs. We will show the world what needs to be done by doing it. Then they will turn to us, and we will be ready. You all are doing your parts. God be with you."

Jensen smirked with glee and continued. "We will join hands now and form our ring of brotherhood to our mighty country. President Quint is ready, are you? Say *YES* with passion countrymen and leaders."

The throngs responded with a unanimous "YES!" The room rumbled with shuffling as the people formed their circle with Jensen and Quint stepping into the center.

"Louder," Quint took over and glowed with his fanaticism. "I can't hear my people!"

"Yes!" They shouted as one.

Quint's voice boomed, "Much louder if we are to be more powerful than the forces which threaten our very lives."

"YES!" They screamed in answer.

"Be ready and take your positions outside by the railings. Lift up your glasses as one and let us propel them overboard to symbolize our attack against the violence by the sheep. We will guide them. Now, countrymen and ladies, throw your drinks into the sea. Go!"

Dignitaries rushed out to outer corridors of the ship and packed against the railings. They whooped with zeal as they pitched their glasses into the raging wind and turbulent waters. Rain drenched their designer clothes, but they were unaware and uncaring. Their only focus was on returning to the room and their circle.

The spotlight came up once more on Jensen and Quint.

Jensen spoke again. "Boats will now take you ashore and planes will carry you over this great country to your destinations, to await the signal."

President Quint grabbed the microphone. "I accept your leadership and I am ready, my sons and daughters."

Lights blackened the room. When they returned, the room was illuminated without the big bosses in the center. The crowd whispered in awe and then dispersed noiselessly.

Gustafson spoke first and broke through the heavy air in a low voice. "Shit, did I hear what I thought I heard or am I dreaming?"

"You heard right," Sam answered. Yep, he could trust Eon. It was no act. The man was as shocked and disgusted as Sam.

ACCELERATION

"Let's get out of here. I have to think." Eon said as he breathed heavily.

"Calm down. I have to learn more first. Are you with me? I want to learn what the signal is?"

"I don't' know. I feel like my life just fell apart." He turned toward Sam. "Why aren't you crazy like the rest of these people?"

"Because I want to stop them, and I'm not taking the drugs. These people wouldn't be so cooperative normally. They've been slowly medicated into submission. They're going to all die. I have to stop it. Do you want to help?" Sam looked at Eon gravely. "We've got to try."

"Yeah, I guess, but I've never been a hero before." Eon smiled nervously.

"Maybe no one will give either of us a medal, even if we succeed. Will that bother you? And you may die?" Sam said.

"Now that last part may just annoy me." Eon said as he shook his head in disbelief. "How do you know you can trust me?"

"I don't," Sam shrugged, "but I've got to trust somebody. Welcome aboard the suicide mission." Sam extended his hand.

"Eon shook it gloomily. "Do you have to put it like that, Adolf?"

CHAPTER 36

"See what you can find out," Sam said to Eon. "If all goes well, I'll meet you at the Macaw on the beach at 7 A.M. It's a little restaurant. I think it's still there. It's been a few years since I've been there. By the way, I'm not Adolf Kristofferson. I'm really Sam Stone. Good to meet you, Mr. Gustafson."

Eon grabbed Sam's arm as he turned away. "I've heard of you. Aren't you dead? And a murderer?"

"Reports were a gross exaggeration." Sam said.

"Clever line, but I've heard that before too." Eon teased.

Sam raised his eyebrows and laughed. "Really? Here I thought I was being original. I'm not a murderer or obviously dead. Jensen is a huge liar."

"I believe you there," said Eon. He looks like a smooth and simpering con job. Is that who beat your face?"

"Yes, but I escaped," said Sam quietly. "Thanks for believing me. Ah, Mr. Gustafson, may I call you by your first name?"

"Please do, Sam. There, we are friends at a horrible event." Eon said sadly.

"Eon, be careful. These people are dangerous."

"Where are you going?" Eon asked.

"I'll let you know after I do it, if I live through it. I'll look forward to seeing you later though. It's good to have a friend."

They shook hands, and Sam took off. Sam headed for the crowds and was swallowed up. He made his way back to the cabins. Some passengers were staying on board. Sam planned to find out who and why. He wanted to do a meticulous search, if possible.

A boisterous group entered the hallway. Sam lowered his head and headed for the linen closet. He dodged the group and plunged inside. He listened to the garbled chatter. He understood nothing so far.

Sam was startled when the door opened and revealed a stunned young cabin steward. Sam quickly feigned drunkenness.

"This is my cabin, have you come to visit?" Sam slurred.

"Sir, let me help you to your room. It's not this one. Do you have your key?"

ACCELERATION

"The one with those pretty orange numbers, no," Sam stammered,

The boy helped Sam from the closet.

"I think it's that one." Sam stumbled on the floor and crawled around sobbing. "But I lost my key, I can't find it."

"I'll open it... here." The door was ajar now. "Let me help you up,".

"Thank you, young man. I shall remember your name? What is it?" Sam mumbled as he was helped up.

"That's kind of you, Sir. I'm Fernando."

He helped Sam onto the bed. "Will you be all right or should I get help?" Fernando asked earnestly.

"I'll be fine." Sam curled up on the bed

"Sir, here's the pillow. It's at the wrong end of the bed.," He said politely.

"Thank you. Every bed needs a pillow. I'll sleep now." Sam closed his eyes.

Fernando quietly left the room.

Sam sprang up and searched the room. It belonged to some Colonel, according to the name on the suitcase. Sam pried it open. Neat, the guy was very neat. Everything looked carefully placed, including a large envelope of papers. Inside were rosters of military and civilian personnel and code names. Codes? For civilians too? He flipped through the pages. There must be thousands of names here. One caught his eye, Silas Jensen, code name- Savior. Sam wanted to choke on that. It should say Devil. He scanned the list with apprehension. No Gustafson. Good. Sam's head came up from the papers. Voices were talking by the door. A key turned in the lock. Sam pitched the suitcase shut and leaped into the small shower stall.

"Silas, we may be moving too fast for Quint." The voice resonated with military authority.

Sam's heart seemed to be exploding in his chest. Jensen was here! He had chosen the right room. Maybe luck was going to sit on his shoulder now.

"Quint will be fine." Jensen responded. "We'll be meeting at the bunker in Idaho on the day after tomorrow. He'll activate the nuclear missiles then. Our personal crew will replace the ones at the site. Quint also will broadcast to the nation from there. I need you to coordinate the event and the replacement of personnel. You do recall the plans, Colonel Pedrosky?"

"Funny, Silas" he snapped. "I know the plans. Are the tranquilizers ready and being pumped into the municipal water system? We can't hold control with our people, if you don't do your part also."

"It's already begun." Silas cooed. "They should be sheep by Friday, the thirteenth. Do you like my choice of dates? The coup has begun. They just don't know it yet." Silas chortled. "It's a big operation. Taking out Washington and Moscow at the same time is inspired. Two centers of countries will be destroyed. This will show our country and the world that we can do anything and anywhere. They'll all fear us. Other nations will bow down to us. Now, logistically, we have control of twelve military installations, fifty city water supplies, and an armed takeover of New York. We couldn't have even considered this magnificent victory without my little drug babies."

"The pills," the Colonel chuckled. "Do the labs think they can keep up the massive production?"

"They have to. We need special people to lead our nation and the world now. We need supreme intelligence. It's the only way. Otherwise we become overpowered by mediocrity, stupidity, and its resident do-gooders. We need super-intelligence, power, strength, and will. This is the way. Don't you feel better since you started the medication, Colonel?"

"Yes, I do. My emphysema has been cured too. It's a miracle, Silas. I owe you a lot. But, what if the people don't want our leadership or they fight back?"

"Colonel, we have had this conversation before. It bores me. With our medicine and our military victory, we will have cut off the people's urges and needs for rebellion. Anyway, who can resist what we offer. We'll end their foolish little global wars, and they'll look up to us, to us, Colonel." Jensen was shouting now.

"But what about Quint?" the Colonel was shaking Jensen. "Stop shouting. You're crazier than he is, Silas!"

"You bet I am, crazy with victory. That's why I can plan all this. Quint is a fool. Anyway he is getting unstable. He was exposed to the early forms of the medication. He will be eliminated as soon as he's done his job. It's amazing what these little pills can do. I've come so far." Silas pulls out a bottle of pills and gulps down a handful. The Colonel hands him a glass of water.

"Silas, you shouldn't take more than two a day."

"I'm the leader. I need the most."

"And what about me?" the Colonel said in a voice that seethed with jealousy.

ACCELERATION

"You are my partner, Old Buddy. You may take as many as you want." Jensen laughed again uncontrollably. "Come on old Bud, let's get off of my ship of geniuses. I think the President's plane can handle this storm."

"You are very confident, Silas. Oh, hell, you're right. Give me your arm, you bastard." The Colonel said. "A drink sounds good before we leave. It may keep us from getting seasick. Let's go to the bar."

"Yes, good," said Silas Jensen. The men walked out and closed the door behind them. The cabin became silent.

Sam emerged from the shower stall. He sat on the bed with hands twitching. He f   forced them to stop. He was shocked and overwhelmed at how far this plot had spread. And Jensen, what a fool he is to take the drug. He knew it was dangerous, but he couldn't resist the power. And the pills are so addictive that now thousands of people have been trapped in their lure? There must also be mighty big factories churning out the pill garbage. Oh, Sean, look what you've done. Scientific discoveries without moral responsibility could destroy us all. Sam buried his face in his hands in despair.

Sam suddenly brought up his head. He needed to get moving and search more cabins. He found the young cabin steward again. He felt badly, but he had to contain his movements so he could explore the other cabins. He bound the boy in the confines of the Colonel's old cabin. He apologized but knew it wouldn't help the poor kid's feelings. He dispatched the youth of his passkeys and thanked him anyway.

The search of the adjoining cabins progressed without fruition. They were starkly empty. Sam found few belongings and no clues. Then he heard a key being inserted into a lock. This time the closet was his refuge. He made it just in time.

There were no voices. A person seemed to be packing his luggage. Sam heard a swish of material and met the eyes of a startled white-haired gentleman. Sam grinned sheepishly and his bent fist jutted out from the enclosure and into the bewildered face. The impact knocked the fellow to the floor. Sam delivered a final blow and the man was out.

"Sorry, Sir, ah- General. Oops, another big shot. Listen old timer, do you mind if I borrow your stunning clothes? Of course you don't. It's a good cause. You see, yours should open more doors and answers for me. Sleepy, huh? It's been a hell of a night. Get comfortable, it's going to get longer." Sam searched his pockets. "Orders! You don't mind if I just take a little peek?"

ACCELERATION

The papers indicated a little town outside in Idaho. The due date for arrival was the thirteenth. Bingo. It had to be the bunker location. Now for the factories. The suitcase gave no further information. Sam unclothed the general and secured him in the closet. He felt rather like a chameleon. The uniform was a close fit, but the decorations were impressive. He pocketed the orders and the wallet. "Good bye, Sir. Thanks for everything. They'll find you, eventually."

Sam picked up the suitcase and strutted towards what he presumed was the exit from the ship. He was then carried along by a noisy group, and into a waiting speedboat. The storm had abated to only a steady rain. The winds still battered the boat but had lost its urge to sink and destroy.

A guard offered the general a poncho.

"Thank you, Mister." Sam barked in his best military style.

The boat heaved itself along with the pull of the waves. The rain had beaten down the voices. Everyone concentrated on holding the rail and seeing through the downpour.

Sam was jolted as the little craft bumped into the floating pier. Stocky guards lifted out the bedraggled elite. One pulled Sam aside and saluted.

"General, the military lodging is at Bluepoint Hotel. Shall I drive you?" he said.

"Sam responded gruffly. "Yes, that's good. Where's the car? I can't see a thing in this
confounded rain!"

"This way, Sir." The man said.

Sam trailed the driver through the cloister of cars. He picked up a fist size rock as he stomped along. The driver soon wiped his wet face, turned the ignition key, and slumped in his seat.

"Sorry. I need the car, but not you." Sam said as he slid the man over.

He drove a few miles and closed in on a solitary tree hugging the highway. He pulled the driver through the mud and up against the tree. He found a rope in the trunk of the limo and tied up his victim.

"I'm getting good at these knots, friend. Don't worry, someone will see you from the road in the morning, I think. Just do me a favor and don't talk too soon. Okay? Just nod your head. Aw, shucks, you can't as yet. Too bad." Sam patted the guy's cheek and sloshed back to his vehicle.

Sam plowed away through the flooded highway towards a little innocent beach restaurant, the Macaw.

CHAPTER 37

Eon Gustafson ran his big hand through his blond hair. He had just turned his life upside down or did he? It wasn't his fault that he was curious. Now here he was at a party that was more like a coven, and it was run by the President of the United States. On top of it all, he had pledged fidelity to a famous dead author who had been accused of murder. He had to get out of here. First, he had to calm down with a stiff drink or something.

Eon looked at the drink tray despondently. "You haven't got a coke, do you?" he said to the waiter. "Scotch would be even better!"

"No," the guy snipped back.

"I already asked." A feminine voice answered.

Eon searched for the source. Yes, it was definitely feminine.

"I love your locks," Elizabeth Martin grabbed onto his arm and swayed. "Oops. I'm tipsy. I've had too much of the orange stuff." She giggled and snuggled along his body. Her long dark hair flowed across Eon's face as he pulled away.

"Sweetheart, let's talk first, although I do find you stunning. It must be that purple dress against all this orange."

"You like this little dress," she rose it slightly. Her beckoning smile vanished. Her slim hands with their deep purple nails clutched against her abdomen.

"You okay, baby?" Eon blurted out.

'Sure," she gulped the air and tore out a bottle of pills from her beaded handbag. "I need more medicine." She fumbled with the lavender capsules.

Eon looked around. "Do you need a drink of water?"

"No," she said as she popped them in her mouth. "I need more." She shook the now empty bottle. "Excuse me, I gotta call this little number on the label." Martin started to walk away but tripped and fell back against Eon.

"I'll call for you, when we get ashore. I'll hold it for you until then so it's safe. How about you getting in one of those little boats with me. We'll leave this bash to the sharks." Eon winked.

"Only if you'll love me," Martin swayed and muttered.

"That won't be hard." Eon replied.

Martin offered her hand and leaned her whole body against him. "I might need a little boost into that boat though and…" she grinned, "And, I might get sick on it. Do you mind?"

ACCELERATION

.

"No." Eon pocketed the empty pill bottle. "I'll probably throw up with you." He guided the lady ahead of him.

They were stopped at the door. "Hold it," the guard sneered. "Oh, Miss Martin. I didn't realize it was you. Go right through."

"Thank you. You look very nice in your uniform, kiddo," she slurred.

"Yes, ma'am. Thanks."

Martin nodded to Eon. "The guard likes me. He wants me, but I'm too good for him."

"Yes, you are." Eon answered, as he helped her into the launch and slipped his jacket over her slim bare arms.

Martin sank against him, as the launch began to move. Something made Eon feel her pulse. It was there but faint. He looked down into her fine features. His eyes bulged open. She was twisting up with pain.

"Honey, what's wrong?"

"I hurt so badly." She began to cry. "I'm sorry to lean on you. I don't even know you."

"Yes, I know. Listen, we're almost to shore. I'll get these guys to get you an ambulance. Just hold on." Eon said.

"Something is stabbing me in the pocket of your coat," she desperately pulled the cell phone from Eon's coat's pocket. "A phone. I hate it. I hate everything. I hurt so bad."

"Give it to me, Elizabeth. "It's mine."

"No no no. It hurt me. No no no." She threw the phone into the ocean, then suddenly sat still, blinked repeatedly, and leaned back against Eon. Her thin shoulders shook as she cried softly. "I hurt. Oh, I hurt so much. I'm sorry, sir. I think I threw your phone away.

"Oh, baby. It's only a phone."

Elizabeth gasped. "Ahhhhh!"

Eon whispered, "Elizabeth, Elizabeth, are you okay?"

She didn't answer, but he felt her breathing beside him. He knew nothing could be done until the boat reached the shore. He felt it shift against the pellets of rain, but it held together. They bounced closer to the unseen docks. He wished it would hurry faster.

Eon looked around impatiently. The lights on the boat grotesquely shadowed the disheveled and diverse group. Two military men were in the rear. The forward hull held two ladies in colorful silk dresses that were now plastered to their shapely bodies. Two business types in suit coats were gritting their teeth impatiently against the cold and rain.

Eon felt his lady suddenly gasp and looked down apprehensively. He didn't like this at all.

Martin was clawing at her face. "This can't be right. No!" she mumbled. No"

That's when he really saw her. "Oh!" Eon pulled away. He starred at the small tortured lady that huddled in his coat. She had changed horribly. The skin on her face was shriveling, even as the rain slid down her sinking cheeks. Her limbs twisted, as pain erupted over her body. Spidery blood vessels climbed and choked her breathing skin. Elizabeth Martin then gasped and slumped forward. Eon caught her and barely breathed. He knew that she was dead. He didn't need to check for a pulse.

He felt the boat suddenly slam against the dock. He pulled his wallet from his coat and eased Elizabeth back against her seat. The pill bottle fell from her lap. He stared in shock and sorrow one last time at the deceased body of Elizabeth Martin and the bottle.

Eon picked up the bottle and ran from the boat. He didn't stop until the rain had swallowed up the voices which called to him. He was not about to return. He saw the flickering lights of the limousines. He hurled himself at one and ripped the driver from his seat. He rammed his fist at the shocked face. He had never hurt anyone before, but now he wanted to strike out at everyone and anything. He banged his huge body on the steering column as he climbed into the car. Eon threw the car in gear and tore through the mud and exploded onto the highway.

Eon Gustafson wanted desperately to put the hellish picture of the dying Elizabeth Martin behind him. He doubted however, that he ever would.

Eon had no idea where the Macaw was located, but he'd find it. He wanted desperately to get the guys responsible for Elizabeth Martin's suffering and cruel death. He hoped he had headed in the right direction. He'd give it an hour and then travel the road again in the opposite direction. The Macaw had to be on this road somewhere. He was desperate to see Sam again. Only Sam could understand what had happened and how he felt. Then they would take action. The bad guys must be stopped and they must pay for the horror and pain they are causing.

ACCELERATION

The longer the rain splashed and the wipers pulled against it, the more the night felt like a bad dream. Eon yearned to open his eyes wide soon and be back in his comfortable ranch house in the Hollywood Hills. A physicist, as mundane and careful as he was, would never stumble upon such a horror as he had just seen. That was too crazy, awful, and unreal.

Eon suddenly looked down at his white knuckles on his hands and relaxed his grip on the steering wheel. He was no coward though. He must calm down. He was not going to run away merely because he was afraid. Fear wakes a person up to reality, but he never wanted this kind of reality No one would. He had never been so horrified and frightened in his life... Eon spent the next hour trying to calm himself.

7 A.M., Sam Stone glanced down at the General's watch that he had confiscated. It had an alarm set for 800 hours on the 13th. Was that the time of the missile launch or the personnel invasion? Whatever. He'd get there early.

Sam stretched his legs under the small restaurant table. He felt somewhat refreshed after pulling up to a motel for the remainder of the night. The shower and couple of hours of sleep had done wonders. He was ready to go. He looked at the single fresh rose on the small table. It brought back sweet memories of Susie. She always had fresh flowers on her table every morning. She would go for a walk in the early morning hours before Sam had stirred. She'd then stop at the corner market. The owner would be just getting in his delivery, and he always made sure he had fresh daisies or roses for his favorite customers. Susie said it meant the day would be lucky. He leaned impulsively over and inhaled the aroma as he reached for his coffee. Nice.

"More coffee, General?" A grey-haired lady in a t-shirt and jeans held the pot of steaming brew aloft of Sam's cup.

"Thanks, I'd like that. You've been here a long time, haven't you?"

"Yes, Sir, it's my second home. I thought you looked familiar, but I couldn't place you. I'm Anna."

"Anna, yes. I used to come here while I was a sophomore at the University. I changed schools for the next two years after that. But, I have great memories of your songs on the guitar, performed right here. You still sing your ballads?"

"That was over ten or more years ago. I was also a good thirty years older than you, even then. It's funny. I thought I was going to bring back the era of Joni Mitchell or Joan Baez.

ACCELERATION

But, I found out that the world didn't want to go back to my youth or change really anything at all. So now I work the early hours to watch the sun come up with my coffee. Anyway, we only have the song-fests on Friday and Saturday nights now. You can still come though. The young people are taught to be tolerant of the older idealists like me. And you're still young enough to sort of fit in, but I'd leave the military uniform at home. Actually, you look pretty young to be a general. You must have gone through some life changes, if you remember my music. Your life must have stories to tell. What did you say your first name was?"

"I didn't. Sorry to be so secretive, but just call me General." Sam looked at her warmly. "You've got a real nice place here. Would you leave the bill?

"Sure thing, handsome. You sure do look young. You must have borrowed that uniform. I like to tease. Did you really win all those ribbons?" She leaned against the table and was enjoying the conversation

Sam gulped the hot coffee and almost choked on the irony of the lady's comments. "Coffee is hot! Anna, are you flirting with me or just being your charming friendly self?"

"A lady is never too old to flirt, and thank you for the compliment. I'll let you read your paper in peace now, sorry, I promise."

"Anna, you may come back, anytime." Sam smiled. The lady was as delightful a touch as any rose on a table. He watched her flounce away like a teenager.

"General, may I join you now? I'm not as pretty, but I like you too."

Sam looked up into the blue eyes of a commanding presence.

"Eon Gustafson. Yes, of course. I've had enough charming chitchat. I'm glad you made it. Do you still feel the same as last night?" Sam eyed him warily; had the man changed his mind or had it been changed for him?

"More so. I've been through hell since I saw you last. A girl died in my arms." Eon lowered his head. "She changed horribly, right before me. I think it was because of the pills. I couldn't do anything to help her. I left her on the boat and ran. I highjacked a car and have been driving around all night. I fell asleep in the car outside here. I feel awful. Mind if I drink your coffee?"

ACCELERATION

"Go ahead. I'm sorry, man. I've seen those pills work too. My brother invented them, and it killed him. I'd like your help in putting the distributors out of business." Sam said quietly.

The din of the restaurant faded into the background, as the men talked and planned.

"I forgot, I have her pill bottle. She said she calls this number for refills."

"Let me see it?"

Eon handed the bottle over to Sam who turned it over gingerly in his hands "Elizabeth Martin! She was the girl who died in your arms?" Sam was stunned. "It's working fast now. She couldn't have been on it that long. I saw her in Chicago. If I read her right, she was clean then. Oh, I probably am wrong. I haven't exactly batted a hundred lately. But meeting you may up the odds. Thanks, Eon.""

Sam started to get up. "Wait. Do you have your cell phone with you?"

"Nope," Eon, shrugged. "Elizabeth tossed mine into the ocean before she died, sorry"

Sam shrugged. "All right, I'll ask Anna and/or the cook if I can borrow a cell phone and call my publisher for money. I'll also get him researching the source of this number, and then perhaps we are in business."

"By the way, who is paying for this gourmet spread?" Eon said with a grin.

"You? Please," Sam chuckled.

Eon nodded, rolled his eyes, and laughed.

"Be right back. Uh, regarding, Anna, the waitress, be careful. She'll be crazy over your blonde good looks."

"Get going, General. I'm starved.". Eon patted his stomach. "Need food now." He laughed as his stomach suddenly rumbled with hunger.

Eon looked up and watched Sam walk over to Anna, who pulled a cell phone from her pocket and hand it to Sam. Sam seemed also to be asking for a pencil or pen. She signaled under the counter and rushed to her next customer. Sam reached under the counter, seemed to pause while thinking, and then put something in his pocket. He then made his call.

Anna spoke to her new customers, a couple with multiple kids and then made her way towards Eon. "Sir, he said you'd pay me for his call." She then winked.

Eon laughed and gave her money for his phone call. He then ordered as if it was possibly his last meal.

ACCELERATION

Sam returned to the table. "Ah, food. I hope half of this is for me. I'm still hungry. I'll pay you later."

"That's what they all say," Eon looked up while munching happily.

"You do eat well," Sam observed all the food with amusement.

"I like to eat for two," Eon said gravely. "For me, and you, if we don't have time. Those men over there are watching us."

Sam looked over at the military men at the counter. The men had turned to stare at them.

"Oh, my, Partner. I think it's time to make an exit. There's a back door. I'll walk that way. You can leave the money on the table, if you don't mind. I'll pick you up in front."

Sam casually got up and headed for the door. He stopped briefly when he got to Anna. "Thank you, special friend. Money's on the table. Love you, Anna." He then strutted out the door and bolted towards his mud spattered limo. Sam jumped in, gunned the motor, and shot to the restaurant door. He slowed briefly as Eon erupted through the door and plunked himself in the front seat. They sped away from the Macaw, whose bird symbol seemed to blink back that they were on their own. Sam looked through the rear view mirror and saw a group of men spew from the small diner. He planned to disappear on side roads at the nearest opportunity. One suddenly   loomed before him, and he took it...Much later, after many winding asphalt arteries, they stopped to catch their breath.

CHAPTER 38

"Sam, I guess I'm a fugitive now also." Eon said with wistful regret.

The torrent of rain water battered the car with a vengeance, as they drove onward.

Finally, Sam spoke quietly, "Eon, they may not know who you are, and that you're from the boat. You might still be able to take off.".

"I'm not so sure they won't figure it out. I'm kind of tall and different looking, Plus I was with you."

"That's true," Sam said sadly.

Sam suddenly saw the Interstate interchange. He was relieved to finally reach it, but the driving was taking too long.

"Search the glove compartment for a map. We need to find an airstrip. Try the GPS also," Sam said. "We've got to make better time. It's been a while, but I can handle a Cessna. We're going to have to borrow one."

"Theft again. I'm getting into this even deeper. Do you think we'll get out alive and be free again?" Eon looked doubtful.

"I hope so. But there's a lot at stake for the country too. A lot of people are getting hurt and will continue so and probably die, if we don't do something," Sam answered with eyes straight ahead. "I'd like my life back too. It seems to have existed so long ago."

They traveled in silence now. Eon continually perused the maps and fiddled with the GPS. Sam drove. The highway seemed to hypnotize and have no ending.

"I found one, an airstrip," Eon broke the curtain of isolation. "It's not far. The turnoff is Brown Road. I wonder if it's really brown? It's probably named after Mr. Brown, an astronaut, who became a noted agronomist and failed. Maybe it takes its name from his experiments, when he made dead grass."

"You're getting slap happy?" Sam laughed. "Oh, this is it!" He veered sharply to make the exit road.'

"Right, go right again," Eon added. "It's about two miles from the main road. "Sam, how do we intend to do this?"

"We just do it."

"You mean, there is no plan?"

Sam caught Eon's shocked look. "It's your basic- Do your best and use your instincts plan. The one that means- Make decisions as you go along. We can do it. We have to."

ACCELERATION

"Sam, you've got guts or you are very crazy, take your pick."

"You too. Eon, hold on, here goes" Sam swerved into the small airport and across the pavement to a small airplane.

"What about a key? Don't you need one?"

"Don't worry. Let's go. They parked beside the plane and jumped into the two-seater.

"Okay, someone is coming." Eon desperately said. Two men in blue overalls were closing the gaping distance between them.

"Patience, I've almost got it. There, we're on," Sam shouted as the engines sprang to life and the propeller turned slowly.

"The guys are getting closer, Boss!"

"We're almost ready to taxi," Sam yelled as the plane began to roll forward and leave the losers in the race now far behind.

"Will we hit air traffic? Isn't this dangerous without a flight plan?" Eon yelled against the roar of the motor.

"Yep, usually, but we are out in the sticks in case you haven't noticed. Also we are in a stolen plane. So if we're going to live as outlaws, we might as well be ones. It's more fun, and we have no choice. When this is over, I promise to return this little baby. You worry too much, Eon. Save it for Idaho, or oops, for running out of fuel."

"Fuel! Are we out?" Eon yelped in agitation.

"Nope, just seeing if you're awake." Sam teased.

"Thanks for the scare." Eon slapped Sam's shoulder. "You mean that I haven't had enough already?"

"Relax. In about three hours we'll land and figure where we are, and how close. We're headed in the right direction," Sam said with assurance. "Why don't you go to sleep?" Sam boomed as he put on the headphones.

"Good idea, if I can calm down!" Eon shook his head and smiled. "All right. Night, Sam Stone." Eon closed his eyes willingly. He was dead tired, and the engines were humming along. Anyway, Sam didn't need him now. He would later, however, and Eon needed to be thinking clearly.

He drifted in and out of cozy visions, but it didn't last. Elizabeth Martin rose up and chased his pleasant dreams away. He woke with beads of perspiration running down his cheeks.

"You sick, Eon?" Sam turned and yelled.

"No, it was just a bad dream."

"I understand. I've had a few of them myself," Sam answered, as his face hardened.

ACCELERATION

"Heads up. I'm landing in that field. It looks rocky. If we don't bounce on our nose, we should be able to push the plane under that grove of trees. Hold on. I'm better at taking off than landing, at least in this little light.

Sam landed smoothly, sort of. The plane jerked over the terrain and tossed its human cargo relentlessly. It finally settled humbly against a boulder.

Eon sighed as he rubbed his aching neck. "That wasn't a good landing, but not bad either."

"Guess I need practice," Sam laughed. "Move, we've got to get this baby under cover." Sam unbuckled his belt and eased out. He stood and inhaled deeply of the cool air and the smell of wild grass. He wished he could hike to the mountains in the distance and just disappear.

Eon caught the longing look on Sam's face. "Later. Then you'll be free to climb that mountain, but then you may not want to. You may have had it with adventures."

"That's very perceptive for a physicist. You ever try psychology?"

"It was my minor," Eon flipped back.

Sam stretched. "That's a potent combination. You are the perfect man for the job."

"What job?"

"To shut down the missiles, or talk the President out of pushing the buttons that open the gates of hell," said Sam solemnly.

"I'm supposed to do that! I'm going home, except I'm stuck." Eon yanked unsuccessfully on the seatbelt.

"Here, let me help, big guy." Sam flipped the catch and helped Eon out. "Now for that favor, listen to me, as we drag this pretty little airplane into those trees.'

Sam started to push on his own, then stopped and looked at Eon. "Well, are you going to help a hopeless do-gooder or not?"

"Yes, okay, go on," Eon said as he began to heave his weight at the craft.

Together, they inched the plane across the yards of rocky field and into the cove of trees that were nestled there, as if together they would protect each other from elements in nature that could so easily go awry. Patches of snow were scattered haphazardly in the distance. The air was still. Was everything waiting a coming storm, whether it be natural or man-made? Sam shivered and buttoned up the general's jacket. He related what he had learned so far. Eon said nothing in response until Sam sat on the ground and took out his maps.

"You make a good case for the accused, and a dangerous mission I might add." Eon crouched next to Sam and looked over his shoulder. "So we are where?"

"Here, we should reach the town of Crystal by nightfall, if we like this way. We can get a room with your money," Sam nodded cheerfully. "And then we'll seek out the President's bunker and sabotage it."

"With what?"

"Oh, this little gun here." Sam waved a small pistol. "Cute, isn't it? I lifted it from Anna when I was looking for a pencil. I kind of remembered she always carried one, with a permit I might add. She had a bad experience with a car jacker once. She incidentally is an excellent shot. At least that's what I overheard her saying. I'll get it back to her or send her a check afterwards…She'll like that. Of course, she liked you best."

"Send the check. I knew I liked Anna, but that is a mighty small gun for your big ambitions here. It's really a tiny gun." Eon groaned and laughed hysterically.

Sam chuckled. "You take what you can get in an emergency. We'll pick up more on the way. I'll get us in. You handle the computers. I know I'm asking a lot of you, Eon. I guess if you want to do so, you can still pull out." Sam hated to do this mission alone, but he would if necessary.

"No, Sam, I'm with you for the duration."

"Good," Sam reached over and shook his hand. "I'll dedicate my next book to you…if we survive."

"And I'll think up somethin g. Ah- I'll name a new law of physics after you. It will be Stone's Law, whatever needs to be done, can be done, come hell or whatever."

"I do like that, Eon." Sam helped the big guy up. "We'll meet here afterwards and then go for the factories. Ben my publisher should have an address by then."

"And money! I hate to see you taking advantage of friends." Eon raised his eyes to the heavens.

"Oh, yes, and money, friend. Let's go." Sam started off and looked back. Eon caught up.

Two lone figures trekked across the empty field towards the dirt road that wound around the hills. It would be another hour until they reached pavement and finally civilization. Of course, it was only a sleazy Last Chance Motel. They pressed the lone chair against the door, in order to keep it closed as the wind roared.

ACCELERATION

"I'll take the best bed," Eon exclaimed, as he sampled both with his huge body. He rubbed his back. "You choose on second thought. The choices are both terrible."

"This is fun, isn't it?" Sam stripped off his clothes and gingerly lay his naked exhausted body between the cool sheets. "Wake me in a couple of hours. Well, actually, I hope you won't," groaned Sam. "But do it anyway, if you can, please."

Both woke at midnight as if some unseen clock had signaled its cue. The men showered, dressed, and departed from the sad simple room with regret and anticipation. The adrenalin rush was only just beginning.

"Do you know exactly where we're going?" Eon asked. Tripping over the rocks and shrubs at night did not make for easy hiking. Also, the temperatures had dropped. It was late, and he was damn cold. "I have one more question, do you have a parka and gloves I can borrow? A pair of hiking boots would be nice too."

"No, on the clothing and yes on the first question," Sam teased, as he plunged onward. Suddenly he reached back and pulled Eon down into the brush. "Shh!"

An engine of a vehicle was coming up fast. Eon heard too now. They hugged the ground as it barreled past within inches of their position. Their prone bodies felt the rush of air as it passed.

"Too close," Sam whispered.

"It looked military," Eon answered.

"Yep, let's get closer." Sam jumped to his feet. "There appears to be a gate and fencing up ahead."

"How did you know where this action was? It didn't show on the maps," Eon pursued.

"I'd read that a missile site was out here and that the President had a bomb shelter type bunker there. They built it years ago in the 1950's during the bomb shelter panics, when everyone was thinking about getting killed. I heard that President Quint was under the control of the military and had a bunker near NORAD. So when Jensen said "Idaho," well, that had to be it. The trick was finding it, and I think that we just did."

"So, which way? Follow that car?" Eon said thoughtfully.

"Let's hope it's going to and not leaving from. But at least we are on a road now, so the hiking should be smoother," Sam said.

ACCELERATION

"Oh, no." Eon landed on the ground.

"What's wrong?" Sam crouched down.

Eon sat back. "I guess I tripped over my big feet. I must be dragging them. He rose and brushed himself off. "You know, General, you could use a good pressing, and I need an appropriate suit. This tux doesn't cut it in the military or for exploring the wilderness. How about an upper class military uniform for me too?" Eon got up and brushed himself off.

Sam suddenly pulled him off the road and down. He whispered and pointed ahead. A man had pulled up in a car from inside the gates. He was talking to the perimeter guards.

"They crept closer. Sam whispered to Eon. "Look. How about a Captain's uniform?" Sam rose and walked forward towards the gate. Here was their opportunity.

"Captain, my car broke down about a half mile down the road. I have V.I.P. passengers and a dazed driver." Sam said in his most General-like manner. It appears that you are heading out. We don't need a medic, just transport. Would you accompany me back to the car with yours and bring us back?"

The young Captain raised his hand in salute. "Certainly, Sir. I was just checking security and heading for my home off base.

My time is yours, General." The Captain stood straight with hands clasped behind his back, in readiness.

"At ease, Captain," said Sam with authority.

The young captain opened the door for Sam, who sat in the back, and then crossed to the driver's door and climbed into his vehicle. They pulled away.

The sky hung over the vehicle like a mysterious black hood.

Eon hid in the darkness beside the deserted road. He speculated that Sam's plan would involve him shortly. It did.

The car came to a stop a few yards from Eon. He wondered what was happening inside. He kept away from the circling search lights of the guard's station, as he made his way towards the solitary car.

He came up upon Sam as he was dragging a very unconscious Captain from the driver's seat.

"Your uniform," Sam said as he began to unclothe the fellow. "He was rather a sweet guy so give him your tux in exchange. He'll wake up confused but not totally humiliated."

"Why Mr. Stone, you still have a heart." Eon said as he climbed out of his elegant trousers. "I'm very glad to let the captain be the black penguin for a change. Anything has got to be more comfortable than this tux. You do realize how long

I've been suffering in it?"

Sam smiled broadly. "Yes. Check his pockets. I'll open the trunk. Take what you need."

A rope and a rifle with a box of cartridges were Sam's presents. Eon chose the Captain's I.D. and pocket knife. They bound the sleeping captive and left him near the road. They turned the car around and made ready their entrance to the base.

Passing through the guard station proved uneventful. It was not the same guard, however, so there was no suspicion. Sam trans-versed a good half mile stretch of uninhabited wilderness until he came upon the second guard gate. This one was manned twice. Sam presented their credentials and groused at the lateness of his visit. Again they met no resistance. Perhaps it would be easy. But, he doubted the luck would last.

Driving through the second guard station, Sam could feel Eon's tension building.

"Relax, Captain," Sam said warmly.

"I'm trying," Eon answered tightly.

"Sam pulled the black sedan into a parking space near a crop of metal barracks. He glanced around at the sleek and deadly missile silos in the distance. He had to admit that he felt a bit nervous. He forced his body to stay calm. Once done, Sam climbed out with authority. He noted the captain's heavy winter topcoat in the back seat and carefully slipped it over it over his arm with the concealed rifle.

"Remember where we parked, Eon, in case we get separated. I'll put this key under the mat by the back seat. Now it's time to do this. Let's go."

The men walked side by side in a direct vector towards the silos. They entered an adjacent structure and asked for a night maintenance director. Sam and Eon silently followed their guide to a small room with a pulsating computer.

"Mister?" Sam said gruffly.

Maddox, sir. What can I do for you? I'm coordinating a shift change right now. I can talk with you in a minute."

"Certainly. May I study a map of the complex in the meantime? I'm doing a readiness check for President Quint's arrival tomorrow.

"I thought it was to be an unplanned secret?"

"It's a secret, but nothing is unplanned, Mister. The maps, now!" Sam barked.

"Yes, General. I apologize for my dalliance."

"Apology accepted." Sam answered sharply and sat stiffly in a chair. He was ready to be served with the maps.

ACCELERATION

The Lieutenant pulled the book of maps on the complex and spread it before Sam. "I'll leave you alone now, sir. If you have any questions, I shall be happy to assist upon my return." The flustered young man delivered his salute and bolted out the door.

Sam grinned at Eon. "I think I'm getting the hang of this General act."

"Most definitely, sir. You even had me cowering in supplication," said Eon in amazement.

General and Captain poured over the maps and memorized the details as quickly as possible. They knew that they should be gone when the Lieutenant returned. Sam tore out one page and jammed it in his pocket. The two carefully restored the large book to its place and slipped out of the office and into the core of the military complex. They had the knowledge now. They just needed to use it.

The night personnel passed the rumpled General and Captain with nary a thought amiss. Salutations were crisply exchanged, and the men walked on.

Their first aim was locating a weapon storage locker.'

"Mister." Eon cleared his throat. "The General needs to do a hands on inspection of your facility. Ready yourself to lead and explain." Eon was beginning to relish his role as Captain.

"Yes, General." The young man snapped back and opened the doors to his armament stash. General Sam passed his coat to his Captain Eon. The guard, with General Sam beside him, proudly explained the contents of the room. Sam carefully examined the instruments of death. Behind them, Eon hovered and silently lifted grenades and a machine gun with bullets and hid them into pockets and under the General's coat. As the tour ended, General caught his Captain Eon's nod, and they concluded the inspection.

Sam saluted and gruffly said, "Thank you, Mister. Well done. We'll move to the next station."

The guard saluted smartly as the General swiftly left the room. Sam and Eon then turned from the corridor and sagged in relief.

"Now what?" Eon said softly.

"The maintenance shafts; it worked last time."

"What last time?" said Eon.

"Later," Sam said. It would take too long to explain. Sam felt a dreaded deja vu. He thought of Caroline beside him as they had tried to get out of the hospital. The memory left a gaping, agonizing emptiness in his gut. It hurt desperately.

They scanned up and down the walls and frantically jumped from corridor to corridor, looking for an entrance to the ducts.

"It's got to be here. There." said Sam as he saw the duck entrance cover. "Good, it's big enough for us, I think."

They pried off the shaft cover. Eon could just barely stuff his huge body through the passageway. Sam handed up the guns and Eon pulled Sam up also. Sam pulled in his legs and yanked up the grate, just as footsteps echoed in the halls. They waited silently.

Sam's hands shook as he unwrapped the technical diagram map from his pocket. Eon squeezed closer to the drawing. "Is it a drawing of the shafts?" he whispered.

"I think so." Sam softly answered. "We seem to be… here. The Presidential shelter with NORAD connections are south. We can make our way to the shelter. Then we'll try to sabotage the computer relays to the missiles and/or kidnap the President at the broadcast and communicate to the networks. I don't know if we can manage it all." Sam sat back against the cool metal walls.

"It all sounds so incredible, just sabotage and kidnap. What if they don't believe us on the broadcast?" Eon asked.

"They'll have to… God, it does sound hopeless." Sam suddenly felt defeat.

"Hey buddy, I was always the doubting Charlie. You're the rock. Remember that, and don't give up, Sam. We got this far; we've got to succeed."

Sam passed his hand over his shaggy hair and threw back his head. "How can anyone believe I'm a General? Look at me. I'm a mess."

"You had me convinced so far. Believe me. You were great. It was quite an award winning performance. Plus, you've lost everything. What else can they take? Well, except maybe your life and mine."

"An interesting argument. Thanks, Eon," Sam sighed and took a deep breath. "Okay, we've got time to disable the computer as a precaution, and then we hide until Quint gets here and shows his true colors. This way."

The men crawled through the conduits and under the semi-red work lights. The red gave their faces an inhuman glow, which added to the nightmare sensations building within them.

ACCELERATION

"Wish we had knee pads, Eon whispered as he paused to rub his aching extremities.

Sam silently nodded. The shafts seemed to unfurled a dizzying array of tunnels which battered and confused them at times, as they tried to increase their pace.

Finally reaching their destinations, they eased their aching bodies out of their frustrating confinement and into the corridor. They had reached the shelter, but stared in discouragement at the door. It bore a computer coded release mechanism.

"Damn!" Sam whispered. "Computer Whiz, can you decode it?"

"I'm a physicist, remember? But, I am terribly bright," Eon grinned. "I can try."

They heard a sound. "Back in the shaft quickly, Sam said hurriedly.

Eon made it on time. Sam did not. He knew he was too late. He shoved back the tunnel cover.

"General we meet again." A voice said crisply.
Sam whipped around. He knew that voice. "Jensen," Sam said with repulsion.

"I'm honored, Mr. Stone, that you remembered me." Silas Jensen laughed harshly. "You got pretty far." Jensen looked at his guards. "Take him."

Sam was suddenly surrounded by bulging muscles in grey suits. His arms were yanked back violently, and his head was pinned against a huge chest.

"Your fan club is getting ugly," Sam grunted through gritted teeth. "What happened to your white-collar thugs? These guys look like stupid weasels. The suits don't help." Sam tried to jerk away but was held fast. "I'll kill you, you know, you scum."

Jensen roared with insane laughter. "You are just an annoying little ant, who I could crush right now by smashing your skull, but I'll wait. I want more time to tear your body apart. Now I have preparations for a President to attend to. Take him to room 7." Jensen waved his arm, and Sam was dragged away.

Jensen surveyed the empty hallway. He glanced at the door and pushed the code. He leaned into the massive cement portal door and stepped into the shelter room. Seemingly satisfied, he stepped back out and heaved the cement door closed. Jensen strolled back down the hallway, and stopped at the end. He patted down his long greying hair, and then turned down the corridor.

Eon had watched Sam's capture in terrified despair. He panicked for a minute, then he calmed. Jensen was out of sight. Eon ran the code numbers through in his mind. He felt that he knew them. It was up to him to finish Sam's mission. He owed him that.

Eon Gustafson slowly pulled his bulk from the tunnel and stood tall. He reached for the computer relay and pushed the sequence of numbers and waited... Nothing! He'd made a mistake. His hands were sweating now. He had to try again and again. Oh God, it wasn't opening! Once more and again. Suddenly he heard something. *A* click. That was it! He pushed hard and the door budged open.

The room was like a darkened cell. He felt for a switch. He pushed a button. The room suddenly became bathed in a garish yellow haze. Eon's eyes swept the room. It was like a tomb. He wondered why the humans who push the annihilation button and launch the fatal bombs should survive, while the innocent ones die horribly. By what right was that justice? And especially if those humans, that lived, were Quint and Jenkins.

Eon paced the room slowly. NORAD computers and vision screens lined the one wall; the other contained shelves of equipment for survival. A small side room swelled with crates of food and water. Pull-down cots and tables lined two walls. A mural of snow-capped mountains and lush green forest covered another wall. Eon stared. It was probably there to maintain sanity from the isolation. A large military clock peeked out at the side of the painting. Was it a reminder of human's mortality? He felt sudden revulsion for this room and all it meant. He totally hated it.

Eon turned to the computers and opened its bowels. He would need more light. He searched, found a flashlight, and balanced the torch as he lay on the hard floor. He snorted at the lack of carpet and other amenities, and then turned back to the intricacies of the monster machine. Was he knowledgeable enough on computer dynamics? He began to finally just snap the wires in frustration. There was not enough time for him to become an expert. Eon snatched a look at the ticking clock. He'd have to leave. He'd been here too long.

Returning the panels over the scramble of wires was simple. Undoing his destruction of the massive computer would not be.

ACCELERATION

Eon smiled in satisfaction. The missiles would either backfire or fail to launch. He felt great with either alternative.

Eon closed down the lights and tugged the huge door closed. He returned to his overhead cave of tunnels, pulled up the maintenance cover, and peered out through the slits in the grate. The deserted hallway seemed to look back, unaware of its previous intruder. It was as if Eon had never been there, but he had.

Now, where was room 7?

CHAPTER 39

"Do you know why you are here, Mr. Stone?"

'No," Sam mumbled groggily, "but I'm sure you'll tell me." Sam felt like he was spinning. They had beaten him severely. "Why don't you just kill me?"

Jensen smiled smugly. "You're my trump card, in case it all falls apart. I doubt it shall. In either case, we will eliminate you, sooner or later. I wouldn't make any plans, if I were you. This may seem like a broken record, but where are the diaries?"

"You mean you still can't find them?" Sam chuckled weakly. "You bastard."

Suddenly Sam felt a bullet rip into his thigh. He wrenched back with the force of the close range impact. Pain shot through his body.

"I repeat, where are the diaries?"

Another shot rang out its deafening sound and shook the air. This time a deadly bullet exploded in Sam's shoulder, and he gasped in shock. He twisted in the chair and slumped.

ACCELERATION

"You noticed that I haven't killed you yet. Are you ready for number three? Where are the diaries?" Jensen yanked Sam's head up and glared into his eyes. "You see why I chose this room? No one will hear the shots. I can blow you to pieces." He began screaming. "Perhaps I have no need for a trump card, you!"

"Go to hell," Sam mumbled, as another shot rang out. Sam braced for the lance of pain, but there was none.

The room exploded with machine gun fire. Men scattered and scrambled for the door. Bullets crashed into the walls and ceiling. Sam watched the madness through glazed eyes and disbelief. It seemed a macabre dance of death. Then the air became still. A large form loomed into Sam's blurred vision. He tried unsuccessfully to make it out and understand.

"Jensen?" He whispered in fear.

"No," a voice said shakily, "he's gone. He and his groupies have run like fat rabbits. It was pretty scary, however."

"Who are you?"

The body knelt beside Sam. "It's me, Eon, Sam. You look a lot worse than before, and I didn't think that was possible. I'm untying you. Lean on me; we are going back into the shafts. Hold this on your leg while I make a tourniquet from my belt.

You are dripping a trail." Eon pulled the belt tight around the leg.

Sam groaned.

"Okay, now get in this little bitty hole, partner. Good, now my turn." Eon moved Sam gently but quickly. There could be no time lost; they must disappear. "We are getting out of here."

"No. Head us back to the Presidential bunker or shelter or whatever. Jensen will think we've run away, I hope. We can wait nearby." Sam said as he leaned back to clear his head. "I'll be fine."

"Sure you will, you'll just bleed to death."

"Eon," Sam grabbed his shirt," we've got to finish this. How much time do we have?" He changed the subject.

"Forty-five minutes. We'll never make it!" Eon said. Sam ignored the comment.

"They'll beef up security, so keep your eyes open wide, for me too." Sam rested his head back and squinted in the half light. "You're going to have to help me get moving. Sorry, Eon."

"Apology accepted, and I hope you're right. Eon ripped off both of his shirt sleeves and placed them on Sam's shoulder wound. He cinched the belt tighter on the leg. "I hope you don't die on me," he muttered.

"Me too," Sam said softly. "We'll hide in the "Presidential Suite."

They made their way, albeit slowly, but did just that.

#

Sam and Eon had almost reached the Presidential bunker. They had heard that a military buildup was coming soon. They were crawling as fast as possible. They needed to fully leave the area near room 7. Sam had a feeling that Jensen suspected they were escaping in the ducts. He probably had men in them Sam hoped they could keep one step ahead until they could sequester in the bunker somewhere, but he was awfully weak.

Sam stopped for a minute to catch his breath. He noted that the shoulder had ceased bleeding. Eon had torn out the lining of his jacket awhile back and packed it solidly in the wound also. Eon reached over to check the tourniquet on Sam's leg, but Sam stopped him.

"Thanks, Eon. The leg's okay. You can stop worrying now. Neither injury will kill me," Sam said softly.

"Yes, but they bleed pretty well, and I bet they smart too."

"Correct assumptions," Sam smiled faintly and then frowned. "We still have a problem with the bunker's coded entrance door."

"Hey, what's a partner for? I already mastered that assignment, sort of. I got in and chewed and scrambled the wiring of the missile firing computer to the best of my amateur ability. We just have the President's broadcast and his credibility to corrupt. Actually he'll probably do the latter all by himself."

"You are certainly picking up on your self-confidence," Sam observed."

"Yes, along with discovering my caveman-like aggressive tendencies."

Sam started to chuckle, but it hurt. "Don't do that, don't make me laugh!" He turned back to the tunnel. "That's it, the bunker is just a few yards ahead, I think."

Sam pushed forward as Eon brought up the rear and helped him with his injured leg which screamed in agonizing protest now, in Sam's head. He strained to concentrate on every movement.

They finally stopped. They were at the grate of their destination. They peered through. It appeared that they were on floor level and that two sets of feet guarded the entrance to the Presidential room.

"Feet are of average size. We might be able to handle them…unless…"

"Unless what?" Eon whispered back.

"They are big guys with little feet." Sam felt cheerful all of a sudden. Why not, the whole mission was for the crazies anyway.

"Oh, deathbed humor is always nice."

"Yep. Okay. Hand me your gun."

Eon handed over the pistol.

"No, the big one."

Eon fumbled and extended the machine gun. "Do little feet need the big guns?"

Sam shrugged and then watched until the feet seemed to be pointed away from the grate. He softly slid the metal covering to the side and eased himself out on his back. Sam positioned his gun up at the guards who whirled at the sound of the gun hitting the side of the tunnel before it had emerged, but Sam had achieved his leverage in time. The gun was aimed at their lower torsos.

"Freeze, gentlemen, unless you want to lose your manhood in a split second. I shoot fast and never miss."

The tall guards held their hands up over their heads.

"Thank you. I detest death and dismemberment, but I won't hesitate to indulge in them." Sam continued sliding on his back the rest of the way out of the tunnel with Eon's help.

One soldier started to test Sam's precarious position by lowering his arms for a brief second. "Don't do it," Sam snapped, "Or I'll blow you apart! I feel really lousy, and when I feel this way, I am nasty. So don't test me."

By now Eon had yanked his body out and was getting to his feet. He held his handgun. "Hands on the wall and high," he ordered.

The men turned to the wall, and Sam stood up. "Eon," Sam said, "remove their guns before I kill them accidentally."

Eon pilfered the deadly metal pieces and waited. Sam gave no other directives. "Now what, boss?"

"Now what? Ah!" Sam paused. He had to do something with them. "Hit them over the heads."

The two captive, bookend-like soldiers exchanged glances.

"Don't do that, keep your eyes on the wall!" Eon turned to Sam. "Hit them how?" he asked under his breath.

ACCELERATION

"Sort of like this!" Sam borrowed the gun from Eon and rammed one now doubting guard over the head. The fellow crumpled to the floor.

"Oh, I like that!" Eon repossessed the gun and incapacitated the second man.

"Very good, check their pulses." Sam said. "They are so young,"

"Yeah," said Eon nervously, "but still big guys. However, they have medium size feet. And they live."

"Yeah, they're dreaming of a nice place and time." Sam looked at his watch. "We don't have much time. Stuff them in the shaft."

"Shouldn't we gag and tie them?" Eon questioned.

"There's no time, quickly!" Sam tugged on one, but he couldn't do it. Eon bounced over and did most of the lifting until it was done.

"The code?" Sam pointed to the door, as he returned the grate to his place.

Eon punched the numbers with precision this time. They swung the huge door open and entered. Suddenly voices echoed down the corridor, as Sam threw himself against the door. He whirled about in despair, as Eon doused the lights.

"Where the hell do we hide?" Sam whispered in confusion.

"The food room- over there!" Eon dragged Sam through the blackness toward the side room. Sam could hear the click of the computerized door release at the same moment that he felt Eon yank him inside the haven and pull the curtain.

News media scurried noisily about, negotiating positions for the broadcast as Sam and Eon jockeyed amongst the shelves. They had only seconds before the President made his royal entrance with his entourage. Sam and Eon were a captive audience, and they had never been so frightened in their lives.

Lights were plugged in and cameras and microphones quickly set up.

Silas Jensen introduced the President to the press, who exploded with questions.

The President interrupted the uproar. "Gentlemen and Ladies, please... I will explain. I am guiding you through this presidential bunker, or some call this room by its softer title, shelter, for a reason. You have all made fun of me in the past. You have said that I was not smart enough to make executive decisions and that my wife and advisors did them for me. You have maligned me as only a charming figurehead. I am here to prove you wrong!"

ACCELERATION

Silence hung over the packed room like a shroud.

"I have increased my intelligence to 160 at my last testing," President Quint continued haughtily. "I am a genius and far surpass you imbeciles of the press. Now that I am more capable than you, I have made a decision for this country. I will lead you all into a new era, one of power and strength. I shall clean the world, and it shall bow down to me and our country. I have thousands of friends that have increased their abilities, just as I have. They will be my ministers." The President smiled with even white teeth in his square jaw. His shock of dyed hair shone in the artificial yellow glow of the room and press lights.

This press was spellbound, as were Sam and Eon. The microphones from each network and newsmen and women were not hustling for position but were seemingly frozen. The President continued to stand with his smile plastered on his perfect features, and then calmly pushed a number of buttons on the computer.

"You," Quint nodded in condescension, "may be watching what I've just done. This control board is the ultimate in military efficiency. With only the touch of my fingers, I can override all "fail-safes" in this missile silo. I just did so. I have released two nuclear missiles for our great country. We shall bring the world to us and we shall rule all."

Carl Crane from NBC broke the stunned silence. "Where are they going?"

The President grinned maniacally. "One, my son, is going to bloom over Moscow and the other over Washington D.C. We will rid our countries of the plague of those of mere average intellect that control them. Our super intelligent people are ready to take over control. In some cities they have already acted. We will then continue to do this around the world. I will continue to be your President, but it will eventually be, of the world. FBI Agent Silas Jensen will provide the drugs for us and any who want to become superior. In the end, however, the inferior will die. It will be a brand new world. My people and I rule now. "Children, it's time to rejoice." Quint stretched forth his hands in supplication to the press, "you are broadcasting live, are you not?"

"Shania Johnson, from CBS, Sir?"

"Yes?" Quint simpered.

"Mr. President, you're crazy!"

Quint's eyes flashed. "Don't you ever call me that" I control you. I could have you all shot. This facility is mine. My people have taken mastery of the cities. We have tranquilizers in the water supplies. We have infiltrated the army bases. We are now taking over the nation's capital in a decisive manner. A nuclear bomb." Quint giggled." You will follow me as before, but now you will be proud. I am in ultimate control."

An older newsman headed for the door. "We don't need another Hitler. I'm getting out of here," he blustered nervously.

"No, you won't, Old Man!" Quint shrieked gleefully. "No one will leave here, until I say so. I say what you do. I am your President. I say, not you. I could squash you all, but I am nice. I'll let you live. I can change my mind, however. I choose…me, me, me!"

Without warning, the President screamed. News people spun frantically to understand why. They returned to the source of the cries, their President. They gaped in horror as Quint clawed at his face and tore out shreds of skin. The President staggered towards the people; the people drew back in repulsion. He was self-destructing before their eyes, and all they could do was watch and recoil.

Then as fast as seizure came, it ceased. Quint stared into the cameras at the faceless men and women and children. His once graceful hands held out a sheet of skin in one hand and a bunch of his hair in the other. They watched the skin and hair slid through his dry bent fingers. Quint quietly said, "I am very smart. I am a genius. You must do what I say."

Suddenly he blinked and stared out in confusion. His pale mutilated face and body twisted in agony. He cried out in anguish as he aged and twisted before their eyes, "I hurt. Help Me!"

The President of the United States fell to the floor. Camera Man Santiago slowly moved up and bent down. He felt his pulse. "He's dead." He said.

The death paralyzed the room except for the two men who crouched in the supply room. Sam and Eon emerged together with guns drawn and leveled them on the stunned crowd.

"Men and Women of the Press," Sam shouted.

The group turned. A woman screamed out," Oh, my God, they're going to kill us all!"

"No," Sam said in a low clear voice, which seemed to mesmerize the group, as much as the violent moments from the minutes before. They were held in the gaze of the tall, dark-hair man with the once handsome face which was now bruised and swollen. Blood had begun to seep through his shoulder and leg wounds and only served to make the scene all the more unreal.

"Guards," Sam continued. "Put down your weapons. You," Sam pointed to a soldier. "You are standing by the leader of this mad conspiracy. He is Silas Jensen of the FBI. He introduced our President here. Restrain him, if you yourself want to continue living. Do not release him, ever."

The young soldier stared in confusion at Jensen, his leader. Jensen slowly started to move his hand into his jacket. Thomas Chin, a newsman, slid quickly beside him and intercepted his hand.

"Jensen," Chin yanked back the hand. "I'm Chin, I was a Marine in Iraq. I know how to deal with an enemy. Donaldson, Chin's black cameraman flew into action and pinned Jensen's other hand behind his back and grabbed the gun from his pocket. "Mr. Jensen," Chin continued. "Donaldson, who holds your gun, is my camera man, but he was with me in Iraq. He is skilled in physical offense and defense. He will break your neck, if you move."

"Thank you, gentlemen," said Sam. "Are the camera's still rolling?"

"You bet, the rest of you are filming, right?" Donaldson answered. The others chimed in with accent, "Ya. You bet. Filming. All shooting."

Sam's heart was beating wildly, but he wanted every minute on tape. He just hoped that it was all getting out.

Shania Johnson spoke again. She looked around as all the camera people nodded. "Yes, Sir." She crossed to Donaldson's camera and began operating it. Nancy Lopez, from another major network waved her hand. "We are all filming, and it is going out all over the world."

Sam felt tremendous relief. "Press and citizens of our country and the world, I'd like to tell you a story about what has happened to the President and many good people throughout our country. We need to see that the conspiracy ends now. Obviously the participants will die, just like our President here. It will be horrifying for them too. Some went into it innocently, some were forced."

"I am Sam Stone, a book writer who has been pursued by Silas Jensen, the man you hold, and other subversives in power, because I wanted to stop the conspiracy, medical experiments on many victims, many murders, and mass addiction to the dangerous Acceleration drug. I was constantly pursued by

ACCELERATION

Jensen and saw him kill too many times to count. You have just witnessed an example of his followers, our President. He believed in power at all cost. The evil manipulator, Silas Jensen, that you hold, was an elite pimp to the President's addiction to a deadly drug. Let me explain further."

The media held their microphones and cameras closer to Stone. They wanted to hear and see every word of the truth. Sam told his story.

"Now, fellow Americans, my friend Eon here has sabotaged the nuclear missiles. I believed that they were not truly released. So it is up to you to take out this story and fight back against the addicted conspirators. Eon and I have done all that we can do." Sam then lowered his machine gun, dropped it to the floor, and collapsed. Eon Gustafson knelt down beside him.

Sam did not see the flurry that was to ensue, but Eon did. He would tell Sam all about it, when he was better, probably tomorrow… maybe.

CHAPTER 40

"I did what?" Sam said as he started to sit up rapidly in the hospital bed. Caught by the constricting tubing attached to his arm and twinging pain in his shoulder, Sam fell back. "I fainted! I've never fainted in my life. I've passed out but never fainted. What is all this stuff in my arm?"

"I can tell that you are going to be a cantankerous patient," the grey-haired little nurse grumbled. "Famous people always are."

"Eh, what am I famous for?" Sam asked cautiously.

"You must have hit your head; you don't even know what you did?" she exclaimed hoarsely, as she started to examine Sam's head for injury.

"No, no, please." Sam batted her hand impatiently. "You mean famous for my writing novels, see I remember."

"I don't know about your writing any books; I only read the good book, newspapers, and tv. I mean you're all over the news," she said.

ACCELERATION

"Am I in trouble, like are there police guards at the door?" Sam asked worriedly.

"Don't be silly. You're a hero, but that doesn't mean you get any special treatment from me. Now turn over for your shot."

"Wouldn't you rather have the arm?" Sam said sweetly.

"No!" she barked.

"All right, I was just asking." Sam turned and suffered the indignity. He pulled his body back carefully, mindful of pain that shot down his leg.

"Do I have any visitors? May I ask also how I'm doing and when I can leave?" Sam asked uneasily.

"Too many questions. Yes, visitors. No, the doctor will see you when he can. Do you need pain medication?"

"No," Sam propped himself up on the pillows.

"Good." She turned and crashed into Eon Gustafson at the door. "Why don't you watch where you walk, young man? It is not visiting hours, you know."

"Yes, I know." Eon displayed his most sexy smile.

"You think you can charm me? Knock off that grin. You men are all alike, only want one thing." The nurse threw shut the door ceremoniously.

"Jeez, you are going to love it here." Eon teased.

"Oh, she means well, I think." Sam shifted in the bed. "So, I missed the climax. What happened after my manly swoon?"

"Nothing. We all yawned and trotted off to bed with each other." Eon said mock seriousness. "No, are you crazy? It was chaos. There was direct satellite feed, so the whole broadcast got out immediately. Jensen was in custody for a while, but somehow he broke away and disappeared. His soldiers got scared, when they realized that they were losing and gave up their guns. The press was great. They went on the air to plead with people to fight the conspirators and assure them that what they saw in the bunker was real. They said that the President was indeed dead."

"Jensen's gone then," Sam pondered.

"Wait, there's more." Eon sat on the bed. Sam cringed at the movement.

"Sorry," said Eon. Anyway, the siege in Washington was short-lived. The Vice President mobilized the remaining forces. People on the drugs got scared when they saw what happened to Quint. They've been flooding the hospitals for help. Families and friends are turning people into authorities for psychotic behavior. They even brought those that are eccentric naturally. It's backfiring. It's McCarthy-ism again.

That's all happened in twenty-four hours!"

"I've been out that long!" Sam said in amazement. "Funny!"

"Yes, you have, but not funny. It's been wild." said Eon.

"What of the suppliers of the drugs?" Sam asked.

Eon shifted his position on the edge of the bed.

"Stay put, will you?" Sam yelped as he gritted his teeth at the stabbing pain in his leg.

"Sorry, Mighty hero. They haven't located the factories yet, but they will. Eon said as he forced himself to stay inert.

"Cut out the hero bit. What of the number on the bottle?" asked Sam.

"It's been disconnected, and there's been a cover-up on leads," Eon said.

Sam jerked. "Eon, it's not finished!" Sam pulled out the I.V. tubing from his arm and started to get out of the bed.

"Sam, you can't leave!"

"I can't stay. Don't you understand? As long as Jensen is loose, it can't end. His plan rose from the ashes before, he'll do it again." Sam staggered to the closet and pulled out his clothes. He examined the blood stained General's outfit and slumped in a chair. "I can't wear these clothes." Sam threw them on the floor by his bare feet.

"Let someone else take over now. You've done enough," Eon said gravely.

"Not if Jensen's still alive. The man won't quit, I know it." Sam said. "Can you get me fresh clothes, like now."

"Okay, Sam." Eon shook his head, but I personally approve of your staying put. The Lone Ranger's smart. But your Tonto has come prepared. Excuse me." He walked past Sam to the closet and reached for a paper bag. He dropped it, in delight, into Sam's lap. "Ask and you shall receive! Did somebody important once say that? Like God."

Sam smiled and pulled out the new clothes, a black T-shirt and jeans. "Good," he said, "I like to be comfortable. And who are the Lone Ranger and Tonto?" Sam rose unsteadily and began changing into the clothes. It was painful moving about, but he was getting used to it.

"Ah," said Eon. "You noticed I bought you a black shirt instead of heroic white. I knew you wanted to not be noticed by the mob of photographers in the lobby of the hospital. Now as for the Lone Ranger and Tonto. You need to watch more old television shows, especially about heroes. The Lone Ranger was an ex- Texas Ranger, like a cop on horseback. Tonto was an American Indian sidekick, also on horseback. Together they were heroes and saved lives. Man, you need me, don't you?"

"Yes." Sam laughed. "Thanks, and hey, you got any money?"

"Ah, Ben sent you funds. It's in the bottom of the bag. We thought of everything. There's a pocket knife too. So you can cut down a tree, if you get bored. We wanted you totally prepared," Eon replied as he flopped back on the bed and stretched out. "So where do we start looking for Jensen?"

"We? No. Not you, me. You've done enough. I'm just relieved you didn't get killed." Sam said as he padded in his bare feet to the closet and pulled out the general's loafers. "These don't go with the jeans, but they're not a bad fit."

"Maybe you'll start a new trend," Eon said cheerfully. He felt rested and relieved at what they had accomplished, but he wasn't sure that Sam should go after Jensen again. He barely survived the last confrontation.

Sam was ready. Eon Gustafson followed his friend into the hallway. He wondered if he would ever see Sam Stone again.

They shook hands. It had meant to be a quick handshake, but they'd been through too much together. Eon grabbed Sam in a huge bear hug. "You take care of yourself, Stone. Give Jensen hell."

"You bet, I'll try. Eon, thanks again. I couldn't have made it without you."

"You sure you don't want me along to the end, for insurance?"

"No, this has become personal. I want to finish this alone," Sam said.

"Where will you look for Svengali Jensen?" Eon asked.

"I'm going back to his house. Maybe I'll pick up a trail there."

Sam turned and looked up into the expressionless faces of two men in plain suits. "Excuse me. Who are you, Gentlemen?"

"We are Baker and Gutierrez, special forces envoy from President Kowalski. Who is Mr. Stone?"

"I'm Stone. Why do you ask?" Sam said warily.

"We'd like you to accompany us. We're looking for the site of the pharmaceutical factory that manufactures the medications for out ex-President and his associates. The new President felt you might wish to assist in our search."

"Yes, I would," Sam said to the men and then pivoted towards Eon. "Looks like I'll have help here. Thanks, Eon. I

ACCELERATION

owe you my life. I'll never forget you." Sam and Eon had built a friendship between them that could not be treated lightly. They nodded with understanding. Sam threw on the jacket that Eon had brought and grabbed his new wallet. The President's men surrounded him. Sam limped slightly, but he was ready emotionally for action. They walked solemnly down the corridor.

Eon remained in the middle of the hospital hallway and watched them go. Something about the men irked him. He couldn't quite explain an uneasiness which settled over him. Maybe it was just the guys' grey suits, or was it the way they wore them- tightly over firm muscles. Eon didn't like it, but perhaps he was just being paranoid. The last couple of days had certainly given him a right to be. He shook off the apprehension and headed for home and his life.

CHAPTER 41

Sam rode in silence between the stone faces. He tested the waters of conversation after he could stand it no longer. "So, how's the nation responding to having a woman President at the helm?"

One guy grunted and actually answered back, much to Sam's surprise. "Shit. We should never have had a female V.P. We deserve this for voting her in."

Sam shrugged. "Isn't she strong enough?"

"That's her problem. She thinks she can change things." The big man laughed with pornographic expletives. "Won't be long. She'll be gone."

Sam caught Gutierrez shooting a look of contempt at Baker.

"What do you mean?" Sam pursued. "How will she go away?"

Gutierrez interrupted as Baker started to speak. "He means we'll vote her out. Right, Baker?"

"Yeah, of course," Baker snorted.

ACCELERATION

Something was wrong, Sam knew it now. He stole a look out the window as the car picked up speed across the airstrip. It kicked up dust as the sleek vehicle than skidded to a halt at a plane, waiting in its path. Sam could almost read the words on the side of the aircraft. Yes, he could almost make it out now. It was "ACC…" That could mean…

Sam exploded from his seat but was pushed back and held by steel muscles that flexed in the suits of Baker and Gutierrez.

"That's pretty bold of you to have that logo on your plane," Sam calmed himself and said as he sat clamped between the two sausage-like thugs. He felt like the Earth had just yawned open and jerked him down into a mad dark spiral.

"Yeah, we are bold," Baker sneered in satisfaction.

"So why do you need me?" Sam continued.

"We don't need you, believe me. The boss wants to give you a special present," Gutierrez announce, with a sneer.

Did Jensen's men have any redeeming qualities? Sam hated them, not because they probably were going to kill him, but because they obscenely enjoyed the idea.

The men strutted with their catch towards the ominous plane. Sam felt like he was being carried despite his height. The guys were not about to let him stumble and jerk away. The huge black plane with its bright orange letters seemed an absurdity amongst the standard shiny aircraft in the field. It was an ugly celebrity. Armed guards secured the area through which Sam was marched. Money can buy an army, Sam thought, and mind-altering drugs can secure devotion.

He was entering once more into the den of dangerous, nasty creeps, and he didn't like it at all. The self-feeding power of this group to keep reshaping was discouraging. Sam felt sickeningly helpless, but then he remembered his old motto- he wasn't dead yet. They'd tried before and failed, perhaps he had one more of his nine lives left. Doesn't the hero always win or is that only in new versions of fairy tales? Sam wanted to laugh; he was definitely not in a fairy tale. Where were the princesses? Dead.

Suddenly Sam's debate within himself was abruptly ended, as he was rudely propelled through the metal doorway and into a second set of vice-like grips. Sam squinted into the semi-light of the plane's interior. "Waiting for me? You shouldn't have," he quipped sarcastically to the shadowy figures before him.

A voice seeped from the form and simpered. "I couldn't leave without you. We owe you."

ACCELERATION

Sam jerked back. It wasn't just the shock of starring into the face of the enemy which clearly formed in front of him. It was Jensen, the man, but he was different. His face had thinned grotesquely.

"Jensen," Sam found his voice. "You've deteriorated. You now look as ugly outside as you really are on the inside."

Jensen's eyes were grey and chilling. "It's a temporary side effect, nothing more." He smiled obscenely through thin peeling skin.

As much as Sam detested the man and believed he deserved death, Sam felt pity and averted his eyes. The feeling quickly abated as Sam's hands were wrenched behind his back and tied, and his feet were bound at the ankles. He was shoved roughly into a seat. The engines engaged, and the aircraft took to the sky.

"We are about to embark on your last few minutes of life, Stone. I plan to give you a proper burial. You will excuse me, however. I have even more important business to attend to."

Jensen sat himself down near one wall of the plane on which computer hardware was mounted. The metal of the machine glittered in the sub light of the cabin. Jensen whispered with a little man who hunched over the center of the dials and gauges.

The craft appeared to be a converted cargo plane. The seating for passengers was sparse. Sam was fastened into one of six places in the rear. The rest of the floor space was occupied by mountains of crates bearing colorful labels. Sam knew what they held. It had to be a new batch of the mind-acceleration drugs. The plane fairly bulged with the cargo; it was enough for hundreds of victims. Sam was struck by the walls of the plane. They were a garish lavender. Jensen must be in the last stages of his addiction, Sam thought. The plane was a tribute to his evil madness.

Jensen caught Sam's observations. "You like my pretty airplane?" he said gleefully. "I also have my new serum. My plans have had only a setback. I am renewed." Jensen rubbed his hands along his body. "I am feeling better than ever. I am smarter than you can ever be." He suddenly closed his eyes, moaned, and then popped his eyes open once again. "I'll show you my little missile control board. I designed it with my brilliant friend here." The huge heavy man at the control's chuckled in a low voice under his breath. He was just as crazy as Jensen, Sam thought.

An insane smile played upon Jensen's thin lips as he continued boasting "I have done the impossible. I will launch those missiles of yesterday from here. Then people will thank me. I will show them that I alone will take care of them all."

Sam felt like his body had stopped functioning, that he had ceased to exist, that he would die right then. He looked at these malignant sick men. Suddenly he felt the hardness of his army knife in his back jean pocket. The guards had foolishly assumed that he had no weapons, since he was picked up in a hospital. He touched the knife and scooted it up in his pocket as he talked. He had hope again.

"Jensen, this is rather uncomfortable, sitting on my hands," Sam said as he squirmed and secured the knife in the palm of his hand.

"Do you really think I care?" Jensen giggled like an ornery child. "I don't. You'll be dead in a minute; it won't then matter. I plan to drop you over the canyons and watch you splat upon the ground." Clapping his hands in delight, he turned back to his computers. "Now shut up, don't bother me!"

Sam felt the ropes on his hands fall into pieces as he split them with the knife. He laid them back over his wrists for effect. The feet would, however, be a problem.

"Now," Jensen spoke into a microphone in the cockpit. "Mr. Krieder and Kaupman, now is the right moment," Jensen turned, "for Mr. Stone's solo plunge into oblivion." He waved his hands, "Goodbye, goodbye."

Kreider and Kaupman emerged from the cockpit and stood with hate seeping from their beings.

"Men," Jensen said, "please carry that creature, Samuel, to the door and toss him out. He is leaving." Jensen then erupted into insane laughter.

Sam was hauled to his feet, as the exit hatch was wrenched open and wind tore at the men and howled in the cabin.

Sam sprang into action as they aimed him for the doorway and the planned abyss. He grabbed the overhead rod at the doorway just as Kaupman pushed Sam. The force caused the Kaupman to lose his balance and plunge forward and out of the plane. His screams ended abruptly in the howling wind. Kreider was stunned, but only for the minute that Sam was able to envelope his tied legs over the man's head and engage him in a headlock. Kreider sputtered and pounded on Sam to no avail. Sam Stone was not about to let go. He held onto the overhead rail tightly and twisted his legs around the neck. Kreider slumped as Sam's previously injured leg throbbed wildly with pain. It all happened within seconds, but Jensen had recovered from his dashed plan.

ACCELERATION

"No!" Jensen shouted, waving a pistol. "You must die. Die, die die!" he shouted shrilly as he shot his gun wildly. Sam yanked Kreider's body as a shield to absorb the impact of the bullet blasts. Jensen continued wildly spewing his remaining bullets about the aircraft. Sam threw Kreider's inert body out of the plane and lunged at Jensen. Sam felt a steel grip around his neck as Jensen hissed and shouted. "Launch the missiles, Snake, we are going to win! You are dying Stone. See how strong I am now!"

Sam felt oxygen deprivation from Jensen's nearly inhuman strength, and his vision blurred. He feared taking his hands off Jensen's almost fatal grip, but his only hope was the knife he had returned to his pocket. Would he die before he reached it again? Sam gripped its cool surface and drew it from its resting place. In a last desperate act of survival, Sam stabbed out. He wasn't at all clear what happened then. Through the haze, he believed he had stabbed Jensen not once but over and over. The grip on his neck loosened until Sam was able to pry off the fingers and slide the body off. Gasping Sam fell back against the maze of controls. He tried to push Jensen's limp body out of his pathway but stumbled onto Snake who had cowered wild-eyed at the foot of the missile board.

Sam regained his balance and threw Snake back into his seat. Sam pulled the knife from Jensen's mutilated body and held it to Snake's throat. "Divert those missiles, you devil, or I'll slit your throat!" Sam's eyes showed the coolness of a killer. He had no longer any reservations about taking the lives of everyone on board."

"It's too late!" Snake stammered through trembling lips.

"No! You can do something. Alter their course to the middle of the ocean." Sam pulled up his knife again, grabbed Snake's head and tipped it back. He carefully drew blood on his neck. He held up the knife and hissed, "Do you see your blood? Do you want to end like Jensen? Your blood is oozing out, you bastard."

"Okay, don't hurt me. I'll do it!" Snake cried out.

Sam released him roughly and returned the knife to the huge man's back. Snake recalibrated the vectors and altered the trajectory. "It should impact as you say. Let me go now. I have parachute. Let me out."

"Where's the chute?" Sam shouted as he moved the knife back to the thin neck.

"In that cabin. I show you. The heavy brut inched backwards towards the metal enclosure. As Snake turned away to open the cabinet, Sam reached for Jenson's gun. He hoped it had one more bullet, just in case.

Snake pulled a chute from the cabinet hole and hurled it blindly at Sam. Snake, in the next split second, pulled out a large knife. With a blood-curdling screech, he charged at Sam with his glistening blade.

Sam caught the chute as he fell but managed to fire the gun repeatedly. The first shot caught Snake full in the chest. He staggered for a moment and continued forward onto Sam's now prone body. The second shot was a click and the third. Empty! Sam registered it furtively as he reached up to block the blow of the large knife which never came. The knife fell to the floor as Snake's fat body plunged down upon Sam. Sam fumbled to raise up the body and met the sightless man's eyes. Sam gasped in relief.

Suddenly Sam was tossed into the metal control center. He grabbed for a handhold as he was pitched forward. My God, the plane was going down, he thought. No wonder there was no reaction from the cockpit to the violence in the cargo/missile control area. Jenson's gunfire must have hit the controls or the pilots. Sam didn't have time to check. He was sliding towards the open doorway. His fingers closed on the parachute. He wound the straps about his arm furiously, and he prayed.

It had been a quick prayer, but he had meant every word. He wanted desperately to live now. He was so close to staying in this world, if the chute would just stay with him and open.

The plane was going down now. He had to escape. Sam pulled himself desperately through the gaping doorway and felt the open air rush into his face. Suddenly he was caught by the wind and hurling through icy air. He stretched out his body and legs to slow the fall and floated. He wasn't afraid. He felt the tangled straps around his arms. He could understand the thrill sky divers must feel. It was glorious to look down upon the earth and feel above it all, above the pain and frustration. He was free!

Sam watched the plane in the distance as it plummeted into the rugged mountains. He felt no pity or hate. Sam wanted to scream with joy, but he knew nothing would come from his voice. It was too exhilarating for such a simple response. He could only gaze in awe at the snow-capped mountains below and shaggy carpet of treetops. It was late afternoon. The sun was creeping into the shelter of the horizon. It would soon be

ACCELERATION

dark, and Sam was falling into a dense forest. He'd better pay attention!

Sam tried tilting his spread eagle form to guide himself into the valley. It had seemed like a good idea, but he got off balance and began spinning. He steadied and straightened his straps and himself, as best he could. Then, it was time. He was closing in on the earth fast now. He grabbed the rip cord and yanked. His arm was jerked by the tangled mesh of the harness. The trees began to explode upon him. He braced for impact.

The body of Sam Stone fell thunderously into the outstretched branches. They cracked and splintered with the plunging weight until he settled amongst them. He had heard something else snap along with the branches. Sam moved his arm gingerly and felt the stab of pain. His arm didn't feel broken, but he was sure that it had been ripped from its socket. The lovely euphoria sense that he had enjoyed in the clouds was now gone. Sam wanted to laugh at the reversal of his fate.

Twisting his neck to see the growth below was nearly impossible. He was trussed in the straps of the chute. If he could just untangle his arm, but it screamed with agony at the slightest motion. Sam thrust his feet sideways and tried to secure balance on a branch somewhere. Maybe he could take some of his weight off the straps. He could then unscramble them with less pain and hopefully fall to freedom. Just how far below that goal of the ground was, he wasn't sure.

Suddenly Sam found it, the leverage he needed. He perched precariously and meticulously and began to remove the bindings from the shoulder. When he had almost given up, he was free, and Sam descended to the earth below and smacked upon it.

"Hey! Mister, you alive?"

Sam tried to breathe. He had fallen hard on the frozen ground. He remembered now. He gulped at the cold air. "I think so," he said. Abruptly an arrow of pain shot through his shoulder. "My shoulder is killing me," Sam sputtered. "You any good at popping them back in place?"

"I can try, just don't hit me when I do it. Ready?"

Sam clenched his teeth.

"Now!"

Sam cried out. It took a moment, but his body finally released him from the excruciating ordeal. "Thanks," he muttered weakly, as he took in the black beard and scraggly hair of his rescuer.

"I'm Cody, Harold Cody. I have a cabin not far from here. I come up every year just to get back to nature. This is the first time I've ever seen any action like today. Was that your plane that crashed into the mountain?"

"Yeah, sort of. Did anyone else make it down?" Sam assumed he was the only one but thought it would look better if he asked. Actually he hoped he was the only survivor. He hated to go through the confrontation all over again in another time or place.

"No, just you." Cody answered sadly. "Sorry."

Sam avoided the man's soulful look. "Thanks," and he meant it in more ways than one. Thank you, Jensen and company, for dying, he thought. Now perhaps Acceleration can end, and I can really live.

Sam smiled brightly. "I'm sort of freezing. Do you have a warm fireplace in that cabin and a pair of long johns that I can borrow?"

"Where are my manners? Sure. Follow me or do you need my help to walk?" Cody said sincerely.

"I'm fine, just fine, now." Sam's dislocated shoulder ached and his recent gun wounds throbbed, but he felt better. He was alive.

He'd be home soon.

Sam slept on the floor beside the fireplace in the rustic cabin. He refused to occupy Cody's only bed, despite the man's repeated offers. Cody had a good heart.

They listened to his radio as the fire flickered shadows around the cabin. The newscasters were broadcasting on every station that they could pick up. It seemed that two nuclear missiles had gone down in the center of the Atlantic. The explosions had created tidal waves that would soon shatter on the east coast. Inhabitants of the United States were banning together and preparing.

It could be worse, Sam mused as he felt himself groggily slipping into much needed sleep. It could be much much worse.

Sam had misgivings about returning to civilization the next day. It was beautiful in the forest, and he was warm and safe. He wished that Caroline or Alex were there. He could feel them next to him. He brushed their memories away into the back

ACCELERATION

recesses of his mind. He would draw from them again someday, but not now. He slept peacefully.

CHAPTER 42

"Susie, it's Sam."

Susie sat on the bar stool perched near her kitchen counter in her designer condo. She held onto her phone tightly. "Oh, thank God. You're not dead! I knew it couldn't be true. Where are you?"

"How about on the corner. I borrowed this cool kid's phone. Say hello to Susie, Jose."

Jose giggled. "Hi, Susie."

Susie smiled broadly. "Jose, hi, and thanks. Tell Sam to come up."

Jose handed back the phone to Sam. "She say to come up. I like her. Is she pretty?"

"Susie, dear Susie, I'm coming." Sam said and turned to Jose and handed back the phone. "Thanks, buddy. She's very pretty."

Susie threw down the phone and ran to the window. Seeing him walk towards the building, she bounded down the stairs in her bare feet, with her long dark hair flying about her slim shoulders.

ACCELERATION

Sam reached for the bell when the door flew open. He drank in the sight of Suzanne, his Susie. Even in shorts and tank top, she was a classy and beautiful lady. He hoped she still felt something for him. He needed to see her. Sam still wasn't sure if it was love. It was not the same as what he'd shared in his brief times with Caroline or Alex. But Susie was special too, and he cared about her deeply. He also needed her badly. He could finally let down his defenses from the last months and feel hope again for happiness.

But he needn't have worried about Susie's reaction to Sam, the disheveled old boyfriend with the long shaggy hair.

"I look a mess," he blurted out. "The other passengers on my flight were more than happy to see me depart. I hope you don't agree." He said nervously. "I've missed you. May I come back?"

Susie pulled Sam inside and then sobbed with joy. She wrapped her arms around him and kissed him passionately. She suddenly interrupted the kiss with the emotional words, "I'm so happy to have you back, Sam."

Suddenly she broke away. "Do you know what you put me through? I never knew if you were alive, and everyone tore your reputation apart on the news. They hounded me for months on who was the real Sam Stone and was he a killer. Now you're a damn hero. Couldn't you trust me to tell me anything?"

She looked so young and vulnerable to Sam. He sat her down on the side of the bed. "I'm sorry," he said earnestly. "I didn't want to get you involved or hurt." Sam said as he lowered himself beside her. He stared ahead into space, seeing the awful memories. "I was usually running blind. I had no idea if it would ever end." His voice grew almost inaudible.

Susie touched his shoulder, and they relaxed. Sam pulled her down onto the bed, kissed her gently, and lay beside her, with her head resting on his chest. "This is nice. I would like to retain this moment forever, if I didn't feel so grubby. Do you think I might clean up in your place?" He looked around for the first time and frowned, "Did you remodel or repaint?"

"Both," she said happily. "Do you like it?"

"You must like orange and purple now. You always liked white walls before. It looks, ah- very royal and happy." The walls and coverings were awash in the colors.

"You don't like it?" she pouted.

ACCELERATION

"It's just so different from before. It's great." Sam kissed her gently and stood up. "A shower and razor would be a gift from heaven."

"Then you have been blessed," she laughed. "There are both in the bathroom. Go. It's been waiting for your return. Give me your clothes, and I'll toss them in my mini washing machine in the kitchen. I added it since your last memorable visit. I must have had déjà vu that you'd return as a mountain man."

"Do you have anything I can wear in the interim?" Sam asked.

"There are towels." Susie answered innocently.

"Oh, thanks. You asked for it!" said Sam as he tried not to laugh.

"I know," she flounced onto the bed. "Hurry and get clean. I'll be right here."

"I'll just do that. I'll be back shortly." Sam sprinted for the shower.

"Hi, darling," Sam said as he joined Susie in the bed. He noticed that she had fallen asleep. He looked around at the wall colors and his stomach turned over. He couldn't stay in this bed and look at those walls. He hated those colors and the death that they brought. He hoped Susie's paint job was just a silly coincidence. She couldn't possibly be under the Acceleration drugs. The drugs are over and gone now. Weren't they? He stared and felt the fear. He got up and walked to the couch in the living room, lay down, and slept fitfully

"Hi,"

"Hi to you," Sam said as he pulled Susie down on the couch next to him.

"Why didn't you sleep with me?" She said as she plopped beside him.

"You were sleeping so soundly. I hated to wake you…Tonight," he said.

"Good. Oh, I forgot to throw your clothes in the dryer." She started to climb out of Sam's arms.

Sam pulled her back. "I already did. Don't go just yet."

"Well, if you insist," Susie teased as she circled his face with kisses. She pulled down the light blanket that he had found in her closet and used for the night. She gazed at his body in delight, and then her face became grave as she noticed the scars. "Are you okay, Sam?"

ACCELERATION

"I'm fine." Sam said. He felt her explore his body lovingly. When he could lay there not one minute more, he pulled her gently beneath him. It was like the best of old times, maybe even better. They were not the same confused people from their past. That was good.

Later they settled back on the couch. Sam clicked on the television.

"I haven't heard the news since the tidal wave was coming. What happened to the coastal cities?" he said.

Susie snuggled against him. "They survived."

Sam hit the remote button and turned up the sound on the news.

"This is Betsy Mallory from Washington. We seem to be weathering the destruction well. The colossal wave has caused an estimated hundred million in property damage, but there have been no reported deaths."

Sam felt relief as he listened further.

"Roger Elliot, reporting here from Boston. The boats in historical Boston are now shelved like children's toys about the streets and foyers of businesses near the harbor."

Sam felt a morbid fascination, but decided to change the station.

"John, was this more of the Quint-Jensen tragedy?

"Yes, David, we think so. It seems the missiles' guidance system was activated from an aircraft and then altered to ditch the bombs in the ocean. It ws undertaken by an amazingly clever technology. We think the missiles were headed for Washington and Moscow as Silas Jensen and President Quint had originally planned. The aircraft is rumored to have been sabotaged at the last minute and crashed into the mountains near Denver."

"John, could Sam Stone be involved again? He supposedly left the hospital in Idaho with government men and hasn't been heard from since."

"Yes, that's true. Whether he went down with the plane or not is unknown. We thought the guy was dead once before, however."

"This has been a nerve-racking couple of days for the news people. We wonder, like everyone- Is it finally over now?"

"Boy, I sure hope so. We have footage of the demolition of the laboratories and hospital in Utah where Jensen and the

Mekka Corporation propagated their conspiracy and produced the mind-altering drugs."

"John, it feels like we're watching the downfall of the Nazi death camps in Europe. Too bad Stone can't see this."

"He can," Susie said softly as she gripped Sam's hand and turned off the television.

Sam stared intently at the blank screen. "I need to return to the family cabin. Will you go with me?" Sam said quietly.

"Of course," She said. She didn't ask why. He had his reasons; she was just glad to be a part of his life again, regardless how small the part was.

CHAPTER 43

"You like these mountains, don't you?" Susie said, as she sat beside Sam as he drove her car and rested her head upon his shoulder. "It's nice, being here with you." She bent over to turn on the radio. There was only static. She felt her pocket. "No romantic music on the radio, and I forgot my cell phone in my other purse in the trunk. That's what I get for bringing two purses. I forget things lately. It must be from worrying about you. So we have no accompaniment. But I still have you."

Sam took one hand off the wheel so as to bring her hand over. He kissed it gently, and then caressed her soft dark hair. "We don't need music. I like this, riding with you again. I actually have been without a phone for so long that I forgot to bring my new one also. We'll rough it." He laughed. "It's like the old days, feels good. No outside world, just you and me and nature."

Susie laughed. "Yeah, just you and me and lots and lots of trees.

Sam was lost in his memories. "I used to come here with my brother and Dad when I was a kid. I thought I was quite the Boy Scout. Sean and I got lost once due to what I thought was my superior sense of direction and pride. Ha! I refused to admit that I was totally confused and scared. I had bent back branches to mark the trail. Then when we'd started back, we left too late and all the branches looked alike. I couldn't tell Sean that his big brother was lost, so we roamed for hours in the dark. When I got totally frightened and started running like a rabid animal, Sean caught up and told me to go slowly, and that I would find the route… I followed his advice. I knew he was right. Finally, about midnight we stumbled back to the cabin."

"Dad went crazy. He was frantic and started hollering at me, but Sean jumped forward and said that he had gotten lost and that I had rescued him. Dad was taken aback but praised me. Then he began chastising Sean. Well, not to be outdone in the honesty department, I piped up and told the truth. Dad was totally bewildered; he didn't know who to believe. He just sat down suddenly at the old wooden table and shook his head. He said, "You guys are too close. Don't worry me so much next time." Then he hugged us both. He never did that before. He wasn't usually demonstrative. I never saw him kiss our mom. He didn't even hold her hand or arm when they walked together."

Susie ran her hand over his chest and slid it under his shirt. "Unlike you."

Sam clasped her hand and kissed it again. "Unlike me." The cabin's just around the bend. Maybe I overcompensate for my dad."

"Definitely not!" A lovely smile played on Susie's fragile features.

"Is that so?" Sam eased Susie's bright orange T-Bird next to the old cabin. I should have taken my car, if I could have found it."

"You don't like my classic car?" She pouted teasingly.

"It's …cute. It's made for petite women. When did you go for aggressive colors You used to be into white in your cars. I seem to remember a new white vehicle each year. You said it was to keep you innocent."

"Ah! I grew up." She winked seductively and sprang from the car. "This is it?" Susie shivered in the cool post winter air and turned back for her jacket. Suddenly she stopped, and her hands flew to her head. "Gee, I've got one angry headache."

Sam joined Susie on the pathway and put his arm around her waist. "Sorry, honey." He guided her to the cabin and pushed open the door.

ACCELERATION

"No key?" she said.

"I left in a hurry."

"Damn!" Susie jerked and clutched her temples. "I just hope that I remembered my medicine."

Sam pulled her back and held her in front of him. "What medicine?" He scanned her lovely but drawn face which abruptly cleared of its pain. '

"It's gone now. Comes and goes. The doctor said it was stress, from knowing you. Silly, don't worry. I'm fine." She dug into her purse. "I have it; here it is, good old modern chemistry." She opened a plastic vile and popped a couple of colorful pills in her mouth.

"I'll get some water for them. Sit down in here," Sam said as he guided her into the room.

"Water is not necessary; they are chewable." Susie beamed and tucked her long hair behind her ears. She threw back her head and laughed gaily. "I feel great now!" She tossed her arms around Sam's neck.

Sam looked at her in amazement. "What is that stuff you're taking? It works fast. Let me see it." He untangled her limbs and reached for the bottle that Susie had thrown back into her canary yellow shoulder bag that swung from her shoulder.

"Hey! Get your hand out of my stuff," Susie's eyes flashed and her face darkened. "Do I go through your personal items? No. Do I ask you a lot of questions? No!" Her voice rose shrilly. "Just because you're some hero, that doesn't mean you can boss me around. I know more than you. You are just a damn stud to me."

Susie instantly cooled her fury. She toyed with her raven curls. Calmly she said, "You thought I couldn't live without you, Mister Big Time. Well, I learned. You were replaced."

Sam was confused. "Susie, I'm sorry if I hurt you." Sam regained his senses. "This isn't you talking. What are you taking? Who is your doctor? I'm going to go to call him."

Susie grabbed his arm and pulled Sam back. "No, you don't! He'll take my pills, and I need them."

"Susie!" Sam pried off her hand and held it. "Let me…" He never completed his plea.

Tearing her hand away, she yelled, "Don't touch me!" She ran to the sink and grabbed a large butcher knife suspended from a peg on the cabin wall. "You can't hurt me; I'm special!"

Sam controlled the despair rising in his throat. "I don't want to hurt you. Give me the knife, Baby." He held out his hand.

ACCELERATION

"Give me the knife, handle first. Or lay it on the counter. Please, I trust you. We love each other."

"You never loved me!" Susie screamed and slapped the blade of the knife across Sam's hand.

Sam yanked back his hand as blood sprang from a gaping slice. "God, honey, what are you doing?" Sam tried to reach for the knife, but she hurled it at him and caught his head. He stumbled backwards as Susie plunged forward. She clawed at his face. Sam grabbed her thin arms and pitched her away. She rebounded with a strength defying her delicate frame. Susie hurled her purse and sprang for the open doorway. Sam batted the purse away, and its contents clattered about the bare floor. A myriad of pill bottles rolled to a stop, and Susie was gone.

Sam breathed deeply and tried to understand the chaos that had exploded upon him so suddenly. His gaze took in the stillness, the small pill bottles, and the blood that spattered from his hand onto the dusty floor. He moved slowly to the sink and pulled an old towel from the drawer. He wrapped it haphazardly about his injured palm.

Sam stepped slowly towards the door, as if in a waking nightmare, where real time stood still. He then walked towards the car and stopped. He opened the trunk and searched Susie's other purse for a phone. "No phone. That's bad news. I can't call the doctor or anyone for help. Stupid of me. I should have brought a damn phone." He searched the road and clearing. Nothing. He must find her. She was running like a wild wounded animal. She would get hurt, he felt it. He had to find her. Couldn't he just help one person that he loved? Must they all suffer and die?

Sam tensed. He knew now what had happened. Jensen had thought that Susie would help capture Sam, so she was unwittingly pulled into the conspiracy. She didn't even know what she had. Damn you Jensen! Even in death, your evil lives. Sam slumped to the ground in grief. He was like the young boy of long ago that was so very lost.

Then Sam jerked up. He must think like that cocky young scout. He began to carefully move about in the trees. His eyes roamed for a sign. The minutes passed. His vision caught the sight of the crushed bit of leaves and the tilt of a broken branch. He had found the trail. He had learned his lesson from the past. He only needed to be calm and determined now. He moved forward silently into the forest.

The skin on Sam's arm tingled. Something had changed. "Susie!" he called and began plunging ahead quickly. He didn't

ACCELERATION

see the drop ahead. He guessed she hadn't either, but Sam was lucky. He had felt the ground disappear from beneath his feet. He grabbed out frantically as he fell, only to jerk to a stop in midair. His hands clung to the tangle of shrubs. Sam clawed at them. He shook off the bothersome towel from his cut hand and managed to solidify his hold. Sam was safe, for the moment. He began to yank his body over the top, and succeeded. He then lay gasping for air on the cold grass.

Sam's body shivered as he dismayed over his lack of a jacket. He wanted to go back. Why had he come to this cliff? Sam's mind had shut itself off. Tears welled up in his deep eyes. Why should laying here bring such sadness? He was alive. Sam closed his eyes and absorbed the motionless surroundings. Was it only a brief time ago that he was hurling through this jungle of wilderness to reach…to reach…? Then it came.

"Oh, God, Susie." He yanked open his eyes and crept to the edge of the overhang. Sam forced himself to look down into the ravine. It was about twenty feet down, and he knew the bright orange glow that flashed in the sunlight below. It was Susic, Susie's jacket. It was like a brand, Acceleration's symbol of conquer and extinction.

Sam rested his face on the rocky edge and then jerked his head up. He squinted up at the sun's radiant attempt to beat the cold cruel earth. Why? His mind screamed out in anger. He fiercely rose to his knees and then swung his legs back over the ledge.

Going around would take too long. He had to get to her. She was not dead; he willed his thoughts to believe this. His shoes slipped briefly; they were far from climbing boots. His mind exploded with memories now. He thought about his escape from the hospital that first time, after the drug had worn off. That cursed drug had made hell out of his life. He began to climb down now with a vengeance. The footholds held, and he made it.

Sam scrambled over to Susie's limp body, so like a rag doll that had been discarded by an angry child. He felt for a pulse. It was there. He wanted to cradle her head in his arms, but what if she had injured her neck or spine. He didn't dare move her. Sam lay down next to her and brushed his hand tenderly across her pale cheek. He knew now that there was real love and need. He was not about to give up.

ACCELERATION

"Baby, I have to go for help," he whispered. "I'll be back. I promise." Sam started to get up but was drawn back when Susie's eyes flickered open and tried to focus.

"Sam," she said softly, "what happened? Are we at the cabin?"

"No," he answered. "You fell off the rocks. You're lying in a clearing."

Susie's eyes darted wildly. "I'm scared. I don't feel anything."

Sam reached out and gently took her hand. "You'll be fine. I just need to get you help. You're in slight shock from the fall. I'm going to…" Sam looked around and held back the panic. "I'm going to pack leaves around you and under your feet to keep you warm and to raise up your legs slightly. Then I'm going to find a phone."

"And dial 911," she flipped back weakly.

Sam smiled as eyes filled with tears. "Yes, honey. That's exactly what I'm going to do, and they'll come running, just like in the movies. You'll recover, and we'll live happily ever after."

"That's the best way," she answered.

"You bet," Sam said as he started to move away, but her voice brought him back.

"I don't know why I went so crazy," she said softly. "I'm sorry; did I hurt you?"

"I know why and no, I'm fine. Sleep now, so I can play hero and rescue you, if I may?"

"Certainly," Susie mumbled as she slipped out of consciousness.

Sam felt a stab of dread but then heard her soft breathing. She was still with him. He'd better get moving. He ran.

Sam had never moved so fast. He piled the cold forest mulch of dead leaves around his lady. He wasn't sure if it would help or lower her body temperature further. He was still no experienced woodman, but surely it had to be better than leaving her exposed to the temperature drop, which would come. When he was satisfied with his meager efforts, Sam rose quickly and began his climb, back up the treacherous overhang. The footholds rang with familiarity as he mounted them firmly. When he was safely over the top, he did not look down. There was no time to waste. He sprinted back to the car. He must hurry.

ACCELERATION

Sam drove madly over the winding desolate road. He reached Jessup's General Store. The storekeeper, his old friend, would he be there? He was.

"Hey Sam, good to see you. It's all over now. You look good. I'm glad you didn't die in that mess with all those bad people. I was watching the news, what I get here. They sure tried hard to hurt you. You're a hero now. I never met a true hero. I'm proud to know you. I'm hugging you, big guy."

Sam laughed as he was clasped in a bear hug. "Thanks." Sam dug in his pocket for his wallet and pulled out a number of bills. Here's the money I owe you. I should have paid you before. I'm sorry." Sam handed Jessup more than enough. He really owed Jessup his life.

"No problem. Thanks. Hey, you want to sit and visit, my boy? I got some good whisky and cigars. You look a little like you fell in a dirt pile though."

"I wish I could stay. Another time, please. I always seem to be coming when I need something. I'm sorry, but my girlfriend slid on a cliff and is hurt. I've got to try to get her more help than just me. May I use your phone, again? This time I'll pay now." Sam handed over a little more money."

"I'm chattering, when you got an emergency. Here, call. I'll save the whiskey and smokes for you later."

Calling 911 was science fiction in so small a populated area. He would need to go through the operator. Sam was connected to the sheriff. He explained his emergency and walked anxiously out of the store. He sank onto the step, Jessup sat quietly beside him. Together they listened to the stillness and waited.

The phone rang. Jessup ran to pick it up, followed by the worried Sam.

"Yep, he's here. Sam." He handed over the phone.

"Sam Stone."

"Yes, that's me."

"I'm Sheriff Henry Giles. We think we know the ravine you were talkin' about on the phone. We figure that there's a back road that should take us pretty close. I got together the emergency medics and rescue crew. We'll get your girl out. Don't get too down now. These guys move pretty fast. Volunteering is something they take real serious, and some are used to also workin' in the big city in the past. They're know-ledge-able." He pronounced the syllables with emphasis.

We're on the way. We'll pick you up, so wait with Jessup at his store."

"Thanks, Sir. I'll be here," Sam said as he hung up the phone and stepped back outside to pace. "I can't sit still. I hope my tramping doesn't make you dizzy."

"Nah! I'll plow along right next to you. Sammy, boy. I heard that you are now a hero."

Sam grimaced. "Not today."

"It weren't your fault that she fell. Anyone can fall." Jessup said.

"By the way, the news fellows have some tall tales goin'. They talk about the President getting old real fast before he died. That ain't true, is it?"

"Yes, it is," Sam said, as he covered his pacing path again.

"How's our lady President doing?" Jessup said. "I'm kinda in to juicy gossip."

"Oh, she's doing just fine- real spunky and bright. Even the Congress likes her, and you know how they like to fight Presidents."

"They sure do." Jessup grinned.

Sam relaxed and sat back down on the store's front step. Jessup joined him. Sam felt that things would turn out for the best with his old friend around. So they talked, really talked, from the heart, and Sam felt encouraged.

The time grew to forty-five minutes since Sam had called. The sheriff and crew arrived, the good guys to the rescue. Sam gladly let them take control.

By nightfall Susie was safely under hospital care. Her skull fracture and bruises would heal. Her spine was only bruised. She would recover. The drug addiction would be the ogre to her recovery. Her survival from its effects were questionable. Was it too late? The medics didn't know, they couldn't. Even with FBI records, it wasn't clear when or if the drug dependency could be turned around. Susie, however, would try, and Sam would support her. Sam called and gave Jessup the update. He treasured his friendship and vowed to see him again in better times.

Darkness huddled around the small house in the deep woods. Sam sat on the floor beside the fireplace. He watched the flames lick impatiently around the small prescription papers and bottles. They were Susie's. The labels blackened and crumbled in its crucible of cremation. Sam doubted the bottles would totally be destroyed, but their essence was gone. Their effects would remain for some time, however, in Susie and others.

Sam sighed. How many more victims were living their briefly normal lives? It was over for him anyway. He would start again to build his life. Sam watched as the flames blinked the image of Susie. He stared as it reformed to Alex and then his Caroline. The forms faded slowly, and Sam closed his thoughts to the many sad parts of the memories. Tomorrow he would turn his back on all but Susie. He prayed that the years would bring no backlash, no aftereffects. They'd just have to see.

There was suddenly a knock on the door. Who knew he was here? Oh, yes, the hospital, but why would they come here? Susie must be worse, and he had no phone. Sam bolted for the door and yanked it open.

Two young people babbled incoherently as they burst through the door.

Heather and Eddie finally caught their breath. Heather sputtered with excitement, "Thank goodness you are not dead. We are lousy sleuths. We got lost and couldn't find any of the bad guys. I'm sorry."

Sam stared at them in disbelief.

Eddie piped up in a small voice. "Is it all over?"

Sam gasped and burst into uncontrollable laughter. "Yes, it is." In between the hugs and kisses, he managed to enunciate further his words of welcome. "Come on in, you goofy kids. My wonderful friends, come in."

CHAPTER 44

"Mr. Stone, your latest book is quite a departure from your usual mysteries. Why did you choose to go for the literary elite? True, you might win the Pulitzer Prize for it, but you may not reap the financial rewards of a bestselling and sizzling mystery story. Don't you want the power of wealth like the rest of America?" the commentator teased.

Sam crossed his legs and tried to gain a comfortable position in the constricting tuxedo. "I've rubbed up against enough power and wealth. I almost overdosed," Sam said patiently.

"You are referring to the Jensen conspiracy. Why have you never written all the details? You know that your public has hoped that you would."

"Maybe I will someday. This book is more important. It stresses happiness, not destruction and death."

"But, violence is more exciting." The commentator's eyes glinted provocatively. "Audience, don't you agree?"

The faceless audience boomed out its affirmation in the dark void behind the camera lights.

Sam sighed wearily. "I've had all the excitement I want for a while."

"Mr. Stone, why did…" The band erupted into a jazzy calliope of sounds that framed the surreal atmosphere. "That's all our time. You will come back, Sir? Thank you for dressing up, by the way."

"Certainly." Sam plastered the requisite grin on his face. He was very tired from the book tour. But the medium was necessary, despite frequently frustrating. "I want to thank you and American for standing by me." Sam shook the M.C.'s limp hand, and the show abruptly ended. Mr. M.C. vanished as if on cue, and Sam made his way into the wings.

"You were great!"

"Thanks," Sam turned at the voice and almost bumped into the source.

"And pretty!"

"Thanks again." Sam chuckled…. "Susie."

"Hi!" She kissed him perkily on the cheek.

"How about some coffee and a chat with an old friend?"

"Sounds good, but I don't drink coffee anymore." Sam said.

"I know," she winked. "Neither do I."

"I thought you didn't want to come on the tour. You wanted to build our nest, so to speak." Sam said with a grin. He was pleased.

ACCELERATION

"I'm finished." Susie said as she pulled Sam forward eagerly.

Sam and Susie emerged from the studio into the bustle of early evening in New York City. She paused to hand Sam a topcoat. The air was still crisp.

"I brought you a coat, but I forgot my own," she laughed.

"No problem. I like this better," Sam put it around them both. He drew her closer.

"What did the doctor say?" he said seriously.

"I'm fine, doing well, and you won't get rid of me this time," she said teasingly.

"I won't and never intended to. I'm truly happy," Sam said as the crowd swelled and life erupted around them. The city vibrated with the cacophony of sounds and rabble of voices. Dirt occasionally flounced from car wheels as they spun by, but Sam didn't notice. He embraced Susie with overwhelming joy. He didn't care if anyone was looking. He was in love again and he was sure that Acceleration would never hurt them again. Pretty sure.

CHAPTER 45

SIX YEARS LATER

"Susie, you're eating again? Didn't we just have that dinner at the Mexican restaurant?" said Sam. He was stuffed. Little Andy was energetic as always, but his happiness was treasured. He was delighted when the waiter let him draw on the child-centered placemat. He even gave him crayons. Sam sat back and watched him. His life felt perfect now. But it was hard to believe that Andy was already in kindergarten."

Susie looked at Sam with irritation. "Don't tease me about eating. I can't help it. I'm still hungry."

"Sorry, honey. Hey, maybe you're pregnant again. I'd like that. We'll have a little girl or boy to go with Andy. He'll be jumping around with excitement." Sam really hoped he was right. He always wanted lots of kids since he married Susie. He had desperately wanted a normal life. He got it finally after his traumatic past years, but he still remembered and missed little Sarah and Alex. Silas had made sure that he punished Alex, by eliminating her cruelly. He didn't want to remember the picture that the police had showed him. It had displayed how Silas had

ACCELERATION

gruesomely placed Alex near the house after her murder. The frozen look on her face had devastated him. They had lived a dream like existence. It ended so awfully. He didn't want to think back on Alex or Caroline either. It still hurt too much. His past with them had been so happy but brief and had ended with such emotional trauma and despair. He never thought he could be this happy again. But he was.

Sam was writing again and enjoying it. That first year after the deaths was difficult. He was recuperating mentally and physically. He could not write. He sat there for months just watching Susie and walking outside with Caesar. Susie got bored with her inactivity and his long periods outdoors, so she built an internet cosmetic company, but she stayed devoted to Sam and Andy.

In the second year, Sam had finally surfaced from his depression and felt healed, and he started writing again. He never wrote about the past conspiracy, however. Not yet, maybe some day. Ben kept saying his fans were waiting for the book. He understood, but he just couldn't write it.

The country had stabilized with its new President. But the news highlighted, for many months, the continuing new deaths from others that had taken the Acceleration drug. The victims' list seemed to have ended now though. Sam was relieved about that. Afterwards, he tried not to read a newspaper anymore. There were many thousands of victims, more than Sam had initially realized. Jensen's spider web had reached very far. But the designers of the plot were dead now. It all seemed like an unreal nightmare.

Sam was able to even begin teaching again. He never mentioned his past to his students, although they eagerly wanted him to. His job was located at a small college in the mid-west again, but not the one of his past. The memories of Alex and Sarah were too painful there. Susie missed city life, however. So eventually, he thought they would move back to New York or LA.

Sam looked at Susie eating a large plate of tacos. She had already consumed her dinner. She had been eating like she was starving. Strange, but again, maybe she was carrying another child.

"Let's take you to the doctor tomorrow. We may be able to get an appointment." Sam said.

Susie laughed. "Do you think I'm going to gain a hundred pounds this time? I hope I have a little boy so Andy will have a buddy. Then again, I could buy cute clothes and play dolls with a little girl." Susie cleaned her plate. Order desert for us, would you Sam?"

"Mommy, do they have ice cream. I want ice cream," Andy looked up from his pictures with a sweet smile and then went back to drawing.

"What's that a picture of, Andy?" said Sam frowning at the orange monster with tendrils.

"It's a nice monster. I like coloring him. He's my friend. He likes me. A man came to school and asked me about my pictures. He said I draw good," Andy grinned.

Sam ruffled Andy's red hair. He loved this little guy a lot. He was surprised at the red hair when he was born, but he was also delighted. He felt like such a lucky dad.

But this picture. It looked like Sean when he died. It sent a chill through him.

Sam turned to Susie. "Did the school call you about that man?"

"Yes, but they said the teacher had told the Principal, and they had consulted with social services to see if there was a problem. They decided afterwards that it was fine and that all kids draw monsters." Susie patted his hand. "Don't worry. He's just being a kid. They were just worried because of your past."

"You're right," said Sam. "But why didn't you tell me? And why are they consulting Social Services without talking to us first? All kids draw pictures of everything."

"It happened fast and I didn't want to upset you. Also, you were on a long walk when they told me on the phone. I'm sorry Sam."

"It's fine, but tell me faster next time. Then I won't feel so left out," He hugged her, but it did bother him, but only because the government may be still watching over him. They had been constantly safeguarding him after the death of the President. They worried that the conspiracy may not be over. Sam couldn't blame the worrying, but it was all over as far as he was concerned. He did wonder about the pictures though.

Sam hailed the waiter. "May we have three servings of ice cream. What kind kids."

Susie laughed. "I want strawberry."

Andy looked up from his picture. "I want strawberry too."

Sam laughed. "I want chocolate. Okay." Sam turned to the waiter, "Did you get that?"

The waiter chuckled. "Yes, sir. Coming up." He walked away still laughing.

ACCELERATION

"I think he was amazed at how much we are eating. Me too," said Sam happily. And yet, it bothered him.

One week later Sam and Susie sat in the doctor's waiting room.

"You look nervous," said Sam. "Or are you just thinking of celebrating with more food?"

Susie smiled. "Both, oh, the nurse just called our names."

Sam and Susie joined the doctor and sat nervously, as they held hands.

Doctor Cruz studied the couple. "Mrs. Stone, you are... pregnant. Congratulations to you both."

Susie jumped up, "YES! Now we can go eat some more. I can't wait to tell Andy."

The doctor was surprised, a bit. "Don't overeat, but I think you'll do well. I'll see you next month, unless there's a problem."

"We'll be here then, Thank you, Doctor. We're thrilled," said Sam happily. But something bothered Sam. He tried to ignore it.

They drove home and told Andy, who jumped up and down with excitement and then drew a picture of Mommy, Daddy, Andy, and a little brother and sister.

"You drew a brother and a sister, why Andy?" said Sam.

"Daddy, I want both, don't you?" said Andy as he jumped into Sam's lap.

"You know, I think that I do, what shall we name them, Andy, although we may get just one?" Sam loved his little boy very much.

"Maybe?" He was thinking hard. "Maybe Andy 2 and Sarah." Andy laughed.

Sam's felt like his heart had stopped. Susie knew about Sarah but shook her head.

"Andy, how did you find out about Sarah?" said Susie quietly.

"I don't know. I just did," said Andy. "When do we eat?"

"Now," said Susie, as she pulled an open bag of cookies from her purse and dropped them on the table. Susie plopped down next to Andy and they both began to gobble them up.

Sam stared with his mouth agape. His heart was pounding. "Is it not over?" he thought. "Please let it be over.

There has to be a simple reason. But what is it?"

The End

ABOUT THE AUTHOR

L L Larson was raised in Rock Island, Illinois. She had happily lived most of her adult life in California, however, but recently moved back to her old hometown. She had missed it and now enjoys the snow, well- most of the time. She has a terrific grown-up son, Timothy, who she loves dearly.

LL graduated from the University of Illinois with a Bachelor of Science Degree and completed two years of post-graduate studies at California State University in Northridge. She worked many years as a teacher and actress. She also has written, produced, and directed her own independent films and acted in small roles on television and all sizes of roles on stage.

ACCELERATION is her first action/adventure/thriller novel. She had a great time writing about her heroic lead character, Sam Stone. She was thrilled by his courage, caring for others, honesty, sense of humor, and his fight for the right against all odds. She hopes you enjoyed Sam and his story.

OTHER BOOKS BY THE AUTHOR

L L has also published the following books in other genres:

1. *You Are Not Alone, Don't Give Up*

2. *Gracie and the Land of the Magical Butterflies*

3. *Without End*

Contact is through the email:

lindasandeelarson@gmail.com

Love to hear from you.

Made in the USA
Columbia, SC
13 March 2021